SCIENCE AND GOVERNMENT

"In any field of human endeavor, anything that *can* go wrong—will go wrong."

—Murphy's Law

"Unfortunately," Zimmermann replied calmly, "you do not have the luxury of choice any longer. You are obliged to react. I am suggesting that since it appears that you must become involved with government departments anyway, we endeavor to make that involvement constructive to our purpose." The professor spread his hands in an appealing gesture. "You have to get involved with them. If you don't they will just squeeze harder."

Dr. Bradley Clifford and Dr. Aubrey Philipsz recognized the government's trap. It was either submit and sacrifice their freedom or stand fast and sacrifice the research that had become their life.

The latter was unthinkable—and so it was that they became both the creators and slaves of the Genesis Machine!

"First-rate scientific speculation embedded in an intriguing story."

—Carl Frederik,
Director of The Boardman Planetarium

THE
Genesis
Machine

James P. Hogan

A Del Rey Book

BALLANTINE BOOKS • NEW YORK

Every child is a born scientist.

This book is dedicated to DEBBIE, JANE, and TINA —the three young scientists who taught me to distinguish reality from illusion by asking always:

       "Who says so?"

       "Who's he?"

and,   "How does he know?"

A Del Rey Book
Published by Ballantine Books

Copyright © 1978 by James Patrick Hogan

Published simultaneously in hardcover by Del Rey Books.

Library of Congress Catalog Card Number: 77-25166

ISBN 0-345-30576-0

Manufactured in the United States of America

First Edition: April 1978
Fourth Printing: November 1981

Chapter 1

The familiar sign that marked the turnoff from the main highway leading toward Albuquerque, some thirty or so miles farther north, read:

ADVANCED COMMUNICATIONS
RESEARCH ESTABLISHMENT

GOVERNMENT PROPERTY

ABSOLUTELY NO ADMITTANCE

TO

UNAUTHORIZED PERSONS

SHOW PASSES—1½ MILES AHEAD

Accompanied by the falling note of a barely audible electric whine, the Ford Cougar decelerated smoothly across the right-hand traffic lane and entered the exit slipway. Without consciously registering the bleeped warning from the driver's panel, Dr. Bradley Clifford felt the vehicle begin responding to his touch as it slipped from computer control to manual drive. The slipway led into a shallow bend that took him round behind a low sandy rise, dotted with clumps of dried scrub and dusty desert thorn, and out of sight of the main highway.

The road ahead, rolling lazily into the hood of the Cougar, lay draped around the side of a barren, rock-strewn hill like a lizard sunbathing on a stone. In the shimmering haze beyond and to the right of the hill, the rugged red-brown bastions that flanked the valley of the Rio Grande stood row behind row in their age-less, immutable ranks, fading into layers of pale grays and blues that blended eventually with the sky on the distant horizon.

The road reached a high point about halfway up the shoulder of the hill, and from there wound down the other side to commence its long, shallow descent into the mouth of the barren valley beyond, at the far end of which was situated the sprawling complex of the Advanced Communications Research Establish-ment. At this time of the morning, the sun shone from the far side of the Establishment, transforming the jumble of buildings, antenna towers, and radio dishes into stark silhouettes crouching menacingly in front of the black, shadowy cliffs that marked the head of the valley. From a distance, the sight always reminded Clifford of a sinister collection of gigantic mutant in-sects guarding the entrance to some dark and cavern-ous lair. The shapes seemed to symbolize the ultimate mutation of science—the harnessing of knowledge to unleash ever more potent forces of destruction upon a tormented world.

About a mile farther on and halfway down to the valley floor, he came to the checkpoint where the road passed through the outer perimeter fence of ACRE. A black Army sergeant, in shirtsleeves but armed and wearing a steel helmet, walked forward from the bar-rier as Clifford slowed to a halt beside a low column. Nodding his acknowledgment to the guard's perfunc-tory " 'Morning," Clifford extracted the magnetically coded card from his pass folder, inserted it into a slot in the front of the box that surmounted the column, and handed the folder to the guard. Then he pressed the ball of his thumb against the glass plate located adjacent to the slot. A computer deep beneath

ACRE's Administration Block scanned the data fed in at the checkpoint, checked it against the records contained in its files, and flashed the result back to another soldier who was seated in front of a display console inside the guardhouse. The sergeant returned the pass folder to Clifford's outstretched hand, cast a cursory glance around the inside of the vehicle, then stepped back and raised his arm. The Cougar moved through and the barrier dropped into place behind.

Fifteen minutes later, Clifford arrived at his office on the third floor of the Applied Studies Department of the Mathematics & Computer Services Building. On the average, he spent probably not more than two days a week at ACRE, preferring to work at home and use his Infonet terminal, which gave him access to the Establishment's data bank and computers. On this occasion he hadn't been in for eight days, but when he checked the list of messages on his desk terminal, he found nothing that was especially pressing; all the urgent calls had already been routed on to his home number and dealt with from there.

So no unexpected panics to worry about before his eleven-o'clock meeting.

No sooner had he thought it, when the chime sounded to announce an incoming call. He sighed and tapped a button to accept.

"Clifford."

The screen showed a momentary frenzy of color, which stabilized almost immediately into the features of a thin, pale-faced individual with thinning hair and a hawkish nose. He looked mean. Clifford groaned inwardly as he recognized the expression of righteous and pained indignation. It was Wilbur Thompson, Deputy to the Deputy Financial Controller of Mathcomps and self-appointed guardian of protocol, red tape, and all things subject to proper procedures.

"You might have told me." The voice, shrill with outrage, grated on Clifford's ears like a hacksaw on tungsten carbide. "There was absolutely no reason for you to keep quiet about it. I would have thought that the least somebody with my responsibilities could expect would be some kind of cooperation from you people. This kind of attitude doesn't help anybody at all."

"Told you what?"

"You know what. You requisitioned a whole list of category B equipment despite the fact that your section is way over budget on capital procurement for the quarter, and without an SP6 clearance. When I queried it, you let me go ahead and cancel without telling me you'd gotten a priority approval from Edwards. Now the whole thing's a mess and I've got everybody screaming down my throat. That's what."

"You didn't query it," Clifford corrected matter-of-factly. "You just told me I couldn't do it. Period."

"But . . . You let me cancel."

"You said you had no alternative. I took your word for it."

"You knew damn well there'd be an exception approval on file." Thompson's eyes were bulging as if he were about to become hysterical. "Why didn't you mention the fact, or give me an access reference to it? How was I supposed to know that the project director had personally given it a priority 1 status? What are you trying to do, make me look like some kind of idiot or something?"

"You manage that okay without me."

"You listen to me, you smart-assed young bastard! D'you think this job isn't tough enough already without you playing dummy? There was no reason why I should have checked for an exception approval against that requisition. Now I'm being bawled out because the whole project's bottlenecked. What the hell made you think I'd want to check it out?"

"It's your job," Clifford said dryly, and cut off the screen.

He just had time to select some of the folders lying on his desk and to turn for the door, when the chime sounded again. He cursed aloud, turned back to the terminal, and pressed the *Interrogate* key to obtain a preview of the caller without closing the circuit that completed the two-way channel. As he had guessed, it was Thompson again. He looked apoplectic. Clifford released the key and sauntered out into the corridor. He collected coffee from the automat area, then proceeded on to one of the graphical presentation rooms which he had already reserved for the next two hours. Since the meeting demanded his presence at ACRE that day, he thought he might as well make the most of the opportunity presented to him.

An hour later Clifford was still sitting at the operator's console in the darkened room, frowning with concentration as he studied the array of multidimensional tensor equations that glowed at him from the opposite wall. The room was one of several specifically built to facilitate the manipulation and display of large volumes of graphical data from ACRE's computer complex. The wall that Clifford was looking at was, in effect, one huge computer display screen. In levels deep below the building, the machines busied themselves with a thousand other tasks while Clifford pondered the subtle implications contained in the patterns of symbols. At length, he turned his head slightly to direct his words at the microphone grille set into the console, but without taking his eyes off the display, and spoke slowly and clearly.

"Save current screen; name file *Delta Two*. Retain screen modules one, two, and three; erase remainder. Rotate symmetric unit phi-zero-seven. Quantize derivative I-vector using isospin matrix function. Accept I-coefficients from keyboard two; output on screen in normalized orthogonal format."

He watched as the machine's interpretation of the commands appeared on one of the small auxiliary screens built into the console, nodded his approval, then tapped a rapid series of numerals into the keyboard.

"Continue."

The lower part of the display went blank and a few

seconds later began filling again with new patterns of symbols. Clifford watched intently, his mind totally absorbed with trying to penetrate the hidden laws within which Nature had fashioned its strange interplays of space, time, energy and matter.

In the early 1990s, a German theoretical physicist by the name of Carl Maesanger had formulated the long-awaited mathematical theory of Unified Fields, combining into one interrelated set of equations the phenomena of the "strong" and "weak" nuclear forces, the electromagnetic force, and gravity. According to this theory, all these familiar fields could be expressed as projections into Einsteinian spacetime of a complex wave function propagating through a higher-order, six-dimensional continuum. Being German, Maesanger had chosen to call this continuum *eine sechsrechtwinkelkoordinatenraumkomplex*. The rest of the world preferred simply *sk-space*, which later became shortened to just *k-space*.

Maesanger's universe, therefore, was inhabited by *k-waves*—compound oscillations made up of components that could vibrate about any of the six axes that defined the system. Each of these dimensional components was termed a "resonance mode," and the properties of a given k-wave function were determined by the particular combination of resonances that came together to produce it.

The four low-order modes corresponded to the dimensions of relativistic spacetime, the corresponding k-functions being perceived at the observational level simply as *extension;* they defined the structure of the empty universe. Space and time were seen not merely as providing a passive stage upon which the various particles and forces could act out their appointed roles, but as objective, quantifiable realities in their own right. No longer could empty space be thought of as simply what was left after everything tangible had been removed.

Addition of the high-order modes implied components of vibration occurring at right angles to all the coordinates of normal spacetime. Any effects that followed from these higher modes were incapable, therefore, of occupying space in the universe accessible to man's senses or instruments. They could impinge upon the observable universe only as dimensionless points, capable of interacting with each other in ways that depended on the particular k-functions involved; in other words, they appeared as the elementary particles.

The popular notion of a particle as a tiny, smooth ball of "something"—a model that, because of its reassuring familiarity, had been tenaciously clung to for decades despite the revelations of quantum wave mechanics—was finally put to rest for good. "Solidness" was at last recognized as being totally an illusion of the macroscopic world; even the measured radius of the proton was reduced to no more than a manifestation of the spatial probability distribution of a point k-function.

When high- and low-order resonances occurred together, they resulted in a class of entities that exhibited a reluctance to alter their state of rest or steady motion as perceived in normal space, so giving rise to the quantity called "mass." A 5-D resonance produced a small amount of mass and could interact via the electromagnetic and weaker forces. A full 6-D resonance produced a large amount of mass and added the ability to interact via the strong nuclear force as well.

The final possibility was for high-order modes to exist by themselves, without there being any component of vibration in normal spacetime at all. This yielded point-centers of interaction that offered no resistance whatsoever to motion in spacetime and therefore always moved at the maximum speed observable—the speed of light. These were the massless particles—the familiar photon and neutrino and the hypothetical graviton.

In one sweeping, all-embracing scheme, Maesanger's wave equations gave a common explanation for the bewildering morass of facts that had been catalogued by thousands of experimenters in a score of nations throughout the 1950s to the 1980s. They explained, for example, why it is that a particle that interacts strongly always interacts in all possible weaker ways as well, although the converse might not be true; clearly the 6-D resonance responsible for the strong nuclear force had, by definition, to include all possible lower modes as subsets of itself. If it didn't, it wouldn't be a 6-D resonance. This picture also explained why heavy particles always interact strongly.

Theory predicted that 5-D resonance would produce particles of small mass, unable to participate in strong interactions; existence of the electron and muon proved it. Further considerations suggested that any heavy particle ought to be capable of assuming three discrete states of electric charge, each of which should be accompanied by just a small change in mass; sure enough, the proton and neutron provided prime examples.

If an interaction occurred between two resonances whose respective components on the time axis were moving in opposite directions—and there was nothing in the theory to say this couldn't happen—the two temporal waves would cancel each other to produce a new entity that had no duration in time. To the human observer they would cease to exist, producing the effect of a particle-antiparticle annihilation.

As a young graduate at CIT in the late 1990s, Bradley Clifford had shared in the excitement that had reverberated around the scientific world after publication of Maesanger's first paper. K-theory became his consuming passion, and soon uncovered his dormant talents; by the time he entered his postdoctoral years, he had already contributed significantly to the further development of several aspects of the theory. Driven by the restless, boundless energy of youth, he thrust beyond the ever-widening frontier of human knowledge, and always the need to know what lay beyond the next hill drew him onward. Those were his idyllic days; there were not enough hours in the day, days in the year, or years in a lifetime to accomplish all the things he knew he had to do.

But gradually the realities of the lesser world of lesser men closed in. The global political and economic situation continued to deteriorate and fields of pure academic research were increasingly subjected to more stringent controls and restraints. Funds that had once flowed freely dried to a trickle; vital equipment was denied; the pick of available talent was lured away by ever more tempting salaries as military and defense requirements assumed priority. Eventually, under special legislation, even the freedom of the nation's leading scientists to work where and how they chose became a luxury that could no longer be allowed.

And so he had come to ACRE, virtually as a draftee . . . to find more effective methods of controlling satellite-borne antimissile lasers.

But though they had commandeered his body and his brain, they could never commandeer his soul. The computers and facilities at ACRE surpassed anything he had ever dreamed of at CIT. He could still let his mind fly free, to soar into the realm of Carl Maesanger's mysterious k-space.

It seemed to him that only minutes had passed when the reminder began flashing in the center of the wall screen, warning him that the meeting was due to commence in five minutes.

Chapter 2

Professor Richard Edwards, Principal Scientific Executive and second-in-command at ACRE, contemplated the document lying on the table in front of him. The wording on the title sheet read: *K-Space Rotations and Gravity Impulses*. Seated around the corner of the table to the professor's left, Walter Massey thumbed idly through his copy, making little of the pages of complex formulae. Opposite Massey, Miles Corrigan leaned back in his chair and regarded Clifford with a cool, predatory stare, making no attempt to conceal the disdain that he felt toward all scientists.

"The rules of this Establishment are perfectly clear, Dr. Clifford," Edwards began, speaking over the top of his interlaced fingers. "All scientific material produced by any person during the time he is employed at ACRE, produced in the course of his duties or otherwise, automatically qualifies as classified information. Precisely what are your grounds for requesting an exemption and permission to publish this paper?"

Clifford returned his look expressionlessly, trying hard for once not to show the irritation he felt for the whole business. He didn't like the air of an Inquisition that had pervaded the room ever since they sat down.

His reply was terse: "Purely scientific material of academic interest only. No security issues involved."

Edwards waited, apparently expecting more. After a few, dragging seconds, Massey shuffled his feet uncomfortably and cleared his throat.

Massey was Clifford's immediate boss in Mathcomps.

He was every inch a practical, hard-applications engineer, fifteen years in the Army's Technical Services Corps having left him with no great inclination toward theoretical matters. When he was assigned a task, he did it without questioning either the wisdom or the motives of his superiors, both of which he took for granted. It was best not to think about such things; that always led to trouble. He represented the end-product of the system, faithfully carrying out his side of a symbiotic existence in which he traded off individual freedom for collective security. He felt a part of ACRE and the institution that it symbolized, in the same way that he had felt a part of the Army; it provided him with the sense of belonging that he needed. He served the organization and the organization served him; it paid him, trained him, made all his major decisions for him, rapped his knuckles when he stepped out of line, and promoted him when he didn't. If he had to, he would readily die fighting to defend all that it stood for.

But Clifford didn't find him really a bad guy for all that.

Right now, Massey wasn't too happy about the way in which Clifford was handling things. He didn't give a damn whether the paper ended up being published or not, but it bothered him that somebody from his section didn't seem to be putting up a good fight to speak his case. The name of the platoon was at stake.

"What Brad means is, the subject matter of his paper relates purely to abstract theoretical concepts. There's nothing about it that could be thought of as having anything to do with national security interests." Massey glanced from Edwards to Corrigan and back again. "You might say it's kinda like a hobby . . . only Brad's hobby happens to involve a lot of mathematics."

"Mmm . . ." Edwards rubbed his thumbs against the point of his chin and considered the proposition. Abstract theoretical concepts had a habit of turning into reality with frightening speed. Even the most innocent-looking scraps of trivia could acquire immense significance when fitted together into a pattern with others. He had no idea of the things that were going on in other security-blanketed research institutions of his own country, not to mention those of the other side. Only Washington held the big picture, and if they went along with Clifford's request, it would mean getting mixed up in all the rigmarole of referring the matter back there for clearance . . . and Washington was never very happy over things like that. Far better if the whole thing could be killed off right at the beginning.

On the other hand, his image wouldn't benefit from too hasty a display of high-handedness . . . must be seen as objective and impartial.

"I have been through the paper briefly, Dr. Clifford," he said. "Before we consider your request specifically, I think it would help if you clarified some of the points that you make." He spread his hands and rested them palms-down on the table. "For example, you make some remarkable deductions concerning the nature of elementary particles and their connection with gravitational propagation. . . ." His look invited Clifford to take it from there.

Clifford sighed. At the best of times he detested lengthy dissertations; the feeling that he was pressing an already lost cause only made it worse. But there was no way out.

"All the known particles of physics," he began, "can be described in terms of Maesanger k-functions. Every particle is a combination of high-order and low-order k-resonances. Theory suggests that it's possible for an entity to exist purely in the high-order domain, without any physical attributes in the dimensions of the observable universe. It couldn't be detected by any known experimental technique."

"This isn't part of Maesanger's original theory," Edwards checked.

"No. It's new."

"This is your own contribution?"

"Yes."

"I see. Carry on." Edwards scribbled a brief note on his pad.

"I've termed such an unobservable entity a 'hi-particle,' and the domain that it exists in, 'hi-space'—the unobservable subset of k-space. The remaining portion of k-space—the spacetime that we perceive—is then termed 'lo-space.'

"Interactions are possible between hi-particles. Most of them result in new hi-particles. Some classes of interaction, however, can produce complete k-functions as end-products—that is, combined hi- and lo-order resonances that are observable. In other words, you'd be able to detect them in normal space." Clifford paused and waited for a response. It came from Massey.

"You mean that as far as anybody can tell, first there's no particle there—just nothing at all—then suddenly—*poof!*—there is."

Clifford nodded. "Exactly so."

"Mmm . . . I see. Spontaneous creation of matter . . . in our universe anyway. Interesting." Edwards began stroking his chin again and nodded to Clifford to continue.

"Since all conventional particles can be thought of as extending into hi-space, they can interact with hi-particles too. When they do, the result can be one of two things.

"First off, the interaction products can include k-resonances—in other words, particles that are observable. What you'd see would be the observable part of the k-particle that was there to begin with, and then the observable part of the k-products that came later. What you wouldn't see is the pure hi-particle that caused the change to take place."

Massey was beginning to look intrigued. He raised a hand to stop Clifford from racing ahead any further for the moment.

"Just a sec, Brad, let's get this straight. A k-particle is something that has bits you can see and bits you can't. Right?"

"Right."

"All the particles that we know are k-particles."

"Right."

"But you figure there are things that nobody can see at all . . . these things you've called 'hi-particles.' "

"Right."

"And two hi's can come together to make a k, and since you can see k's, you'd see a particle suddenly pop outa nowhere. Is that right?"

"Right."

"Okay . . ." Massey inclined his head and collected his thoughts for a moment. "Now—in idiot language—just go over that last bit again, willya?" He wasn't being deliberately sarcastic; it was just his way of speaking.

"A hi can interact with a k to produce another k, or maybe several k's. When that happens, what you see is a sudden change taking place in an observable particle, without any apparent cause."

"A spontaneous event," Edwards commented, nodding slowly. "An explanation for the decay of radioactive nuclei and the like, perhaps."

Clifford began warming slightly. Maybe he wasn't wasting his time after all.

"Precisely so," he replied. "The statistics that come out of it fit perfectly with the observed frequencies of quantum mechanical tunneling effects, energy-level transitions of the electron, and a whole list of other probabilistic phenomena at the atomistic scale. It gives us a common explanation for all of them. They're not inexplicable any more; they only look that way in lo-order spacetime."

"Mmm . . ." Edwards looked down again at the paper lying in front of him. The administrator in him still wanted to put a swift end to the whole business, but the scientist in him was becoming intrigued. If only this discussion could have taken place at some other time, a time free of the dictates of harsher realities. He looked up at Clifford and noted for the first time the pleading earnestness burning from those bright, youthful eyes. Clifford could be no more than in his mid to late twenties—the age at which Newton and Einstein had been at their peak. This generation would have much to answer for when the day finally came to count the cost of it all.

"You said that there is a second possible way in which hi- and k-particles can interact."

"Yes," Clifford confirmed. "They can also interact to produce hi-order entities only." He looked at Massey. "That means that a hi plus a k can make just hi's. You'd see the k to start with, then suddenly you wouldn't see anything at all."

"Spontaneous particle extinction," Edwards supplied.

"I'll be damned," said Massey.

"The two effects of creation and extinction are symmetrical," Clifford offered. "In loose terms you could say that a particle exists only for a finite time in the observable universe. It appears out of nowhere, persists for a while, then either vanishes, or decays into other particles, which eventually vanish anyway. The length of time that any one particle will exist is indeterminate, but the statistical average for large numbers of them can be calculated accurately. For some, such as those involved in familiar high-energy decay processes, lifetimes can be very short; for radioactive decays, seconds to millions of years; for the so-called stable particles, like the proton and electron, billions of years."

"You mean the stable particles aren't truly stable at all?" Edwards raised his eyebrows in surprise. "Not permanently?"

"No."

Silence reigned for a short while as the room digested the flow of information. Edwards looked pensive. Miles Corrigan continued to remain silent, but his sharp eyes missed nothing. He smoothed a wrinkle in his expensively tailored suit and glanced at his watch, giving the impression of being bored and impatient. Massey spoke next.

"You see, like I said, it's all pure academic stuff.

Harmless." He shrugged and showed his empty palms. "Maybe this once there's no reason for us not to have Washington check it out. I vote we clear it."

"Maybe isn't good enough, Walt," Edwards cautioned. "We have to be sure. For one thing, I need to be certain of the scientific accuracy of it all first. Wouldn't do to go wasting Washington's time with a theory that turned out to be only half worked out; that wouldn't do ACRE's image any good at all. There are a couple of points that bother me already."

Massey retreated abruptly.

"Sure—whatever you say. It was just a thought."

Clifford noted with no surprise that Massey had been simply testing to see which way the wind was blowing. He would go along with whatever the other two decided.

"Dr. Clifford," Edwards resumed. "You state that even the stable particles possess only a finite duration in normal spacetime."

"Yes."

"You've proved it . . . rigorously . . . ?"

"Yes."

"I see . . ." A pause. "But tell me, how do you reconcile that statement with some of the fundamental laws of physics, some of which have stood unchallenged for decades or even for centuries? It is well known, is it not, that decay of the proton would violate the law of conservation of baryon number; decay of the electron would violate conservation of charge. And what about the conservation laws of mass-energy and momentum, for example? What happens to those if stable particles are simply allowed to appear and vanish?"

Clifford recognized the tone. The professor's attitude was negative. He was out to uncover the flaws—anything that would justify going no further for the present and sending Clifford back to the drawing board. The mildly challenging note was calculated to invoke an emotive response, thus carrying the whole discussion from the purely rational level to the irrational and opening the way for a choice of counterproductive continuations.

Clifford was on his guard. "Violation of many conservation laws is well known already. Although the strong nuclear interactions do obey all the laws listed, electromagnetic interactions do not conserve isotopic spin. Furthermore, the weak nuclear interactions don't conserve strangeness, nor do they conserve charge or parity discretely but only as a combined product of C and P. As a general principle, the stronger the force, the greater the number of laws it has to obey. This has been known as an experimental fact for a long time. In recent years we've known that it follows automatically from Maesanger wave functions. Each conservation principle is related to a particular order of resonance. Since stronger interactions involve more orders, they obey more conservation laws. As you reduce the number of orders involved, you lose the necessity to obey the laws that go with the higher orders.

"What I'm saying here . . . " he gestured toward the paper "is that the same pattern holds true right on through to the weakest force of all—gravity. When you get down to the level of the gravitational interaction—determined by lo-order resonances only—you lose more of the conservation laws that come with the hi-orders. In fact, as it turns out, you lose all of them."

"I see," said Edwards. "But if that's so, why hasn't anybody ever found out about it? Why haven't centuries of experiments revealed it? On the contrary, they would appear to demonstrate the reverse of what you're saying."

Clifford knew fully that Edwards was not that naive. The possibility that conservation principles might not be universal was something that scientists had speculated about for a long time. But forcing somebody to adopt a defensive posture was always a first step toward weakening his case. Nevertheless, Clifford had no option but to go along with it.

"Because, as I mentioned earlier, the so-called stable particles have extremely long average lifetimes. Matter is created and extinguished at an infinitesimally small rate—on the everyday scale anyway; it would be utterly immeasurable by any laboratory experiment. For matter at ordinary density, it works out at about one extinction per ten billion particles present per year. No experiment ever devised could detect anything like that. You could only detect it on the cosmological scale—and nobody has performed experiments with whole galaxies yet."

"Mmm . . ." Edwards paused to collect his thoughts. Massey sensed that things could go either way and opted to stay out.

Clifford decided to move ahead. "All interactions can be represented as rotations in k-space. This accounts for the symmetries of quantum mechanics and the family-number conservation laws. In fact, all the conservation laws come out as simply different projections of one basic set of k-conservation relationships.

"Every rotation results in a redistribution of energy about the various k-axes, which we see as forces of one kind or another. The particular set of rotations that correspond to transitions of a particle between hispace and normal space—events of creation and extinction—produces an expanding wave front in k-space that projects as a gravitational pulse. In other words, every particle creation or extinction generates a pulse of gravity."

There were no questions at that point, so Clifford continued. "A particle can appear spontaneously anywhere in the universe with equal probability. When it does, it will emanate a minute gravity pulse. The figures indicate something like one particle creation in a volume of millions of cubic meters per year; utterly immeasurable—that's why nobody has ever found out about it.

"On the other hand, a particle can vanish only from where it already is—obviously. So, where large numbers of particles are concentrated together, you will get a larger number of extinctions over a given period of time. Thus you'll get a higher rate of production of gravity pulses. The more particles there are and the more closely they're packed together, the greater the total additive effect of all the pulses. That's why you get a gravity field around large masses of matter; it isn't a static phenomenon at all—just the additive effect of a large number of gravity quanta. It appears 'smooth' only at the macroscopic level.

"Gravity isn't something that's simply associated with mass per se; it's just that mass defines a volume of space inside which a large number of extinctions can happen. It's the extinctions that produce the gravity."

"I thought you said the creations do so, too," Massey queried.

"They do, but their contribution is negligible. As I said, creations take place all through the universe with equal probability anywhere—inside a piece of matter or way outside the galaxy. In a region occupied by matter, the effect due to extinctions would dominate overwhelmingly."

"Mmm . . ." Edwards frowned at his knuckles while considering another angle.

"That suggests that mass ought to decay away to nothing. Why doesn't it?"

"It does. Again, the numbers we're talking about are much too small to be measurable on the small scale or over short time periods. As an example, a gram of water contains about ten to the power twenty-three atoms. If those atoms vanished at the rate of three million every second, it would take about ten billion years for all traces of the original gram to disappear. Is it any wonder the decay's never been detected experimentally? Is it any wonder that the gravity field of a planet appears smooth? We have no way of even detecting the gravity due to one gram of water, let alone measure it to see if it's quantized. You could only detect it at the cosmological level. At that level, totally dominated by gravity, conservation laws that hold good in laboratories might well break down.

Certainly we have no experimental data to say they don't."

"That means all the bodies in the universe ought to decay away to nothing in time," Edwards pointed out. "They've had plenty of time, but there still seem to be plenty of them around."

"Maybe they do decay away to nothing," Clifford said. "Don't forget that spontaneous creation is going on all the time all over the universe as well. That's an awful lot of volume and it implies an awful lot of creation."

"You mean a continuous process in which new bodies are formed out of interstellar matter by the known sequences of galactic and planetary evolution; the newly created particles provide a source to replenish the interstellar matter in turn."

"Could be," Clifford agreed.

At last Edwards had drawn Clifford into an area in which he was unable to give definite answers. He pressed the advantage.

"But surely that requires some resurrection of the Continuous Creation Theory of cosmology. As we all know, that notion has been defunct for many years. The overwhelming weight of evidence unquestionably favors the Big Bang."

Clifford spread his arms wide in an attitude of helplessness.

"I know that. All I can say is, the mathematics works. I'm not an astronomer or a cosmologist. I'm not even an experimental scientist. I'm a theoretician. I don't know how conclusive the evidence for Big Bang is, or if there are alternative explanations for some parts. That's why I need to publish this paper. I need to attract the attention of specialists in other areas."

The string of admissions gave Edwards the moment he was looking for, a moment of weakness that could be exploited. It was time to move in the hatchet man. He half-turned toward Corrigan.

"What do you have to say, Miles?"

Miles Corrigan's official title at ACRE was that of

Liaison Director, a euphemism for watchdog. Aloof
from the hierarchy of line managers who reported to
Edwards, Corrigan took his orders directly from the
Technical Coordination Bureau in Washington, an
office of the Pentagon that provided a rationalizing interface between the Defense Department and the various centers of government-directed scientific research.
Through the Bureau, the activities of practically all
the nation's scientists were controlled and coordinated,
both among themselves and with the activities of the
other allies in the Western Democracies. The payer of
pipers was firmly calling the tune.

   Corrigan's job was to make sure that the right things
got done and got done on time; that was the publicized
part anyway. The unpublicized part involved simply
maintaining a political presence—a constant reminder
that whatever things went on in the day-to-day world
of ACRE, they were always part of and subordinate
to the grand design of loftier and more distant archi-
tects. His brief was to watch for, track down, and ex-
orcise "counterproductive influences," which meant
wrong attitudes, uninformed opinions, and anything
else of that nature that threatened to affect adversely
or undermine the smooth attainment of the Establishment's assigned objectives. Corrigan could track a sub-
versive rumor back to its source with all the skill and
tenacity of an epidemiologist tracing an outbreak of
typhoid to its prime carrier. To avoid any witch hunts,
it was safer just to say the kind of things you were
supposed to say, or at best, not to say the kind of
things you weren't. The scientists at ACRE called him
the Commissar.

   By temperament and background he was well qualified for the job. After walking through a first-class
honors degree in law at Harvard, he had set up a
lucrative practice in Washington, specializing in defending the cases of errant politicians—at which he
had demonstrated a prodigious skill. In the course of
a few years he had incurred the lifelong indebtedness
of a long list of fixers and string-pullers—the only

kind of friends that meant anything on his scale of values—and their tokens of gratitude soon added up to a permanent end to all of life's potential financial problems.

He married the daughter of a senator who had made his first million in a series of clandestine arms deals that had involved the offloading of whole shiploads of substandard ammunition on unsuspecting recipients in Burma and Malaysia—or so it was said. The allegations of the senator's involvement were never proved after becoming bogged down over a legal technicality. Miles Corrigan had seen to that.

Through the influence of his father-in-law and the goodwill of a number of friends with the right contacts, he entered government service at the right level to further his ambitions. His assignment to ACRE represented the final stage of his grooming before he made his debut on the international political scene. He had made it while still in his prime and was all set to fly high.

He took the cue, sensing a turkey being set up for the kill. When he spoke, his voice was icy and menacing, like the hiss of a cobra measuring its distance. "I'm not interested in k-spaces, hi-spaces, or any of the other buzz-phrases. If all this boils down to saying that you've got something that serves the national interest, then tell us about it. If you haven't, then why are you wasting our time?"

He confronted Clifford with the sneering, unblinking stare that had destroyed innumerable confused and hostile witnesses. His eyes were mocking, inviting the scientist to court disaster if he dared; at the same time they were insistent, demanding an immediate reply. He caught Clifford completely unprepared.

"But . . . that's not the point. This is . . ." Clifford was surprised to hear himself stumbling for the right word. Even as he spoke he realized he was on the wrong foot and walking straight into the trap, but it was too late. "We're talking about fundamental knowl—"

"Will it help us kill Commies?" Corrigan cut him short.

"No, but . . ."

"Will it help stop Commies from killing us?"

"No . . . I don't know . . . Maybe, someday . . ."

"Then why are you fooling around with it? How much time and resources has all this stuff taken up? What effect has all this had on the work you're paid to be doing? Massey describes it as a hobby, but I don't believe it's quite as simple as that. I've checked the amount of computer usage you've logged over the past six months and I've checked the current status of the projects you're supposed to be working on. They're all way behind schedule. So, where's all the computer time going?"

"I don't suppose Einstein had the A-bomb in mind when he developed special relativity," Clifford retorted, ducking the feint and walking straight into the uppercut.

"Einstein!" Corrigan repeated the word for the benefit of the jury. "He's telling us he's another Einstein. Is that right, Dr. Clifford—you consider yourself to be on a par with Einstein?"

"I didn't say anything of the kind, and you damn well know I didn't." Clifford had recovered sufficiently to return Corrigan's look with a glare that could only be described as murderous. He knew that he was being drawn on to Corrigan's home ground. Somehow he didn't really care much any more.

"You're saying that we ought to allow you to dabble around with anything that takes your fancy and at whatever expense, simply in case you happen to hit upon something useful. Is that how we're supposed to preserve the security of the West? Doesn't the concept of organized professional objectivity mean anything to you people? How long do we have to protect you and the freedom that you're always talking about before you wake up to reality?"

Edwards stared uncomfortably at the table, having

joined Massey in abdication. It was all up to Corrigan now.

"This isn't some kind of philosopher's utopia where anybody is owed the right to any living he chooses," Corrigan continued. "It's a dog-eat-dog jungle; the strong survive and the weak go to the wall. To stay strong we have to get our priorities straight. Your priorities are all screwed up. Now you're asking us to follow suit and compound the offense by approving it."

He took a long, deep breath for effect. "No way. There's no way I'm going to tell Professor Edwards to give a carte blanche for even more time-wasting and misuse of funds and resources."

Actually, Corrigan couldn't tell Edwards to do anything. His use of the word was deliberate, however, serving as a gentle reminder of his own power, if not authority, at ACRE. Edwards didn't argue the point. He knew that Corrigan's reports back to the Bureau would have a lot to do with whether he ever moved on to become chief at ACRE or something similar, or whether he ended up running a backwater missile test range on the northern coast of Baffin Island.

When the victim has been battered to a pulp and stripped of every shred of dignity, he becomes highly suggestible and will respond eagerly to even a slight gesture of friendship. Prison guards had been well versed in the technique throughout history. And Corrigan understood psychology well; he knew what made people tick all right.

His tone softened a fraction. "Everyone's out of step except you, Dr. Clifford. We're all a team here, trying to do a good job. Why make it difficult? Once you make the effort to fit in, you might find that life's not really that bad.

"Don't you feel you owe it to this country and all it stands for—the way of life we all believe in? Isn't it worth a few sacrifices to protect all that? Right now half the world out there is sitting and waiting for us to ease up for just one second so they can blow us all off the face of this planet. Are you just going to sit there and let it happen? Do you want them to come walking in here without having to lift a finger?" Corrigan finished on a note that oozed all-in-it-togetherness. "Or are you gonna join the team, do your share, and help us go out there and zap those bastards?"

Clifford had turned white. Corrigan and his propaganda epitomized everything abhorrent in a world that was going insane. And now he was expecting to enlist Clifford in the ranks of the mindless, brainwashed millions who had toiled and bled and died believing that line ever since the world began. There would always be Corrigans to ride on the backs of the masses—for as long as there were willing backs to carry them. Clifford's voice fell to a whisper as he fought to control the anger that boiled inside, churning his stomach and bubbling up into the back of his throat like waves of nausea.

"I'm not interested in zapping anybody, mister . . . not for you or for whatever you represent. Your system put me here; don't you tell me I'm screwed up now because I don't belong. Don't you tell me I owe anything to your system to help straighten out its mess. Save your garbage for the morons." Without waiting for a reply he got up and strode toward the door. Edwards and Massey remained silent, staring fixedly at the table. If Brad was flushing himself down the tubes, they weren't going to get caught in any of the backsplash.

Clifford, still shaking when he slammed the door of his office behind him five minutes later, began hammering a brief code into the keyboard of the desk terminal. At least he had tried the official channel. The outcome hadn't really been a surprise; that was why he had already prepared a long file in the data bank, ready for immediate transmission.

A woman's face appeared on the screen.

"Message Center. Can I help you?"

"I need an immediate outgoing channel. The destination code is 090909-73785-21318."

The woman began keying the code automatically, then hesitated.

"Triple-09 prefix is extraterrestrial, sir—for the lunar bases."

"I know."

"I'm sorry, but those channels need special authorization from grade 5 or over. Do you have a clearance reference?"

All the frustrations of the last half-hour boiled over.

"Listen, damn it, and store this on file. This is absolutely top priority. I take full responsibility. I don't care if you need clearance from the President, the Pope, or God Almighty himself. GET ME THAT DAMN CHANNEL!"

Chapter 3

". . . Proxima Centauri, 4.3 light-years away from us, has at least three planets of significant size, the largest of them having a mass of 0.0018 times that of the sun and an orbital period of 137 years. Slightly farther away, at 6.0 light-years, Barnard's Star again has at least three planetary companions, B1, B2, and B3, of masses 0.0011, 0.0008, and 0.0003, periods 26, 12, and 14.3 years respectively; we strongly suspect others as well. Beyond these systems, the stars Lalande 2115A, 61Cygni, and Kruger 60A, to name just three, also possess planets that have been positively observed and whose main properties have been accurately measured. In fact, more than thirty planets of stars other than our own sun are known to exist within a radius of twenty light-years from us."

Professor Heinrich Zimmermann pointed out the last item on the list and then turned away from the three-dimensional model of the local regions of the galaxy to look directly into the camera. The camera trolley rolled noiselessly forward to close in on his tall, immaculately dressed figure, dignified by a lean, angular build and a crown of silvery hair.

"Thus some of our work here at the Joliot-Curie Observatories on Lunar Farside has added immensely to our knowledge of the Sun's neighboring planetary systems. If these statistics are extrapolated to cover the whole galaxy, they indicate the existence of billions of planets. If only one in every thousand were to be similar to Earth in temperature and surface chemistry, we are still left with millions of worlds on which life as we know it could emerge. Furthermore, as you saw earlier, the emergence of life is not, as was once supposed, a billion-to-one freak occurrence; as the experiments of such scientists as Okoyaku and Skovensen have shown, it is virtually a certainty once the right conditions are established." He stepped aside to allow a zoom-in for a close-up of the model while he delivered his final words. "I will leave you to draw your own conclusions as to the implications of these statements. Despite the exciting things that we have seen in this program, it could be that the real excitement is yet to come."

"Okay. Cut it there." The floor director's voice sounded from the wall of darkness behind the arc lights. "That was fine. Take a short break, but be ready for another take of the first part of sequence 5 in five minutes. Harry and Mike, don't go rushing off anyplace—I need to talk to you for a second."

The lights dimmed and a hubbub of voices broke out on all sides. The floor around Zimmermann was transformed into an arena of bustling technicians. He paused to allow his eyes to readjust to the comparative gloom of normal lighting, acknowledged the thanks from the film team, and moved away from all the activity to stand by one of the dome's viewing ports. While he dabbed his forehead lightly with a pocket handkerchief, he stared silently out at the harsh, bleak landscape of the lunar surface.

Beyond the litter of assorted engineering and latticework that marked the environs of the observatory complex and base, the soft, rolling dunes of ash-gray dust lay seared beneath the direct rays of lunar noon, pitted here and there by the ink-black shadow of the occasional crag or boulder. Above the featureless horizon, a million blazing jewels lay scattered on a carpet of velvet infinity. Joliot-Curie was without exception the loneliest center of human habitation in the universe. Here, shielded by the body of the Moon itself from Earth's incessant outpouring of electronic caterwauling, gigantic radio dishes listened for the whisperings that brought the secrets of the cosmos; unhampered by any atmosphere and all but free of the weight-induced distortions that had crippled their Earth-bound predecessors, enormous optical telescopes probed the very limits of the observable universe. The Joliot-Curie observatory complex was distant; it was isolated, but it was free—a surviving outpost of unfettered science where the pursuit of knowledge constituted its own ends.

A shadow from behind him darkened the wall by the side of the viewing port. Zimmermann turned to find Gus Craymer standing there; Craymer was Assistant Producer of *Exploding Horizons*—the documentary they were making. Craymer peered past the professor to take in the scene from the outside and pulled a face.

"How come you guys don't go nuts in this place?" he asked. Zimmermann followed his gaze, and then turned back smiling faintly.

"Oh, you would be surprised, Mr. Craymer. The solitude and peace can be quite stimulating. It really depends on what you see when you look out there. Remember the rhyme about the two men and the prison bars? I wonder sometimes that you don't all go nuts on Earth."

"You see stars, huh," Craymer grinned. "Literally." He indicated the far side of the room with a nod of his head. "There's coffee going over there if you'd like some." Zimmermann folded the handkerchief and replaced it in his breast pocket.

"Thank you, no. I'll enjoy some in comfort when we have completely finished. How near the end are we?"

Craymer consulted the typed schedule that he was holding.

"Well, there's some outside shooting to be done now that the Sun's at the right angle . . . some close-ups of instruments to go with the commentary we recorded

yesterday. Lemme see now, where are your parts . . . ?
Here we are—there's only one more shot that involves you and that's coming up right now. That'll be
a retake of the beginning of sequence 5 . . . the one
where you talk about radiation from black holes."

"Ah, yes. Very good."

Craymer closed the folder and turned to look out
across the floor with Zimmermann.

"I guess you'll be glad to get back to your work
without this bedlam going on all the time," he said.
"You've been very patient and cooperative while
we've been here. I'd like you to know that all the
people on the team appreciate it."

"Quite the contrary, Mr. Craymer," Zimmermann
replied. "It has been my pleasure. The public has paid
for everything here, including my salary; they have a
right to be kept informed of what we are doing and
why. Besides, anything that popularizes the true nature of science is worth a little time and trouble, don't
you think?"

Craymer smiled ruefully as he recalled the problems
that they had encountered with petty bureaucrats in
Washington six months before, when they had tried
to put a documentary together on spacecraft naviga-
tion and propulsion systems. In the end they'd had to
abandon the project, since what was left after the cen-
soring wouldn't have made a lesson fit for elementary-
school students.

"I wish more people thought that way these days,"
he said. "They're all going paranoid back home."

"I can well imagine," Zimmermann replied, moving
aside to make room for a technician who was positioning a spotlight according to directions being shouted
from across the room.

As they began threading their way toward the area
where the next shooting sequence would take place,
Craymer asked: "How long have you been up here
now?"

"Oh, eighteen months or more, I suppose . . . although I do visit Earth from time to time. It may sound

strange but I really miss very little. My work is here and, as I said a moment ago, the environment is stimulating. We have no interruptions and are largely left free of interference of any kind."

"Must be nice to be able to do your own thing," Craymer agreed. "You steer clear of all the sordid political stuff then, huh?"

"Yes, I suppose we do . . . but it has not always been so. I have held a number of government scientific positions, over several years . . . in Germany you understand, before the formation of U.S. Europe. However . . ." Zimmermann sighed, "when it became apparent that official support would be progressively restricted to activities of the kind in which neither my conscience nor my interests made me wish to participate, I resigned and joined the International Scientific Foundation. It is completely autonomous, you see, being funded entirely from private and voluntary sources."

"Yeah, I know. I'm surprised the USE government didn't try and make things difficult . . . or maybe you don't push around easy?"

Zimmermann smiled and scratched an eyebrow.

"I think it was more a question of persuading them that neither I nor my particular kind of knowledge would have been of very much use to them," he said.

Craymer reflected that the more he saw of life, the more he became convinced that the quality of modesty was the preserve solely of the truly great men that he happened to meet. The amplified voice of the floor director boomed around the room, curtailing their conversation.

"All right, everybody. In your places for the sequence 5 retake now. This will be the last one today. Let's make it good." The murmuring died away and the arc lights came on to flood a backdrop set up against one wall. To the right of the backdrop, banks of instrument panels and consoles carried a colorful array of blinking lights and display screens. Zimmermann moved forward from the jumble of cameras, microphone booms, chairs, and figures, to stand in the semicircle of light in front of the consoles. A short distance to his right, Martin Borel, compere of the documentary, took his position in front of the backdrop.

The floor director's voice came again. "Mart—this time, start moving to your left as soon as you say '. . . the most perplexing phenomena known to man.' Take it at the same speed as last time—that way the professor will appear on camera just as you introduce him. Okay?"

"Sure thing," Borel acknowledged.

"Professor?"

"Yes?"

"When you refer to the equipment behind you for the first time, do you think you could move back for about five seconds so that we can pan in on it, please? Then close back in with Mart and resume the dialogue."

"Certainly."

"Thank you. Okay—roll it." Borel straightened up and assumed a posture with his hands high, near his shoulders. The clapperboard echoed. "Action."

"The black hole," Borel began, speaking in the firm, resonant tones of the professional. "Strange regions of space where matter and energy are lost forever without trace, and time itself stands still. We have traced the history of black holes through from early speculations all the way to the confirmed realities of the present day. Scientists can now draw for us an incredible picture of the bewildering laws of an unfamiliar physics, that dominate these mysterious bodies. But despite all this new knowledge, unexpected riddles continue to emerge. The black hole is still, and will continue for a long time to be, one of the most perplexing phenomena known to man."

Borel began walking slowly across the front of the backdrop toward Zimmermann.

"To give you an idea of the kinds of riddle that investigators into black-hole physics are meeting today, let me introduce Professor Heinrich Zimmermann of ISF, Director of Joliot-Curie and perhaps one of the most distinguished physical astronomers of our time.

"Professor, the receiver that we saw outside is collecting radiation from the vicinity of a black hole in space. Down here you are analyzing the information that the computers have extracted from that radiation. Could you summarize for us, please, what you are finding and what new questions you are being forced to ask?"

By now Zimmermann had been through this routine three times.

"The receiver is at this moment trained on a binary system known as Cygnus X-1," he replied. "A binary system is one in which two stars are formed very close to one another and orbit about a common center of mass under their mutual gravitational coupling. Most binary systems comprise two ordinary stars, each of which conforms to one of the standard classifications. Some binaries, however, contain only one normal, visible star, the second body being invisible. The so-called dark companion emits no light but can be detected by its gravitational influence on the visible star. In many cases, they are known to be neutron stars as described earlier in the program. In a number of confirmed instances, however, collapse of the companion body has continued beyond the point at which a neutron star is formed, which results in the condition of ultimate degeneracy of matter—a black hole. Cygnus X-1 is an example of precisely this."

"In other words, you have an ordinary star and a black hole orbiting each other as a stable system," Borel interjected.

"That is so. However, the system is not quite permanently stable. You see, the gravitational attraction of the black hole is strong enough for it to draw off gaseous material from the surface of the star. The system thus comprises three parts essentially: the visible star, the black hole, and a filament of stellar material that flows out of the former into the latter, connecting them rather like an umbilical cord. The filament spirals around the black hole as the particles contained in it acquire energy and accelerate down the gravitational gradient. In a somewhat simplified way, you might picture it as bathwater spiraling down into the drain." He paused, allowing Borel to pose the next question.

"But straightforward as this might sound, it is producing results that you are having difficulty in explaining. Isn't that so?"

"Very true," Zimmermann agreed. "You see, the matter that is being drawn off of the visible star is extremely hot and therefore in a highly ionized state. In other words, it is made up of strongly charged particles. Now, charged particles in motion give rise to electromagnetic radiation; calculations predict that a characteristic spectrum of broad-band radiation, extending up into the x-ray frequencies, should be observable as a halo around the black hole. Indeed, we do observe radiation of the general nature that we would expect. Precise analysis of the spectrum and energy distributions, however, reveals a pattern that is not at all in accordance with theory."

Zimmermann moved to one side and gestured toward the instrumentation panels behind them. "The equipment that you see here is being used for this kind of investigation. From here we can monitor and control the receiving equipment, direct the computers, and observe what they are doing.

"Many years of observations and measurements have enabled us to determine the characteristics of several black-hole binaries with sufficient accuracy for us to compute precisely a mathematical model that should give us the pattern of radiation that each should produce." He moved forward to indicate one of the monitor screens on the console. "In fact, this is a picture of the theoretical distribution pattern computed for Cygnus X-1." The screen showed a wavy green line, annotated with captions and symbols; it rose and fell in a series of peaks, valleys, and plateaus, like a cross-sectional view of a mountain range.

"This is what we should expect to see. But when we analyze the data actually received from Cygnus X-1 . . ." he touched a button to conjure up a second, red curve, "we see that there is a significant discrepancy." The screen confirmed his words. The red curve was of a different shape and lay displaced above the green curve; only in one or two places did the green rise high enough for the two to nearly touch.

"Both curves are to the same scale and plotted from the same origin," Zimmermann commented. "If our model were correct, they would be approximately the same. It means that the amount of radiation actually measured is much greater than that which can be accounted for by theory."

"Actual measurement shows more radiation than predicted," Borel repeated. "Where does the excess radiation come from?"

"That, of course, is what intrigues us," Zimmermann replied. "You see, there are only three objects in the vicinity—the star, the filament, and the black hole. We are quite confident that we know enough about the physics of ordinary matter—as exemplified by the star and the filament—to exclude them as possible sources. That leaves only the black hole itself. But how can a black hole produce radiation? That is the problem confronting us. You see, all our theories of physics, based on general relativity, tell us that nothing —matter, energy, radiation, information, or any kind of influence—can escape from a black hole. So how can the black hole be responsible for the extra energy that we detect as radiation? But there is nothing else there for it to come from.

"The answer to this question could have very far-reaching consequences." The camera pulled in for a close-up. "Let us ask the question: What happens to matter when it falls into a black hole? We know that it disappears completely from the universe of which we have any knowledge. Logically, one must conclude that it exists thereafter either in some other part of our own universe or in some entirely different universe. There would appear to be no other possibility. If you reflect for a moment on the implications of what I have just said, you will realize why it is that we get excited at the discovery of what could turn out to be a process operating in the reverse direction. Something that contemporary theory declares impossible is being observed to happen. Behind it, we see hints of a whole new realm of physical phenomena and laws, of which we must at present admit an almost total ignorance. And yet we have strong reasons to suspect that within this mysterious realm, things that we consider to be impossible could turn out to be commonplace."

Borel waited a few seconds to allow the professor's words time to take effect.

"I find this absolutely fascinating, and I'm sure the viewers do too," he finally said. "There are one or two questions about what you've said that I'd like to come back to in a moment. But before we do that, for the benefit of the more technically minded among those watching, I wonder if you would describe in a little more detail the exact function of each of the pieces of equipment that you have assembled behind us here."

"Okay. Cut." The director's voice called again. "That was good. We'll splice the rest of take 2 on from there to complete that sequence. That's all for today, everybody. I'd like all the people who are involved in tomorrow's outside shooting to stay on for a schedule update. Everyone else is free to enjoy the J-C nightlife. Thanks. See you all at dinner."

The arc lights went out and Zimmermann spent a few minutes discussing technical details with the direction team. Then he left the room, traced his way through to the door that gave access to one of the interdome connecting tubes, and followed the tube through to Maindome, which stood adjacent. From there he descended by elevator to emerge four levels

below ground in the corridor that led to his office
suite. His secretary was watering the plants in the
outer office when he entered.

"Hi," she greeted with a freckled grin over her
shoulder. "All through?"

"Hello, Marianne. Yes. I must confess I'm not terri-
bly sorry either." He looked at what she was doing.
"My goodness, look at the size of those plants already.
I'm sure that even your fingers can't be that green. It
must be the gravity." Casting a casual eye over the
notes and papers on her desk, he inquired, "Anything
interesting?" She turned and creased her face into a
frown of concentration.

"Mellows called and said that the replacement
photomultiplier has been fitted in C dome—he said
you'd know what it was all about. Pierre's come down
with a bug and is in sickbay; he won't be able to make
the meeting tomorrow."

"Oh, dear. Nothing serious, I hope."

"I don't think so. I think it was something he ate.
Doc said he looked distinctly hydroponic."

"Uh huh."

"And there was this long message that came in,
addressed to you by name . . . from a Dr. Clifford at
some place in New Mexico."

"Clifford . . . ? Clifford . . . ?" Zimmermann shook
his head slowly. "Who is he?"

"Oh." Marianne looked surprised. "I assumed you
knew him. I took a hard copy of it . . . here." She lifted
a thick wad of closely printed pages out of a tray and
passed them across. "Came in about an hour or more
ago."

Zimmermann ruffled curiously through the sheets of
mathematical equations and formulae, then turned
back to the top sheet to study the heading.

"Dr. Bradley Clifford," he read aloud. "No. I'm
sure I have never heard of him. I'll take it though
and have a look at it later. In the meantime, would
you get Sam Carson at Tycho on the screen for me,

please. I'd like to check the schedule for incoming flights from Earth."

"Will do," she replied as the professor disappeared through the door into the inner office.

Chapter 4

Nothing happened for about a month.

Then they threw the book at Clifford. They hauled him up in front of panels who lectured him about his obligations to the nation, reminded him of his moral responsibilities toward his colleagues and fellow citizens, and described to him all the things that they assumed he felt about his own career prospects. They brought in a couple of FBI officials who questioned him for hours about his political convictions, his social activities, his friends, acquaintances, and student-day affiliations. They said he was irresponsible, he was immature, and that he had problems in conforming, which they could help him with. But, to his unconcealed surprise and mild regret, they didn't fire him.

Just when it seemed to be approaching its traumatic peak, the whole affair was suddenly dropped and apparently forgotten. It was as if somebody somewhere had quietly passed down the message to ease off. Why this should be so, Clifford could only guess, but he didn't imagine for a moment that such old-fashioned sentiments as charity or philanthropy had very much to do with it. Something unusual had happened somewhere, he was sure, and for reasons best known to others, he wasn't being told what. But he didn't waste too much time worrying about such matters; he had found other, more absorbing, things to occupy him.

Edwards's remarks about Steady State and Big Bang theories of the universe had stimulated Clifford's curiosity with regard to cosmological models. Accordingly, Clifford applied himself to refreshing his knowledge of the subject. In due course, he was intrigued to discover that, while the weight of observational evidence amassed over the decades strongly favored Big Bang as Edwards had pointed out, a comparatively recent theory of quasars had been published that seemed to threaten seriously one of the traditional pillars upon which the Big Bang model rested.

It was a question of the amount of helium present in the galaxy. Both cosmological models—Big Bang and Steady State—enabled mathematical predictions to be made of how much helium there ought to be.

According to the generally accepted Big Bang model, most of the helium that existed had been produced during the phase of intense nuclear reactions that accompanied the first few minutes of the Bang. Calculation showed that as a consequence of the processes involved, one atom in every ten that went to make up the galaxy would be a helium atom. During the twelve billion years or so that followed the Bang, this amount would be increased slightly by the manufacture of helium through stellar fusion.

On the other hand, the Steady State model, by that time largely discredited, was obliged to assume that all the helium observed had been produced by the fusion of hydrogen nuclei in the interiors of stars. Measurements of such fusion reactions in terrestrial laboratories and nuclear reactors, when combined with the data that had been accumulated through years of astronomical observation, gave a figure for the total rate of helium production for the whole of the galaxy. When this figure was multiplied by the accepted age of the galaxy, the answer provided an estimate of how much helium there should be in total; it came out at about one atom in every hundred.

Here, then, was a relatively clear-cut method of testing the validity of the two models: Big Bang predicted ten times the amount of helium that Steady State did. Many such tests had been performed, all with a high level of confidence. They all gave a result in the order of ten percent. Big Bang, it appeared, passed the test extremely well.

Or so it had seemed before the Japanese theory of quasars was announced and confused the issue. The theory explained the phenomenal amount of energy radiated by quasars as the result of the mutual annihilation of enormous quantities of matter and antimatter. Quasars were viewed as the scenes of cosmic violence on an unprecedented scale, where armies of matter and antimatter numbering billions of solar masses each were locked in a ruthless battle of extermination, destined to continue until one or the other adversary was completely eliminated. Eventually a galaxy would condense out of the ashes of the conflict—a normal galaxy or an antigalaxy, depending on the flag of the survivors.

The detailed mechanics of the process as presented by the two Japanese cosmologists involved the production of large amounts of helium as a by-product. That put a new light on the question of cosmological models.

Because of their enormous distances, quasars provided, in effect, a window into the past—a view of events that had taken place billions of years previously. If the Japanese theory was correct, the Milky Way Galaxy too would have been formed from the debris of a cataclysmic quasar event that had occurred during some earlier cosmic epoch. The quasar had burned itself out, but its residues still remained—including the helium.

So that could be the answer. Maybe the observed amount of helium didn't require the primordial inferno of a Big Bang to explain it at all. At least, now there was an alternative explanation that needed looking into.

Even if the theory eventually came to be fully substantiated, vindication of the Steady State model would not follow automatically. For one thing, the time-window provided by long-range astronomical observations revealed an evolving universe—evolving from a population of quasars to a population of galaxies—and not one that remained unchanging in its general appearance throughout the whole of time, as seemed to be demanded by a Steady State definition; indeed, the new theory itself required an evolutionary sequence.

But Clifford was less interested in the issue of Big Bang versus Steady State than in that of Big Bang versus his own theories of k-space rotations and spontaneous particle events. Edwards had been sceptical on the grounds that Clifford's theories seemed irreconcilable with Big Bang. However, if Big Bang were superseded by something else, Clifford could be right. Here was a hint that the ground upon which the edifice of Big Bang had been erected might not be solid bedrock after all; it made Clifford wonder how firm the foundations of its remaining pillars might turn out to be.

Whether Steady State became resurrected or not as a consequence was a separate, and largely irrelevant, matter.

Chapter 5

Clifford rested his elbows on the edge of the table and cocked his head, first to one side and then to the other, as he studied the checkered board being displayed on the Infonet screen. If he advanced his pawn to King 5 as he had been preparing to do for the last four moves, Black could initiate a series of exchanges that would leave Clifford with a weak center. So Clifford had no choice but to postpone the pawn move yet again and cramp Black first by pinning the knight on . . . no, he couldn't; Black's last move had unmasked the queen, protecting the square that Clifford wanted to move his bishop to. Damn! The machine had seen right through it. He sighed and began to explore possible ways of opening up his king's bishop's file to bring some rook power to bear on the problem.

Suddenly a flashing message in bright red letters appeared across the middle of the board:

> YOU'RE IGNORING ME!
> AND YOUR DINNER'S READY!!
> AND I'M FED UP!!!
> AND IT'S NOT GOOD ENOUGH!!!!

He grinned, keyed the terminal into *Local Override* mode, and tapped in the reply:

> ARMIES MIGHT MARCH ON THEIR STOMACHS
> BUT HAVE YOU EVER TRIED IT?
> OK—I'M COMING DOWN.

"I should think so." The voice of his wife, Sarah, chided him from the audio grille. "I wonder if computers have ever been cited in divorce cases before."

"As core-respondents?" he offered.

"You idiot."

"What's to eat?"

"Bits, bytes, and synchronous whatsits—what else? Oh—and *processed* veg. There—how's that?"

"Not bad."

He canceled the override, stored the present position of the game, and cleared the connection, having been informed that the session had cost him $1.50 of network time. As he rose from the chair amid the shambles of books and papers that he had long come to feel at home in, he noted absently that the chart of elementary-particle decay processes was coming away from the wall above the desk and resolved for the fourth time that month to do something about it sometime.

Sarah came from an English family that had once been reasonably prosperous. Her father had risen from Marketing Assistant to Managing Director of a ladies-fashion business that owned a number of factories in Yorkshire and Lancashire, with its head office and showrooms in London. His life had been one of ceaseless work and total dedication; spending twelve hours a day at his desk—frequently more—and logging hundreds of hours flying time across the air lanes of Europe, he had transformed a demoralized sales force and a collection of antiquated mills into a vigorous, professionally managed and profitable business operation. On one occasion, in the early days when the going was tough, he had mortgaged his own house as security for a bank loan to pay that week's wages.

But as the country stagnated under the burden of its own brand of socialism and everybody clamored for a more equitable distribution of a wealth that became steadily more difficult to create in the first place, the fruits of his labors were milked away and poured into the melting pot of free handouts and subsidies from which the new utopia was to emerge.

Although she had stayed with him through the rise and fall of his dreams, Sarah chose not to join her father's business, preferring instead to pursue a career in medicine, in which she had developed an interest at an early age. She studied at London University and Charing Cross Hospital during the day and helped her father with his administrative chores in her spare time. A year before she was due to complete her studies, her parents parted amicably; her mother went north to join a Scottish company director in the oil industry while her father, leaving the carcass of his own enterprise to the squabblings of the vultures from various government ministries, cashed his shares and was last seen heading south for sunnier climes, accompanied by a glamorous Italian heiress. Sarah went to live with an aunt in California, where she continued studying medicine and qualified as a radiologist. It was there, while taking a short refresher course in nuclear medicine at CIT, that she met Clifford. They were married six months later. When he moved to ACRE, she obtained a job at the local hospital, working three days a week; the money helped and the job kept her from becoming bored and getting rusty.

She was garnishing two juicy steaks when he entered the kitchen door behind her and pinched her sides just below her ribs.

"Eek! Don't do that when I'm cooking—it's dangerous. Come to think of it, don't do it at all."

"You're funny when you squeak like that." He peered over her shoulder. "Hey—I've been conned."

"What do you mean, conned?"

"You said it was ready. You're only just dishing it out. You might have cost me the game busting in on my concentration like that."

"Good. Concentrate on me instead." She carried the plates over to the table. They sat down.

"Looks good," Clifford commented. "Where'd it come from?"

"A cow of course. Oh, I forgot. They wouldn't have taught you things like that in physics, would they?"

"Where'd you get it, you dumb broad?"

"Same place as usual. I'm just a good choose-ist."

"I already know that. Look who you married."

Sarah raised her eyes imploringly toward the ceiling. They ate in silence for a while. Then she said:

"I called Joan and Pete about those theater reservations while you were upstairs. It's all right for Friday night."

"Mm . . . good."

"George is coming too. You remember George?"

Clifford frowned at his plate while he finished chewing.

"George? Who's George?" He thought for a second. "Not Joan's brother George?"

"That's the one."

"The one in the Army. Big guy, black hair . . . likes music."

"I don't know how you do it."

Clifford frowned again. "I thought he was overseas somewhere."

"He was, but he's home on leave at the moment. He's with a missile battery in eastern Turkey."

"Great." Clifford attacked his steak once more. "He's good fun. Haven't seen him for . . . must be around a year now." He didn't pursue the subject further. Sarah watched him in silence, her face serious.

Eventually she said in a strangely sober voice: "Joan told me he's been talking about the situation out there. They're on stand-by alert practically all of the time now. They have combat patrols airborne around the clock, and the mountains are full of tanks ready to move at a moment's notice."

"Mmm . . ."

"She's worried sick, Brad. She says he's convinced there'll be a showdown before long . . . everywhere. And now that she's expecting, it's really getting her down. . . ." Sarah's voice trailed away. She continued to stare at Clifford, looking for some sign of reassurance, but he carried on eating stolidly. "What do you think'll happen?"

"No idea . . ." He realized reluctantly that something more was called for, but was aware that Sarah knew him too well to be taken in by the clichés that immediately sprang to mind. "It doesn't look too good, does it?" he conceded at last. "Our esteemed and inspired leaders have their righteous cause to protect. I've got mine."

When Clifford and Sarah conversed, most of the dialogue was unspoken—and instantly understood. In these few words he had told her that as far as he was concerned, even one human life was too high a price to pay for any political or ideological crusade. In anticipation of her next question—whether he would go into the armed services if drafted—the answer was no. Doing so would help solve nothing. If half the world had been brainwashed into becoming zombies, the answer was not to go backward a hundred years and emulate them. Man had to move forward. Universal education, awareness, and knowledge offered the only permanent solution. Bombs, missiles, and hatred would only drag the agony out longer, giving people a tangible threat to unite against. If war came, he would find a way to survive and to be himself in whatever way was left open to him. That would be the only meaningful way of fighting for something that was worth preserving.

She looked hard at him for what seemed a long time, then her face softened into a wry half-smile.

"What would we do then—head for the hills?"

He shook his head and replied lightly, "Everybody and his brother would have the same idea. You wouldn't be able to breathe up there. Death trap— right in the middle of the fallout zone from the West Coast. You'd need to get away from the wind system of the northern hemisphere completely. Head south— more privacy in the jungles."

"Ugh!" Sarah pulled a face. "Nasty crawly things there . . . and slithery things. Don't like them."

"Nor do most people. That's why it would be the thing to do. Anyhow . . ." The chime of the Infonet extension in the den interrupted him. "Hell—who's that?"

"I'll get it. You finish that up." Sarah rose and disappeared through the door. Clifford could hear the muffled tones of one end of a brief dialogue. Then she came into the kitchen again.

"It's somebody asking for you. I've never seen him before—a Dr. Phillips from California?"

"Phillips?"

"He seems to know you."

Clifford contemplated his fork quizzically for a moment, then set it down on his plate and strolled through into the den. He sank into a swivel chair and swung round to face the screen.

The apparition confronting him looked like a cross between something out of a rock opera and a reincarnation from Elizabethan England. His hair fell in flowing blond waves almost to his shoulders, forming an evangelical frame for his medieval pointed beard and shaped mustache. The part of his body that was visible was clad in a loose silky shirt of vivid orange, with ornate designs in gold thread embroidered about the shoulders and the long, tapering collar. Clifford's first guess was that he was about to be the victim of a harangue by some kind of religious freak.

"Dr. Clifford?" the caller inquired. At least there was no hint of fanatical zeal in the voice.

"Yes."

"Dr. Bradley Clifford of Advanced Communications Research?"

"No less."

"Hi. You don't know me. My name's Philipsz—Dr. Aubrey Philipsz of the Berkeley Research Institute. I'd better spell that: P-H-I-L-I-P-S-Z. Most people that like me call me Aub. I work on the experimental side at Berkeley—high-energy particle physics."

"Uh huh." Clifford was still trying to orient himself toward the probable direction that the conversation would take, but no particular direction seemed to suggest itself. The voice issuing from the grille sounded out of character with the face on the screen. If it hadn't been for the synchronization, Clifford could have believed that the audio and visual components of two different conversations had somehow gotten scrambled in the network. Aub sounded confident, composed, and totally rational, though without any trace of arrogance. His eyes were shrewd and penetrating, yet sparkled at the same time as if suppressed mirth were bubbling up to break free.

"You're the guy who wrote the paper that connects gravity with k-space transitions," Aub confirmed.

Clifford straightened up in his chair. "That's right . . . but how come you know about that?"

"You don't know we know about it?"

"No, I don't. Who are you and where does Berkeley fit in?"

Aub nodded slowly, half to himself, as if Clifford's response had somehow been expected. "Just as I thought," he said. "Something smells about this whole business. You couldn't imagine the problems I've had trying to get hold of your name."

"Suppose you start at the beginning," Clifford suggested.

"That's a fantastic idea, man. Why don't I?" Aub thought for a split second. "Part of the paper talks about sustained rotations of k-functions. In it you derive the criteria for stability and frequency for different rotational modes."

"That's right. It follows from conservation of k-spin. What of it?"

"Your mathematics implies that certain sustained rotations can take the form of continuous transitions between hi-order and lo-order dimensional domains. In normal space the effect would appear as a particle repeatedly vanishing and reappearing, like a light flashing on and off."

Clifford was impressed, but dubious. For the moment, he'd reserve judgment.

"That's correct. But I still don't see . . ."

"Take a look at this." Aub's face disappeared and was immediately replaced by an irregular pattern of thin lines, some straight and some curved, traced in white on a black background. Clifford recognized it as an example of computer output from a high-speed ion chamber; this was the standard technique for capturing details of high-energy particle interactions, and was used by experimentalists worldwide. Aub's voice continued: "You see the track marked G to H, down at the lower right of the picture?"

"Yes." Clifford picked out the detail indicated. It was not a continuous line, but comprised a string of minute points of white.

"That's the track of an omega-two minus, resolved at maximum power. As you can see, the particle was only detected at discrete points along its trajectory. In between those points nothing was detected at all. It was continuously vanishing and rematerializing in flight—exactly as you'd expect a sustained rotation to appear. I've analyzed the momentum and field vectors, and from the measured mark-space ratio of the track, it appears to conform to a mode 3 rotation with negative phi; all the even terms of the k-spin function come out at zero. Exactly like your theory predicts."

Clifford quickly realized that he was talking to no fool. He sat forward to study the picture more closely while his mind wrestled with the implications. He was looking at positive experimental proof of some of the predictions that followed from his theoretical work. How had this come about? Was his work being taken seriously after all—so seriously that actual experiments were being conducted to test it? If so, why did he know nothing about it?

After a few more seconds, Aub inquired, "Okay?"

"Okay."

Aub reappeared on the screen. The mirthful twinkle was gone from his eyes.

"That picture was produced six months ago, at Berkeley."

Clifford stared back at him, aghast and incredulous.
"Six months! You mean somebody else already . . ."
Aub guffawed suddenly and held up both hands.

"Relax, man, it's okay. Nobody beat you to it. The
picture came up during some experiments having to
do with something else. At the time nobody realized
what the *G-H* line meant. We all thought it was due
to some kind of fault in the computer. We figured out
what it really meant only when we read your paper
about, aw, two, maybe three weeks ago."

Clifford was still nonplused.

"Look," he protested. "I still don't know who you
are or what in hell's been going on. What happened
two or three weeks ago?"

Aub nodded vigorously and held up a hand again.

"Okay, okay. It really goes back a bit before that.
I run a small team of specialized physicists at Berkeley. We handle all the way-out jobs—the oddball projects that are about as near as you can get to research
these days. Well, round about a month or so ago, I
was told I had to drop what I was doing and take a
look at something new that was important, and very
hush-hush. They gave me a copy of the paper you
wrote, but without any name on it, plus some comments and notes that a few other people had produced,
and told me they were interested in finding out if any
of it could be tested experimentally. Could I look into
it and see if I could devise some ways of checking it
out? So, I took a look at it."

"Yes."

"And . . . well, you've seen the result. One of the
guys in my section remembered something we had done
about six months ago and spotted the connection.
When we dug the picture up out of our records and
re-examined it according to your formulae—zowie!
We hit the jackpot. Here was a prediction we didn't
even have to look for; we'd already found it."

Clifford followed the story, but his bewilderment
only increased.

"That's great," he said. "But I'm still not clear.

Where did the . . ." He turned to look inquiringly at Sarah, who had appeared at the door.

"Dessert?" she whispered.

"What is it?"

"Fruit 'n ice cream."

"Dish it out. I'll be a coupla minutes."

She nodded, winked, and vanished. Clifford looked back at the screen.

"Sorry 'bout that, Aub. I was saying—where did the paper come from?"

"That's what I wanted to know. Naturally I wanted to talk to whoever wrote it, but when I tried to find out who it was, nobody would tell me. They just said that that didn't matter, that I had to talk through them, and that the whole thing was top-security classified. But lots of things that I asked—simple things—they didn't seem to be able to get answers to. That's when I thought the whole thing was starting to smell . . . you know—it was as if they weren't really talking to the guy who wrote it at all."

Clifford's expression made any comment unnecessary.

Aub continued. "So I started getting curious. Like I didn't like the idea of being just some kind of barrel organ that you turn the handle on and tunes start coming out. I started digging around on the quiet for myself—contacts, whispers, guys who know guys who know guys—you know the kind of thing; there are ways and means. Anyhow, to cut out all the details, I traced the paper back to the place you work— ACRE. You know a guy there called Edwards, and another one called Jarrit?"

"Edwards is number two there," Clifford confirmed. "Jarrit's his boss."

"Yeah, they were mixed up in it. Seems they got contacted by the famous Fritz on the back of the Moon . . ."

"Zimmermann?"

"Zimmermann. That's him. I couldn't find out how he got to know about it but . . ."

"That's okay; I know that much myself," Clifford told him. Unable to contain a grin, he went on to describe briefly how he had been driven by pure exasperation to bring the whole thing to Zimmermann's notice by decidedly irregular channels—an action that Aub seemed to approve of wholeheartedly and without hesitation.

"What happened after that?" Clifford asked.

"Well, it looks like your pal Zimmermann and his bunch had been hitting all kinds of problems to do with cosmic background radiation." Aub went on to describe how the astronomers at Joliot-Curie had been involved with measurements of the spectrum of background radiation that pervades all of space and is absolutely regular in whatever direction one cares to choose. The Big Bang theory of the origin of the universe required the early stages of the Bang to be characterized by a totally radiation-dominated situation. In the expansion and cooling that followed, the radiation would become decoupled from matter and continue to exist as a steadily cooling background field, exhibiting the energy distribution spectrum of a blackbody radiator. Calculations based on this model showed that in the course of the twelve billion years thought to have elapsed since the Bang, the temperature of this background radiation would have fallen to somewhere in the region of fifteen degrees Absolute.

Measurements taken from the late 1960s onward had indeed established the existence of an isotropic background field having a temperature of three degrees Absolute—close enough to the theoretical figure when allowance was made for all the uncertainties involved. It all seemed to be very much as Big Bang predicted.

Because of the relatively narrow radio "window" through the Earth's atmosphere, however, the range of these early measurements was necessarily confined to the band of wavelengths between 3 millimeters and 70 centimeters; inside this range the agreement between the observed energy distribution and that of an ideal blackbody was good. But later on, as more information became available, first from satellite-borne and subsequently from lunar-based instruments, a steadily increasing departure from the theoretical values became evident. The further the range was extended, the larger the error became. Big Bang Theory was meticulously re-examined, but still the answer came out the same—the energy distribution of the cosmic background radiation ought to be as for a blackbody. But it wasn't. Could it be then that the radiation being detected hadn't come from any Big Bang after all? If not, where did it come from?

"Then," Aub explained, "your paper appeared. It described particles appearing and disappearing spontaneously all through the universe, with each such event producing a pulsed k-wave which, in normal space, would be detected as radiant energy. Particle annihilations were concentrated in masses and resulted in the phenomenon of localized gravity; what about the particle creations, spread evenly and diffusely all through space? What kind of radiation would they produce?"

Clifford had become mesmerized by Aub's account.

"At that point," the young man continued, "Zimmermann became interested and instructed his mathematicians to run computations of the cumulative energy-distribution profile that should follow from your equations. The results matched extremely well with the observed data that classical Big Bang models couldn't explain. That was when Zimmermann became excited.

"He passed details of his findings and their implications back to the senior management at ACRE, at the same time urging that attempts be made to test other aspects of the theory. Since much of the theory concerned basic particle phenomena, ACRE reported back to the folks in Washington, who then brought in Berkeley plus a few other places. That's how I came to be involved and how, as you've already seen, another prediction of your theory was found to have been already proved.

"And while I was finding out all that, I found out who you were too," Aub concluded. "You didn't seem to be in on the project, and the more I thought about it, the more that bugged me. I figured somebody ought to tell you, and so I called." He shrugged. "I'll probably get my ass kicked, but what the hell?"

Despite Aub's casual manner, Clifford had grown increasingly aware that behind the outlandish exterior was a mind that could work at lightning-fast speed. The piece of detective work that Aub had dismissed in a few matter-of-fact sentences would have won a commendation for a whole squad of the FBI. There were probably only a few scientists in the country who could have appreciated fully, let alone grasped instantly, the implications buried in those pages of mathematics. Clifford thought he had a good idea just who it had been that had "remembered something we did about six months ago and spotted the connection."

Clifford sat back and digested the information for a while. Aub watched in silence, having said all he had to say.

"It smells right enough, Aub," Clifford agreed at length. "I haven't a clue what's going on behind all this, but I'm really glad you called. What's the latest at Berkeley? Is that it?"

"That's about it. We're setting up some experiments specifically to look for more examples of sustained k-rotations. I'll keep you posted, huh?"

"You do that. Keep in touch. I'll see what I can find out at the ACRE end."

"Best not to say too much about us talking direct either, okay?"

"Check."

"Well, nice talking to you at last. What does everybody call you anyway?"

"Brad."

"Brad. Okay, Brad, I'll keep in touch. See you."

"Thanks again, Aub."

The screen blanked out. Clifford remained staring at it for a long time until a voice from the kitchen jolted him back to reality.

"How would you like fruit and white-stuff soup instead?"

"Uh. Why?"

"That's what you've got."

"That's no good. I only eat that with gravy."

"Not in my kitchen. Who's Dr. Phillips?"

"It's a long story . . . something funny going on. Put some coffee on and I'll tell you about it." He added absently, "He spells it with a z."

"What?"

"Philipsz. P-H-I-L-I-P-S-Z."

She looked at him curiously as he walked back in and sat down.

"How strange. I wonder why there's a z at the end."

Clifford pondered the question. "If it were at the front, nobody'd be able to pronounce it," he said at last.

Chapter 6

In the days that followed Aub's call, Clifford's attempts at ACRE to evince an open acknowledgment of the things that had been happening met with no success at all. Restricted to cautious questioning and discreet probing since the risk of repercussions falling on Aub ruled out any form of direct confrontation, he met only with what appeared to be a conspiracy of silence. Nobody reacted; nobody knew what he was talking about; nobody volunteered any information at all on the matter. Only in one or two instances did he detect an attempt on somebody's part to conceal embarrassment, or an abnormal haste to change the topic of conversation.

Then things took a strange and unexpected turn. Clifford received a call from Edwards's secretary informing him that the professor would like Clifford and Massey to join him for lunch in the Executive Dining Suite on the following day. Edwards was a formalist with a strict regard for protocol so it was not in his nature to socialize with the lower echelons of ACRE's political hierarchy. He dined fairly regularly with Massey, it was true, but that was to be expected since their day-to-day business relationship demanded a constant dialogue and they were both busy men. The occasions on which they invited individuals of Clifford's grade to join them were few and far between, and inevitably, when they did, there was a special reason—usually when Edwards had something particularly delicate to sell.

Clifford, predisposed by long experience to regard credibility as inversely proportional to seniority, was suspicious. But although the message was couched in phrases appropriate to an invitation, the unspoken words behind it came through loud and clear: BE THERE.

Edwards did not look directly at Clifford as he spoke, but kept his eyes fixed on the wine glass in his hand while he absently swirled the contents round and round inside.

"One of the subjects that I wanted to raise with you, Dr. Clifford, was the matter of . . . ah . . . the technical paper of yours that we discussed some time ago . . . the one dealing with rotations in k-space and so on."

"I mentioned it to Walter a day or two ago," Clifford replied, then added pointedly: "He said the matter was closed and that was that." Clifford had learned enough from Aub to guess that a sudden change of attitude was being hinted at, although at that stage he had no clues as to the form the change might take. He made the comment to angle the impending conversation from his perspective of the situation—his "official" perspective anyway.

"Yes, I know." Edwards frowned at his glass for a second. "But at that time Walter was not fully up to date on the latest discussions I've been having with Washington."

"I was only handing down the policy I'd been given up to then," Massey added, taking his lead dutifully. "But it seems like the prof's been putting up a good fight for you behind the scenes after all."

Clifford ignored the sycophancy and asked simply: "So?"

A demonstration of candor seemed called for. Placing his hands palms-down on the table, Edwards looked up at Clifford. "I admit that our reactions to your request were somewhat, shall we say, negative . . . too much so. I've had second thoughts on the subject since and have mentioned it . . . confidentially, you understand . . . to one or two of my acquaintances at the Bureau." He paused, waiting for an appropriate response, but Clifford continued to sip his drink and said nothing. "Opinions there are that, as you said, the subject is of academic interest and should therefore be pursued further, but that it has no immediate military or security significance. In other words, they are favorably disposed toward the idea of publication . . . in order to attract the attention of other scientific bodies, as you asked." He sat back in his chair and regarded Clifford expectantly.

Clifford set his glass down slowly on the table and did not answer at once. From the things that Aub had already told him, he was pretty certain that the matter had been raised in Washington in ways that represented far more than confidential words with one or two acquaintances. The subject was no doubt causing quite a stir in high places, but Edwards was not saying so. Why? Several major scientific institutions were becoming actively involved at a time when a world crisis was approaching fast. That situation could never have come about if the military was not interested— very interested. And yet Edwards was declining to admit this side of the issue and was attempting instead to push the academic implications as an excuse for reversing his earlier decision and taking things further. Why?

A waitress appeared at the table to clear the main-course dishes. They sat in silence until she had finished and departed.

"That's fine then," Clifford said. "I've already signed the request. All you have to do is get on with it."

"Well, it's not quite that simple," Edwards answered. Clifford sighed. Nothing was ever simple. "Some of the statements that you make are rather provocative, to say the least, and there are parts that, as I'm sure you would agree, do contain some still somewhat speculative assertions. What I'd like you to do is spend some time going over those areas more

thoroughly and producing more in the way of sub-
stantiating evidence. Also, there are a few mathematical points that I think ought to be expounded more
clearly. If you could manage that, I think we'd see
a clear way through to getting the paper published."

"It wouldn't look good for Washington to bounce it
back for the same reasons," Massey supplied. "Much
better if we got it absolutely clean here first."

"In fact, I'm now prepared to authorize you full
access to whatever facilities you need at ACRE to get
on with it," Edwards added. "Also, we can assign
somebody else to take over the projects that you're
running . . . to give you more of a free hand. Right,
Walt?"

He directed the last question to Massey. Massey
nodded firmly and leaned forward to prop his elbows
on the edge of the table. "Right. Bill Summers is up
to speed now and needs more to keep him occupied.
He'd be ideal."

Edwards had definitely overplayed his hand, Clifford decided. Acknowledging a matter of scientific but
academic interest was one thing; suddenly playing
down all the things that had previously been considered more important was another.

"How will Corrigan feel about that?" Clifford asked,
keeping his tone deliberately nonchalant.

"You needn't worry about him," Edwards said reassuringly. "I can guarantee he'll stay out of the way
and not interfere."

Edwards had taken the bait. He had just told
Clifford that the whole subject had already been discussed and agreed at the highest levels within ACRE,
and no doubt beyond as well—hardly fitting for a topic
of mere academic interest, one would have thought.
The whole setup, then, was a device to keep Clifford
working on the theory, to keep the ideas flowing. But
at the same time he was not being informed openly
that those ideas were attracting a lot of serious attention already. The action had started, but he was being
left out of it.

"Sounds like a good deal, Brad," Massey commented. "I'd have thought you'd be jumping at it by now."

Either Massey hadn't seen through all the persiflage, or he was playing back the party line exceptionally well. Clifford decided to give Edwards one last chance to come clean. He held the professor's eye and said in a soft, curious voice: "That's all very nice to hear. But theories aren't much use without some kind of evidence to back them up. If Washington is sufficiently interested to go ahead and you're as interested as you've indicated, why can't we simply organize some tests of some of the predictions? They don't have to be all that elaborate or time-consuming. There are places around with the equipment for setting up suitable experiments. If some of the simpler things could be proved—or disproved, as the case may be—right now, it could save a lot of wasted time in the long run."

Clifford watched the reactions of the other two closely as he posed this suggestion. For a split second a hint of guilt flashed across Edwards's eyes before he brought it under control. At the same time, Massey turned toward the professor and shrugged. "Sounds a good idea to me," he commented.

In that split second Clifford learned two things. First, Massey was not in on the conspiracy. His remark had been genuine, and in any case his taking up of Clifford's point in that way would have been inconsistent with his situation had he known that such experiments were already in progress. He would not, knowingly, have made Edwards's position more difficult. Second, there was no question of Edwards's failure to mention the experiments being accidental, since Clifford had just provided an unmistakable cue for him to put right the omission. Clifford was being squeezed out.

Edwards then supplied all the confirmation Clifford needed. "Mmm . . . You have a point, Dr. Clifford. I agree, once we know that the theoretical arguments are on completely solid ground, yes, perhaps something along those lines might be in order. But for the time being, certainly until Washington is involved officially and has had a chance to comment, I feel that such measures would be . . . er . . . somewhat premature."

Massey turned his gaze from Edwards to Clifford and performed his inevitable about-face as surely as if Edwards had been working the levers.

"It's a bit early yet, Brad, see?" he said. "Maybe later on when Washington has gotten into the act. What d'you say, huh?"

In the end Clifford agreed. Nothing he could have said without involving Aub would have changed the politics, and at least Edwards had given him unrestricted access to the facilities that he needed to do the things he wanted to do. Also, he would be relieved of doing the things that he didn't want to do. As Massey had said, it was not really so bad a deal. Clifford was not particularly interested in the politics anyway—just curious. He could sense the sticky glue of officialdom beginning to congeal and felt better off staying clear of it . . . up to a point. Every man, after all, had his pride.

So, for a while, Clifford was free to pursue his own research without interruption. But although he had dreamed of a life in which he could devote all of his hours to his own work using facilities like ACRE's and without the mundane distractions of other tasks, now that it had come about he found the job far from satisfying. He was being used to foster other men's ambitions, and that irked him. His brain, it seemed, was useful, but he didn't fit with the team.

One morning Clifford stood by the window of his office, contemplating the view outside while mentally going over his schedule of activities for the day, when a sudden shadow in the sky above caused him to glance up involuntarily. A medium-size aircar bearing the markings USAF was slowing down to hover above the executive parking area preparatory to landing. He watched as the vehicle completed its descent and a half-dozen or so dark-suited figures emerged, disappeared into a waiting limousine, and were whisked out of sight around the corner of the building toward the main entrance of ACRE's Admin Block. He noticed too that several other aircars were already parked near where the one he had seen had landed. An hour or so later, when he was on his way through the Admin Block to collect some books he had requested from the library, he noticed two armed military policemen stationed outside the door of the Main Conference Room.

"What's going on?" he asked Paul Newham, one of the senior mathematical physicists, later on in one of the cafeterias over lunch.

"Oh, just another closed-doors meeting, I guess," Newham told him.

"Another one?"

"Washington bigwigs. They've been coming and going all week. Must be something big in the wind; Jarrit's been involved in all of them from what I hear. You didn't know?"

Clifford sat frowning uneasily with his fork frozen in midair.

"No, I didn't," he said slowly. "So, what's it all about?"

"Haven't a clue. Bill Summers did ask around but was politely advised to mind his own business. I guess whatever is going on doesn't concern the likes of us, Brad." Newham started to drink his coffee and then looked up suddenly as if he had just remembered something. "Although Edwards's secretary did mention something when she was having a drink with one of the guys the other day. What did he say she said now . . . ? Something to do with k . . . k . . . k-something or other. Didn't ring a bell at the time."

Two days after that, Sarah mentioned that she had made an Infonet call to Lisa Clancy, the wife of Clifford's former tutor at CIT and an old friend of the family. Lisa had told her that Bernard—her husband

—was due to travel to New Mexico to attend a scientific conference of some kind. He hadn't been very forthcoming as to exactly where he was going or what the purpose of the conference was, but she had a feeling that the meeting might be at ACRE. Eager to renew his old acquaintanceship and, perhaps, at last to get access to some inside information, Clifford called Bernard that same evening.

"Well . . . that's a bit difficult, Brad . . ." Bernard's face contorted with visible discomfort as he looked out of the screen. "It's a pretty tight security issue . . . know what I mean? Don't get the wrong idea, I'd love to see you again but . . ." he shrugged and made an empty-handed gesture, "you know how it is."

"Hell, I don't want to know what your business is," Clifford protested. "All I wanted to know was if you'd be in the area and if so, whether we could get together for a beer."

"Yeah, I know." Bernard was looking acutely embarrassed but at the same time helpless. "It's awfully nice of you to think of it, but really . . . I can't. Some other time when I'm traveling that way socially, sure, but . . . this'll be business and the schedule's pretty tight." Bernard suddenly tightened his features into an expression of seriousness. "Give my regards to Harry Cottrill if you see him around there." Then he relaxed. "Well, gotta go, Brad. Nice to hear from you again. Keep up the good work, eh? Look us up if you find yourselves back in California. Regards to Sarah."

"See you around." Clifford accepted the situation and flipped off the terminal irritably. He sat for a while staring moodily at the blank screen.

"Who's Harry Cottrill?" Sarah asked from the far side of the room. "We don't know anybody by that name, do we?"

"Huh . . . ?" Clifford half-turned and sat back to face her. "That's the funny part. I was just wondering about it. . . . We don't know him, but I do. He was a guy I used to know at CIT."

"CIT?" Sarah looked puzzled. "Why should we see him around here? Did he move here or something?"

"Not that I know of. Last place I saw him was CIT."

"That's crazy." Sarah returned Clifford's nonplused look. "Why should Bernard go and say a crazy thing like that?"

"I don't know," Clifford said slowly and thoughtfully. "But I think he was trying to tell us something. His face became rather serious as he said it—you know—as if he was trying to make a point."

"Who was this Harry Cottrill?" Sarah asked after a few seconds of silence. "Another physicist or suchlike?"

"No, nothing like that. . . . He was a biologist . . . had a thing about termites. He was an entomologist there . . . always talking about termites . . ."

"Bugs. Ugh. Nasty things."

"Bugs!" Clifford looked up abruptly. *That's* what it was. Bernard was afraid of his line being bugged. That's why he wouldn't say anything." He stood up and sent the chair spinning on its swivel with a sudden blow of his fist. "Bastards! What are they turning this damned world into?"

Bernard Clancy did come to ACRE. Clifford was walking along the corridor outside the conference room when the door opened and a party of visitors, several of whom he recognized as prominent mathematicians and physicists, was ushered through. Clancy just had time to catch Clifford's eye and shrug with a brief apologetic grin before he and the rest were herded hurriedly away by Corrigan and a troupe of minions. They departed from ACRE within minutes.

"Hey, I'm sure that's Walter Massey and his wife over there, Brad." Sarah's voice came down at him from the same direction as the heat bathing his prostrate body. He mumbled something unintelligible and raised his head a few inches to scan the nearby parts of the sloping tiled area that surrounded the pool. Everywhere was a sea of tanned arms, legs, and bodies, sunshades, and a few tables; the pool was crowded and noisy.

"Mmm . . . where?" he asked after a second.

"There . . ." She pointed. "Walking this way from the pool. She's got a blue bikini on."

"Yeah . . . I think you're right." He allowed his head to flop back on the towel, closed his eyes again, and gave every indication of having dismissed the matter from consciousness.

"Want me to call them over?" he heard Sarah ask, and then, before he had made any reply: "Hey! Sheila . . . Walter . . . Over here . . ." She turned back to her husband. "They've seen us. They're coming over."

Clifford flinched as drops of icy liquid peppered his skin. He opened his eyes to find the lower half of Sheila Massey's bikini—surely it had been sprayed on —staring down at him over the top of a magnificent pair of suntanned thighs. A few seconds later he noticed that Sheila was there too, removing her swimcap to allow cascades of jet-black hair to tumble out onto her shoulders. Walter was close behind.

"Hi," Sarah greeted, gathering together some of their things to make room. "Come and make it a party." Sheila sat down, accepted a towel from Sarah's outstretched hand and began drying herself.

"Thanks," she said. "Hi, people. Just enjoying the sun?" She looked up. "Pull up a pew, Walt."

Walter Massey was looking toward where they had been heading. "I'll just go on up and get my cigarettes," he said. "Be back in a minute." With that he disappeared from Clifford's field of vision.

As the girls began chattering back and forth over him, Clifford became acutely aware of Sheila's sinuous movements on one side and Sarah's curvaceous form on the other, and he began suddenly to wonder if, perhaps, the Arabs had got it right all along after all. What was so bad about camels and tents anyway?

Who needed civilization? Maybe polygamy ought to be compulsory—then perhaps everybody would forget about making bombs. Interesting thought. His reverie came to an end when he realized that Sarah was speaking to him.

"Did you know that, Brad?"

"Uh . . . ? What?"

"What Sheila just said—about the big stir-up at ACRE."

"Stir-up?"

"Walt's been saying he thinks there are big changes in the offing," Sheila told him. "Some big new project connected with scientific outfits all over the place . . . Moonbases . . . Some people somewhere out in California. Stuff like that."

"Oh . . ." Clifford's tone made light of it. "Yeah—I heard one or two things."

"Never told me," Sarah said.

"Just rumors," he murmured vaguely. "I didn't take a lot of notice."

"Walt doesn't think they're just rumors," Sheila added. "He thinks a few of the top guys at ACRE have been interviewed for jobs on it . . . top scientific guys."

"Him too?" Clifford tried to sound less interested than he was but couldn't prevent himself from half sitting up as he spoke.

"I don't think so . . . at least, if he has, he hasn't said. The project's supposed to be very secret—security and all that stuff. But he figures there's going to be a major reshuffle right down through ACRE. All kinds of promotion prospects for everybody . . . That's what he's interested in. He could use a change."

"Well nobody's talked to me about it," Clifford declared, falling back again to gaze up into the sky. "When somebody does, I'll tell you about it. Until then it's just rumors."

But there was anger burning in his eyes. Harems, he had somehow suddenly decided, were strictly for other times and other places.

Chapter 7

"Mode 3 with positive phi. Again all the even terms of the k-spin function come out zero. How about that?" Aub stared out of the screen in Clifford's den and waited for a response.

"What's he talking about?" Sarah whispered from the chair that she had pulled up next to Clifford.

"They've been running more experiments at Berkeley," he whispered back. "It looks as if more of the theory's predictions are coming out okay. It's fantastic news." He looked back at the screen. "That's great, Aub. Sustained rotations are real then, eh? How about mode distribution frequencies?"

"Well, we haven't done a lot of tests yet, so the statistical data's still pretty thin, but from the figures we've got it looks as if it might check out fine. I'll keep you posted on that; we're scheduling another run for tomorrow."

"I'll call you again tomorrow then, okay?"

"Great, man. See ya."

"S'long Aub." Clifford slipped an arm round Sarah's shoulder and gave her a compulsive hug as he switched off the terminal. "Everything's working out fine, baby," he said, laughing. "We're gonna be famous yet." She brought her hand up and squeezed his fingers reassuringly. Her mouth smiled but she kept her eyes averted. In his excitement Clifford had momentarily forgotten their conversation with Sheila Massey, but Sarah hadn't.

The following evening Aub called in again.

"Man, we have news!" he announced jubilantly. "Another couple of positive tests today and mode distributions as predicted. The statistics are still from a small sample, but it's looking good. Opinion here is starting to firm up that the theory is well on its way to being validated." His expression changed to a frown. "Surely they *must* have told you about it at ACRE by now?"

Clifford shook his head.

"But *Jeez* . . . they sure know about it," Aub protested. "We've been sending the data through all along . . . . I know for a fact that that guy Edwards is up-to-date. Why are *you* of all people being kept in the dark, for Christ's sake?"

"Don't ask me, Aub," Clifford said wearily. "Maybe I've told them too often what I think of their system. But there's no way they're gonna make me live in nice straight lines."

"So what's bugging you? You wanted out and you got out. Sounds like it's okay."

"I just feel I might have something to contribute," Clifford answered with a trace of sarcasm. "On top of that, I just don't trust them not to screw the whole thing up somehow. You know how their minds work . . . or don't. They'll sure as hell find a way."

The next day a more subdued Aub called. "All kinds of rumors flying around here—something to do with people being selected as candidates to work on some new top-security thing. My boss hinted this morning that I might be lined up for a move, but clammed up when I tried to pump him."

"We had something similar going on at ACRE," Clifford said. "Any idea what's up?"

Aub grimaced. "Couldn't get a lead on that . . . it's all political and everybody's getting neurotic about security. I'm pretty sure it's being set up from somewhere high up though—probably Washington." He frowned and cocked his head to one side. "So what's the score at ACRE? A reshuffle in the wind there?"

"Looks like it," Clifford replied. "Some other places too, I hear."

"Are you involved in it?"

"What do you think?"

Aub shook his head in despairing incredulity. "It's crazy," he declared. "What kind of an operation are those nuts going to be able to run with all wheels and no engine? Do you think they're doing what I think they're doing?"

"Don't tell me, Aub," Clifford sighed. "Right now I don't wanna hear it."

A few minutes later, after he had cleared down the call, Clifford turned toward Sarah, who had been watching from across the room.

"Have I got two heads or something?" he demanded.

"Not that I've noticed," she replied, then became more serious. "Oh, Brad, how can people be so stupid?"

He thought for a second and growled. "I guess it doesn't matter which way the wheels go round, as long as they're all going round the same way together."

The Aub that Clifford grew to know better during this time turned out to be even better than his first impressions had suggested. Like Clifford, he was preoccupied, almost obsessed, with a compulsive urge to add further to the stock of human scientific knowledge; he had no political persuasions and few ideological beliefs, certainly none that could be classed as part of any recognizable formal system. He accepted as so self-evident that it was not worthy of debate the axiom that only the harnessing of knowledge to create universal wealth and security could provide a permanent solution to the world's problems. It was not, however, the desire to discharge any moral obligation to the rest of humanity that spurred him onward; it was simply his insatiable curiosity and the need to exercise his own extraordinary inventive abilities. He had no interest in impressing his beliefs on those who were not disposed to listen; in the end they would come to think his way anyhow, and whatever he did or didn't do in the meantime would make no difference that mattered.

Unlike Clifford, Aub was not unduly perturbed by a situation in which the interests of pure science were subordinated to those of politics, a state of affairs that he looked upon as transient and one that would change nothing in the long-term history of the universe. He reacted to the warped world that others had shaped by extracting from it and using the things that he needed while remaining indifferent to and, for the most part, uninfluenced by the rest. Life was to be made the most of despite the follies of others, not by their license. Aub, the individualist, the opportunist, and the eternal optimist, would pursue unswervingly the path he had elected to follow, happily riding the tide when its direction happened to coincide with his own and just as easily striking out on his own when their courses diverged. For the time being, life at Berkeley suited him by affording ample opportunity for him to develop and refine his talents. Tomorrow—who could tell?

Everything came to a head one day when Clifford was working at home in his study at the top of the house. He was staring at the screen of the upstairs terminal, digesting the meaning of a group of tensor equations out of ACRE's computers, when the chime sounded and a message superimposed itself on the display to inform him of an incoming call. He cursed, suspended the program, and touched a key to accept. It was Aub, looking angry and disturbed in a way that Clifford had never seen before.

"I've just been talking to my boss and his boss," Aub informed him without preliminaries. His voice was seething. "So now I know what gives."

"Hey, calm down, buddy," Clifford answered.

"What's with all the bosses? Now you know what, what gives?"

Aub seemed to take a second or two to compose himself. His heavy breathing came through clearly on audio. Then he explained. "There was a zombie from Washington here too. They want me to take another job."

Clifford sensed the connection immediately. His brow creased into a frown of suspicion. "What kind of job?" he asked.

"They didn't come too clean with the specifics, but it was obvious they intend taking further—a lot further—the experiments that we set up to prove *your* theories. They want me to set up a team and head it . . . to manage the whole thing formally and more thoroughly." He moistened his lips and asked: "Do you know anything about this yet . . . officially?"

"No way."

"That's what I thought. That's just what I damn well thought." Aub continued to glower while Clifford thought over what he had just said.

"Where abouts is this going to take place?" Clifford asked at last.

Aub showed his hands and sighed. "Again, they wouldn't say. But what I did gather was that there are going to be lots of people in on it . . . from all kinds of places. Not just experimental particle guys like me, but the works—mathematical guys, physics guys, cosmology guys . . . you name it. They're getting a whole circus together."

"I see . . ." Clifford murmured slowly.

"But *do* you, Brad . . . really?" Aub's beard quivered with his indignation. "You can see what they're doing—they're setting up a whole high-power scientific team, on the quiet, to take your work apart and go through it with a fine-tooth comb. But they're not even telling you it's happening, let alone inviting you in on it. It's plain piracy. Next thing, they'll be setting up some stooge with his name in big lights all over as having started the whole business. You won't buy their apples so they're cutting you out."

Clifford's initial calm began changing to a cold, creeping anger that climbed slowly up his spine until it filled his whole being. The picture that he had long suspected deep down inside was now laid bare before his eyes. Fighting to keep himself under control, he asked through gritted teeth: "So, what'd you do—take the job?"

Aub shook his head firmly. "If I didn't know what I know I probably would have—it would have sounded pretty interesting—but as things were, I wanted to check out the score with you one more time. They told me the whole thing was politically sensitive and all that junk and not to breathe a word about it, but what the hell? I'm damn glad I did check it out too. Right now I'm in the right mood to go straight back upstairs and tell 'em to upstick it ass-wise."

Clifford was still in an ugly mood ten minutes later when, downstairs in the living-room, he recounted the conversation to Sarah.

"It's the end," he fumed, pacing from one side of the room to the other. "This time I've had it. First thing tomorrow I'm going straight in to see Edwards—and Jarrit too, if he's around—and I'm gonna spell out to the two of 'em just what I know about their setup and their neat little plans and their . . . their bullshit! They can throw me out if they like, but just to see their faces will be worth it . . . just to see them scurrying for the woodwork."

Sarah contemplated the ceiling stoically and drummed her fingertips lightly on the arm of her chair until the pounding of his footsteps had stopped. When she sensed that he was looking at her again she lowered her eyes to meet his and shook her head slowly from side to side, at the same time smiling with a mixture of despair and amusement.

"Now, Brad, you know you can't do that," she said. "Assuming, that is, you don't go and have a coronary or burst a blood vessel first. It's just not practical."

"Oh? And why not?"

"Because . . ."

"Because what?"

She sighed a sigh of infinite patience. "Because of Aub," she told him. "To be credible, you'd have to tell them where you got the information, and that would drag Aub into it. The only other way would mean you'd start a big scene and then have to admit that you'd got nothing to back up your accusations, in which case you'd end up looking silly. Either way, it's not practical." Sarah also knew, but didn't say, that whatever satisfaction such an action might have bought Clifford in the short run, ultimately it would achieve nothing significant. Even if such a showdown resulted in his being offered, belatedly, his rightful place in the operation, he would never accept it—not now; the price would be more than his pride and his principles would allow him to pay.

"Yeah . . ." Clifford mumbled after a while. "Yeah, I guess maybe you're right." He walked across the room and stood staring out of the window for a long time, unsure of what he was going to do next. Sarah said nothing but sat soberly contemplating the toe of her shoe.

She had a fairly good idea of what he was going to do.

"You can't," Corrigan declared flatly. "Your contract says so."

"That stuff's academic now," Clifford retorted. "I've already told you—I have."

A long table was set at right angles to the desk in Jarrit's office to form a T—useful for impromptu conferences and small meetings. Jarrit was leaning forward at the desk, fists clenched on the surface in front of him, while Edwards and Corrigan were seated next to each other on one side of the table. Clifford sat opposite them. All four faces were grim.

"There has been no formal request and therefore no approval," Edwards pointed out. "The matter will have to be considered in the regular manner."

"Screw the regular manner," Clifford said. "I've quit."

"I don't think you fully realize the gravity of the issue, Dr. Clifford," Jarrit stated. "This is not some trivial question that can be settled by local procedures. You are employed under the terms of a special federal directive which states, quite unequivocally, that you do not have the right to terminate your contract unilaterally. Surely I don't have to remind you that we—the whole Western world—are facing a crisis. We are living in an emergency situation."

"The screw-ups that brought it on had nothing to do with me. I've quit."

"Maybe not," Corrigan said. "But the same could be said for everybody else. Nevertheless, you'd agree that you have a share in the obligation to protect the nation from their consequences, wouldn't you?"

"That's what your book says. I never said so."

"Oh, is that so?" Corrigan felt himself getting into stride; the old familiar feeling of limbering up before launching into the devastation of another awkward witness was coming back. "Are you telling us that you are above the law of this country? Do you consider yourself . . ."

"I'm telling you I'm not an object for compulsory purchase," Clifford cut him off short. "The goods aren't for sale."

"You're copping out then, huh? That's what you're saying?" Corrigan's voice rose uncontrollably. "Democracy can go to the wall."

"What do *you* know about democracy?" Clifford made no atttempt to hide the contempt that he felt. His tone was close to a sneer.

"I believe in what it says, that's what I know," Corrigan snapped back. "People have a right to choose how they want to live, and I'll fight any bastards who try to come here and take that away . . . there's a billion of 'em out there. Nobody's gonna ram some crummy ideology I don't want down *my* throat, or tell me what to or what not to believe. I make my own decisions. That's what I know about democracy and that's what I say you've got a duty to defend."

"That's okay then." Clifford's voice sank abruptly to almost a whisper; the contrast to Corrigan's shouting added emphasis. *"I've* chosen. *You're* doing the ramming." Corrigan's face whitened and his lips compressed into a tight line. Before he could form a reply, Clifford went on, his voice rising. "There's no difference between you and them. You're all preaching bundles of canned delusions, and it's all the same crap! Why can't you all go home and forget about it? The people of this planet have already chosen how they want to live, but the message doesn't suit you so you don't hear it—they want to be left alone."

"People!" Corrigan's complexion changed to scarlet. "What do people know? Nothing! They know nothing!" Jarrit and Edwards began fidgeting uncomfortably, but Corrigan had become too heated to notice. "They're just goons," he shouted. "They've never had a thought in their tiny lives. They don't know what they want until somebody strong enough stands up and tells them what to want. And when a million of 'em want the same thing they've got power and that's what it's all about . . ." He checked himself, realizing that for once he had let his mouth run away, and subsided into his seat.

"And that's democracy?" Clifford challenged.

Jarrit cleared his throat loudly and broke in before the exchange could escalate further.

"You realize, of course, Dr. Clifford, that if you insist on pursuing the course of action that you have indicated, the financial consequences to yourself would be quite serious. Your severance pay, outstanding holiday pay, retirement contributions, and all other accrued benefits would automatically be forfeited."

"Naturally." Clifford's reply was heavy with sarcasm.

"What about your security classification?" Corrigan asked, still smarting. "That would be reduced to the lowest a man can have and still walk the streets. It'd be the next thing to having *Commie* painted across your forehead."

"That would deny you any prospect of future employment in government service," Edwards added. "Or with any approved government contractor, for that matter. Think about that."

"And you'd lose your draft-exemption status," Jarrit said.

"You'd be jeopardizing your whole future career," Edwards added.

Clifford looked slowly from one to another of the three and accepted the pointlessness of long speeches or explanations.

"Stuff all of it," he said. "I've quit."

Suddenly Corrigan exploded again.

"Scientists! You wanna pick daisies while the whole world's up for grabs. You're telling *me* about delusions . . . and all the time you're chasing after reality and truth and all that shit! Let me tell you something, mister . . . *that's* the biggest delusion. There is no objective reality. Reality is whatever you choose to believe is real. Strong wills and cast-iron beliefs make the reality happen. . . . When a hundred million people stand up together and believe strongly enough in what they want, then it'll happen that way. That's what defines truth. Men who were strong built the world; the world didn't build them. Truth is truth when enough people say it is—that's the reality of the world we live in. *Your* world is the delusion. Numbers . . . statistics . . . pieces of paper . . . what have they to do with people? It's people that make events, and it's about time you made it your business to grow up out of your fairyland and tried to understand it. *We* made you what you are and *we* own you. . . . You exist because your toys are useful to *us*. We don't exist through any of your doodlings. You think about *that!*"

Clifford let the silence hang for a second to accentuate the embarrassment now evident on the faces of Jarrit and Edwards. Turning away from Corrigan to exclude him pointedly from the remark as an object no longer worthy of consideration, he quietly concluded, "I've quit. I couldn't put the reasons into better words than that."

A couple of hours later, as Clifford steered the Cougar up the climbing road along the valley side and looked back at ACRE for the last time, he became aware of something that he had not noticed for a long time: The air of the mountains tasted clean and free.

Chapter 8

Sarah looked at the numbers displayed on the screen and pursed her lips ruefully. After a few more seconds she switched off the terminal and swiveled her chair round to face across the room.

"So, what happens now, I wonder," she said. "We're broke."

Clifford, sprawled in an armchair by the opposite wall, scowled back at her.

"Dunno," he confessed. "I guess I could still get some kind of job—nothing spectacular, but worth something."

She cast an eye round the room, with its tasteful decor and comfortable furnishings.

"I suppose all this will have to go."

"Reckon so." His voice was matter-of-fact.

She swung the chair through a full circle and came back to face him again.

"Perhaps we should take that jungle trip that you talked about. Who knows—peanuts and berries and things might not be too bad after the first twenty years or so."

He managed a grin; she tried to return it, but her heart wasn't really in it.

The news had come as no surprise. Not once had she questioned what he had done; she knew that he had done what he had to. He knew that she shared his values and would accept philosophically whatever sacrifices were necessary to preserve them. There was no need for long and elaborate explanations or justifications.

She swung the chair to and fro in a slow rhythmic motion and pressed her fingers into a point in front of her nose. "Just for once, let's be logical and objective. We ought to set out some sort of plan of where we go next."

"We *ought?*"

"Of course we ought to. The world hasn't ended, but there are still a lot of things that are going to need straightening out. Now, what's the first thing we need to do?"

"Get drunk."

"See, no objectivity. That's the American male's eternal solution to everything. All it does is shovel the problems into tomorrow."

"Best place for them to be isn't it? It never comes."

"Only if you get drunk tomorrow too, and we can't afford that. Let's be serious. For a start, I'll see about switching to a full-time week at the hospital. That'll help."

Clifford saw that she was making an honest effort to be constructive. He straightened up in the chair and his mood changed abruptly.

"That'd help a lot," he said. "You're great."

"We should start looking for somewhere cheaper to live too," she continued. "Perhaps a small apartment. I think there are one or two quite nice ones going over near Hammel Hill. If you could find a temporary job, we should be able to balance things and stay fairly comfortable until we've decided what we really want to do. What d'you think?"

"Absolutely right, of course," he agreed. "In fact, Jerry Micklaw was saying the other week that they've got some vacancies at the place he works. It's long hours and hard work, but the pay's good . . . and they get plenty of bonuses. If I got fixed up there it would give me a chance to look around for a while. Come to think of it, maybe we wouldn't have to quit this place in such a hurry after all. I reckon if we cut down on a couple of the . . ."

The chime of the doorbell sounded.

Sarah was nearest. She left the room to answer the door while Clifford contemplated the carpet. Absently he heard the door being opened while he thought more seriously about the things they had been discussing. Then Sarah's incredulous "Good heavens!" brought him back with a start. Suddenly the hallway outside the door was filled with a laughing, reverberant voice gushing through the house and dispelling the gloom like a flood of aural sunshine. Clifford looked up and gaped in disbelief as Aub's lean wiry figure strode through the door. Sarah stood framed in the opening behind him, her hands spread wide apart in an attitude of helplessness.

"Dr. Clifford, I presume." Aub beamed down and then burst into laughter at the expression on Clifford's face. Clifford managed to rise halfway before finding his arm being pumped vigorously up and down. "Seemed about time," Aub said, turning to shake Sarah's hand as well. "Couldn't think of any good reason for putting it off. So . . ." He shrugged.

Clifford shook his head in bemusement.

"Aub . . . what in hell's name? It's great to see you at last but . . . what the hell are you doing here . . . ?"

Aub laughed again.

"I just followed my feet, and this is where they came." He looked around him. "Man, what a pad . . . Fantastic! You know something, I really dig that mural . . . kinda soul-touching. Who's the artistic one?"

"Enjoy it while you can, Aub," Sarah said. "We may have to move out of here before very long. Brad quit his job today."

Aub's face radiated sheer delight.

"You don't say!" He made it sound like the best news he had heard for weeks. "I don't believe it. You mean you finally told those ACRE bums to go get lost. Hey, Brad, that's just great, man—really great!"

Clifford regarded him sourly.

"Why so funny?"

"You're not gonna believe it. We both arrived at the same conclusion—I quit Berkeley too!"

Clifford gaped for a second or two. As the message sank in his features slowly broadened into a smile.

"You did? You too? That's crazy . . . Why?"

"They tried to make me take that job again—the one I told you about—the secret project. But by that time I'd already figured the whole thing was a messy, lousy business and I didn't want to get mixed up in it. So I told them I wasn't interested. Then they tried using muscle and said they were empowered to order me to take it under special security legislation. I said I sure as hell hadn't empowered them, and not long after that it occurred to me that the time had come for me and them to go our own separate ways."

"Brad's cleaned out," Sarah told him. "They've cut off everything—all the benefits. He won't be able to get a decent job either."

"Yeah, me too." Aub grinned, shrugged, and showed his empty palms. "So, who cares? Just remember the ice ball."

"Ice ball?"

"Twenty billion years from now the whole world will be just one big ball of ice, so it won't make any difference. I always think about the ice ball when Murphy's around."

"Murphy?" Sarah was getting rapidly confused.

"Murphy's law of engineering," Aub explained, then looked at her expectantly. She shook her head.

"In any field of human endeavor, anything that *can* go wrong . . ."

"*Will* go wrong," Clifford completed for him. Suddenly they were all laughing.

"Well . . ." Clifford shook his head as if still trying to convince himself that life hadn't taken a sudden turn into dreamland. "I suppose the cliché for the occasion is, 'this calls for a drink.' What'll it be? Better make the best of it while the stuff lasts."

"Rye 'n dry," Aub told him. "Cheers."

"Vodka with Bitter Lemon," Sarah added.

"So what the hell made you come here?" Clifford asked as he walked across to the bar and began pouring the drinks. "I was just about to give you a call."

Aub collapsed untidily into an armchair and stretched his legs out in front of him, already seeming at ease and at home.

"That's a good question," he conceded as if it had occurred to him for the first time. He rubbed his beard reflectively. "I guess the thought never occurred to me to do anything else. It kinda seemed the obvious thing to do."

"You make a habit of just, sort of . . . appearing in places?" Sarah asked, perching herself on the arm of the chair opposite Aub's.

"Never really thought about that either," Aub answered. "But I suppose, yeah . . . maybe you're right. Good way to stay clear of getting in ruts . . ." He looked across at Clifford. "Oh—there was another reason I came here too . . . the best reason I find for doing anything."

"What?"

"I felt like it."

They all laughed again. Aub's very presence seemed to fill the room with a charge of optimism and confidence that, whatever might come next, they could handle it. Suddenly everything was going to work out in the end . . . somehow.

"So where do you go from here?" Clifford inquired as he came over with the glasses. "Any plans?"

"None." Aub shrugged and accepted his drink. "This is where I hitch up to serendipity, I guess. What about you?"

"No idea. Looks like maybe we hitch up to serendipity together."

"I'll drink to that, Brad," Aub said readily. "Cheers."

"Cheers."

"What about your things, Aub?" Sarah asked.

"Things?"

"Possessions . . . from wherever you were living in California. Where are they?"

"Oh those." Aub shrugged again. "I sold everything that wouldn't move to the guy I was sharing the apartment with. Traveling light suits me. The rest of it's in a couple of bags outside the door."

"That's your world, eh, Aub?" Clifford said.

Aub made a wide circular motion with his arm. "No way, man. The whole world's still out there any time I want to use it, only this way they can't take any of it away. I can enjoy a swim without having to buy the Pacific." He thought for a moment, then added: "Did you know that 12 percent of all suicides are people with over a million bucks? I'm not taking any chances."

Clifford pursed his lips.

"The logic doesn't follow," he said. "You're taking a big risk the way you're going."

"Huh—how come?"

"Because that means that 88 percent must be people with under a million," Clifford answered with a grin. "Try thinking about it that way."

Aub roared with laughter and slapped his thigh.

"I like that. But don't get carried away—figures can lie."

"And liars can figure," Sarah came in, looking pointedly at her husband. "I'm just about to start dinner. I'll make it for three . . . chicken okay, Aub?"

"You've talked me into it. How can a man argue with that kind of persuasion?"

"Oh, dear," Sarah sighed apprehensively. "I can see I'm going to have problems with you two."

"Never mind her, Aub," Clifford said. "Have another drink."

"*Big* problems," Sarah decided, and got up to go into the kitchen.

"So what could they do?" Aub rested his elbows on the table amid the dinner debris and spread his palms upward. "They're three miles from the road, their car's gone, all their clothes are gone . . . man, it's a problem." Sarah wiped a tear from her cheek and tried to stifle a giggle. Clifford spluttered over his coffee and placed the cup unsteadily back on his saucer.

"So what happened?" he asked.

"Well, they had to hike it back to the road . . . that or stay out there and start Adam and Eve again all over, and Robbie never really had much time for any of that kinda thing."

"What—all through the forest?" Sarah said disbelievingly. "Without any clothes on at all?"

"What else could they do?" Aub demanded. "Like I said, they couldn't stay out there forever. Anyhow, that wasn't the really funny part. When they got to the road, they stumbled on it all of a sudden—there was this kinda wall of bushes and greenery and stuff, and when they went into it and came out the other side, there they were, right out on the road with traffic going past with heads going round inside . . . real crazy." Aub held up a hand to stop Clifford and Sarah's laughter from rising any higher for a second. "And right in front of them were these two ladies—you know the kind, about middle-aged, hair done up in buns, thick tweed skirts, that kinda thing—obviously teachers since they had this bunch of schoolkids all tagging along behind . . ."

"Oh, no!" Sarah shrieked. "I don't believe it."

"Really . . ." Aub grinned and nodded emphatically. "So here's these two good ladies, very staid and proper, taking all these nice kids for a walk out in the country . . ." he started to laugh himself, "and suddenly the bushes open up and out comes Robbie and this girl, both naked as the day they were born and holding hands . . ." Aub paused, giving the picture time to register, then changed his tone abruptly. "What would you have said? You've got five seconds which is all Robbie had."

"Wha . . . I dunno . . ." Clifford shrugged helplessly. "What is there to . . ."

"Times's up," Aub announced. "Know what Robbie said? Talk about quick thinking . . . he said, absolutely seriously and with his face dead calm: 'Excuse me, but have you seen a flying saucer parked around here? We seem to have lost ours.' "

Clifford and Sarah collapsed in hysterics. Aub joined in and added between gaspings for breath: "And Robbie swore they believed it. He said one of them—very concerned—suggested that he ought to contact the Air Force. The other one wanted to know where they came from. Robbie told them: 'Venus, but we always come here for a holiday because it gets too cloudy there.' "

"You're making it up," Clifford said after he had calmed down a little.

"So help me, I am not. There was this other guy there who . . ."

"Before you start another one, have another drink," Clifford interrupted. He picked up the bottle, then frowned as he realized it was empty. "That all we've got?" he asked Sarah.

"We *did* have a lot more," she told him. "I think you two are getting pretty close to cleaning us out."

"*Us?*" Clifford pointed at her accusingly. "You haven't been doing too badly either." He placed his hands firmly on the table. "That settles it. Tonight we're going out to celebrate and show Aub the town. Woman—upstairs and make yourself presentable. We'll clear up this mess."

"Never thought I'd see the day," she said. "Okay, why not? We can worry about the expense tomorrow."

Chapter 9

Clifford awoke the next day feeling very sick and very fragile. It was past twelve o'clock and Sarah was already up. He lay immobile for a long time, recollecting disconnected fragments of the hilarious night that had brought him to the painful condition in which he now found himself, wondering how anyone could possibly conceive that what he had been having should be considered a good time, and collecting the will power he would need to do anything else.

At last he half sat up, groaned, collapsed back onto the pillow, tried again, and made it. A little later, after shaving, showering, and dressing, he emerged still semisomnambulent from the bathroom and made his way slowly downstairs to face stoically whatever the new day, what was left of it, had in store for him.

An ashen-faced Aub was sitting woodenly in an armchair when he entered the living-room. Assorted clatterings and tinkling from the kitchen told him that Sarah was at least still capable of purposeful activity. Clifford sank into the armchair opposite Aub and joined his silent contemplation of the meaning of the universe.

"Ma-an . . ." Aub said after a thousand years or so had passed.

Another thousand years dragged by.

Sarah appeared in the doorway bearing a mug of steaming black coffee. "Oh, so the other half of the dynamic duo finally made it," she said, looking at

Clifford and pressing the mug into Aub's motionless hand. "I was just going to call the undertakers in for an estimate. Then I thought that perhaps I could make something by selling you for medical research. I know just the people who'd be interested."

"Don't scream."

"I'm not. I'm just talking."

"Then don't talk. Whisper. Buzz saws don't make noise like that."

"Like some coffee?"

"Mmm, yeah . . . please."

Sarah left the room and resumed riveting a boiler in the kitchen. Aub returned at last to the confines of his physical body and brought his eyes to focus on the mug clasped in his hand. He studied it curiously for a while as if aware of its existence for the first time, then raised it to his lips and sipped the contents gratefully.

"Some night," he pronounced finally.

"Some night," Clifford agreed.

Another silent communion ensued.

Eventually Aub frowned. "What was it we were celebrating?"

Clifford's brow contorted with the effort of concentration.

"Can't remember . . . wait a minute . . . we quit our jobs. That was it—we're both out of work and we're both out of cash. That's what we were celebrating."

Aub nodded slowly, his inner suspicions evidently having been confirmed.

"That's what I thought. You know something . . . when you really get to figuring it out, there's another side to it." Aub delivered the ultimate secret that had been revealed to him during his meditations: "It really ain't all that funny."

Sarah came in again, handed Clifford his mug and settled herself down in the swivel chair with her own. She peered over the rim of her cup as she drank and shifted her eyes from one specimen of virile masculinity in its prime to the other.

"Let's sing songs," she suggested. Clifford growled something obscene. "Brad doesn't want to sing songs. Something tells me that my man isn't his usual exuberant self today. I wonder if Avis hires out temporary replacements."

"If they do, don't forget to give them our number," Clifford said. "I might apply for a job."

"Pig."

"A job's only part of the problem," Aub said. "At least you've got a place. I'm not even sure where I'm going next yet."

Sarah swung the chair round to face Aub. She looked surprised.

"You're not going anywhere. You've got the spare room for as long as you want it. As far as we're concerned, this is just as much your place now. I thought that was obvious."

Aub smiled with a rare show of awkwardness. "Well, if that's okay . . ."

"Sure," Clifford confirmed. "Feel at home for as long as you want. It hadn't occurred to me to think anything else."

"Man, that's just great." Aub relaxed visibly, but he still seemed vaguely unhappy about something. "But hey, you know . . . I couldn't take you up on that without paying in my share, especially now that you've got problems too. . . ."

Clifford held up a hand. "It's okay, Aub. What you're really saying is you need a job—then there'd be no problem. Right?"

"Well . . . guess so."

"Maybe we can fix that. There's this place just outside of town that happens to have some vacancies right now. It's long hours and . . ."

"Brad," Sarah broke in. "You're not serious about that place, are you? I mean . . ." She looked from Clifford to Aub, then back again. "You're good scientists, both of you. You couldn't just forget about everything. That wouldn't be right, and besides, you'd never stick it out for more than a week."

"It'd only be for a while," Clifford insisted. "Just till we've had a chance to look around. Maybe we'll move away from here if something better shows up somewhere else. Maybe we'll even quit the country."

Sarah shook her head. Though she had previously encouraged Brad to take a temporary job to tide them over, she now realized that was the means to no end. "I think you'd do better starting the way you mean to go on," she declared. "Even if doing so takes a little while longer. Surely with your knowledge and academic record you can find something suitable without too much trouble."

Clifford sighed and scratched the back of his neck, as if deliberating how to phrase a delicate point without giving offense. "Look, dearest heart," he said. "You're a great gal and all that, but sometimes you have this tendency to forget things, you know. Aub and I are both what you might call *persona non grata*. As far as scientific appointments go from now on, we have had it; we've been blacklisted . . . out . . . kaput . . . finished. Remember?"

"Of government-controlled positions, yes," she persisted. "But the government doesn't own the whole of science, or the whole of the country, for that matter . . . yet. Try somewhere outside their sphere of influence."

"Like . . . ?"

"Well—what's wrong with ISF? I'm not an expert on these things, but they are involved in lots of the kind of work you're interested in, aren't they? How about them?"

"ISF!" Aub laughed out loud. "Excuse me—I don't mean to be rude. But do you have any idea how many scientists—top scientists—are waiting for a chance to get in with that outfit? It was the first place everybody scrambled for when things started tightening up. There's a waiting list years long and they're very selective. Guys with strings of letters a mile long are queuing up to get in, right, Brad?"

"It's like a free-handout day at Fort Knox," Clifford said.

"But you're already well in with ISF," Sarah pointed out. "Couldn't you try talking to that Professor Zimmermann? He was obviously more than impressed by the work that you did. Surely it's worth a try. Even if you get nowhere, you'd be no worse off than if you hadn't tried it."

"Zimmermann!"

Aub looked at Clifford. Each seemed to ask the other with his eyes why they hadn't thought of it before. Then Clifford sank back and began rubbing his chin.

"I'm not so sure," he finally said. "Zimmermann has to be involved in all the business that's been going on at ACRE and everywhere else. His buddies down here will have fixed it. I don't think we'd have a snowball in hell's chance. What d'you reckon?"

Aub rested his elbows on his knees and chewed his lower lip while he appeared to turn the question over intently in his mind. "I think you might be wrong there," he answered. "You've got to hand it to Sarah —she's a genius. Thinking about it now, I'm not convinced that Zimmermann was all that involved. All he did was respond positively to the information that you sent him. As he saw it, the paper had come from ACRE, and so that was where he sent his response. He contacted the senior management there because it seemed the natural thing to do. He would have assumed that you would automatically be involved in whatever happened after that." Aub looked up. "You know what, it wouldn't surprise me if Zimmermann doesn't know a thing about what's been going on down here. I vote we give Sarah's suggestion a try. Like she says, if he tells us to get lost, we're no worse off."

Clifford was already persuaded.

"Okay," he agreed. "So how do we get in touch?" Aub shrugged and inclined his head in the direction of the Infonet terminal.

"We call him."

"But it's not that simple. From a domestic terminal you can only get extraterrestrial access through privileged codes. I don't know the sequences."

"I think I do," Aub informed him. "I went through a phase of being a network freak once, you know . . . figuring out how to crack the system just for kicks. I got some data out of one of the lunar nodes a couple of times. I reckon I could do it again to get us a com channel. I don't mind—the call will only trace back to your number if it gets intercepted."

"Thanks a lot." Clifford looked at Sarah, speechless.

"Don't mention it," Aub returned cheerfully. "Who's going to do the talking? I guess you should. At least he knows your name; I wouldn't imagine he's even heard of me. So, what d'you say?"

"All right. But at this point I can't even think straight, let alone talk sense. How about rustling up some breakfast? Then we'll give it a try."

"See," Sarah said, pointedly. "You do need me."

"I know I do. Who else would fix breakfast?"

"You'll be sorry when I've found my millionaire and gone," she said, rising from her chair and moving toward the door.

"Aw, you wouldn't know what to do with one. They're all fat, bald, and fifty. Fix the food."

An hour later the three of them huddled around the Infonet terminal. Clifford and Sarah watched in fascinated silence while Aub played the keys swiftly and surely with practiced fingers, pausing from time to time to study the codes that appeared intermittently on the screen. Three attempts had aborted so far, but Aub seemed to be just warming up.

"Aha! We're into the ET trunk beam," Aub finally announced. "From here on it oughta be smooth sailing. They must have altered the timeout settings. That's what screwed it last time."

"How much do these calls cost?" Sarah asked.

Aub chuckled and continued working. "To you, not a cent. The call's routed via the message-switch complex at Berkeley. I got into there on a straight domestic call and rigged it to copy into the outgoing queue buffer. It's easier to get through to ET from there because I know the access procedures. It'll be logged as originating locally, so Berkeley pays the charge. You just collect the domestic tab to California."

Clifford started to say something but the screen suddenly cleared and caused him to stop. A short header message appeared up near the top of the display.

"I think we're through," Aub informed them. "Over to you, Brad." He moved the terminal round on its jointed supporting arm so that the screen faced Clifford. After a few seconds it came to life to reveal a man's face.

"This is ISF at Joliot-Curie, Luna. Hello."

"I'd like to speak to Professor Zimmermann, please."

"Can I say who is calling?"

"Clifford. Dr. Bradley Clifford."

"Of what organization, Dr. Clifford?"

"It's a private call."

"Private." The man's eyebrows raised slightly. Either he was suitably impressed or he was suspicious. "One moment please." The screen blanked out for what seemed an eternity. Then the man reappeared. His face gave away nothing. "I'm sorry, Dr. Clifford, but Professor Zimmermann is unavailable at the moment. Can I pass on a message or get him to call back?"

Clifford's heart sank. It was a brush-off—polite, but a brush-off. He exhaled in one, long, hopeless breath all the tension that had built up inside him during the last few minutes.

"Okay, ask him to call," he said dejectedly. "You'll have the callback code logged." With that he cut off the screen.

Clifford got up, swore, and pounded the back of an armchair with his fist. "The bastards!" he grated, his breath coming heavily. "They've got everything taped up. I knew it . . . I knew it all along." The other two remained staring at the lifeless screen.

"Well, we did say we'd be no worse off," Sarah reminded him after a while. She tried to sound soothing but could not hide the disappointment in her voice. "At least it was worth a try."

"One hell of a letdown all the same." Even Aub sounded bitter.

"He might call . . ." Sarah said, but the words trailed away.

"And pigs might swim the Pacific." Clifford paced over to the far side of the room. "The bastards!"

Sarah and Aub remained silent. There was nothing more to say.

They finished off another pot of coffee and began discussing without very much enthusiasm plans for the future. Clifford thought of teaching somewhere in South America; Aub had always wanted to spend some time in the Antarctic. Sarah again changed her mind about the local vacancies and thought that taking them wouldn't be too bad as a short-term measure after all. By late afternoon they had all cheered up somewhat and were swapping stories of days gone by.

Then the Infonet chime sounded.

Clifford still retained a secret shred of hope deep inside, which he would not admit to the others and which he only partly admitted to himself. His inner psychological defenses were shielded from the possibility of further disappointment by refusing to allow him to acknowledge that he really expected anything to happen at all. He had resolved inwardly, therefore, that in the event of any incoming calls, he would react without any display of emotion or excitement. In that way, anything he felt as a consequence would at least be private. Even so, before he realized it, he found that he was the first to reach the screen, his hand shooting out instinctively toward the *Accept* key.

Sarah and Aub were close behind.

A dignified countenance, topped by a crown of elegant silver hair, looked out at him.

"Dr. Clifford?"

"Yes."

"Ah, good. It is a pleasure to see you at last. I am Heinrich Zimmermann. I do apologize for not being available earlier; we were right in the middle of some extremely critical observations. May I congratulate you on your astonishing contribution to science. I was fascinated to read your paper, and delighted that you should think to bring it to my attention.

"Now, Dr. Clifford, what can I do for you?"

Chapter 10

The meeting in the Main Conference Room at ACRE had been in session for over two hours. About two dozen people were present, seated around the long rectangular table that stood in the center. Representatives from the Technical Coordination Bureau and some officials from various other federal departments were arrayed along one side of the table, facing a row of scientific personnel, many of them from ACRE itself, lined up on the other. Sitting at one end, Jarrit, flanked by Edwards and Corrigan, was presiding over the meeting. The atmosphere was tense and humorless. Dr. Dennis Senchino, a nuclear physicist from Brookhaven, was remonstrating from a place roughly in the center of the scientific side.

"I'm sorry, but I can't accept that," he said. "What you're asking is, if I might put it bluntly, naive. We are talking about a whole new range of physical phenomena that nobody even understands yet. It's completely new uncharted territory that we've only just come to realize exists at all. It's true that in time concrete applications of some kind may come out of it, but there's simply no way that anybody can tell how long that might take. The only thing we can do is pursue further research on an open-ended basis and wait and see what happens. You can't just produce new discoveries to order against some kind of timetable, as if . . . as if you were planning to put up a building or something."

Johnathan Camerdene of the Bureau was not satisfied. *"Can't, can't, can't* . . . All we hear is *can't.* When will somebody try applying some positive thinking for a change and admit that maybe he can do something? I don't see how a scientist is any different from any other professional person. If I ask my lawyer if he can have my case prepared for a date in court that's been fixed for next month, he tells me he can. My doctor shows up on time when I'm sick; my bank manager makes payments on the days I tell him to; my kid's teachers get their timetable organized before the start of a semester. Everybody else in the world accepts time as a real part of life that you have to take along with the rest of it. They all meet their deadlines. What's so different about your people?"

"It's not the people; it's the subject." Ollie Wilde of ACRE fought hard to conceal his rising exasperation. "You can't tell a Rembrandt to go paint a masterpiece today. You can't tell a gambler to come back a winner. Those things can only happen in their own time, not yours." He looked for support to his right and left. Heads nodded their mute assent.

"But how much time is their time?" Camerdene demanded.

"That's what we're trying to get through to you." Senchino joined in again. "Nobody knows. Nobody can even say at this stage whether there are any defense or military applications potential in it at all . . . never mind what they might be, never mind when they might happen."

"All we've got are the beginnings of a fundamental theory," Wilde added.

"I must agree that all this sounds extremely negative," Mark Simpson, another of the Bureau men chimed in. "But this is characteristic of the way the scientific mind has worked throughout history." He swept his gaze coldly along the line of faces confronting him from the other side of the table. "Didn't scientists state, even right at the end of the nineteenth century, that heavier-than-air flight was impossible?

Even after World War II, wasn't it the scientists who were saying that man would never reach the Moon and that artificial satellites would never happen before the year 2000?"

"Some of them might have said so," a voice growled. "But who do you think *made* things like that happen?"

Simpson ignored the remark and went on. "I think that what we're hearing here today is just another example of the same thing." His words were met by stony glares from across the table. One of the ACRE scientists lit a cigarette and threw the pack irritably back down in front of him.

Another Bureau man spoke up. "Let me try to put it more constructively. I agree with what Mark's just said. Although scientists are proficient in their own specialized fields, they do have certain characteristic weaknesses. One of the biggest is their inability to organize their thinking and their activities into any kind of methodical and objective program."

"For Christ's sake . . . !" One of the scientists was unable to contain his outrage. "What do you mean— incapable of being objective? Science *is* being objective! You don't know what you're talking about . . ."

"Please," the Bureau man said, holding up a hand. "Let me finish. I am talking about methodical ways of planning toward specific objectives, not about methodical ways of assembling data."

"You think that's all there is to science," the previous speaker asked derisively. "Assembling data . . . tables of numbers?"

"Whether there's more to it or not, traditional scientific practice has not evolved ways of planning methodically towards specified goals," Simpson insisted. "What I am trying to draw attention to is the fact that other professions have been forced by necessity to develop such skills, and the techniques involved are well known." He cast a pleading look along the table as if his message were so obvious that it needed no spelling out. "Over the past few weeks we have drawn up a list of what appear to me to be perfectly reasonable objectives. To achieve those objectives would seem to require two things: your technical knowledge plus the organizational and planning skills needed to wrap the whole thing up into a practical implementation framework. All I'm saying is, let's pull together and do it."

One of the scientists shook his head.

"It won't work that way. You can do that once a branch of science has developed to the level of engineering technology—that is, when you understand it properly and can formulate all the rules for applying it. But we're not anywhere near that point yet; we're still in an early phase of basic research. You've got to distinguish between the two. The things you've been saying just don't apply to the stage we're at."

"Maybe because nobody has ever tried it before," Camerdene suggested.

"Hell, no," Senchino came in. "You're missing the whole point. The question is . . ."

"Before we go off into any more technicalities, let's just remind ourselves of the real importance underlying this issue." Corrigan spoke from the end of the table. "This information is strictly within these four walls. Latest intelligence reports confirm that both the Chinese and the African-Arab Alliance have developed fully operational satellite-based laser capability for deployment against our Orbital Bombardment System. With full anti-ORBS capability, they are more or less on a par with us in terms of the strategic balance."

"There's no need to tell you then how grave a situation we're facing," Jarrit came in. "I'm sure you can also see the possible significance of the matter we're talking about."

"Industrial disruption in South Korea is rife," Corrigan continued. "Intensive subversion of the population is being organized systematically and the government is becoming unpopular as a result of very effective left-wing propaganda." He paused and looked about him to give his words time to sink in. Then he resumed. "We've all seen the pattern before. All the signs are that the stage is being set for a so-called war of liberation in the classical style, and world opinion is being preconditioned to make it difficult for the West to react effectively. We think they're going to take us on in a trial of strength in that area and we think it will happen within the next six months."

A few murmurs greeted these revelations. Camerdene waited until they had subsided and nodded his head gravely. "That's the general picture," he said. "At the technological level we're more or less even and at the grassroots level we're being outmaneuvered. That means that the superiority in numbers gives the advantage to the other side."

Camerdene then began his summation. "To restore and preserve the balance, we must pull ahead significantly in the technological area. You have told us that we appear to have made a breakthrough in a totally new aspect of science. Whenever that has happened in the past, it has always resulted in new, often revolutionary, military capabilities. If that's true in this case, we need those results fast."

Corrigan nodded his endorsement of Camerdene's remarks and, indicating Simpson, said, "As Mark just pointed out, in the past the professional and managerial skills that we have at our disposal today were unknown. The processes for developing raw scientific ideas for useful applications depended on the whims and fads of unguided amateurs." A few mutters of protest broke out, but he took no notice. "Today we have the skills and techniques necessary to guide those processes efficiently."

"It seems to me that the scientific fraternity is sadly behind the times in its thinking." Simpson elaborated on Corrigan's statement. "If they would only adjust their outlook to accommodate a more realistic appreciation of the facts, they would see that the measures we are proposing are perfectly feasible and attainable. In view of the extremely serious situation that has just been described, I find it amazing that things as elementary as this should have to be spelled out in this way."

Murmurings of approval came from the Washington side. When they had died away Senchino sat forward and turned imploringly toward Jarrit.

"We've already said you can't command people to have new ideas. The discoveries in the past that led to technological revolutions were almost all made by a few very exceptional individuals. That's the whole point these people are missing. You can't take just anybody and make him exceptional by telling him to be exceptional." A row of blank stares came back across the table. He looked down at the wad of papers in front of him and pushed them out to arm's length.

"I've read what Bradley Clifford produced and, yes, I follow what he's done. But I couldn't do it, no way. I'm essentially an applications man; I can take the rules that somebody else figures out and apply them to a specific range of problems. I accept that I'm not a creative thinker; that requires a completely different kind of mind. I can follow Clifford's work as far as it goes, but there's no way I could work out what comes next. There's just no way that anybody here or anywhere else can command me to be creative."

"Clifford needs to be part of this project," another of the scientists declared. "Lots of us here could serve on the team, but somebody like him has to head it."

"Why isn't he here anyhow?" the man next to the speaker asked.

"He quit," Senchino answered.

"I know, but why?"

"That's a separate matter that doesn't concern this meeting," Corrigan broke in. "Let's just say for now that despite his intellectual talents, he would not have fit in because of the project's sensitive nature. He exhibited distinctly undesirable ideological and temperamental traits; in a nutshell, he was unstable, rebellious, and had all the makings of a high-security risk. As a matter of fact, he deliberately and openly defied security directives." The looks from the scientific side of the table were sceptical. Nevertheless, Corrigan pursued his point. "The topic we are discuss-

ing could result in a decisive trump card for the West.
To involve somebody of Clifford's disposition would
have been unthinkable. He might well have ended up
making a present of the whole package to the other
side."

Camerdene read the expressions that greeted Corrigan's explanation.

"Clifford had his strengths, but only in his own
narrow field," he said. "He was just a man, not a su-
perman. Nobody is indispensable. I can't see any reason why we shouldn't be able to set up a nucleus of
specialists who can carry on just as well as he could.
You've only got to look at the amount of talent in this
room right now, never mind the whole country . . ."
He waited a second for some reaction to the compli-
ment but it had no visible effect. "After all, a scientist
is a scientist; you're all familiar with the same facts
and possess comparable skills. You're all trained to
understand a specialized jargon, it's true, but no more
so than an accountant who knows how to read a balance sheet . . ."

"Clifford was an innovator," one of the scientists
insisted wearily. "People can't be trained to innovate.
You've either got it or you haven't."

"I refuse to accept that there was anything so special about Clifford that you can't get along without
him," Corrigan retorted sharply. "If a surgeon becomes sick before an operation, the hospital can
always find somebody else to perform it. If Clifford
hadn't stumbled on a new piece of theory when he
did, somebody else would have done so sooner or
later . . . and still might. If that somebody else turns
out to be in Peking or somewhere, then we're in real
trouble." He screwed up his face as if experiencing
a nasty taste. "And yet all we've heard all day has
been lame excuses."

Senchino took a deep breath and clenched his fists
until the knuckles showed white.

"You can't treat the human mind like some kind
of machine that you pour raw material into at one end

and get finished products out the other. The only way you can . . ."

And so it went on . . . and on . . . and on.

Meanwhile, in the Clifford household, Aub and Sarah were watching intently as Clifford finished describing the sequence of recent events to Zimmermann. Throughout, Zimmermann had listened attentively and without interrupting, though his face became increasingly more troubled as the details unfolded.

"Well, Dr. Clifford . . . I really don't know what to say," he replied. "The whole situation is deplorable . . . disgraceful."

Clifford hesitated, wondering if the question was too presumptuous, but asked anyway. "Can . . . can I take it then that you didn't know this was happening?"

Zimmermann's eyebrows shot upward in momentary surprise.

"Me? Good heavens, no! I knew nothing of these things. We are rather isolated here and have more than enough work to keep us busy. I had assumed that after my reply to ACRE a program of investigation would have followed as a natural consequence. That, I'm afraid, Dr. Clifford, is why you never received any reply from me; it must have seemed most discourteous, and I do apologize, but, you understand, it did not occur to me that my reply to ACRE would fail to be passed through to you. Disgraceful!"

"So you really haven't had anything more to do with the project since you sent that reply?" Aub asked, edging into the viewing angle.

"Certainly not with the politics," Zimmermann said. "But as far as the scientific aspects go, you didn't really expect me to forget all about it, surely—not something like that." He grinned in a vaguely mischievous way that enhanced the warm feeling they already had toward him. "My goodness me, no. I have had several of my astronomers doing observational work in connection with the paper ever since I realized its significance. In fact, we have a team working on it at this very moment."

"You have!" Clifford was excited. "Anything to report yet?"

"Mmm . . . not yet . . ." Zimmermann gave the impression that he knew more than he was prepared to talk about for the time being, but his manner was cautious rather than furtive. "Certainly we cannot yet offer any evidence as conclusive as the experiments of Dr. Philipsz that you described, but . . ." his eyes twinkled mischievously again, "we are working on it."

"So you haven't gotten involved in a dialogue with any other institutions about it?" Clifford inquired.

"No, we have not, I'm afraid," Zimmermann replied. "I did urge that other organizations should be encouraged to test out those parts of the theory that we are not equipped to investigate, but after that I left the matter in the hands of the powers that be. I had assumed that, should any of those organizations wish to discuss anything with us here, they would contact us accordingly. It was my intention to compare notes when we had a full set of confirmed results to report, but we have not quite reached that position yet."

A brief pause followed while Clifford wrestled in his mind with the problem of how to broach the object of his call in a tactful manner. Before he had formed any words, Zimmermann's expression changed to a shrewd, penetrating stare, but his eyes still sparkled. When he spoke his voice was soft and had a curious lilt. "But your immediate problem, of course, is that of deciding where you go from there, is it not?"

This piece of mind reading caught Clifford unprepared.

"What . . . well . . . yes that's right," was all he could manage.

Zimmermann finished the rest for him. "And you called me in the hope that I might be able to help."

So the problem was solved; there it was, said—over. Clifford nodded mutely. He could sense Aub and Sarah tensing on either side of him.

Zimmermann gazed out of the screen for a long time without speaking, but they could tell from his face that his mind was racing through a whole list of undisclosed possibilities.

"I do not make promises unless I am certain of my ability to honor them," he said finally. "Therefore I will not promise anything. I want you to stay near your terminal for the next twenty-four hours. During that time—and this I do promise—either I or somebody else will call you. That is all I am prepared to say for now. And the sooner we finish this call, the sooner I will be able to do something about the things I have in mind. Do you have any further pressing questions?"

The three looked at one another. There were no questions.

"I guess not, Professor," Clifford answered.

"Very well then, good day. And remember—make sure at least one of you stays home."

"We will. . . . Good-bye, and thanks again . . . thanks again very much."

"Thank me when you have something to thank me for," Zimmermann said, and with that the screen went dead.

"You did it, Aub!" Clifford exclaimed. "How about that—you damn well did it."

"Not me, man," Aub said and pointed a finger at Sarah. "I just pressed the buttons. It was her idea, I seem to recall. She did it."

"Thank you, Aub; you're a gentleman," she pouted. "See, Brad, you just don't appreciate me."

"Where'd you learn to do it?" Aub asked.

"Oh," she said. "When you're married to Brad you soon learn to do all the thinking around the house."

Late afternoon the next day, while Clifford and Aub were engaged in a chess game and Sarah was reading, the Infonet chime sounded. In the scuffle to get to the terminal the two men knocked the board over between them and by the time they had sorted themselves out

Sarah had already accepted the call. The screen showed a dark-haired man, probably in his mid forties and evidently of Mediterranean extraction, speaking from what appeared to be a room in a private house; there was a window behind him through which they could see part of an expanse of water with pine trees bordering its far shore.

"Mrs. Clifford?" he inquired. His voice was light and cheerful.

"Yes."

"Ah . . . is your husband there, please?"

"He's untangling himself from a coffee table right at this instant. . . ." The man on the screen looked puzzled for a second, then grinned. "Oh, he's okay now," Sarah said. "Here . . ." She moved away and allowed Clifford to take her place. Aub moved forward to stand beside her expectantly.

"Hello, sorry about the fuss. I'm Bradley Clifford."

"That's okay," the caller said, grinning again. "No need to demolish the furniture on my account." His tone became more businesslike. "My name is Al Morelli—Professor Al Morelli. I'm a very old friend of somebody who, I understand, you've only just gotten to know—Heinrich Zimmermann."

"Yes . . . ?"

"I thought there were two of you." Morelli frowned slightly. "Isn't there a Dr. Philipsz there too . . . spells it funny?"

"I'm right here." Aub moved round to join Clifford.

"Great. Hi." Morelli thought for a second. "Heinrich has been telling me something about the work that you guys have been doing on k-physics. Sounds pretty staggering, to say the least. I was especially interested in the part about gravity impulses—you've actually checked that out?"

"Not exactly," Clifford answered. "But Aub ran some experiments while he was at Berkeley that verified the predictions of sustained rotations. The gravity-impulse conclusion ties in closely with that part, so the signs are encouraging. That's about all we can say for now."

Morelli looked back and nodded slowly as if satisfied about something.

"Well, there's no need for us to go into all the details right now," he said. "Heinrich gave me a pretty good run-down, and if he's convinced, that's good enough for me." He paused for a second, then went on. "You've probably guessed why I'm calling. I understand you two guys are looking for jobs and are having a pretty tough time getting fixed up. That right?"

"Yep. That's about it," Clifford told him.

"Okay, I know about the reasons," Morelli said. "And I don't blame either of you for acting the way you did. I think maybe I'd have done the same thing. Anyhow . . . I run a research project for ISF. It's located in Sudbury, Massachusetts, at the Institute for Research into Gravitational Physics. You may have heard of it."

"Heard of it . . . I sure have." Clifford sounded impressed.

"Gravitational physics . . ." Aub sounded intrigued. "So that's why you were particularly interested in the gravity pulses, right?"

"Right," Morelli confirmed. "But in more than just a casual way. From what Heinrich said, it sounds as if the work we're doing here could have a direct bearing on it."

"What kind of direct bearing?" Clifford asked. "You mean you're working on something that ties in with the gravity aspects of my theories? That's fantastic."

Morelli held up a hand to caution him.

"Well, it's a bit early to say yet. Let's just say for now that I'm pretty certain you'd find our work at Sudbury interesting. Now, obviously, I didn't call just to talk about academic stuff. It so happens that I'm looking around for people who are suitably qualified and experienced in our particular field, and from what Heinrich said, I think you two might just fill the bill.

I'd be interested in talking to you about it. Also, if you're in the kind of jam he says you're in, then . . ." He left the sentence unfinished but his expression said the rest. "Well, how about it. Interested?"

"You mean there's a chance we might get into ISF?" Clifford sounded incredulous.

"That's about it."

Aub was gaping unashamedly.

"Yes," he said after a few seconds. "We're interested." It was a masterpiece of understatement.

"Fine." Morelli looked pleased. "How about two days from now? Could you get here by then? Don't worry about the cost or anything—ISF will fly you here and back, naturally."

Clifford and Aub looked at each other, nodded, and turned toward Sarah. She nodded back vigorously.

"Seems fine," Clifford said. "No problem there."

"Fine," Morelli declared again. "I'll get my secretary to log in a couple of reservations and call you back with the details. See you both Thursday then, huh? Have a good trip."

That night Clifford, Aub, and Sarah had another wild celebration out on the town. They drank to the future of ISF, to the health of German astronomers, to the ghost of Carl Maesanger, and to network freaks wherever they might be. But most of all, Clifford and Aub toasted the pure, unsuspected genius of a certain young English lady.

Chapter 11

Clifford and Aub caught the early-morning suborbital shuttle from Albuquerque to Logan Airport, Boston, where they landed just under thirty minutes after takeoff. Sarah was needed at the hospital that day and was unable to accompany them. They received a smiling welcome from Morelli's secretary, who flew them the rest of the way to Sudbury in an ISF airmobile.

The Institute for Research into Gravitational Physics comprised an aesthetically pleasing collection of functional buildings, all clad in a mix of pastel plastics to add a splash of vivid but tastefully balanced color to the browns and drab greens of the surrounding pine woods. A large lake bordering one edge of the Institute's grounds appeared like a pool of liquid sky among the trees as they descended toward the landing pad. But better still than all these things, there were no wire fences and no armed guards.

Morelli was a stockily built, energetic, and purposeful man, endowed, as had been evident from his image on the Infonet screen, with a swarthy complexion and deep-brown eyes that had evidently been handed down to him along with his name. By midmorning Aub and Clifford were seated in his spacious and comfortable office overlooking the lake, while Morelli told them something about the kind of work that he and his researchers had been engaged in for the past few years. He had described to them how, through the 1990s, he had worked in many areas of particle physics, his main specialty being the phenomenon of particle-antiparticle annihilation. Near the end of that decade he had discovered to his astonishment that he could set up an experimental situation in which particles could be induced to self-annihilate —to vanish without the involvement of any antiparticle at all. Even after Morelli had spent some time explaining how this was achieved, Aub still found it amazing.

Aub leaned back in the deep armchair and gazed at Morelli with unconcealed awe. "I still can't get over it," he declared, shaking his head. "You mean you can actually produce conditions in a lab that cause particles to vanish—not just to annihilate mutually with an antiparticle—to do so on their own? I've never heard of anything like that."

Morelli looked back across his desk with evident amusement. "Sure we can," he said, as if making light of it. "We do it every day. After lunch I'll take you to have a look at how we do it."

"But it's fantastic," Aub insisted. "Nobody at Berkeley ever talked about that kind of thing. I never read about it. . . . How come the results have never even been published? Surely that kind of thing should have been published all over."

"I was working in a government-controlled research program at the time," Morelli explained. "The whole project was subject to strict security. The details are no doubt filed away somewhere where nobody can get at them . . . you know the way it is."

"And yet you can work on the same kind of thing here at ISF . . . where you're not under federal control." Clifford spoke from a chair beneath the window. "Seems kind of . . . strange."

Morelli pursed his lips and raised his eyebrows, apparently weighing his reply before speaking. "Well . . . we don't exactly go out of our way to broadcast what we're doing here. That was the first thing that I learned when I made the move—if you want to be left alone these days, don't attract attention."

"But people can just walk in and out of this place," Clifford said in mild surprise. "I'm amazed word never leaked out. I mean . . . what about the people who work here; they never talk to anybody outside?"

Morelli smiled the curious smile of somebody who knows more than discretion permits him to say.

"You know, in World War II the English sometimes sent absolutely top-secret information through the ordinary mail, especially when they knew that the enemy was making great efforts to get their hands on it. It's a funny thing, but when something's sitting there right under somebody's nose and there's no attempt made to hide it, he often walks right on by . . . particularly if he's been conditioned to be neurotic about security. I suppose you could say that we operate along that kind of principle . . . in an informal kind of way. As for the people here . . ." Morelli shrugged as if to indicate that the point did not require elaboration. "Oh, they're pretty smart. If they weren't, they wouldn't be here." After a pause he added in a quiet voice: "You'd be surprised at some of the work that goes on around the world inside ISF."

Clifford got the message that further questions on that subject would not be in order. It was time to get back to the main topic of conversation.

"You were starting to tell us about your experiments here," he said.

"Right." Morelli sat forward and cleared a space in front of him for his arms. "We've been running experiments on induced annihilation on a large scale for about a year now. The building you came past after you landed—you may have noticed the big storage tanks by the wall outside it—houses the equipment."

"The whole building?" Aub asked.

"Yes, it's pretty big machinery; as I said, we're working on large-scale annihilation here, not just small lab tests. Anyhow, the setup is essentially as I de-

scribed a few minutes ago—we project a beam of
particle matter into a reaction chamber where the annihilation takes place . . . induced by the principles
I've described. Our main work at present is to
measure everything associated with the process and
to try to understand the physics of it better. I won't go
into too many details right now—you'll see it all for
yourselves before you go." Then he grinned. "You can
see how hung-up we are about security."

"What kinds of things are coming out of all this?"
Clifford asked.

"This is where I think you'll start to get interested,
Brad," Morelli replied. "And Aub, of course. You
see, since we've been running large-scale tests, we've
discovered a remarkable thing—we can generate a
gravity field artificially!" He paused and looked from
one to the other to invite comment.

"You mean that when you annihilate large numbers
of particles, you detect a gravity field?" Clifford spoke
slowly and thoughtfully; the implication was immediately clear. Aub stared incredulously at Morelli for a
moment and then swung sharply round to face
Clifford.

"Hey, Brad!" he exclaimed. "That's fantastic. It's
just what you'd expect from your theory. It's a part of
it that we didn't even think there *was* any way to test."
He gestured toward the professor. "And he's already
tested it!"

Morelli quickly confirmed what Aub was saying.
"The particle beam is induced to annihilate inside a
fairly small volume in the reaction chamber. When we
wind the beam up to a relatively high intensity, we
detect a well-defined gravity field around the annihilation volume. It's exactly as if there was a large, concentrated mass present there . . . which, of course,
there isn't. In other words, the process simulates the
gravitational effect of mass."

Clifford and Aub were stunned when they recognized the connection between Morelli's work and their
own. Clifford had already concluded from purely

theoretical considerations that what appeared to be
an annihilation of a particle was really a rotation in
k-space—a rotation that shifted the particle fully into
the unobservable hi-order domain of k-space. This
event would generate a k-wave pulse that, projected
into normal lo-order space, would be detected as gravi-
tation; lots of annihilations together would add up to
an apparently continuous field.

Aub had already produced conclusive evidence of
such k-rotations and his example had shown the sustained rotation—in effect, the continual annihilation
and re-creation—of just a single, isolated particle,
which constituted far too tiny and insignificant an
event for there to have been any hope of detecting
its supposed gravity pulse. Nevertheless, it had fur-
nished positive support for the theory.

And now Morelli, pursuing a completely different
and independent track, had discovered a way to force
annihilations in enormous numbers. Sure enough—just
as would be expected from the theory—he had found
that an apparently smooth gravitational field was produced in the process. Surely this could be no mere
coincidence; Zimmermann must have known exactly
what he was doing.

"It's the theoretical aspects that have been holding
us up," Morelli told them. "When I first stumbled on
the way to make the thing work, I was trying to do
something else entirely; it was mainly an accident.
Since then, here at ISF we've refined the process, but
we're still not too sure of what's behind it. We know
how to make it work, but we don't know *why* it
does." He threw his hands out and shrugged unashamedly. "I guess you could say it's been largely
trial and error, a few inspired guesses, and more than
a fair share of luck. Anyhow, it seems to work okay."
He glanced from Clifford to Aub and stated what was
by that time clear. "So when Heinrich told me about
what you two have been doing, naturally I was interested . . . to put it mildly. He could see the connection

too, which is why he got in touch with me. The rest you know."

"That's what surprises me," Clifford said. "Zimmermann spotted the connection straight away, and yet nobody from the government—the Bureau, for example—has even followed it up, not even recently." Morelli pulled a face and inclined his head to one side.

"I know what you're gonna say," he nodded.

Clifford said it anyway. "They're getting all worked up about the paper I wrote, especially where I talk about annihilations. Also, they must have details on record of the work you did before you came to ISF— work on inducing annihilations. Yet they never put the two together . . . ? Seems crazy. They've got thousands of asses warming chairs all over the country. What do they do all day?"

"It figures," Aub interjected.

"They don't have records that talk about the gravitational simulation though, remember," Morelli pointed out. "That only turned up in the work we've been doing here. So they'd have nothing to suggest that the connection between matter annihilation and gravity pulses that your paper predicted might actually have been demonstrated experimentally."

"Yes, but even so . . ." Clifford waved his hand in the air to indicate despair.

"I agree," Morelli nodded. "You'd have thought somebody would have been on the ball. But . . . I guess I don't have to tell you anything about the way those balls of fire zip around the place." The irony in his voice raised brief smiles. "Anyhow, to change the subject back again, I seem to have been doing most of the talking so far. I'm supposed to be interviewing you about possible positions here, so why don't I shut up and let you tell me some more about yourselves and the work you've been doing together. It already looks to me as if you're just the guys to fill in where we seem to be falling short, but let's go through the thing properly. After that I'll take you along the corridor to meet Peter Hughes, who wants to talk to you both individually. He's Director of the Sudbury Institute, and nobody gets hired without talking to Peter. After that I've fixed lunch for the three of us."

For about the next half-hour Clifford and Aub explained in detail the nature of their own work and its relevance to Morelli's experiments. As they spoke, Morelli became excited. From his comments, there seemed little doubt what the outcome of the interview would be. By the end of the discussion Morelli was speculating on a whole new branch of science that might grow from the pioneering at the Sudbury Institute.

"In a way, I suppose you could say it's analogous to what happened before," he said, settling back in his chair once the serious talk was over.

"How do you mean?" Clifford asked.

"Well, take those guys in Europe around the beginning of the nineteenth century—Faraday and the rest —when they first worked out the connection between magnetism and electricity . . ." Morelli glanced from Clifford to Aub and explained: "Before then the only kind of magnetism that anybody knew about was the kind that occurred naturally—in certain types of rock, such as lodestone. Well, don't you think we're doing exactly the same kind of thing all over again, but with gravity?"

"You mean they couldn't *manufacture* magnetism before then," Aub replied. "They couldn't turn it on and off or control it in any way. It was just . . . *there.*"

"Exactly." Morelli nodded vigorously. "It was just there—inseparably tied up with a chunk of matter. If you wanted magnetism, you went out and you dug it up. There was no other way." He paused and shifted his eyes toward Clifford. "But . . . when people started playing around with electrical currents and coils of wire and that kind of thing, they found they could make their own magnetic fields artificially, *and* they could then control them—make them bigger, smaller, turn them on and off at will. . . ." He threw his arms out wide. "And out of their work we got the whole science of electrical engineering—and later on electronics."

"And you think this could go the same way?" Clifford followed what Morelli was saying but this was the first time that his mind had been fully opened to the long-range possibilities. Morelli's enthusiasm for his work was irrepressible, his optimism, unbounded—which almost certainly explained how the project at Sudbury had advanced as far as it had without any firm theoretical understanding on the part of the researchers. It provided a stimulating contrast to the environment that Clifford had so recently left. He became aware suddenly of his keen desire to become part of ISF and of Morelli's team. It wasn't just the work that attracted him; he knew that here was something to which he could belong.

"Yes, I think it easily could," Morelli told them. "Like I said, the analogy is pretty close. Gravity has always just been there—inseparably tied up with a chunk of mass, hasn't it? We've only known it in its naturally occurring form; if you want gravity, go find a big mass. There's no other way . . . or there hasn't been up until now."

"But now you can make your own artificially," Aub completed.

"That's right. We can make our own and we can control it . . . and we don't need big bulky lumps of mass to do it either. We can do it in a lab and in a way that's relatively easy to handle," Morelli said. "To me that adds up to all the beginnings of a whole range of solid, down-to-earth engineering applications. How does that grab you guys? Interested?"

"Interested!" Aub turned to Clifford and back while he sought suitable words. "Just show me where I start."

"I can't add anything to that," Clifford said. Morelli grinned and held up a restraining hand.

"I wish it was that easy too, but let's wait and see how your interview goes. Peter's the guy you have to convince now, not me." He glanced at the clock on

the wall opposite the desk. "In fact, we'll have to
make a move in a minute or two. But before we go,
I'll just tell you a bit about our latest experiments
here—just to whet your appetites some more." The
sudden change in his tone hinted that he had saved
the best until last. The other two became instantly
attentive.

"We'd already guessed, of course, that the process
of particle annihilation inside the reaction chamber
somehow induces a curvature in Einsteinian spacetime
around the volume in which the process takes place.
In other words, it mimics the effect normally produced
by a large mass, which is not news to you any more.
From what I know now about Brad's theoretical work,
I can see now how it does it—qualitatively at least,
that is."

"What you're really doing is amplifying by a factor
of a few billion what happens naturally anyway," Aub
supplied.

"That's a good way of putting it," Morelli agreed.
"If I've understood what you've been telling me, the
gravity field around an ordinary mass results from the
tiny fraction of particles inside it that are annihilating
spontaneously at any instant. Okay?"

"That's right," Clifford confirmed. "Only a very
small proportion of the mass contributes anything to
the field . . . is gravitationally active if you like. Most
of it is purely passive; it takes up space and has bulk
but contributes nothing to the field. As we said earlier,
that's the part that really departs from classical ideas
—gravity turns out to be a dynamic effect, not static."

Morelli nodded and then turned his head toward
Aub, who was obviously about to add something. He
took up the point. "In fact, your experiments are a
good demonstration of just that. What you've effectively done is scrap the passive mass entirely. The
particles that annihilate inside your reaction chamber
can be thought of as a mass that's 100 percent gravitationally active. Every one of them is involved in
the process, unlike in ordinary mass."

"You're just doing what Nature does anyway, only on a much more concentrated scale," Clifford commented. "You're concentrating inside a few cubic centimeters the same number of annihilations every second that would normally take place in . . . oh, I don't know . . ." he shrugged and turned up his hands, "a whole mountain or something."

"And we get a smooth, detectable resultant field," Morelli concluded. "Yeah, that's what I meant when I said I can see better why it works now. It also explains more specifically why we can increase the strength of the field by increasing the beam density or by focusing into a smaller volume—they both give you more annihilations per cubic centimeter per second, which brings me back to what I was about to tell you." Clifford and Aub waited expectantly.

Morelli went on. "Recently we've been pushing the limits to find out how far we could take it . . . how far we could bend Einsteinian geodesics. The result has been pretty sensational—something we sure didn't bargain for. You see, fellas, what we've managed to do is generate a field so strong that nothing can get out of the annihilation volume at all—not even light! We have to push the volume right down to microscopic dimensions to do it, but it sure works okay. The space-time curvature at that level is so great that everything gets bent right back in to the middle. What do you say to that?"

For a few seconds that seemed a lot longer, the two young scientists stared at him in mute astonishment as their minds struggled to take in his meaning. Here was something that had been widely talked about for decades, it was true, but all the same, to be told quite matter-of-factly that it had actually become a reality and was just part of a day's work at Sudbury . . .

"A black hole!" Clifford's jaw sagged. "You mean you've produced an artificial black hole here . . . ?"

"*Jeez*," Aub exhaled slowly. "Man, have I been wasting my time. . . ."

Morelli smiled, unable to conceal his amusement.

"Thought you'd be impressed," he said. "We may not be theoretical hotshots here, but we haven't exactly been standing still all the same." He looked from one to the other and nodded his head. "Yes, we can produce black holes artificially if we go to high enough power; they're tiny, but they're genuine. But these are black holes with a difference. We don't need enormous amounts of mass to make them, and we can switch them on and off when we feel like it. Now, did you ever hear of a black hole like that before?"

Two silent stares greeted his words. He waited a moment for possible questions and then, seeing that none would be immediately forthcoming, turned toward the display terminal situated on one side of his desk.

"I'll leave you to think about that for a minute," he said. "It's time we were making tracks. I'll just call Peter and make sure he's free."

Two hours later, after what had seemed to them to be satisfactory and promising talks with Peter Hughes, Clifford and Aub were having lunch with Morelli in the Institute's Social and Domestic Block. By this time Morelli was painting vivid pictures of his visions of the future of gravitic engineering, and his two guests found themselves being infused and excited by the torrent of ideas that poured, seemingly inexhaustibly, from their host's fertile and imaginative mind.

"Artificially induced weightlessness?" Clifford repeated incredulously. "You really think it could work?"

"Aw, at this stage I can't really say," Morelli conceded candidly. "But just suppose for a moment that it did. It'd revolutionize the whole business of transportation. Just imagine—if you could move big loads effortlessly anywhere . . . all over the world. Why bother building bridges and things when you can simply float things across rivers on a g-beam? Who needs roads and rails? They're only ways of cutting down friction, and this way there'd be no friction—only inertia."

"You'd be able to move a ten-ton block of stone around with a push of your hand," Aub joined in. "Man, that's incredible."

"As long as you weren't in too much of a hurry to get it anywhere," Morelli said. "Not much acceleration, but yeah—sure—you could do it."

"What about static fields?" Clifford asked as another possibility dawned on him. "You know—for supporting structures and such. Think that might work too?"

Morelli shrugged as he began refilling the three coffee cups from the pot that had been left on the table.

"Who knows? Why not? Anything's possible until somebody proves it isn't . . . not so? Structures . . . ? Sure—maybe one day we'll even figure out how to hold up structures."

"Hey, that could change the whole of architecture," Aub whispered. In a louder voice he went on. "There'd be no limits of loading to worry about . . . weight-induced stresses and that kind of stuff. You could put up buildings any size or shape you wanted —all kinds of things—right up into the sky. You could make skyscrapers look like mud huts. It's crazy."

"Buildings . . . ? Skyscrapers . . . ?" Morelli threw out an arm to indicate there were no limits to what he could see. "Why mess around with buildings? Why not whole cities? String 'em together up into the sky like something you never dreamed of. Why not?"

Why not . . . ? Clifford found the unbridled enthusiasm of the extraordinary man that he had just met infectious. His mind soared with Morelli's unbelievable cities as new, undreamed-of possibilities tumbled before his mind's eye.

"And what about earth-moving?" he said. "You could move mountains maybe—literally. Resculpt the whole planet . . ."

"Move mountains? Resculpt planets?" Morelli's voice rose to a resonant crescendo as he threw the vision out to infinity. "Think big, Brad! Move planets! Resculpt the Solar System! Do you know there's an asteroid out there that's reckoned to contain enough iron to meet the world's needs at today's rate for the next twenty thousand years? Cost a bomb to ship it back in worthless pieces though; so why not ship the whole thing back and break it up in our own back yard? Overpopulation problems? Break up another planet and park the bits in orbit round the Sun here, where it's nice and warm; that'll keep us going for a while. How do you break a planet up? Answer: gravitic engineering! You set up an unbalanced field around it that makes it spin faster until it pulls itself apart. Easy! Want me to go on?"

Clifford and Aub just sat and stared at him wide-eyed. Yes, it could all happen. As long as there were people with the vision and the will to make it happen, a new age of human achievement could come true. And perhaps the first hesitant steps toward such a future were already being taken right there at Sudbury at that very moment. Things that had been just dreams for centuries might come true because of what they were doing.

Why not?

After lunch, Morelli conducted them to a large building, situated on the far side of the Institute, to let them have a look at the GRASER—Gravity Amplification by Stimulated Extinctions Reactor. They entered an area of conventional office suites and from there proceeded through a labyrinth of corridors and instrumentation labs to the heart of the project itself.

They found themselves standing on a metal-railed catwalk, looking down across a large, windowless, concrete-walled area, most of which was crammed with a chaotic tangle of machinery, electronic equipment racking, cables, and pipework. At the center, a spherical metal construction reared up out of the mess caged in steel lattices and festooned with electrical harnesses. A bright silvery tube, about three feet in diameter, connected the sphere to an enormous and complicated rig of some kind, which in turn appeared to be only part of something larger that was built through the far wall. About half a dozen technicians and scientists were engaged in various tasks about the floor. Morelli was pointing toward the tube and talking in a louder than usual voice to make himself heard above the background of subdued whining and humming.

"The beam is formed and accelerated in a generating setup located next door," he said. "We use hydrogen as our starting material; the feed-stock is held by the side of the building in big tanks that you may have noticed as we came in. That tube conveys the beam into the annihilation chamber. Actually, the core of the tube—where the beam itself is—is only six inches in diameter. The rest of the thickness that you see is mainly made up of focusing and control coils. The chamber is shielded inside that sphere; we get a fair amount of heat and radiation as a side effect of the process."

"Have you got a black hole in there now?" Aub asked. Morelli shook his head.

"Not at the moment," he said. "They're only doing some calibration tests this afternoon. Pity you won't be around next Tuesday; we should have one then."

Clifford was leaning on the guardrail and looking thoughtful. After a while he turned toward Morelli. "The radiation you mentioned just then, Al—does it come simply from losses inside the chamber, or is it produced by the annihilation process itself?"

"There are some losses, sure," Morelli answered. "It's pretty straightforward to calculate what they are. But on top of that, yes, there is a residual amount left over that must come from the annihilation process."

"So you not only create a gravity effect; you generate other kinds of radiation as well," Clifford checked.

Morelli nodded and replied: "That's correct. From what you said this morning, it's what you'd expect from your own k-theory. Why—what's on your mind?"

Clifford appeared not to hear the question but went on. "What about when you go all the way to a black hole . . . what happens then?"

Morelli raised his eyebrows and nodded approvingly. "It's funny you should mention that," he said. "That's exactly one of the things that's been bothering us. When we set up a black hole in there, we detect a definite radiation flux emanating from the hole itself. According to classical relativity, that shouldn't happen; nothing should be able to escape from a black hole—energy, radiation, light—nothing. But . . ." Morelli shrugged and spread his arms, "there it is. No question."

"Hawking Effect?" Aub suggested, referring to the idea of quantum-mechanical tunneling, first proposed by the English theoretical physicist Steven Hawking of Cambridge, back in the 1970s. The theory postulated a method by which black holes might be seen effectively to emit radiation. It required the spontaneous production of a particle-antiparticle pair somewhere in the vicinity of the black hole. Occasionally one particle of the pair might fall into the hole while the other escaped in the opposite direction to be detected by a distant observer. The net effect that he would observe would be a flux of particle radiation apparently produced by the hole itself.

"We thought of that too," Morelli replied. "You could be right, but I don't think we've got enough data yet to be certain one way or the other. That's one of the things we mean to look into." He looked at Clifford. "What does your theory say about it?"

"I haven't really gotten round to considering the k-physics of black holes," Clifford said, turning his back on the rail to face the other two. "But now that you mention it, it's an interesting point. According to k-theory, a particle appears to be created when two hi-domain functions interact to produce a k."

Morelli held up a hand to interrupt. "Just a second.

Hi-domain . . . that's the higher order of existence outside normal spacetime. Check?"

"Check," Clifford agreed. "A k-function exists in both hi- and lo-domains together. Now, the large number of annihilations taking place inside the reactor back there will produce a flux of hi-domain particles —a kind of radiation, if you like, not detectable in normal space. Since this radiation is not subject to the limitations of ordinary spacetime, it will be capable of escaping from the black hole." Clifford nodded to himself. "Yes. Outside the hole there will be a flux of hi-particles. These can interact with each other to produce k-particles, which are detectable. What you would see are particles apparently appearing spontaneously . . . looking like conventional radiation coming out of the hole. As I said, I haven't gotten round to working out the details, but qualitatively the theory sounds okay."

"So there are two possible explanations for it," Morelli summarized. "Hawking Effect and k-theory."

"That's about it." Clifford seemed pleased.

"The first involves conventional quantum probabilities; the second doesn't but talks about hi-radiation instead . . . as an intermediary agency."

"Uh huh."

Morelli seemed very interested. "It would be something if we could figure out some kind of experimental test to see which one fits," he said. "Any ideas?"

"Difficult," Clifford admitted. "In either case you'd expect to see the same thing. I guess the only approach would be to calculate precisely the intensity of the observed field that each theory predicts. Several people have already done that for Hawking Effect; when I've had a chance to think about it, I could probably give you some numbers for the other. Then we'd just have to do some accurate measuring to see which one fits best."

"Aren't you forgetting something?" Aub asked him. "What?"

"The hi-radiation. That's the big difference between

the two theories. Yours says that there ought to be an intense source of hi-radiation inside that thing; the other one doesn't. So why not simply test for that?"

Clifford looked at him quizzically. "How can we test for it? It doesn't exist in ordinary spacetime. It doesn't interact with our universe in any way, except when it produces k-functions, but they appear as conventional forms of energy. So we can only infer the existence of the hi-radiation indirectly . . . which is what we've been saying all along. We don't have any kind of instrument that can respond to it directly."

"That's my whole point," Aub insisted. "I think I could make one that does."

"Make one?"

"Yeah, I've been thinking about it for a coupla days now. Remember that picture I showed you when I called that first time? It was a track of a particle rotating continually through hi-space and normal space . . . vanishing and reappearing all the time."

"Okay. So?"

"Well, the mode of rotation should be influenced by hi-radiation. That means that it does interact in an observable fashion with our universe. I figure I could design an instrument based on that principle. Essentially it would be a special kind of ion chamber in which you could measure the effect of incident hi-radiation on the tracks of particles with full k-spin. To test out the idea, I knew that we'd need a concentrated source of hi-particles." He gestured downward in the direction of the reactor sphere. "Now it looks as if we've got one."

Clifford stared at him in astonishment. "A hi-radiation detector . . . ? You're joking."

"I am like hell."

"Any idea how long it'd take?" Morelli joined in, becoming intrigued.

"Depends how soon you tell me I can start," Aub replied, grinning unashamedly. He didn't believe in beating around the bush.

It was early evening by the time they left. Morelli walked with them to the pad where the airmobile was waiting to take them back to Logan. As they were about to turn to climb aboard the vehicle, he shook hands with both of them.

"Well, I've never had too much time for being secretive and all that. We'll be sending you formal letters and that kind of stuff, but I don't see any doubt about it. I'm looking forward to working with you guys. It's gonna be a great team."

They arrived back at Clifford's house at nine o'clock. Sarah couldn't really feign surprise at the news. She was already dressed to go out.

Chapter 12

The day after they returned from Massachusetts, Aub had already begun making preliminary notes for the design of the detector. He worked through the following night, hogging the upstairs terminal and amassing a mountain of notes and diagrams, and seemed only to have whetted his appetite for more by the morning.

That same morning the formal job offers came through from Sudbury and were promptly accepted. By late afternoon Aub had, via the Infonet, found himself an apartment in Concord, within easy reach of the Institute, and by evening he was packed and ready to go.

"That's one of the problems about having houses to sell and being married," he grinned as he bade Clifford and Sarah *au revoir* from the doorway. "Like I always said, it suits me to travel light. See you both back East when you've sorted out all the chores, huh?"

Sarah turned from the door after he had gone and shook her head wonderingly.

"What a character," she mused to Clifford. "I've never seen anybody so eager to start a new job. He won't sleep for weeks."

"You haven't met Al yet," Clifford told her. "Once the two of them really get going together, anything could happen. If those two had been the Wright Brothers, World War I would have been fought with supersonic jets."

Just over a month later, Clifford and Sarah moved into an attractive house on the outskirts of Marlboro, within easy distance of both Sudbury and Concord. Sarah had already gotten a job at the Marlboro General Hospital, and for once everything seemed to be going smoothly.

By the time Clifford arrived at the Institute to commence his first day's work there, Aub had already persuaded Morelli to assign a team of technicians and junior scientists to assist full-time on the project. Clifford met the group later that morning at one of the informal meetings that Aub had instigated as a means to review regularly the progress of design work on the detector—which was proceeding in leaps and bounds.

"Brad, this is the crew," Aub said as Clifford nodded in response to the "hi's" from around the table. "Alice, Sandra, Penny, Mike, Joe, Phil, and Art." They acknowledged their names in turn as Aub pointed them out. "Crew, this is Brad—the guy you've been hearing about for the last month or so. And now that the team is at last complete, to business." Aub opened a folder that was lying in front of him, extracted a sheet titled *Action Points,* passed a copy to Clifford without comment, and glanced briefly at his own. Clifford had only been in the room for a minute, and yet already they were at work. He was impressed; if this was typical of how Aub's enthusiasm was rubbing off, it was small wonder that the project was racing at breakneck speed. Somehow Aub had never before struck Clifford as an effective manager of people; Clifford wondered how many more unsuspected talents lay beneath that outlandish exterior.

"It says here *Mode-Hold Synthesisers,*" Aub stated. He looked up. "Mike, how's it going?"

"I've got a prototype circuit breadboarded in the lab downstairs," a red-haired young man dressed in a Pendleton shirt and green jeans replied from the far end. "It's going to need tighter tuning at the h.f. end, and there's still some stray leakage capacitance somewhere that needs tracking down, but I think it'll be okay. Gimme . . . say . . . another week on it."

"Review again next Monday," Aub mumbled, marking the margin of the paper. "Okay?"

"Sure."

"Mode Interpretation Routine, Alice?" Aub read the next item and shot an inquiring look at one of the girls.

"Bit of a problem there," she replied. "I need to know more about the mathematical derivation of the phase functions."

"Well, we now have just the guy with us," Aub said, looking over to Clifford. "Brad, how about sitting down with us after we break up and going over it?"

"Sure thing," Clifford answered.

"Special analogue IC chips from Intercontinental Semiconductors," Aub went on. "Did you get any joy on those, Joe?"

"No dice," Joe answered. "They're on a six-month waiting list. Nothing they can do about it."

"Shit!" Aub began drumming his fingers on the table irritably.

"But . . . despair not," Joe added. "I tracked a dozen down in a surplus shop in Boston, and Penny's going over to pick them up tomorrow. Cheap too."

"Fantastic." Aub brightened up again. "Next . . . Penny . . . two hundred feet of low-loss cable . . ."

The meeting was rapid-fire all the way through and lasted less than forty minutes. By the end of it Clifford felt completely at home. As Al had said just before Clifford and Aub departed on the first day they had come to Sudbury, it was a great team.

"I knew you were here so I brought you a coffee." The voice from behind him made Clifford look round from the screen with a start. Standing just inside the door of the office, Joe was holding a steaming cup in each hand. The time was twenty minutes before midnight; three months had gone by since Clifford's arrival at Sudbury.

"You must be a mind reader, Joe," Clifford said.

"Thanks, put it down there." He indicated a spot on the table next to his chair, amid the disorderly piles of folders and papers. "What's the matter; can't you sleep these days either?"

"I got a bit carried away with testing out that stabilizer subsystem," Joe said, putting down one of the cups. "Today was the first time we've had a chance to try it out on-line. I couldn't wait to see the results."

"How'd they come out?" Clifford asked.

"They're looking good. I think we've got the compensation derivatives right now. Aub and Penny are downstairs now tuning it in."

"Doesn't anybody ever go home in this place?" Clifford asked with a sigh. "You know, Joe, if we were paid overtime, we could all have retired by now."

"Yeah, well . . . I guess we'd all find we've forgotten how to spend time any other way if we did," Joe said. "Besides, this is more fun."

"You like it still, eh? That's good."

"Beats baseball," Joe declared. "How about you . . . things working out?" He slid into an empty chair beside Clifford's and gestured toward the strings of equations frozen on the screen at which Clifford had been working. "What are you into here now, for instance?"

Clifford returned his gaze to the screen and relaxed back in his chair. "If this detector that Aub's making works, we will have for the first time ever an instrument that responds directly to hi-radiation. We'll actually be able to observe effects taking place in the universe we know, that are the results of causes taking place in a domain that can't be perceived directly. That'll be a pretty significant thing."

"Okay, I'm with you," Joe said, nodding. "So what's all that on the screen?"

"Its part of a theoretical analysis to predict exactly the pattern of hi-radiation we ought to get for different annihilation rates, volumes, beam power settings . . . that kind of thing."

"Oh, I get it," Joe said after a moment's reflection. "Once you've got some firm numbers to work with, you'll be able to test the predictions by means of the detector. If Aub's readings confirm that you get what the calculations say you ought to get, then the theory's on pretty solid ground."

"Exactly," Clifford confirmed. "It's the only motto to go by, Joe—always check it out. It's the only way I know that you can be sure you know what you're talking about. That's what science is all about."

"I thought you were mixed up in something to do with secondary radiation too," Joe said, sipping his coffee slowly. "This Hawking Effect business . . . isn't that so?"

"That's so," Clifford agreed. "But that's another part of it. We already know that the annihilation process produces a fair amount of conventional classical radiation as a secondary effect. What we don't know for sure yet is how it happens. Classical quantum mechanics—in the shape of the Hawking Effect hypothesis—gives one explanation; secondary reactions among hi-particles offer another. What I'm trying to do is work out exactly the pattern we ought to see if the hi-particle explanation is correct. Al has already run some experiments on black-hole situations to see how well Hawking Effect predictions stand up. They don't come out too well at all."

"Oh?" Joe sounded interested.

"No," Clifford said. "There was a lot more radiation detected from the hole than quantum mechanics said there should have been."

"You reckon the other explanation will do better then?"

"I don't know yet . . . not until I've finished working out the model. Then there's nothing to stop us testing it out. We won't need Aub's detector for that since we're talking about conventional radiation that we can detect and measure without it."

"What about the other thing—the pattern of pure primary hi-radiation?"

"That's a different matter," Clifford told him. "That

detector of Aub's is the only way of measuring it. So let's hope he can make it work."

Three months later, Peter Hughes and Al Morelli were standing beneath the reactor sphere of the GRASER amid the collection of electronics racks, cubicles, and tangles of wire that had gradually come together in the area of floor which had been cleared for it. It looked more like a collection of technological junk that had been thrown haphazardly together and had somehow, miraculously stuck than anything designed for a purpose, embodying all manner of components and assemblies as a consequence of Aub turning to whatever sources of materials were available or improvising alternatives—another of his talents, Clifford discovered. In front of them, quite unperturbed, Aub was keying some final settings into a console while Clifford and the rest of the team stood watching intently.

"The beams's on and running," Morelli said to Hughes. "So annihilations are in progress in the reactor now."

"What power are you running?" Hughes inquired.

"Black hole," Morelli said.

"You're testing for pure hi-radiation then?" Hughes looked intrigued but at the same time cast a dubious eye over the chaotic and improbable mixture of equipment around him.

"First live test," Morelli confirmed. "That's why we brought you down."

Morelli noticed that Aub had half-turned from the console and was looking very glum. "What's up?" Morelli called. "Problems?"

Aub gestured at the screen above the keyboard he had been operating. "It's screwed up somewhere," he informed them. "We've either got a hardware fault or there's a bug in the initialization routine. It's hanging up and I can't get into the Command Interpreter." He exhaled a long sigh and turned to look at the disappointed faces on the other side of him. "Sorry, people, but the show's off for today. Can you come back next week?"

A week later it was.

"Something's screwed up somewhere . . . I hope. The system checks out okay, but it's reading zero. That either means we've got some obscure fault that the diagnostics aren't picking up or it means hi-waves don't exist. For the sake of Brad's theory, I hope it's the first."

Hughes and Morelli walked toward the exit. "How the hell can they trouble-shoot in all that mess, Al?" Hughes remarked in a low voice. "It looks like a cross between a bombed computer factory and a combined harvester."

"Yeah, but they've done it all in six months and on a shoestring," Morelli replied. "There have to be teething problems. I'll let my money ride on that bunch for a lot longer yet."

At half past three the morning of the following day, Aub withdrew his head from the signal-processing sub-system cubicle and held out his hand triumphantly to present a tiny silver object to Clifford, Phil, Art, and Sandra, whose eyes were red-rimmed from hours of studying the circuit diagrams and wiring lists that littered the area around the detector.

"It was a break in the a.c. signal path to the third differential," he announced. "The diagnostic only checked out the d.c. Just imagine—all that trouble over one lousy open-circuit capacitor. It's enough to make you want to throw up."

And so, later on that same day, Peter Hughes and Al Morelli returned once more to the GRASER building to witness a repeat performance. This time, after Aub had keyed in the final command sequence and while the rest of the team waited and watched with bated breath and crossed fingers, a column of numbers appeared on the display screen of the master console. Aub gave out a whoop of jubilation and turned in his seat to face toward where Hughes and Morelli were standing.

"That's it!" he shouted, gesticulating wildly at the screen. "It's responding! We're getting a response! Those readings are pure, 100 percent hi-radiation."

Peter Hughes stepped forward to peer at the display, his face wreathed in a smile of pure delight.

"They've done it, Al!" he exclaimed, turning toward Morelli. "Well I'll be doggone . . . they've actually gone and hit jackpot!"

Morelli moved forward and gazed at the screen in disbelief.

"You're absolutely certain that that's what you're measuring," he said to Aub. "That really is hi-radiation doing that? It's not just some indirect measure of secondary reactions or something like that?"

"It sure as hell is not," Aub stated in a tone that left no room for doubt. "What we're measuring here is coming straight from the middle of that black hole in there." Just to make sure the message was loud and clear he added a few more words. "And to get from in there to out here, it isn't traveling through any of the dimensions of ordinary spacetime. It's coming through the hi-order domain of k-space."

Peter Hughes was studying the screen closely, his brow knitted into a frown of concentration. Eventually he caught Aub's sleeve lightly and pointed to the display in front of them.

"If that data relates to hi-waves that are propagating through a domain of k-space unknown to conventional physics, then surely none of the units of conventional physics can be used to measure it," he said.

"Absolutely right," Aub agreed.

"That's what I thought," Hughes informed him. "So in that case, what units do those numbers represent?" Aub beamed a wide grin up at him.

"A new unit that we've defined specifically for the purpose," he said. "The first unit ever defined for measuring pure hi-phenomena."

"What do you call it?" Hughes asked. "Have you thought of a name yet?"

"Of course we have, man." Aub's smile broadened. "Milliaubs—what else?"

The first major hurdle had been cleared. Hi-radiation had not only been demonstrated positively to exist, but an instrumental technique for detecting and measuring it had been found. The project team was naturally in high spirits after these developments, but as further experiments were conducted to exploit the new knowledge, Clifford became even more troubled by the difficulties he was running into on the theoretical side. The detector had provided a complete vindication of his predictions concerning the existence and nature of hi-radiation, it was true, but measurements of the secondary radiation—conventional electromagnetic radiation—showed repeatedly that there was a flaw in his mathematical model somewhere. The amount of radiation measured always turned out to be far greater than his theory predicted. He found himself describing the problem to Sarah one evening, while they were out having a few drinks in the bar of one of the local hotels.

"You really wanna know?" he said, leaning forward across the table of the booth in which they were sitting. Sarah whisked his glass out of harm's way a spit-second before his elbow reached the spot. "It's all kinda technical . . . I'm not sure I know how to put it."

"I really want to know," she told him. "I know there's something not quite right, and I'd just like some idea of what it is. Try me anyway—I'm interested."

Clifford folded his arms on the table in front of him, buried his chin in his chest for a moment, then looked up at her and began. "We've talked before about k-space, hi-space . . . that kind of thing. Just tell me first what you understand about it."

"Any prizes?" she asked hopefully.

"Not today. Just testing."

"Okay," she said, then thought for a second. "As I understand it, there's more to the world around us than we can see. Didn't you say once that you can think of the normal world as some kind of 'shadow' existence—a 'projection,' I think you said, of something bigger—like shadows on a wall being projections on a flat world of solid things in a real world? Wasn't it something like that?"

"You've got the general idea," he said, nodding. "We can perceive—in other words, we know about—the things that happen in space and time, which turn out to be different aspects of the same thing anyway—"

"Four of them aren't there?" she interrupted. "Dimensions, right?"

"Right. At least, physics has always dealt in terms of four. But in fact there are more . . . to be precise, six of them."

"That's the bit I thought was strange," Sarah came in again. "Four I can visualize okay, but six . . . ? No way. Where are the other two?"

"That's the whole point. There *is* no way anybody can perceive the higher ones . . . either by their senses or by instruments. We've got no way of knowing about them . . . no more than a shadow man on the wall can know about up or down out of his flat world. He not only can't move out of it, he can't even see out of it, so the words just don't mean anything."

Sarah held up her hand to prevent him from going any further and sipped her drink while she reflected on what he was saying. At last she put the glass down. "I don't know if I'm missing something, but if all that's as you've said, how do *you* know about them . . . the higher dimensions? I thought you just said nobody could."

"Mmmm . . ." He studied the tabletop pensively, "that's where the problem gets technical. If I just say that the mathematics of a lot of physical processes—down at the subatomic level—makes sense when the extra dimensions are assumed and don't make sense when they aren't, would that be good enough? You'd buy that?"

"Suppose I'll have to," she accepted. "But you said 'assumed.' That's not good enough, surely. Aren't you supposed to be able to *prove* things like that?"

"Absolutely right! And that's what we've been trying to do, and that's where we're hitting problems."

She rested her chin on her knuckles and said again:

"Well—I'm interested. Tell me."

"Okay," he agreed. He was beginning to enjoy the conversation. "Let's play a game . . ."

"What, in public?"

"I'm serious. There's a flat universe." He indicated the top of the table. "Forget we're solid 3-D people and imagine we're shadow people that live in that universe—as we said a minute ago. Now . . ." he pointed at one of the coasters lying between them. "That's an object that exists in our flat universe . . . it's got no thickness at all, okay?"

"Okay," she agreed.

He picked up the coaster and turned it at a right angle so that its edge rested on the table.

"Now I've rotated it so that, although it still exists, it now lies completely in the dimension that we—the shadow people—don't know about. How much of it do we see?"

"It's got no thickness at all, you said?" she checked.

"That's right."

Sarah shrugged and opened her fingers.

"We don't see any of it," she said. "It's vanished."

"Precisely. The tabletop is lo-order space . . . normal space. The up-down dimension is hi-space, and all of them together is k-space. Get it?"

A light of sudden comprehension glowed in Sarah's eyes.

"Just a second, before you say any more," she said excitedly. "Let's see if I can fill some of it in for myself. If you didn't just rotate that, but spun it over and over all the time, the shadow people would see it disappearing and reappearing all the time, wouldn't they? That's the thing that Aub and you were getting worked up about when Aub was at Berkeley . . . those things you called k-space rotations. He showed us a picture of a particle doing just that."

"Absolutely right," Clifford confirmed. "It was doing just that. And that was the first concrete proof that it all really was real." Sarah had nothing to add at that point and seemed eager for more, so Clifford went on. "Now suppose we have two objects, both of which exist purely in hi-space . . ." he picked up a second coaster and held it parallel to the first so that they were both standing edge-on to the table. "We don't see anything in the shadow universe . . . normal space, right?"

"Right," Sarah agreed.

"Now, if they collide and one or both of them flip over . . ." He went through the action and left her to complete the sentence.

"We'd see one or two of them appear from nowhere," she observed at once. "Hey, this is fun. More, please."

"Yes, exactly. In fact that machine that Al Morelli built does both those things. It makes lots of particles flip from normal space into hi-space . . . vanish . . ."

"Which makes gravity."

"Right. And it also generates a big output of pure hi-space particles that aren't detectable—or weren't until Aub made his detector . . ." He paused as he realized that Sarah was signaling again. "Uh?"

"How does that thing work?" she asked. "I thought you said that nothing in the hi-space place could be detected by senses or instruments. . . . Doesn't Aub's thing do just that?"

"You're right," Clifford conceded. "But before that there was no known way of doing it. What Aub found was that he could set up a system of spinning particles—appearing and disappearing in the way you said a minute ago—and that the way in which they spin . . . the spin mode . . . changes when pure hi-particles interact with it. That's what we call hi-radiation. By monitoring the changes in spin modes, Aub can measure certain things about the hi-radiation that's causing the changes."

"Okay," Sarah said slowly. "I don't get all of that, but I see the general idea. Where were we?"

"Morelli's GRASER makes lots of hi-radiation."

"Yes, that was it," she said. "So this machine of Al's is throwing out these hi-particle things that nobody can know about except by using Aub's detector thing. Joe told me that you'd calculated what the detector should have detected, and sure enough it did. So what's the problem?"

"Up to that point, no problem," Clifford agreed. "I worked out a math model of black-hole conditions and you're quite right—as far as the predicted hi-radiation went, sure, it checked out fine with what we measured when Aub finally got the detector working."

"So?"

"But pure hi-radiation wasn't the only thing that the model predicted. Remember the collisions . . . ?" Clifford repeated the action of colliding and flipping over the coasters. "The hi-particles can interact among themselves to produce particles that we can detect by ordinary methods . . . in other words, ordinary, conventional radiation. So we ought to see conventional radiation—apparently coming from nowhere—around Morelli's black holes."

"And you don't," she guessed.

"We do, but the pattern and the amount are wrong. The frequency spectrum is wrong, and there's more of it than the model says there should be."

Sarah looked slightly disappointed.

"Is that all?" she said, raising her eyebrows. "I mean, that doesn't sound like the end of the world. You've proved the main point. Are the exact numbers that important?"

"Yes, they are," Clifford told her. "For one thing, the only way you can be sure you've got the theory right is if the numbers come out the way the theory says they should. If they don't, that means there's something there you don't understand that you should understand. And the second thing is that there is another possible explanation for the radiation around the black holes that doesn't require k-theory at all; it's called 'Hawking Effect' and involves just conventional physics. You have to get the numbers right to be able to choose which explanation fits. Otherwise you'll never know. Right now we've tested both predictions and neither fits. K-theory comes closer to the number that we actually measure, but it still predicts less radiation than is there. That's the problem."

"But you're closer, you said," Sarah pointed out. "Isn't that good enough for you to choose?" Clifford shook his head.

" 'Fraid not," he said. "The error's too big. Until we know why, both theories could be equally wrong and the fact that one comes nearer could be just a coincidence . . . certainly not grounds for saying it's right." He sighed. "As I said, you have to get the numbers right."

Chapter 13

Aub, however, was as usual completely unperturbed by such academic details. Leaving Clifford to ponder them, he abandoned himself ecstatically to the task of fully mastering and further refining his latest toy. Gradually he found ways of improving the sensitivity of the instrument so that it would register reliably the levels of annihilation-generated hi-radiation even when the GRASER was running at comparatively moderate power, and the mass concentrations simulated inside the reactor sphere were nowhere near black-hole intensities.

Aub was busy in his office when he received a call from Alice, who was downstairs on the reactor floor debugging a program that had recently been added to the system.

"There's something unusual happening here, Aub," she said, looking puzzled. "I don't understand it. Can you come down and have a look?"

Fifteen minutes later, Aub joined her beside the reactor sphere, at the master console of the detector and cast an eye quickly over the familiar clutter of equipment around them.

"What's the problem?" he asked cheerfully. She pointed at a column of numbers glowing on the main monitor screen. Almost at once Aub's face knotted into a puzzled frown as he realized that it was unusually quiet; there was none of the humming and whining that signaled when the GRASER was running.

But before he could speak, Alice offered an explanation. "I had to switch on the detector to run the program. It seems to be measuring hi-radiation, but the GRASER is shut down this morning. What do you make of it?"

Aub sighed and sank into the operator's chair. Late the night before he had installed an additional rack of hardware to improve the sensitivity of the instrument still further and had gone home without testing it out, having wasted half the night tracing an intermittent fault.

"I guess I musta screwed up somewhere last night," he said in a resigned voice. "It looks like we're in for another day of trouble-shooting. Better hook into the main computer and start calling down the diagnostics."

But by mid-afternoon, at which time they had been joined by a curious Sandra, Joe, and Art, Aub was still disturbed. "This is crazy. The system checks out okay, the GRASER's not running, so we're not generating any hi-waves, but we're still measuring them. Let's start up the GRASER and run a few standard calibration routines. There has to be something screwy somewhere."

Later that evening the whole team, including Clifford, was gathered round the console while Aub repeated the tests that he had performed time and time again. Still the results came out the same. They were detecting hi-waves where there were no hi-waves to be detected. Clifford took the logical view that if the waves were there and they were definitely not coming from the GRASER, then they had to be coming from somewhere else. No sooner had he said it when the truth dawned on him. Five minutes later he was on the line to an astounded Al Morelli, who was half-shaved and wearing a bathrobe.

"The detector is definitely responding, Al," he said, his voice quivering with excitement. "But what it's responding to has got nothing to do with the

GRASER at all. It's coming from the whole of the universe!"

"Universe? What universe?" Morelli looked bewildered. "Brad, just what are you talking about?"

"*The* universe!" Clifford exclaimed. "All over the universe you've got particle transitions going on all the time, right? You've got creations happening all the time, everywhere, and you've got annihilations happening mainly inside masses."

"Sure, but . . ." Morelli's eyes widened. "You're not saying . . . ?"

"That's just what I'm saying," Clifford affirmed, nodding violently. "Every single one of those events generates hi-waves just as surely as those same events taking place inside the GRASER do. What Aub's done is wind the sensitivity up so high that we're actually getting a reading from it. We're reading the hi-wave background noise from the *whole* universe."

Morelli's face just gaped out of the screen.

Before he could formulate a coherent reply, Clifford went on. "I'll tell you another thing too. There's every reason to suppose that the background hi-wave noise also produces a background of ordinary radiation through secondary reactions. That gives us a possible alternative explanation for the three-degree thermal background radiation, so maybe we don't need the Big Bang model to account for it at all now. How about that? Here's something we've got to talk to Zimmermann about right away."

"What do you mean—'k-astronomy'?" Peter Hughes looked suspiciously over his desk at Aub and Morelli, who hadn't stopped babbling excitedly since they sat down. "If you're telling me you want more money for the project . . ."

"Hear us out first, Pete," Morelli said. "This could be the greatest thing since Galileo. That machine over in the GRASER building is picking up hi-waves from everywhere in the universe—stars, black holes—everything everywhere . . ."

"I know that," Hughes replied. "But . . ."

"It wasn't designed for anything like that, but it works," Morelli went on.

"Now, suppose we developed an instrument specially to do that kind of thing," Aub chimed in. "An instrument to observe the universe in terms of its hi-wave radiation instead of its electromagnetic spectrum . . . by 'hi-light.' "

"But I still don't see . . ." Hughes began again, but Morelli cut him off again.

"We think this could open up possibilities you never dreamed of. Brad's come up with an analysis of how hi-waves propagate through k-space. It's enough to blow your mind."

"K-space points don't correlate with geometric points in normal space," Aub said. "Or even with Einsteinian point-events. There's no tie-in between the separation of k-points and everyday 'distance' . . ."

"So velocity doesn't transform up from lo-space," Morelli said.

"Not in any physically meaningful way, anyhow," Aub added, just to make it clear. Hughes looked helplessly from one to the other and suddenly held both hands up protectively in front of his face.

"Stop!" he bawled. The office at once fell silent. "Thank you," he said in a calmer voice. "Now, why don't you just calm down, think about it, and then tell me from the beginning exactly what the hell you're talking about?"

Aub and Morelli turned toward each other with questioning expressions.

"You tell him," Morelli suggested.

"No, you tell him," Aub answered. They both began speaking at once and Hughes stopped them again. Eventually Aub began the explanation.

"A hi-wave can be generated at some particular point in normal space . . . such as inside the reaction chamber of the GRASER. It can also be observed— or at least its effects can—at some other particular point in normal space . . ."

"Such as in your detector," Hughes completed. "Fine. Go on."

"That's right," Aub nodded. "But what happens in between is not something you can visualize. It doesn't *mean* anything to say that a hi-wave goes from point A to point B at any particular speed."

"You mean it just happens . . ." Hughes looked mystified. "How can something get from A to B without going from A to B?"

"That's the whole point that comes out of Brad's analysis," Morelli supplied. "To talk about going from A to B in the everyday sense implies the notions of direction, distance, and time. Brad's equations do contain variables that play similar roles, but they relate to k-space. . . . They don't have any direct interpretation in ordinary spacetime."

Aub waited a few seconds and then elaborated. "Direction, distance, and time come out simply as projections into the lo-order domain of normal space, of quantities that exist in k-space but which can't be experienced as total impressions. The only way, for example, that a two-dimensional being could perceive a 3-D object—a sphere, say—would be to cut it up into slices and attempt to integrate all the pictures into one total concept, but he couldn't really do it accurately since he wouldn't have the right mental equipment to construct 3-D models."

"What he'd have to do would be to inspect each separate slice in *sequence*," Morelli came in. "That implies he could only perceive the object as a *series* of impressions. In other words, he would have to *manufacture* the *illusion* of time, in order to make up for his inadequate sensory equipment."

In spite of himself, Hughes began to look interested.

"So what are you saying then?" he asked. "We're like that, but with regard to k-space? Time and all the rest of it are subjective illusions?"

"In terms of the real k-universe, yes," Morelli said simply. "The conceptual model of the universe that we perceive is a product of the limited awareness that we've so far evolved."

"But the important point is that ideas of time, direction, and distance are products of *our* universe, not realities of the *true* universe," Aub said. "If you like, k-waves aren't restricted by things that are really constructions of evolving but imperfect minds. Hence, those quantities are irrelevant when you talk about k-space propagation. A light wave is a projection of a k-wave into normal space, and its finite velocity results from the restrictions of the lo-domain that it's projected into. A pure hi-wave doesn't project into lo-domain space at all, and therefore its observed propagation isn't restricted."

"What Aub is saying, Pete, is that when a hi-wave is generated, say, in the GRASER, and picked up, say, in the detector, the time delay between the two events is zero . . . to an observer in normal space who records it as two events. The propagation is instantaneous!"

Hughes looked at them incredulously. The reason for their excitement when they had first burst into his office was now becoming clear.

"And you say you're now receiving hi-waves from all over the universe," he said slowly. "Are you getting at what I think you're getting at?"

"K-astronomy!" Aub confirmed. "Or hi-astronomy, whatever you want to call it—yes, that's exactly what we're getting at. With telescopes you can get information from stars and galaxies and stuff, but most of it's millions of years out of date. But with hi-waves you can get information on what's going on out there *now* . . . without any time delays! And distance is no object either, since the same thing applies!"

Hughes frowned disbelievingly.

"But that's faster-than-light," he told them. "It implies all kinds of causality paradoxes. Relatively says so. You're being absurd."

"No Pete," Morelli answered. "We're not talking about something moving *through* normal space at some high velocity. We're not talking about anything moving *through* normal space at all. Think of it in an instantaneous . . . *transformation,* if you will . . . from one point in space to another. Forget anything like 'velocity' being involved at all."

Aub thought about that for a moment then turned to Morelli. "Relativistic causality paradoxes all stem from the fact that two observers moving faster-than-light couldn't even agree on the *order* in which two events happen, let alone on the time-interval between them."

"Well doesn't that apply here?" Hughes asked.

"No," Morelli replied. "You see Pete, for paradoxical events to be observable, there'd have to be some period of time for them to be observed in. In the process we're talking about, the transformation happens in zero time, and there's no opportunity for paradoxical events to happen." He shrugged. "If there's no way you can detect a paradox, then there isn't any paradox."

"And since we're not introducing the notion of velocity, there's no problem with acceleration either," Aub added. "All the problems about an infinite mass needing infinite energy to accelerate it—they go away too."

Hughes blinked at him in astonishment. For a while his mind struggled to come to terms with the things he had been told, but when he spoke his tone betrayed that he was as good as sold on the idea.

"So what happens next?" he asked. "Where do we go from here?"

"Well, you can't just make a telescope or something you can point at places in the sky," Aub answered. "From the things we've been saying, a hi-wave doesn't do anything simple like come at you from any particular direction. That background noise that we've been picking up contains information from everywhere and every direction all at once . . . all scrambled together."

"So what do you do to get round that?" Hughes queried.

"Aub's not sure yet," Morelli said. "But he's been talking to Brad about it, and Brad thinks there might be ways of computer-processing the information to somehow isolate the part of the signal that comes from a given object of interest—say, a star. Then it might be possible to construct some kind of image out of it . . . we don't know yet. Brad's still working on it." Morelli paused and rubbed his chin for a moment. "They proposed a schedule of modifications to the detector to make it better suited for responding to external hi-waves rather than GRASER hi-waves, but when Aub and I discussed it, we figured we'd do a lot better if we started out from scratch with something new, designed especially for the job."

"A Mark II detector," Aub came in. "One built for just this kind of work. It would give us a chance to cash in on all the lessons we've learned with the one we've got and to add some features that we haven't got."

"So we came to see you to talk about it," Morelli added needlessly.

"You want to build another machine," Hughes finished for them.

Morelli and Aub glanced at each other.

"Yes," they said both together. Hughes sat back in his chair and nodded slowly as if his worst suspicions had just been confirmed.

"I knew it was more money," he told them. He thought for a few seconds. "Tell you what I'll do. You get your heads together and produce a preliminary cost breakdown of what you think you'll need. After that, if you convince me, I'll talk to ISF headquarters in Geneva about it. Fair enough?"

Morelli opened the folder that he had been resting on his knees, extracted a wad of typewritten sheets of columns and figures, turned them around, and slid them on to Hughes's desk.

"Funny you should mention that, Pete," he said,

keeping an absolutely straight face. Hughes stared disbelievingly down at the papers and then back up at
the two earnest faces confronting him from the other
side of his desk.

"Okay," he sighed, resigned. "Let's go through it
now."

A week later, Hughes and Morelli flew to Geneva.
The week after that, three directors from ISF headquarters came to Sudbury to obtain firsthand background information on what had been going on and
what the possibilities for the future were. A few days
after the matter had been discussed in Geneva, Peter
Hughes called Morelli and gave him the good news.
"I've just had Maurice on the line from Geneva.
You'd better tell the team right away—we're going
ahead with Mark II."

The first thing to do was place orders for a long list
of equipment needed for the construction of Mark II.
Hughes and Morelli had decided that, however gifted
with talents for the unorthodox Aub might be, the new
instrument would be designed and built according to
accepted practices. In that way it would be easy to
expand, modify, and trouble-shoot; parts would be
readily replaceable; and regular maintenance by suppliers would be feasible, enabling Aub and the other
scientists at Sudbury to concentrate on the jobs they
were there to do. It would take longer to get off the
ground that way, but thereafter progress would be
faster. Besides that, they had Mark I to occupy them
in the meantime; without doubt it still had enormous
potential for improvement that they were only beginning to appreciate.

But at about that time the first signs started to appear that on other fronts things were not running
normally.

"Yes, Professor Morelli?" The face of the official from
the State Department local office in Boston stared im-
passively out of the screen.

"I want to know about this inquiry you've sent us,"

Morelli replied from his Sudbury office. "And the questionnaire that you've attached to the back of it. What's it all about?"

"Purely a routine formality, Professor," the official replied smoothly. "A matter of keeping records up-to-date, you understand."

Morelli waved the paper in front of him. "But what is the purpose of all these questions?" he demanded. "Personnel working here and a list of the projects they're working on . . . declaration of capital equipment and the use that's being made of it . . . major research projects funded during the last two years . . . What in hell's going on? I've never seen anything like this before."

"Perhaps we have been a little more lax in the past than we should have been," the face replied. "I assure you that such information is pertinent to our duties and that we are empowered to request it."

"Empowered by whom?" Morelli asked angrily. The man's manner was beginning to irritate him.

"That I can't disclose, I'm sorry. I can only give you my assurance."

"Damn your assurance! It's either hogwash or you don't know what you're talking about. Let me talk to your boss."

"Really . . . I can hardly accept the necessity of . . ."

"Put me through to your boss," Morelli stormed.

"I'm afraid that Mr. Carson is unavailable at the moment. However, I . . ."

"Then tell him to call me," Morelli said and flipped off the screen.

Morelli glowered at the blank display screen for a long time while he tried in his mind to fit some kind of pattern to it. That had been the third such probing inquiry in two weeks. All kinds of obscure officials in obscure places were, it seemed, suddenly taking a lot of interest in Sudbury and what was going on there. He didn't like it.

"Okay, Alice, this guy in a gray suit and wearing a

collar and tie started talking to you in the club,"
Morelli said. They were with a group relaxing and enjoying the sun during the lunch break by the shore of
the lake outside the Institute. "What happened?"

"Well, at first I thought it was a pickup," she told
him. "You know, some guy out on the town . . . He
looked a bit out of place there, but you get all kinds,
I guess."

"Uh huh . . . go on."

"But it turned out he really wasn't interested in me
at all," she said. "Only in the place I worked at. He
wanted to know if I worked for a Professor Morelli,
who used to specialize in gravitational physics and who
had discovered how to force particle annihilations
some years back. It was a funny kind of conversation
for a place like that. . . . He seemed to be trying to
make it sound casual, but it came across all artificial,
you know?"

"So what did you tell him?" Morelli asked.

"Well, I said, yes I did, but then he started asking
if you were still working on the same thing and how
much further you'd gone with it. That was when I got
suspicious—really suspicious—and got out. Later on,
Larry—he's a bartender there—said the guy had been
asking around all night trying to get ISF people
pointed out. I thought you should know."

"You did the right thing," Morelli told her. "Don't
worry about it; just forget the whole thing. But if anything similar happens again, you let me know right
away. Okay?"

Later that afternoon, Morelli went to find Peter
Hughes. "Me being pestered is bad enough, but now
they're starting on the juniors. What in hell is going
on?"

"Sorry, Mr. Hughes, I'm afraid I can't help you." The
man from the Technical Coordination Bureau in
Washington looked dutifully concerned, but somehow
the sincerity didn't come through. "I really don't know
anything about anything like that."

Hughes stared back at the screen dubiously. "I'm not saying your department is actually doing it," he said. "I'm simply asking what you know about it. The Bureau seems to have at least a finger in most of these kinds of pies."

"As I said, Mr. Hughes, I know nothing about anything like that," the Bureau man replied. "I will make inquiries though, I assure you. I'm sure you appreciate that there are many departments that require all types of inputs for statistical purposes and so forth . . . nothing sinister. If any of their people have been a little, shall we say, overzealous, I apologize, and if I can find out who it is and bring some restraining influence to bear, I certainly will. Thank you for calling. If you'll excuse me, I think I have another call holding."

Meanwhile, down in the basement room that housed the central node of the Institute's computer complex, the computer operations manager was frowning over the weekly activity analysis that had just been dropped on his desk. The numbers on the sheet told him that the surveillance programs running in the preprocessor that interfaced the system to the outside world via the Infonet lines had trapped and aborted no fewer than fifty-seven illegal attempts to gain access to the Sudbury database from anonymous places elsewhere. It had been the same the week before, too, and nearly as bad the week before that. Somebody was apparently trying very hard to find out what information and records were stored in that database.

But all this interference proved nothing more than a distraction—an irritation that didn't really affect the work on Mark II. Then things took a more serious turn. The first intimation that the project was in trouble came when Mike and Phil drew up a detailed list of required equipment and components and began contacting suppliers for technical information, prices, and delivery estimates.

"I'm sorry," the secretary to the sales manager of Micromatic Devices, Inc., advised. "But Mr. Williams isn't in right now. Can I take a message?"

"You've taken about a hundred messages already," Mike told her irritably. "I've been trying to talk to him for two days. When will he be back?"

"I really can't say," she replied. "He really is busy these days."

"Damn it, so am I," Mike protested. "What's the matter with everybody these days—don't they want to do any business? Look, you find him, please, and tell him to give me a call, urgent . . . day or night, I don't care. Got that?"

"Well, I'll see what I can do." The secretary didn't sound very optimistic. "Leave it with me, okay?"

"Okay," Mike sighed as he cut the call.

"I want to try something," Clifford growled from where he had been watching at the back of the room. "Key the same number again, will you." As he spoke he moved forward and pivoted the Infonet terminal around so that the view from it would show a different background. Mike rekeyed and, as Clifford slipped into the chair, another female face appeared.

"Micromatic, hello," she announced.

"Ron Williams, please," Clifford answered.

"Putting you through to Sales," she said. A second later the same secretary that had spoken to Mike was staring out at Clifford. He repeated the name.

"Who's calling Mr. Williams?" she inquired.

"Walter Massey of ACRE, New Mexico."

"One moment."

The screen blurred for a moment, then stabilized to reveal the smiling features of a man probably in his late thirties.

"Walt . . ." he began, then his face fell abruptly. "Oh . . . Bradley Clifford . . . It's been a long time . . . I thought you'd left ACRE a long time ago."

"I did," Clifford said curtly. "I'm at ISF, Sudbury. What the hell are you playing at?"

"I'm not sure I know . . ."

"Sure you're damn well sure. We've been calling for two days and getting the bum's rush. All the time you're sitting on your ass there. What are you playing at?"

Williams looked confused and tried to smile weakly.

"We've been having a bit of a communications problem here," he said. "Sorry if it's been a pain. What did you want?"

"Model 1137-C pulse resonators," Clifford said. "How much and how long to deliver?"

"Oh, gee . . . well . . . ah . . . that might be a problem. I don't think that model is available anymore. They're on engineering hold at Manufacturing pending design mods. Could be a while before they're released."

"How long is a while?" Clifford demanded. "And what do you have in the way of alternatives?"

Williams was looking distinctly uncomfortable. "I really can't say how long," he pleaded. "It all depends on our engineering people. We've withdrawn all the other models from the list." Without waiting for further comments he went on hastily. "It looks as if we can't really help you this time. Some time in the future though, maybe."

After he had cleared down the call, Clifford scowled at Mike. "Something very strange is going on. I've never known that outfit play hard to get before; usually they're very helpful. If it's not because they don't want to do business, then somebody somewhere is getting at them and warning them off for some reason. I'm beginning to get a good idea who."

"They were advertising them less than a month ago, and now they're saying it'll take twelve months at least." Clifford slapped the paper down on Morelli's desk and turned angrily away to face the window. "It's the same thing everywhere we go, Al. Everything is unavailable or reserved for government priority or out of stock. The only way we'll get those modulators is from that company in France that Aub mentioned. Have you had any luck with that approach yet?"

"Forget it," Morelli said gloomily.

"Why? What's happened now?"

"We need an importation license and we can't get one. It's been refused."

"Why, for Christ's sake? Aub says all the ones they used at Berkeley came from France, no problem."

"No reason offered," Morelli said. "It's just been refused outright. Anyhow, the matter's academic now since the French outfit won't play ball."

"What d'you mean—won't play?" Clifford asked. "I thought they said they'd be happy to oblige."

"A week ago they said they would be," Morelli agreed. "But when I talked to them yesterday, it'd all changed. Jacques muttered something about having to reserve a stock for spares and said they couldn't let any go. He said they'd been misled by an incorrect stock count."

"Bullshit!" Clifford raged. "They've been got at too. Isn't anywhere in the world safe from those bastards and their grubby fingers? All we wanted to do was be left alone!"

"But it looks as if somebody doesn't want to leave you alone," Sarah commented when Clifford brought her up-to-date that evening. "You always said we'd be famous one day."

"The whole thing's childish and stupid," Clifford declared moodily. "Presumably the idea is to show to the world that you can't beat the system. If you look like you're doing a good job of getting along without them, they make it their business to screw it up for you. That way the world gets the message. It's typical of the way their tiny minds work. Jesus, no wonder the world's in such a mess!"

"I suppose it's a gentle reminder to ISF to stay in line too," Sarah added. "If the system pronounces you undesirable, then that's the way you're supposed to stay. In other words, taking in the outcasts isn't the way to keep friends."

"Yeah, that too, I guess," Clifford agreed. "Al's

pretty fed up with the whole lousy business too. I've never seen him low before. It's ridiculous."

"Do you think they might reconsider your employment contracts then?" Sarah asked hesitantly. "I mean it must be affecting the work of the whole place."

"If they've thought about that they haven't mentioned it," Clifford said. "But I can't say I'd blame 'em." He thought deeply for a long time and then said suddenly in a brighter voice:

"Oh, I forgot to tell you, there is a piece of good news as well."

"I don't believe it. What?"

"Professor Zimmermann is due to take a couple of weeks vacation down on Earth sometime in the near future. Al said so today. Apparently Zimmermann wants to come to Sudbury for a day or two to see for himself what we're doing at the Institute. You always said you wanted to meet him. It looks like maybe now you'll get the chance."

Chapter 14

The screen and its associated electronics had been salvaged from a basement room of the Institute that had become the final resting place for a bewildering assortment of dust-covered hardware left over from one-time projects whose purpose was long forgotten. The minicomputer that provided local control for the screen and in addition linked it into the Institute's main computing complex had originally formed part of a body scanner at Marlboro General Hospital; it had been scheduled for the scrap heap when the hospital made a decision to replace the scanner with a more up-to-date system, but had found its way to Sudbury on the back seat of Aub's car. The control console had been built mainly from panels of roughly cut aluminum sheeting, and included in its list of unlikely component parts: pieces of domestic Infonet terminals, microprocessors from household environmental-control units, Army-reject bubble memory modules, a frequency synthesizer from a sale of surplus stocks by a marine radar manufacturer in Boston, and a selection of items from various do-it-yourself hobby kits. The whole assemblage was housed in a small room adjoining the GRASER and connected by a multitude of cables to the clutter of cabinets and racks that formed the main body of the detector situated out on the large floor, in a space cleared immediately beside the reactor sphere itself.

Professor Heinrich Zimmermann stood back a few paces from the screen, a faint smile of amusement playing on his lips as he contemplated the image being displayed, and accepted good-naturedly the challenge that it implied. Most of the screen's area was taken up by a plain circular disk of dull orange, showing no internal detail or pattern but lightening slightly to become just a shade more yellow toward the center. The background to the disk was at first sight completely dark, but closer inspection revealed the merest hint of a tenuous blood-red mist to relieve the blackness. At length Zimmermann shook his head and looked back at Aub, who was sitting on a metal-frame stool in front of the console and watching him with mischievous, twinkling eyes that failed to conceal his suppressed mirth.

"I thought that you had shown me everything. Now it appears that you have saved some sort of mystery until the very end. I am afraid I shall have to acknowledge defeat. What is it?"

Aub's face split into a wide grin. From behind the professor, Clifford and Morelli stepped forward to complete the semicircle around the display.

"Well, since you're an astronomer, we thought we'd better lay on something that would have the right kind of appeal," Clifford replied. "As we said earlier, Aub's been spending quite a lot of time modifying the detector to give an improved response to cosmic hi-radiation. Okay?" Zimmermann nodded. Clifford continued, "The most intense sources of naturally occurring hi-waves are the concentrated annihilations produced in large masses. Now, what's the biggest mass you can think of very near where we're all standing?"

Zimmermann frowned to himself for a moment.

"Near here . . . ? I suppose it would have to be the foundation and base supporting the reactor sphere out there . . ." He caught the look on Clifford's face. "No . . . ?"

"Much bigger 'n that. Try again."

"Bigger by lots of orders of magnitude," Morelli hinted, joining in the game.

"You don't mean . . ." Zimmermann pointed down at the floor while the others nodded encouragingly. "Not Earth?" He looked from one to another, astonished.

"That's what you're looking at, all right," Clifford confirmed. "That image is produced from data processed out of hi-radiation being generated right through this whole planet."

Zimmermann stared again at the screen while his mind raced to comprehend fully the thing he was seeing. He knew that the hi-waves received by the detector did not arrive through normal space and could not be associated with any property of direction. He also knew that the everyday notion of distance had no direct counterpart in hi-space and that the information arriving at the detector was a summation of hi-waves originating from every part of the cosmos. How, then, could a representation of Earth be extracted from all that, and just what viewpoint did the image on the screen signify?

As if he could read the questions forming in the professor's mind, Clifford picked up his explanation. "Distance does play a part in the k-equations, but not in the sense of determining any propagation time. It comes in as an amplitude-modulating coefficient."

"How do you mean, Dr. Clifford?" Zimmermann asked.

"The total signal that's picked up by the detector is made up of components that originate all over the universe," Clifford replied. "The distance of a given source from the detector does not affect the time at which the hi-waves generated by it are received. In other words, all the components that are being picked up *now* are being generated *now;* whether the source is the GRASER or a star at the other end of the galaxy makes no difference."

"Extraordinary," Zimmermann mused. "So if somebody made a GRASER a thousand light-years from here and switched it on, information from that event would be buried in the signal that you detect here—at the same instant."

"Yes, indeed," Clifford confirmed. "But you'd have to be very clever to see it. You see, although components in the signal do exist from sources all over the universe, their strength falls off rapidly with distance. It's the nearer and larger sources—big masses—that dominate in the equations. So it's not impossible to single out the components that originate in Earth's mass and use them as starting data to construct an image. The strength of the signals from other places falls off rapidly as they get farther away, and you can soon ignore them for all practical purposes. In theory, in the signal that produced the image on the screen there were components that originated, say, in the Andromeda Galaxy, but in practice they existed only as mathematical terms with values approximating to zero. There's the cosmic background that we talked about, which is the sum of all the things like that, but we get rid of it by tuning in above the background-noise threshold."

"Fascinating," Zimmermann said, staring at the image again. "So presumably, from the information that you select out of the composite signal, you've developed some method of projecting directional representations." He pointed at the screen. "I mean, that image presumably represents some aspect or other of this planet, seen from some particular direction or other." His brow creased into an apologetic smile. "I must confess that what it is and where I'm looking at it from are questions that I find myself still unable to answer."

"That was a big hassle," Clifford admitted. "The information carried by a hi-wave contains timelike and spacelike data all scrambled together with other things you can't really interpret. It took a while to figure out how to extract the spacelike data from all that stuff, but . . ." he gestured toward the display, "I guess we managed it in the end okay."

"So what are we looking at?" Zimmermann inquired. Aub joined in at that point.

"Here we're tuned to resolve a perpendicular plane anisotropic to the detector and extending for ten thousand miles. It's a cross section right through the center of Earth. Doesn't show a lotta detail but . . ." he shrugged, "it's only our first attempt, after all."

"Actually, if you look at the numerical data, you'll see that it's possible to distinguish the crust, upper and lower mantle, and the core," Clifford informed him. "It just doesn't show up too well on the picture."

Zimmermann was speechless.

Aub noted his puzzled expression and began operating keys on his panel, causing the disk on the screen to shrink to a fraction of its previous size, though remaining unchanged in general appearance.

"Rotating the sectional plane to lie perpendicular to the axis," he sang in the tones of a fairground showman. "The plane now coincides with the circle of latitude eighty-five degrees north—just below the pole. Hold on to your seats for an instant trip right through the world." He commenced playing the keys casually. The disk swelled slowly, then stopped at a size that almost filled the screen. "Now you're at the equator," Aub announced. The disk shrank once more and finally condensed rapidly to a tiny point of orange. "South Pole."

"We can do better than that, too," Morelli added, encouraged by Aub's performance. "The dominant hi-wave components received here are naturally the ones that come from the mass of Earth. However, once we've computed the matrix that defines that mass, we can negate it and feed it back into the equations to cancel itself out. That leaves only the lesser hi-wave components that come from other places. Once they're isolated, they can be amplified and used to compute spacelike images in the same way as you've seen. Aub . . ."

Aub took the cue and conjured up another disk,

similar to the previous one but exhibiting a less pronounced variation in color from edge to center.

"That's the Moon," Clifford stated. This was the most impressive item of the demonstration, but out of sheer devilment he forced his voice to remain matter-of-fact. "We could do the same thing with other bodies as well, but there'd not be much point with the setup we've got at the moment. As you can see, it gives little more than a smudge. Doesn't tell an awful lot."

"With Mark II you'd really see something," Aub added. "For instance, I reckon we could chart all the black holes in the neighboring parts of the galaxy—directly; you wouldn't have to rely on their effects on companion bodies to detect them the way you have to now."

"And don't forget," Clifford rounded off. "You'd see all those things like they are *now* . . . no time delay."

Zimmermann continued to stare back at them silently. Never before in his life had so many staggering revelations been compressed into such a short interval of time. His mind reeled before the vision that was unfolding of the unimaginable potential of the things he had just witnessed. Surely the first acquisition of the sense of sight by the early multi-celled organisms in the seas had been no more revolutionary in terms of its impact on the evolution of an awareness of the universe. He was present at the birth of a new era of science.

The others watched him in silence. They knew full well what he was thinking, but overdramatization and plays of emotion were not their style.

"This is incredible!" Zimmermann managed at last. His voice was barely more than a whisper. "Incredible . . ." He looked back again at the image on the screen as if to make sure that he had not dreamed the whole thing. After contemplating it for a while longer, he had another question. "Do you really believe that you could resolve detailed images . . . ones that carry information? We could really gaze down to the core of

Earth and for the first time actually see what is happening in the world beneath our feet? We could look inside the planets . . . inside the stars . . . ?"

"It's possible," Clifford nodded. "The only way we'd know for sure, though, would be with Mark II. This system was never meant for that kind of thing."

"Incredible," Zimmermann said again. "I gathered that you were making progress here, but this . . ." He gestured toward the screen and shook his head, as if still having difficulty believing what he had just seen. "It will change everything."

"Those images you just saw weren't being processed in real time, of course," Morelli explained. "You're not seeing something that's actually being picked up at the detector right this instant. They were simply playbacks of images that had already been computed. That's the main problem with the system so far—the amount of computer power needed to generate those outputs is absolutely phenomenal. These two guys have just about monopolized the machines in this place for the past few weeks. We've had to offload nearly all of our normal work on to the net."

"Extracting the spacelike information that you need out of the k-functions is a tedious business," Clifford explained. "The equations involved have an infinite number of solutions. Obviously we don't try to solve for all of them, otherwise we'd never finish, but it's still a hell of a job just to calculate the sets of limits needed to generate whatever spatial projection you want. Planar cross sections is only one possible category of solutions, yet imagine the number of different sections of, say, Earth that could be specified . . . taking into account all the possible angles and viewpoints. It blows your mind."

"I think mine has already been blown sufficiently for one day," Zimmermann replied, smiling. "May I relax now, or do you three gentlemen have still more surprises up your sleeves?"

Morelli went on to describe the difficulties that they were experiencing in obtaining the components needed

for Mark II. He mentioned the questions that were
being asked, the snooping, the general harassment
they were being subjected to, and gave his guesses as
to the reasons behind it all. Zimmermann already
knew much of the earlier part of the story, of course,
and the rest quickly fell into place. As he listened, his
face grew dark and angry.

"The damn fools!" he exclaimed when Morelli had
finished. "There is more future in what you are doing
here than will ever come out of all their budgets put
together. God knows, I'm no militarist, but if that's
what they want, this is where they should be putting
their backing. Have they any idea what this could
lead to? Have you tried to tell them?"

Morelli shook his head slowly.

"We wouldn't want them muscling in," he said.

"They would," Clifford said, suddenly in a sober
voice. "You see, we know what it could lead to."

"And we're outa their line of business," Aub completed.

Later on that evening, accompanied by Sarah, they all
went for dinner to Morelli's spacious home on the
shore of Lake Boone at Stow. Nancy Morelli, Al's
cheerful, homely wife already well known to all the
guests, produced a delicious German meal of veal in
wine sauce followed by Black Forest cake, with plenty
of Moselle Golden Oktober and a selection of liqueurs
to finish. Throughout the meal they talked about life
at Lunar Farside, Sarah's work at Marlboro, Nancy's
memories of childhood in New York, and Clifford's
rock-climbing experiences at Yosemite. Zimmermann
and Morelli swapped stories of the times they had
spent in Europe, Sarah talked about England, and Aub
raised roars of laughter with accounts of his hilarious
escapades at Berkeley and before. Not once did the
men deviate from their dutiful observance of the un-
written rule that declared the earlier events of the
day—if the truth were known, still the most pressing

topic in the mind of each of them—strictly taboo for this kind of occasion.

After the dishes had been cleared away and everybody had spent another half-hour chatting and joking over drinks, Nancy took Sarah outside to show her the lake and the surrounding pine woods by sunset. As soon as the back door to the kitchen clicked into place, an entirely different atmosphere descended upon the room before anybody had said anything. Nobody had to broach the subject; they all felt it. Zimmermann was the first to speak.

"I suppose you did think of bringing the affair to the attention of ISF headquarters in Geneva, Al. One way round some of the difficulties might have been to have other ISF locations place your orders for you, and then have the material shipped to Sudbury as an internal transfer."

"Yeah, we thought of that," Morelli said. "But this is our own matter . . . local. If I've gotten into the bad books of the powers that be, I figure we oughta keep it that way. It would do more harm than good in the long run to go dragging the whole of ISF into it. Besides . . . as Brad said earlier today, if they get wind of what we're working toward, the place would be swarming with them." He took a sip of his drink and frowned into his glass. "In fact, from the things that have been happening lately, it wouldn't surprise me if they've gotten some kind of a sniff already."

"I suppose I must agree with you," Zimmermann said with a sigh. "Were I in your place, I would come to exactly the same conclusions. By and large, ISF enjoys an extraordinary degree of independence in its activities, which it is naturally very anxious to preserve. We must not do anything that might prejudice relationships between ISF and government—any government." The professor reflected upon what he had just said, then shook his head. "No, you are right. We cannot go higher in ISF."

"Then where do we go?" Aub asked.

"I have been considering that question ever since

this afternoon," Zimmermann replied. "Gentlemen, you have a problem. To solve it, it will be necessary for you to sacrifice at least some of your commendable ideals and come to terms—at least to some degree —with some of the less appealing realities that surround us. I have seen this kind of thing before. Believe me, you will not beat the system. This is only a beginning; it will get worse. Don't underestimate the people you are up against. Many of them are stupid, but they have power—and that is a fearsome combination. They will destroy you if they can, spiritually if not physically. Destruction is their business."

"So, what do we do?"

"If you continue to refuse to acknowledge that the power to make or break your project ultimately lies outside your own immediate sphere of influence, it will grow until it overwhelms you. Therefore, you must accept that it exists and will not go away by being ignored. That is the first step. Only when you accept that it exists can you think of using it to your own ends."

"Using it?" Clifford was confused. "How d'you mean, 'using it'?"

"Quite simple. You are obviously aware of how much the state commands in terms of resources, finance, and sheer weight of influence. Just think of the difference it would make to your research program if all that were to be harnessed to help it along."

"But that would be going backward, Professor," Aub protested. "We don't need their kind of help. Brad and I burned all our boats getting out of there not so long ago. The whole point is, we want to stay clear of them. We've done fine up to now with ISF providing all the resources and stuff."

"But that is precisely the point I am making," Zimmermann replied calmly. "Unfortunately, you do not have the luxury of a choice any longer. The sentiments that you have expressed are fine just as long as the decision for you and the system to ignore each other and go separate ways is mutual. But when they begin to take notice of you, I am afraid that an attempt on your part to continue ignoring them will lead only to disaster. You are obliged to react. I am suggesting that, since it appears that you have no choice but to become involved with the government departments anyway, we endeavor to make that involvement constructive to our purpose." The professor spread his hands in an appealing gesture. "You have to get involved with them. If you don't, they will just squeeze harder. Use it."

Clifford stared out through the window for a few seconds, then turned abruptly to face the room.

"That's all very well as a theory," he said. "But we already know their attitude. It's totally destructive, probably because they're worried how it might look if two guys who had told them to screw themselves got the edge on the bunch of whiz-kids they were getting together when we left. I just don't see any way they're gonna suddenly like us. I don't see any reason why they should want to."

"That is where I might be able to help," Zimmermann stated softly. "As you know, my position with ISF causes me to maintain regular contact with high-ranking people in the government, many of whom are close personal friends of long standing. Even before I joined ISF, my work with the federal European Government involved considerable dealings with persons in Washington who are very close to the President."

Zimmermann paused to let the gist of what he was saying sink in. Three pairs of eyes watched him intently. "I hope all this does not sound too immodest, but perhaps you can now see my point. Don't be misled by the people who you have had to put up with. Thankfully, there still are some extremely intelligent and perceptive individuals in charge of this country, where you would expect them to be—at the top, where the real power lies. I'm not talking about the petty tyranny that is reveled in by the riffraff and exalted office clerks whom you have had the misfortune of running up against. Now, suppose that I could open the right eyes to what you are doing here . . ." Zimmermann left the sentence unfinished.

Morelli looked at him with a new respect. Certainly if some kind of involvement was the only alternative to wrapping the whole thing up, then that would be the kind to have. Even if some form of commitment to more mundane objectives were called for, at least their basic research would have to continue before such could be realized. That meant they would be able to carry on unhindered, and in the long term . . . what the hell?

"What do you plan on doing then?" Morelli asked Zimmermann.

"First thing in the morning I will rearrange my schedule," Zimmermann answered. "Then I will make some appointments and fly to Washington—I hope straight away. That part you must leave to me. As for you . . ." his gaze swept the room to take in all three of them. "You will need to take off your scientists' hats for a short while. I want you all to get used to the idea of becoming salesmen."

Clifford and Aub looked at each other mystified. They both shrugged together.

Zimmermann grinned. "It is very simple," he said. "What we have to arrange is . . ." The noise of the kitchen door closing interrupted him. Feminine laughter flooded the room. He glanced over his shoulder. "Oh dear me. It would appear, gentlemen, that business for today is over. I will explain everything in the morning. Ah, there you both are at last. We had almost run out of things to talk about. What do you think of the lake?"

Late that night, while Clifford and Sarah were driving Aub home, the two scientists explained to her the gist of what Zimmermann had said.

"Sounds as if he's offering to wheel in some big guns for you," she commented after they had finished. "Things could get interesting. Do you really think he could pull off something like that?"

"Well, Al reckons he knows all the right guys, all

right," Aub answered from the back seat. "And it didn't take him any time at all to get us into ISF when we had the whole world on our backs. I'd give him my vote. What do you think, Brad?"

"I remember a long time ago—that first time we called him—he said he'd never make promises he couldn't be sure of keeping," Clifford replied. "I don't think he would, either; he doesn't seem to be that kind of person. That's what this world needs more of—more credibility in high places. He's got it, and that's why he is where he is and knows who he knows, and the rest are a load of bums." He became quiet for a while and then his face broadened into a smile of gleeful anticipation in the darkness of the car. "Boy," he said over his shoulder. "I can't wait to see the carnage when Zim's big guns start blasting. If this all works out the way I'm beginning to think it might work out, I think I'm gonna enjoy it."

"Yes," Sarah agreed. "Minions and office boys have been a pain in my life lately. I think I might enjoy it too."

Chapter 15

The world of 2005 had polarized itself into virtually a lineup of the white versus the nonwhite races, a situation that had been developing for the best part of a century.

The buildup toward a final showdown had really begun to gather momentum in the early 1980s when, after a spasmodic series of clashes and coups among the emerging African nation-states, the white regimes in the South were finally overwhelmed and the continent began welding itself together into a closely knit alliance of anti-West, antiwhite African powers. In 1985, the Treaty of Khartoum cemented relationships between this bloc and the Federation of Arab Nations, popularly known as the Afrab Alliance, and marked the intensification of a joint economic campaign against the Western world. In the second half of that decade, Israel was overrun by Afrab armies, during the course of which tactical nuclear weapons were employed in the Sinai by both sides and the U.S. Mediterranean Fleet went into action. As a direct consequence of the war, forces from the American mainland invaded and occupied Cuba.

China had allied herself firmly with the Afrab powers; a major East-West confrontation at that time was averted only by an unexpected attitude of moderation from Moscow. By 1990, the Persian Gulf states had sided with the China-Afrab consortium and from that time onward a never-ending series of border skirmishes and local wars continued along India's eastern and western frontiers, ostensibly over disputed territories that were claimed by her neighbors on both sides. In the Far East, Australia, New Zealand, Japan, South Korea, and Indonesia concluded mutual defense pacts to counter the relentless spread of Chinese influence southward and eastward.

During all this time, the split in the Russian ranks that had first showed itself during the final Middle East War had widened progressively. European Russia, following the lead set by the Moscow government, embarked on a policy of a growing understanding with the West, while the Eastern Siberian Provinces retained a hard-line Marxist posture, aligned with that of China. By 1996, the Eastern Revolt had spread to Central Siberia, and regular Chinese forces were fighting alongside the rebels against the Moscow Army. The war reached its peak in 1999 and after that died down to a succession of skirmishes roughly along the line of the Urals. Siberia declared Vladivostok its new capital and moved rapidly from there toward full integration with the Afrab-China consortium, the conclusion of which process was proclaimed as The Grand Alliance of Progressive Peoples Republics in Canton in 2002.

European Russia, encouraged by the fruitful results of operating manned orbiting laboratories and lunar bases, developing nuclear-powered spacecraft, and staging a manned mission to Mars, all as joint ventures with the West, finally merged into the Federation of Europe that had been established in 1996. In 2004, an integrated command structure was established for the armed forces of America, the Australian Federation, and the new, Greater Europe. Thus the Alliance of Western Democracies formally came into being.

The stage was thus set. Both sides possessed nuclear spacecraft, had achieved permanent lunar bases, and were deploying the latest in a long list of strategic deterrents—the Orbital Bombardment System, ORBS, consisting of swarms of orbiting fractional nuclear bombs that could be brought down at any point on Earth's surface in minutes.

And then the news flashed round a tense world that Act One was beginning.

The unrest that had been smouldering in South Korea burst into flame spontaneously all over the country, like the reappearance of a forest fire that had been festering in the roots. Within the space of a few weeks a fiendishly planned epidemic of riots, strikes, ambushes, and guerilla operations consolidated into a nationwide orchestration that left the Army with no coherent strategy to implement, no secure place for regrouping, and no way to turn. The Seoul government was deposed and replaced by the so-called People's Democratic Assembly, whose first task in office was to appeal for aid to defend the populace against the continued oppressions of the regular forces that were still fighting. The Chinese divisions massed along the thirty-eighth parallel were quick to respond, and inside a matter of a few more days the takeover was complete.

Powerless to act in the face of such a widespread popular movement and left at a complete standstill by the speed at which these events had unfolded, the Australian and Japanese forces stationed in the country had played no active role. Ignominiously, under the stony stares of lines of heavily armed Communist combat troops, they queued up in front of the waiting air transports that would fly them to Japan.

Morelli, Clifford, Aub, and a group of other scientists and senior personnel from Sudbury stood in front of a reserved landing pad in the Institute's airmobile parking area and watched the steadily enlarging dot that was descending from the sky above them. Zimmermann was not with them, having returned to Luna the previous week after spending a month with them. Three medium-size skybuses, painted white and carrying the words MASSACHUSETTS STATE POLICE DEPARTMENT, were lined up together along one side of the parking area. Their occupants had taken up posi-

tions around but at a respectable distance from the
landing pad, at various strategic points around the
grounds of the Institute and at doors inside some of
its buildings.

The dot gradually resolved itself into the snub-
nosed shape of a Veetol Executive jet bearing the
colors and insignia of the U.S. Air Force Transport
Command. It slowed to a halt and hovered a hundred
feet above the pad while the flight-control processors
obtained final clearance from the landing radar and
the pilot made his routine visual check to see that the
site was unobstructed. Then the jet sank smoothly
downward to come to rest amid the falling whine of
dying engine noise. The door swung open and a short
stairway telescoped down to the ground.

After a few seconds two men dressed in civilian
suits, presumably FBI, emerged and stood on either
side of the foot of the steps. They were followed by
a powerfully built individual wearing the bemedaled
uniform of an Army major general; it belonged to
Gerald Straker, a Presidential adviser on strategic
planning and an authority on advanced weapons systems. Behind Straker came General Arwin Dalby, U.S.
Representative to the Coordination Committee of the
Integrated Strike Command of the Allied Western
Democracies; General Robert Fuller, of the Strategic
Planning Commission; and General Howard Perkoffski, second in command of the North American global
surveillance, early-warning, and countermeasures system. Next came two civilians, both from the Pentagon; one was Professor Franz Mueller, resident
consultant on security of military communications systems, the other, Dr. Harry Sultzinger, the architect of
ORBS.

General Harvey Miller, USAF, Deputy Chief of Orbital Bombardment Command, was followed by a trio
of Air Force aides and then by a navy contingent
headed by Admiral Joseph Kaine, chairman of a presidential advisory committee charged with investigating
methods to improve submarine detection from satel-

lites. Three more civilian technical advisers came hard on the heels of the Navy: Patrick Cleary, computer technology; Dr. Samuel Hatton, military lasers; and Professor Warren Keele, nuclear sciences. Finally there emerged the instantly recognizable, lean, balding but vigorous figure of William S. Foreshaw, Secretary for Defense of the United States.

When introductions had been completed, the two groups merged and made their way over to the Administration Building of the Institute where, in the Large Conference Theater, Morelli started off the program for the day with a presentation of the things his team had achieved to date.

"We've invited you here today to bring to your attention some new discoveries in science that can only be described as astounding," he told them. "In our opinion, the work that we have done over the past couple of years represents a breakthrough in human knowledge that is possibly without parallel in history."

He waited for the air of expectancy to rise to an appropriate level and then continued: "All of you gentlemen are, I'm sure, conversant with the notion that the universe in which we live exists within a framework of space and time. Everything that we know, everything that we see, even the most distant object that can be resolved by our most powerful telescopes or the tiniest event observable inside the atom —all these things exist within the same universal framework." The rows of faces watched him expressionlessly.

"We now have not only a working theoretical model but also firm experimental evidence that this universe is only a tiny part of something far vaster . . . not merely vaster in size, but far, far vaster in terms of the conceptual entities that inhabit it and the totally new range of physical laws that govern the processes taking place inside it." Sudden interest began creeping into some of the faces in front of him as a few of the individuals present got their first inkling of where he was about to take them. Morelli nodded slowly.

"Yes, gentlemen. I am talking about a completely new domain of the universe that lies beyond the dimensions of space and time—a domain so strange that we are only beginning to glimpse some of the possibilities that are waiting to be uncovered. But even this first glimpse has revealed facts so staggering as to fundamentally change and in many cases dispose of practically every currently accepted law of physics. The whole universe that has been revealed up until now by all our instruments turns out to be nothing more than a pale shadow of an infinitely more exciting and infinitely vaster superuniverse. Let me tell you about some of the workings of this superuniverse."

Morelli went on to describe in nontechnical terms the theory behind particle extinctions and creations, and the interpretation of these events as transitions of basic entities between the various dimensions of k-space. He described the generation of k-waves and explained how all the known forces and forms of energy of physics could be interpreted in terms of them, and led from there to the notion of gravity as a discontinuous, dynamic phenomenon that resulted from the slow decay of matter particles.

"But gravity waves are just projections into our universe of a more complex k-wave," he told them. "In the superuniverse there exists a form of superwave that defies all powers of imagination and has the property of being able to pervade all the points of our ordinary space simultaneously. These superwaves are produced continuously in every piece of matter in the universe—in the planets, the stars, and even in the voids between—and every tiny particle-event taking place at any point in the cosmos makes itself known instantly at each and every other point." Surprised mutterings ran through the audience. Morelli chose that moment to make his first announcement concerning the practical relevance of it all.

"Here at Sudbury, we have constructed an instrument that not only responds to these superwaves coming from everywhere in the universe, but in addition enables them to be processed into meaningful visual images." He paused to allow time for the impact of that statement to take effect, and then gestured toward the large screen behind him, which he had used earlier to present diagrams illustrating the basic concepts of k-theory. He operated the controls below the edge of the lectern in front of him and immediately the screen came to life to show a bright orange-yellow disk.

"That, gentlemen, is a cross-section view right through the center of Earth," he informed them. Gasps of astonishment erupted.

Warren Keele, the nuclear sciences expert, was unable to contain his amazement. "You're saying that's a real, live view through the Earth?" he said, his voice straining with disbelief. "You mean your instrument can actually pick up these waves coming from all through Earth and make pictures out of them?"

The comments from around the room had risen to a steady murmur. Morelli seized the chance to capitalize on the mood of the moment. "Yes, we can do exactly that. We can do much better than that, too." He changed the view to that of another, similar-looking disk. "And that is another sectional view, but this time one of our Moon!" He repeated the procedure with a flourish to show a third disk, this time one that became noticeably brighter towards its center. "And that's the Sun!" His voice rose above the ensuing clamor to drive home his point. "Every one of these images was obtained from within a hundred yards of where you are sitting, and every one of them shows the object as it was at the instant the information was received. Later on today, we will take you into another building and show you the screen from which these pictures were taken. You will be able to sit in front of it and gaze into the heart of the Sun!"

Morelli then kept them at fever pitch by going on to describe the operation of the GRASER and dropped his second bombshell when he announced that gravity could be produced and controlled artificially.

"At any other time this would be a stupendous achievement in itself," he said. "It's something that men have dreamed about for a hundred years. As things are, it comes as a mere by-product of something that's bigger and even more stupendous by far."

When Morelli had finished, excitement and enthusiasm bubbled on every side. Some of the generals were still looking bemused and a miniature instant conference began around William Foreshaw. Morelli waited patiently.

Then, as the hubbub of voices began dying away, Patrick Cleary turned back to face the stage. "Professor Morelli, what you've described to us is obviously a much-extended extrapolation of Maesanger's Field Theory."

"That's correct," Morelli agreed.

"What is incredible is not only the extension of the theoretical concepts, but also the experimental support that you've been able to demonstrate."

"Never mind all that," Samuel Hatton threw in. "They're already turning out solid applications. That's what blows my mind."

"Sure," Cleary acknowledged. "I didn't mean to play that down." He turned to face Morelli again. "What I was about to ask, Professor, was: Is this by chance the famous hyperspace of science fiction that we've all been waiting for?"

Morelli grinned briefly.

"Better ask our theoretical king about that," he said, then called toward the back of the room, where Clifford was sitting with the Sudbury contingent. "Brad, what would you say to that one?"

"Depends on which of the many varieties of hyperspace you have in mind," Clifford replied. "In the sense of dimensions existing beyond the accepted ones, I guess, yes, it could be. If you're thinking of instant star-travel or something, I think you'll be disappointed. Certainly we've not got that on today's schedule."

Dr. Harry Sultzinger spoke next.

"This business about instant propagation intrigues me," he said. "Are you saying that Special Relativity's gone out the window . . . or what?"

"Actually, it doesn't really go against Special Relativity," Morelli said. "Relativistic physics puts an upper limit on the velocity of energy through ordinary Einsteinian spacetime. Hi-waves exist in another domain entirely—one to which the laws of conventional spacetime don't apply. I guess you could say that Einstein's traffic cops patrol the public highways only, but hi-waves travel cross-country."

"But what about information?" Sultzinger insisted. "If a hi-wave goes from here to there in zero time, it's carried information in zero time. Relativity says you can't do that."

"Only because all methods for moving information that have been known up to now invariably involve moving through classical spacetime," Morelli said. "But with hi-waves we're effectively bypassing that, so the problem doesn't arise."

"Actually, it does get slightly more involved than that," Clifford called again from the back. "Some people have put together all kinds of complicated cause-and-effect arguments to show that instant information transfer gives rise to all kinds of logical paradoxes. My own view is that the difficulties lie in the logic and the conceptual limitations rather than in anything factual. We're working on that at the moment, and I wouldn't be surprised if a number of old ideas about simultaneity end up having to be re-examined."

"How detailed could the information be that could be carried on these waves?" Admiral Kaine asked.

"The pictures you've just seen are pretty crude because we've only got a first-attempt lab lash-up instrument that was never designed for that job in the first place," Morelli answered. "How far we could push it, we don't know yet. That's one of the main things we mean to find out."

"The whole thing reminds me of the first crude spark-gap experiments of Hertz," Cleary declared, sounding impressed. "And that led to the whole science of radio, radar, TV, and electronic communications. Have you got any ideas what kind of technology might grow out of what you're doing here?"

Morelli launched into a vivid account of the possibilities of gravitic engineering that he never tired of discussing, especially with Aub. The questions poured out incessantly all through lunch, all of them positive, imaginative, and obviously prompted by genuine desires to learn more.

"Could there be a way of focusing artificial gravity into some kind of beam that could be directed remotely," General Perkoffski asked Clifford at one point, "so that you could direct it at a target?"

"It's too early yet to say," Clifford replied. "What did you have in mind?"

"I was wondering if you could use it to disorientate a missile's inertial guidance system," Perkoffski said. "It wouldn't need to be too powerful."

"Say, I never thought of that angle," said Arwin Dalby, who had been following from the opposite side of the table. "A localized gravity beam . . . if it was possible, I wonder how strong you could make it and how localized."

Clifford was about to reply when Robert Fuller broke in: "To hell with screwing its guidance system. If you can make the beam strong enough, why not simply pull the whole damn missile down?"

"Or even stop it from getting off the ground in the first place?" Dalby suggested. "You know . . . the more I think about this, the more I like it."

"Perhaps we could even bring down an ORBS satellite," General Straker joined in. "That would really be something to shout about." He reflected on the idea for a moment, then had another thought. "Or maybe bend spacetime to divert it away into space permanently. How about that?"

For the first hour after lunch the visitors saw the GRASER running and crowded four at a time into the monitor room to sit spellbound in front of the display screen of the detector. The image did not tell them much, but the very thought of what it meant was enough to keep them speechless for many minutes.

After the demonstrations, they returned to the Conference Theater to listen to Aub. Morelli had devoted most of his time to recounting the history of events and developments that had culminated in the then current state of the art. Aub allowed himself to plunge ahead and speculate on some of the things that might follow.

"The GRASER that you have all just seen produces a strong output of hi-waves," he said. "In other words, it's a transmitter. The detector that you've looked at is a receiver." He gazed around the room, inviting them to fill the rest in for themselves.

"We've got both ends of a communications system," someone observed after a second or two. The visitors were joining in and interacting—a good sign.

"Yes indeed," Aub agreed, nodding with satisfaction. "But this communication system is unlike anything that's ever been dreamed of before. It uses a transmission medium that is utterly undetectable by any means known to contemporary science. Also, there is no means known to contemporary science by which any disturbance can be impressed upon that transmission medium." He dropped the formal language that he had been using up to that point and put it another way: "Nobody else in the world has a way of listening in on it or a way of talking through it."

"Completely espionage-proof," Franz Mueller commented, nodding vigorously. "The perfect military communications vehicle . . . absolute security."

"And jam-proof," Perkoffski added. "That's what you were getting at, isn't it, Dr. Philipsz? There'd be no way anybody could jam it . . . or even interfere with it?"

"Just that," Aub confirmed.

"That's all I need to hear," Perkoffski remarked

with a smile. "Just tell me where to sign for a system like that. I'm sold."

"But more than that," Aub resumed. "It also has zero transmission delay, remember. Now imagine what we could do if we could add control functions—feedback, that is—to the data-communications capability that we've been talking about. Now, I'm sure you can all see immediate possibilities for a feedback control technique that has zero time delay in the loop . . . . over *any* distance!" He paused again to let them think about it. After a second or two, low whistles of surprise came from the audience. Excited muttering broke out on one side.

"Long-range space probes!" a voice exclaimed suddenly. "Holy cow, we could monitor them and control them in real time from right here on Earth—interactively."

"That means that Earth-based computers could be used for all kinds of things involving fast-response processing in remote places," a second came in. "How about a Mars-Rover being driven directly by a PDP-64 sitting right here? I don't believe it!"

"Yes, that's the kind of thing I had in mind," Aub said when the buzzing had died down. "But why shouldn't we look a little further ahead than that as well . . . just for a second? Suppose I were to suggest that one day the arrival of the first robot starship might be witnessed *and controlled* from a mission-supervision center here on Earth . . . second by second, *as it was actually happening,* light-years away!" He surveyed the wide eyes around him. "Why not? The basic techniques to do it are already with us. You've seen them today."

Before they could recover, Aub used the large screen to bring up again the hi-wave image of Earth that they had seen that morning.

"And finally, think about this," he said. "That image was generated from a kind of wave that emanates from every object in the universe, large or small, to a greater or lesser degree. Visualize then what it might look like if we were to develop ways to refine the image, to resolve more detail—details of the surface, for instance. Suppose we could select any part of the surface and zoom in instantly on any place we chose . . . or any place above the surface . . . or below it . . . or maybe on the Moon. . . ." Aub reeled off the possibilities slowly, one at a time, dangling each for a few seconds tantalizingly before the mind's eye of his listeners. The expressions on their faces told him they were with him all the way.

"All that and more, from a single point somewhere, say, in the U.S.A.," he concluded. "What kind of impact would that have on the global strategic balance . . . ? Just imagine, gentlemen, a radar—if you wish to think of it that way—that can 'see' below the horizon, through a mountain . . . even right through a whole planet!"

When Aub was finished, Peter Hughes spent ten minutes summing up the major items of the day, then ended with a flash. "As you are all aware, the International Scientific Foundation chooses to conduct its affairs independent of government backing and involvement. In view of the extremely important nature of the things that my colleagues have described today, it is our considered opinion that an exception to this general rule is clearly called for. The potential that we have heard explained impinges directly on the future not only of this nation but of the whole of the Western world. To realize this potential, however, it is clear that a great amount of further development will be necessary. Time is not on our side, and to use effectively what little there is, it is imperative for this field of research to be supported and furthered vigorously and without delay. To progress we need backing on a scale that only the nation can provide."

After a brief muttered conversation with his aides, William Foreshaw, the Defense Secretary, looked up at where Hughes was still standing. "Thank you, gentlemen. I don't think we have any further questions at this point." He cast an inquiring eye round the faces from Washington just to be sure. "Before we commit ourselves to any kind of formal reply, we'd appreciate a half-hour or so to talk a few things over among ourselves. I wonder if your people would be kind enough to leave us alone in here for a while, please?"

"Certainly," Hughes replied. He gazed toward the Sudbury personnel at the back of the room and inclined his head in the direction of the door. They filed out and Hughes followed. Outside in the corridor they all found they had the same thought in mind and made their way toward the coffee lounge a few doors farther along for some badly needed refreshment. Forty-five minutes later, they were still sitting there, the conversation having degenerated to a few spasmodic syllables as their impatience began to make itself felt.

At last Aub got up and ambled over to join Clifford, who was staring morosely out of the window and who had not spoken since entering the room. "Cheer up, Brad. It all went pretty well. Don't you think so?"

"It went okay." Clifford's voice was neutral.

"So what's eating you, man? You look kinda bugged."

Clifford turned his back to the window and braced his arms along the sill, at the same time emitting an exasperated sigh.

"Just remind me, Aub, why are we doing all this? What are those people doing here anyway? Christ . . . didn't it cause us enough trouble trying to get ourselves away from all that? Now we're tying ourselves in knots trying to set it all up again the way it was. It just doesn't make any sense."

"But it's not like it was, is it?" Aub answered. He obviously harbored few doubts. "Like Zim said, we're talking to the right people now. We couldn't have left things the way they were going—they weren't going anywhere at all. This way we look like we might end up back in business again. That can't be all bad."

"I just don't like it. I don't trust them, and I don't like being mixed up with people I don't trust. I've seen too much of how they work."

Aub clapped him encouragingly on the shoulder.

"Maybe you're looking at it the wrong way. We got out before, sure, but they weren't on our side then. Since then, we've come a long way all on our own. Now we've still got all that, but we've got them on our side too. That changes everything. That bunch next door could fund Mark II by pooling their salaries. That's what this is all about, don't forget."

"You're right, but I still don't like it. . . ." Clifford didn't seem cheered.

At that moment one of the police guards who had been posted outside the door of the Conference Theater came into the lounge and exchanged a few words quietly with Peter Hughes. Hughes nodded, stood up from the chair in which he had been sitting, fidgeting nervously, and spoke in a raised voice.

"Well, it looks as if this is it. The jury seems to have reached a verdict. I don't think it would be appropriate for all of us to go crowding in, so if you don't mind, I'll just take Al, Brad, and Aub. No doubt we'll see you all here when we come back out."

"Do you think they'll buy it?" Hughes muttered under his breath as they followed the burly figure of the guard back along the corridor.

"If they do, I'll know to apply to IBM for my next job," Aub replied cheerfully.

They went back into the Conference Theater and sat down facing the august gathering. William Foreshaw waited until the door had been closed before addressing them.

"First of all, I would like to express our appreciation for the efforts that you have made today. Any words I might choose to attempt to describe our impressions would be an understatement. Therefore I'll just settle for 'thank you all.' " A murmur of assent rippled round the rest of the delegation. Foreshaw continued. "Second, we'd like Mr. Hughes to convey our appreciation back to ISF headquarters in Geneva. We are gratified by this demonstration that an independent scientific organization will rise to meet its national obligations. And now, to business. First, I have one or two questions I'd like to ask. . . ." He paused and looked slowly from one to another of the four people sitting in front of him. There was a curious look in his eyes.

"Would it come as a surprise to you gentlemen," he said at last, "to learn that the same line of theoretical work is also being pursued elsewhere in this country? I should add that it has not progressed to anything near the things you have showed us today, but the basics are there."

Nobody spoke. The Sudbury group looked slightly uncomfortable.

"They ran into a problem," Warren Keele supplied, more to ease the silence. "Some bum who was key to the whole thing walked out on them. They're still trying to ungum the mess he left them with."

"You mean at ACRE," Clifford said quietly. He never could stand pretense in any form.

Foreshaw looked disturbed. "How do you know about ACRE?" he asked. Puzzled looks from around him punctuated the question.

"I used to work there. I was that bum."

In the next fifteen minutes the story came out. Clifford and his colleagues had not intended to raise this issue, having determined to let the water that had flowed under the bridge go its way and to concentrate on the future. But the questions were insistent. As it became apparent just how much a key to the whole thing Clifford had been, and exactly how the mess had come about, the Defense Secretary's eyes hardened and his mouth compressed into a thin, humorless line.

"Looks like somebody goofed," General Fuller mused when the meeting was finally over. The menace in his voice hinted strongly that the somebody wouldn't do very much more goofing in future. Foreshaw completed the copious notes he had been making throughout, capped his pen, replaced it in his pocket, and closed the pad. He straightened up in his chair and regarded the scientists again, his change of posture signaling an end to that part of the proceedings.

"I think we've heard all we need to for now on that topic," he said. "What we do from here on is not a matter for this meeting. Let's get back to the point." He leaned forward and placed his elbows on the edge of the table.

"Gentlemen, you have asked for our support and backing. We are unanimous in voting our total commitment to expediting your work in any way we can. You tell us what needs to be done to get you moving at maximum possible speed. What is your biggest problem area right now?"

Morelli answered that one. "The main bottleneck with the system as it stands at present is computer power. As I mentioned when I spoke this morning, the amount of processing you have to do to get just one of those images is fantastic. Until we can come up with a better way of extracting meaningful information from the raw data, we're not going to move any faster than a snail's pace. The rate of progress of the past six months isn't the thing to go by; we're up against different requirements now. That's our biggest single problem."

"We had already gathered that," Foreshaw nodded. "It was one of the things we discussed while you were outside. We think we can help. For instance, what would you say if I were to offer to make a BIAC available?"

Morelli looked incredulous. Clifford and Aub gaped. Even Peter Hughes suffered a visible momentary loss of composure.

"A BIAC!" Morelli blinked as if trying to convince himself that he wasn't dreaming. "I guess that would be . . . just fine. . . ." His voice trailed away for lack of an appropriate continuation. Foreshaw's expression remained businesslike, but his eyes were twinkling.

"Very well," he said. "That's settled. It will be done.

Now, Professor Morelli, are there any other things that look as if they could slow you down?"

"Well . . . there are one or two suppliers we seem to be experiencing difficulty with. I've got a hunch that one or two people whom you might have some influence over aren't being as cooperative toward us as they could be."

"Do you have details?"

Morelli slipped a wad of handwritten sheets of paper out of the folder he had brought in with him and began reciting the items in a monotone. He had gotten to number seven when Foreshaw stopped him, his face dark with anger.

"Wait," he said, taking his pen out again and opening his pad. "Now go back and start again would you please. I want the facts."

"There's a Mr. Johnson on the line from Weston-Carter Magnetic," Morelli's secretary called through from the outer office. "What d'you want me to do?"

"Put him through," Morelli shouted back. He turned away from the window through which he had been admiring the lake and, still humming softly to himself, returned to his desk and sat down facing the Infonet screen. Within seconds the features of Cliff Johnson, Sales Director of WCM, had materialized.

"Al," he said at once, beaming. "How are you? Hope I'm not calling at an awkward time. I've got some good news."

"I'll always listen to good news," Morelli said. "Shoot."

"Those special transformers you wanted wound— we can do 'em inside two weeks." He waited, looking slightly apprehensive as if he expected some embarrassing questions, but Morelli replied simply, "That's great. I'll have one of the guys get an order out today."

"No need, Al," Johnson said. "I'll get a salesman from our Boston office to call in and collect it. That way he can check over the technical specs too. I wouldn't want there to be any mistakes."

"As you say then," Morelli shrugged. "That's fine by me."

"Fine. If there are any problems at all, call me personally. Okay?"

"Okay. See ya around."

Morelli cleared down the call, got up, walked across to the window and resumed admiring the lake. That had been the third such call he had taken that morning and it wasn't even ten o'clock yet. Amazing, he thought.

"I got a letter from Sheila Massey today," Sarah remarked one evening about a week later as Clifford was eating his dinner.

"Sheila with the legs . . . how's she getting on?"

"Trust you to remember the legs. She's fine. I thought you'd be interested in what she had to say."

"Me?" Clifford stopped chewing for a second and looked puzzled. "Why should I be interested?"

"Listen to this," Sarah told him, unfolding the sheets of notepaper in her hand. She read aloud from part of the letter: " 'Walter has gotten himself a good promotion at last . . .' "

"Good for Walter," Clifford threw in.

"Shut up and listen. Where was I . . . ? 'Walter has gotten himself a good promotion at last. In fact, everybody seems to be moving around in ACRE because there has been the most almighty shakeup there you ever did see . . .' " Sarah glanced up and noticed that Clifford was looking at her with evident interest. She read on. " 'Walter isn't too sure what's behind it all, but he says there are all kinds of rumors about really big trouble behind the scenes. He thinks a lot of the top guys are getting hell from Washington about the way they've been handling something or other—all the usual secret stuff. Jarrit—he was the big boss there if you remember—has gone, but nobody is sure where. Prof Edwards has been moved up to take his job. That smart-aleck guy, Corrigan I think it was, has gone too. Walter thinks that Edwards got to Washington and demanded that they throw him out. Rumor has it he's been shifted to a missile test range or some such thing —somewhere on Baffin Island.'" Sarah lowered the letter and looked across at Clifford. He threw back his head and roared with laughter.

"That's all I needed to make this a perfect week," he managed at last. "Well, how about that? Wait till I tell Aub." He began laughing again.

"Zimmermann certainly wasn't kidding when he said he'd wheel in a few big guns," Sarah chuckled. "I think he's done rather well, don't you?"

"Big guns?" Clifford laughed. "Them minions haven't been gunned, baby. Zim's pals have carpet-bombed the bastards!"

Chapter 16

Voice recognition by computer had begun in a crude way during the early 1970s. Not long afterward, experiments conducted at the Stanford Research Institute demonstrated that parts of the electrical brain waves associated with the faculty of speech could be decoded and used to input information directly from the human brain to the machine. The method utilized mental concentration on a particular word to trigger the word's characteristic pattern of neural activity in the brain, without the word's actually being voiced; once a pattern had been detected, it could be matched against those stored in the computer's memory—each human operator having his own unique prerecorded set—and translated into machine language. The operation of the computer or whatever it was controlling was then determined by the machine-language command. By the early eighties, a sizable list of experimental machines of this type had appeared in research laboratories around the world, initially each with its own very restricted command vocabulary, typically: *On, Off, Up, Down, Left, Right,* and so on. But the vocabularies were growing. . . .

These early beginnings broke the trail for the developments that began appearing over the next thirty years. Other centers of the brain, such as those relating to visual perception, volition, and abstract imagination, were also harnessed as direct sources of data and command information for computer processing.

Later on, techniques for accomplishing the reverse process—of enabling the brain to absorb data from the machine independent of the normal sensory channels—were added.

The result of all this was the Bio-Inter-Active Computer—the latest word in computer technology, offering perhaps the ultimate in man-machine communication. The BIAC eliminated the agonizingly slow traffic bottleneck that had always plagued the interface between the superfast human brain on the one hand, and the hyper-superfast electronics on the other. For example, a straightforward mathematical calculation could be formulated in the mind in seconds, and its execution, once inside the machine, would occupy microseconds; but the time needed to set the problem up by laboriously keying it in character by character and to read back the result off a display screen was, in relative terms, astronomical. It was rather like playing a game of chess by mail.

But the BIAC did much more than simply enable data and instructions to be fed into the machine more quickly; it enabled the machine to accept input material of a completely new type. Whereas classical computers had required every item of input information to be explicitly specified in numerical or encoded form, the BIAC, incorporating the most up-to-date advances in adaptive learning techniques, could respond to generalized concepts—concepts visualized in the operator's mind—and automatically convert them into forms suitable for internal manipulation.

It thus functioned more as a supercomputing extension of the operator's own natural abilities, its feedback facilities evoking in him a direct perceptual insight to complex phenomena in a way that could never have been rivaled by mere symbols written on pieces of paper. The dynamics of riding a bicycle can be represented as a complicated string of differential equations, the solutions of which will infallibly tell the rider what he should do to avoid falling off when confronted by a given set of conditions—speed, curve of road, weight of rider, etc. The young child, however, does not concern himself with any of this; he simply *feels* the right thing to do—given some practice—and does it. In an analogous fashion, the BIAC operator could *feel* and *steer* his way through his problem. It was the perfect tool for handling Clifford's k-function solutions.

Only a handful of BIACs had been built, and all of them were undergoing government evaluation trials under conditions of strictest security. The offer to make available to Sudbury one of the next three scheduled to be built provided, therefore, as convincing a measure as anyone could ask for of the significance attached to the Institute's work. Even so, it would take three months or so for the machine to become available.

Security of the BIAC posed a problem that had to be solved during that period. Dismantling the GRASER and the detector and shipping them elsewhere would have been possible as a last resort, but the magnitude of the task promised to be horrendous. Eventually Peter Hughes suggested an arrangement that, although falling below the requirements usually stipulated for that type of situation, was granted a special dispensation. Structural alterations were made to the GRASER building to seal off all entry points apart from the main door and a fire exit at the rear, which was operable from the inside only. Everything and everybody not directly involved with the project were moved into other accommodations elsewhere at the Institute. Then, finally, access to the building was severely limited to a few specially designated people, and two officers of the State Police were to be stationed at the door around the clock to insure that the rules were observed.

Clifford saw these developments as portents of things to come, and his misgivings intensified. Life took an unexpected turn, however, and soon he was too preoccupied with other things to brood about such matters. He was sent away for six weeks to undergo an intensive course in BIAC operation on a machine already installed at the Navy's equipment evaluation laboratories in Baltimore. Aub remained at Sudbury, being too immersed in the design details and preparations for Mark II to afford any time away. He would follow later.

For the first couple of days after his arrival in Baltimore, Clifford sat through a series of lectures and tutorials aimed at imparting some essential concepts of BIAC operation and at giving the class some preliminary benefits from the techniques that others had developed.

"The BIAC becomes an efficient tool when you've learned to forget that it's there," one of the instructors told them. "Treat it as if you were learning to play the piano—concentrate on accuracy and let speed come in its own time. Once you can play a piano well, you let your hands do all the work and just sit back and enjoy the music. The same thing happens with a BIAC."

Eventually Clifford found himself sitting before the operator's console in one of the cubicles adjacent to the machine room while an instructor adjusted the lightweight skull-harness around his head for the first time. For about a half-hour they went through the routine of calibrating the machine to Clifford's brain patterns, and then the instructor keyed in a command string and sat back in his chair.

"Okay," the instructor pronounced. "It's live now. All yours, Brad."

An eerie sensation instantly seemed to take possession of his mind, as if a bottomless chasm had suddenly opened up beside it to leave it perched precariously on the brink. He had once stood in the center of the parabolic dish of a large radio telescope and had never forgotten the experience of being able to shout at the top of his voice and hear only a whisper as the sound was reflected away. Now he was experiencing the same kind of feeling, but this time it was his thoughts that were being snatched away.

And then chaos came tumbling back in the opposite direction—numbers, shapes, patterns, colors . . . twisting, bending, whirling, merging . . . growing, shrinking . . . lines, curves. . . . His mind plunged into the whirlpool of thought kaleidoscoping inside his head. And suddenly it was gone.

He looked around and blinked. Bob, the Navy instructor, was watching him and grinning.

"It's okay; I just switched it off," he said. "That blow your mind?"

"You knew that would happen," Clifford said after he had collected himself again. "What was it all about?"

"Everybody gets that the first time," Bob told him. "It was only a couple of seconds . . . gives you an idea of the way it works, though. See, the BIAC acts like a gigantic feedback system for mental processes, only it amplifies them round the loop. It will pick up vague ideas that are flickering around in your head, extrapolate them into precisely defined and quantitive interpretations, and throw them straight back at you. If you're not ready for it and you give it some junk, you get back superjunk; before you know it, the BIAC's picked that up out of your head too, processed it the same way, and come back with super-superjunk. You get a huge positive feedback effect that builds up in no time at all. BIAC people call it a 'garbage loop.' "

"That's all very well," Clifford said. "But what the hell do I do about it?"

"Learn to concentrate and to continue concentrating," Bob told him. "It's the stray, undisciplined thoughts that trigger it . . . the kinds of thing that run around in your head when you've got nothing in particular to focus on. Those are the things you have to learn to suppress."

"That's easy to say," Clifford muttered, then

shrugged helplessly. "But how do I start?" Bob
grinned good-humoredly.

"Okay," he said. "Let's start by giving you some
easy exercises for practice. Try ordinary simple arith-
metic. Visualize the numbers you want to operate on,
concentrate hard on them and also on the operation
you want to perform, and exclude everything else.
Get it fixed in your mind before I switch you in again.
Okay?"

"Just anything?" Clifford shrugged. "Okay." He
mentally selected the digits 4 and 5 and elected to
multiply them together, just to see what happened. The
torrent of chaos hit him again before he realized Bob
had hit the key.

"That was a bit sneaky of me," Bob confessed.
"The best time to slot in is often when the problem
is clear in your mind. Try again?"

"Sure."

After three more excursions round the garbage
loop, Clifford sensed something different. Just for a
split-second it was there; the concept of the number
20 seemed to explode in his brain, impressing itself
with a clarity and a forcefulness that excluded everything else from his perceptions. Never before in his
life had he experienced anything so vividly as that
one simple number for that one brief moment. Then
the garbage came at him again and swallowed it up.
For a while he just sat there dumbstruck.

"Got it that time, huh?" Bob's voice brought him
back to reality.

"I think so, at least for a second."

"That's good," Bob stated, encouraging his pupil.
"You'll find for a while that the shock of realizing it's
working distracts you enough to blow it. You'll get
over that though. Don't try and fight it—just ride it
easy. Try again?"

An hour later Bob posed the problem, "Two hundred
seventy-three point five six multiplied by one hundred
ninety-eight point seven one?"

Clifford gazed hard at the console, visualized the

numbers, and almost immediately recited, "Fifty-four thousand, three hundred fifty-nine point one zero seven six."

"Great stuff, Brad. I reckon that'll do for a first session. Let's break off for lunch and go have a beer."

A week later Clifford was learning to cope with problems in elementary mechanics—situations involving concepts of shape, space, and motion as well as numerical relationships. He found, as his skills improved, that he could create a dynamic conceptual model of a multibody collision and instantly evaluate any of the variables involved. Not only that, he could, by simply willing it, replay the abstract experiment as many times as he liked from any perspective and in any variation that he pleased. He could "feel" the changing stress pattern in a mechanical structure subjected to moving loads, "see" the flow of currents in an electrical circuit as plainly as that of liquid in a network of glass tubes. By the end of the fourth week he could guide himself through to the solution of a tensor analysis as unerringly as he could guide his finger out of a maze in a child's coloring book.

The BIAC's adaptive learning system grew steadily more attuned to his particular methods of working and automatically remembered the routines that it had flagged as yielding desired results. As time went on it proceeded to string these routines together into complete procedures that could be invoked instantly without their having to be assembled all over again. In this way the machine automated progressively more of the mundane mechanics of solving a whole variety of problems, leaving him ever more free to concentrate on the more creative activity of evolving the problem-solving strategy. It therefore built up its own programs as it went along; and it was all the time expanding and refining its collection. Programming in the classical sense, even with respect to the parallel programming used in the distributed computing systems of the 1980s and '90s, no longer meant very much.

Clifford imagined a single cube. He imagined that he was looking at it from the direction of one of the corners and down on to it. Having fixed the picture in his mind, he opened his eyes and found a fair representation of it staring back at him from the BIAC graphic screen. It was not bad—a bit ragged at one of the corners and the lines were a little wavy here and there, but . . . not bad. Even as he thought about it, the subconscious part of his mind took its cue from his visual perceptions and the imperfections in the displayed image subtly dissolved away.

"Try adding some color," Aggie suggested. She was the graphics instructor taking Clifford through the final part of the course. He mentally selected opposite faces red, blue, and green, consolidated the thought, then used the knack that he had developed and projected it at the view in front of him. The hollow cube promptly became solid—and colored.

"Good," Aggie pronounced. "Now try rotating it."

Clifford hesitated for a second, felt the first surge that forewarned the bio-link was beginning to become unstable, and caught it deftly before it could run away into positive feedback. The reaction was by now purely reflex. He settled down again and tried lifting one corner of the cube, but instead of pivoting about its opposite corner as if it were a rigid body, the shape deformed and flowed like a piece of plasticene. He emitted a short involuntary laugh, reformed the smear of colors back into a cube, fired a command at the BIAC to lock the display, relaxed and sat back in his seat.

"Went off the rails there somewhere," he remarked. "What should I do?"

"You let the idea that it was rigid slip," Aggie told him. "But even if you hadn't, trying to rotate it by stimulating external forces is a pretty difficult thing to get right at first. That's what you were trying to do, isn't it?"

"Yes." Clifford was impressed. "How could you tell?"

"Oh . . ." She smiled and gestured as if throwing something away. "You learn to spot such things. Now, when you try it again, don't think of actually moving the cube. Imagine it's fixed and you're walking around it . . . as if it were a building and you're in a hoverjet, okay? You'll find that if you do it that way, rigidity and all the other implied concepts take care of themselves subconsciously. Right. So, unlock it and give it another whirl."

Three days later, early in the evening and after their serious business for the day was over, Aggie showed Clifford some games based on animated cartoons that she had produced to amuse herself during her spare time. The difference with these cartoons was that the sequence of events unfolding on the screen could be modified interactively from second to second by the players.

Clifford's mouse scurried along the floor by the baseboard with Aggie's black-and-white cat pursuing close behind. He instinctively read the speeds and distances and sensed via the BIAC's responses that his mouse would just make it with two point three seven seconds to spare. He slowed the mouse slightly to take the corner at the bottom of the stairs and then raced it flat out along the last straight to where its hole, and safety, lay.

Suddenly he screeched the mouse to a halt. The entrance to the mouse hole was barred by a tiny door bristling with solid-looking padlocks.

"Hey, that's cheating!" Clifford roared indignantly. "You can't do that!"

"Who says?" Aggie laughed. "There's no rules that say I can't."

"Christ!" Clifford accelerated the mouse away as the cat pounced on the spot it had just vacated. He ran it round behind the cat, who immediately began turning after it. For an agonizing second he stared helplessly searching for a way out, and then, seized by sudden inspiration, he created a second mouse hole in the baseboard and promptly shot the mouse through it.

"That's not fair!" Aggie shrieked. "You can't change the house!"

"There's no rule that says I can't," Clifford threw back. "I win."

"Like hell. That was a tie."

They were still laughing as they removed the skull-harnesses and shut off the operator station to finish the day.

"You know, Aggie," he said, shaking his head. "This really is an incredible machine. I'd never have dreamed this kind of thing could work."

"It's primitive yet," she replied. "I think all kinds of applications that even we can't imagine will grow out of this some day. . . ." She gestured vaguely in the direction of the screen. "For example, I wouldn't be surprised if a whole new art form developed from little things like that. Why hire actors to try and interpret what's in the scriptwriter's mind if you can get straight into his mind?" She shrugged and looked sideways at Clifford. "See the kind of thing I mean?"

"Make movies out of peoples' heads?" He gaped at her.

"Why not?" she said simply.

Why not? Somewhere, he remembered, he had heard that said before.

The final thing they showed him in Baltimore was the way in which the BIAC could function as a communications intermediary between man and man. Two or more human operators interacting simultaneously with the machine were able to exchange thought patterns among themselves in a way that was uncanny, using the computer as a common translator and message exchange. Even more remarkable was the fact that there was no particular reason why these operators had to be in close proximity to one another, and a number of experiments of this kind had been conducted in which the machine in Baltimore was

linked to another BIAC, owned by the Air Force and
located in California, thus coupling operators three
thousand miles apart. Clifford found this the most astounding thing he had seen since coming to Baltimore.
He thought about it all the way back to Boston.

Clifford returned to Sudbury to find that installation
of the Institute's own BIAC was well under way and
that construction of the Mark II had commenced. The
latter operation would require far more time to complete, however, and as an intermediate measure to
gain some preliminary experience in using BIAC techniques to interpret k-functions, the new computer
was connected on-line to the Mark I prototype.

He slowly learned to steer his way through the
masses of data to ferret out and manipulate the spacelike solutions of the equations and to project them as
visual displays. To his astonishment he found that he
could "move" his vantage point at will throughout the
body of Earth and about its surface. The resolving
power of the Mark I was still poor, preventing him
from distinguishing much in the way of meaningful
detail, but he did succeed in producing recognizable
images of some prominent geographic features such as
mountain ranges, continental margins, and ocean
trenches. He managed to obtain some surface views
of the Moon too, in which the ghostly outlines of the
larger craters and ring-walled plains could just about
be discerned. It was somewhat like viewing the transmission from a remote-TV space probe that could be
moved instantly from place to place—a tantalizing
foretaste of what might be possible with Mark II.

One evening, while they were out for a few drinks at
their favorite bar in Marlboro, Clifford was describing
his experiences in Baltimore to Aub and Morelli.
Aub had at last reached the point of being able to
leave the immediate work on Mark II in the hands
of the rest of the team and had made arrangements
to go on a BIAC training course himself, starting the

following week. Naturally, he was interested to learn about what the Navy had in store for him.

"You mean there's this guy in Baltimore and there's this other guy out in California someplace, both plugged into BIACs that are hooked together, and they can exchange thoughts?" Aub stared over his beer in astonishment. "Man, that's crazy."

"You've gotta be joking, Brad," Morelli said.

"Really." Clifford nodded emphatically. "I've seen them doing it. One of them can read a list of numbers off a piece of paper and the other one will tell you what they are. . . . They can send pictures—one guy imagines a face that they both know and the other guy identifies it . . . all kinds of things."

"Sorta like telepathy by the sound of it," Morelli remarked. "I never had much time for that kinda stuff."

"It's not really, though, is it," Clifford pointed out. "Not in the way that people usually mean the word."

"How d'you mean?" Morelli asked.

"Well, usually they're talking about paranormal phenomena . . . things outside known science. But this isn't like that—it's all based on things we know about and understand."

"It achieves the same sort of effect, though," Aub broke in.

"Which is my whole point," Clifford declared. "It's just another example of the kind of thing that's happened over and over again through history." Two pairs of eyes looked back at him blankly. "Every day," he explained, "we take it for granted that we can do things that people five hundred years ago dreamed about, but could only think of in terms of magic. We can fly through the air, stare into magic mirrors, and watch things going on in other places. . . . We can even talk to people all over the world. . . ." Clifford opened his hands expressively. "We've made all those things happen, but we've used methods of doing it that people from way back could never have imagined."

"Yeah, I'm with you," Aub said, nodding. "Because they had no idea about electronics and the like."

"Yes, that's what I'm getting at," Clifford told him. "They imagined flying and talked about levitation, because they couldn't see in advance the kind of engineering needed to make the idea work."

"Okay, I'll go along with that," Morelli agreed. "You're saying that people made the mistake of imagining telepathy, thinking it had to be some kind of magic. Now that the effects they talked about are actually starting to happen, it turns out you don't need anything magic to do it—just a couple of BIACs."

"That's exactly it, Al," Clifford confirmed. "Talking about something paranormal is just a way of discussing something you don't properly understand . . . yet. The operative word is 'yet.' In the end, the idea all becomes part of what's normal. Nobody thinks now that there's anything mysterious about talking across country by Intonet. And effectively, this is no different, except that the talking uses a BIAC instead of a regular Intonet terminal."

"Well . . . I guess that doesn't leave much over outside orthodox science," Aub mused after reflecting for a while. "I guess maybe that's what everything we do is about—turning paradox into orthodox."

Chapter 17

Through Zimmermann, the ISF astronomers at Joliot-Curie had been kept updated on developments at Sudbury. Excited by the way in which k-theory had accounted successfully for the observed distribution of the three-degree cosmic background radiation, a group of them had begun reappraising other outstanding problems in the light of the new theory. This led to their formulating a new system of k-conservation principles and enabled them to explain at last, among other things, why the amount of conventional radiation produced in the vicinity of the Cygnus X-1 black hole was larger than classical quantum theory predicted it should be.

Essentially, the new conservation principles stated that when matter/energy 'vanished' out of normal space to exist totally in hi-space, as happened when a particle annihilated or matter fell into a black hole, then an equivalent amount of energy had to reappear in normal space somewhere. Calculation showed that this 'return energy' would appear in a distribution pattern that gave the greatest intensity in the immediate vicinity of the point at which the original annihilation had taken place, but which fell away exponentially all the way to infinity. This led to the remarkable conclusion that when matter annihilated, say in Cygnus X-1, or in Morelli's GRASER, energy reappeared instantaneously at every point in the universe as a direct consequence of the event. The amount of return energy that would appear, for example, some-where in the middle of the Andromeda Galaxy as a result of one gram of matter being consumed in the GRASER in Massachusetts would thus be immea-surably and unimaginably small; nevertheless, mathe-matically at least, it would be there.

All this was really another way of stating Clifford's laws of hi-wave propagation, which showed that the hi-radiation produced by any event of creation or an-nihilation would manifest itself instantaneously all through space, the intensity decreasing sharply with distance. Indeed, the equations describing the two processes were soon shown to be mathematically iden-tical. What the astronomers had done was to compute the amount of conventional radiation that would be produced at every point in space by the process of hi-particle interactions. When this quantity was integrated across the whole volume of the universe, the re-sult showed that the total amount of energy produced throughout this volume equaled the amount originally destroyed. Hence the new conservation laws followed.

It was just as well that it worked out this way. The rate of destruction of mass sustained in the GRASER was far higher than that attained in the largest H-bomb. Only a tiny proportion of its energy equiv-alent was delivered back into normal space within the reactor sphere however, the rest being distributed across billions of cubic light-years of space. Had it been otherwise, they would easily have blown Massa-chusetts off the map the instant they switched on.

The pattern of return energy therefore explained the observed radiation from Cygnus X-1. When Clif-ford examined the forms of the equations derived by the scientists on Luna, he discovered that they in-cluded terms which made allowance for the distri-bution of matter in the surrounding volume of the universe—terms which he had neglected in his own treatment of the problem. Using the more compre-hensive equations, he recalculated the radiation that should be expected from an artificial black hole in the GRASER—the quantity that had previously contradicted both his own predictions and those based on classical quantum theory and the Hawking Effect. This time it came out right. K-theory, it appeared, was well on its way to being fully validated.

In the course of all this experimentation, Clifford developed a regular working relationship with the astronomers and cosmologists at Joliot-Curie, and together they began to explore some of the deeper implications of the theory that Clifford had not thought very much more about since his days at ACRE. From the Japanese model of quasars, it was evident that these objects were the scenes of mass annihilation on a truly phenomenal scale. According to the new conservation principles, the energy equivalent of the mass being destroyed ought to be returned into normal space, most of it being concentrated around the quasars and the rest of it diffusely scattered everywhere else. Throughout the 'everywhere else,' therefore, there ought to exist a steady background flux of particle creations attributable to distant quasars. But all the annihilations taking place inside the ordinary masses and black holes scattered throughout the universe would, by the conservation principles, contribute to this background flux as well. Thus there were three known mechanisms for destroying mass: quasars, black holes, and spontaneous annihilations, most of which took place inside masses. Also, there was one known mechanism for creating it: the universal background of spontaneous creations. The crucial question was, did the two balance?

It was important to know this because the very fabric of spacetime itself—the lo-domain aspects of Clifford's k-functions—came into the equations. It was possible for one of these two quantities to exceed the other without violating the conservation principles provided that the volume of the universe adjusted to compensate and maintain a constant average density. In other words, in a universe heavily populated by quasars, the rate of mass annihilation implied would be too large for return energy alone to provide the balancing mechanism, and space itself would grow to accommodate the excess. The expansion of the universe followed directly from k-theory, and came about as a consequence of an earlier cosmic epoch of quasar formation.

So, was the universe still expanding? Nobody knew because all the data that told of the fact—red shifts of distant galaxies, for example—came from millions of years in the past. Were there quasars still there *now?* Again, nobody knew, for the same reason. Could the balance be tested? How many black holes were there in sample volumes of the universe? Nobody knew. But the new science of k-astronomy enthusiastically anticipated by Aub and Morelli promised a means of answering all these questions.

What fascinated the cosmologists—and began to infect Clifford as well the more he talked with them—was the prospect of a new and revolutionary cosmological model. It was purely hypothetical at that stage, but somebody on Luna had suggested that if the quasars had ceased to exist *now,* and if the expansion had stopped as a consequence, and if creations turned out to predominate in the balance, a new epoch of quasar formation might be induced. This gave rise to a new picture of cosmology in which phases of quasar formation and expansion alternated with phases of galaxy manufacture . . . for ever. Thus the notion of a continuous "Wave Model" of the universe was born, superseding, if it could be proved, both the Steady State and the Big Bang models. It required neither the singularity in the laws of physics that characterized Big Bang and about which a number of leading physicists still felt a trifle uneasy, nor for the universe to appear the same at all times, as was required by Steady State but which observation had shown to be manifestly untrue.

All in all, there was a lot of exciting work already lined up waiting for Mark II.

But as Mark II neared completion and the first tests

of its subsystems commenced, world events cast a deepening shadow over the project. Anti-West policies intensified in South America, threatening closure of the Panama Canal, and the Urals border war escalated to include the use of massed tanks and ground-attack aircraft as regular features. The long-drawn-out civil war in Burma finally died out as the revolutionary factions effected a shaky compromise and took over the country, while the exhausted remnants of the right-wing government forces retreated to seek sanction in neighboring India. Soon India itself became the object of renewed border pressures from both east and west as Chinese and Afrabs resurrected long-standing griev-ances. Hong Kong, having been reduced to a state of economic impotence and famine by a systematic stranglehold of sanctions and blockade, was taken over uncontested. Within three days, China announced its claim for Taiwan.

"Yeah, I know it's a pain, Brad, but that's the way it is," Morelli said across his desk. "It'll only take, say, a day at most. Get a couple of the team to give you a hand with it."

"But . . ." Clifford waved the wad of forms that Morelli had given him in front of him. "What is all this crap? I haven't got a spare day. . . ." He glanced down at the schedule sheet attached to the front. *"In-ventory of Capital Equipment Advanced . . . Projected Purchase Breakdown . . . Accumulated Maintenance Debits . . ."* Clifford looked up imploringly. "We've never had anything like this before. What's going on all of a sudden?"

Morelli sighed and scratched the side of his nose.

"I suppose Washington is trying to bring it to our attention that they've poured a lot of hardware into this place and it's costing them a lot of bucks," he said. "I think maybe it's a little reminder that they haven't seen much in the way of results yet . . . you know how they work—subtly."

"This won't help get results," Clifford fumed. "It'll

just soak up time." He halted for a second, then continued. "Who says we're not getting results, anyway? We've solved the secondary-radiation problem . . . untangled the cosmic background problem . . . postulated new k-conservation principles. That's what I call results."

"I know," Morelli agreed, holding up a hand. "But it's not what *they* call results. "Remember, we sold them on supercommunications and superradar and all kinds of other superstuff? That's what they're waiting to see."

"Aw, but hell . . ."

"I know what you're gonna say, Brad, but don't say it." Morelli placed his hands down in a gesture of finality. "They're paying for the tunes, and I guess we have to play. Fill it in as they ask and keep it short, okay? Like I said, get some people to help you and I bet you can clear it up in half a day."

"Bureaucrats!" Clifford snorted to himself as he closed the door behind him and began walking down the corridor. Washington, it appeared, was not wildly excited about quasar distributions or Wave Models of the universe.

"Next Thursday, I'm afraid," Peter Hughes said to Morelli as they were walking across the grounds of the Institute away from the GRASER building. "They really didn't leave me any choice."

"Thursday?" Morelli looked dubious. "Brad will be pretty mad about that. He was planning to devote the whole of Thursday to checking out the BIAC interface to Mark II."

"He'll have to postpone that, then," Hughes said. "Sorry, Al, but our friends in Washington were adamant."

"But hell . . ." Morelli protested. "Why a progress review meeting . . . and all day at that? The team is perfectly capable of reviewing its own progress, and they can do it in half an hour. Brad and Aub spent four hours last week preparing that progress report for Washington. Wasn't it good enough for them or something?"

Hughes threw his arms wide open in front of him as he walked and sighed heavily. "I don't know, Al. They said it wasn't detailed enough. They say they need to send some of their people here to go right through the whole project . . . from top to bottom. As I said—I didn't have much choice about it."

Morelli shook his head apprehensively.

"Brad'll be pretty mad," he repeated.

"Aub's not bothered about it," Clifford told Sarah later on that night. "He's only interested in getting his Mark II up and running and keeping the funds flowing in to do it. He said we shouldn't waste time on any of that nonsense but should just keep feeding back whatever fiction's needed to shut them up."

"That's not your way though, is it," Sarah said, stating the fact rather than asking the question. He shook his head slowly, looking deeply worried for the first time in months.

"No, it's not," he said. "I don't like deception. But there's something more than that. It's ACRE closing in all over again . . . I can feel it."

Chapter 18

"No, I'm serious, Aub. One of the doctors at the hospital was telling me yesterday—first aid, casualty evacuation, and precautions against fallout and radiation hazards. They're working out the details of the courses now. Within three months they'll be compulsory in every school in the state and in every company that employs more than twenty people in one place. You wait and see." Sarah spoke as she set three places on the dining-room table. Aub, perched precariously on a stool at the breakfast counter and sipping from a can of Coke, watched her from the kitchen.

"Back to the Boy Scouts, eh," he said. "Reckon we'll get badges to put on our shirts too?"

"I don't think it's funny. It proves things must be getting bad. I heard on the news this afternoon that somebody exploded a tactical nuke in an arms factory somewhere just outside Calcutta. Nearly two thousand dead. What kind of people do things like that?"

"Yeah, I heard about it. Head cases. Seems to be the in-thing."

Sarah placed the napkins and glanced at the clock. "Six twenty-five. I'd have thought Brad would be back by now. What was it you said he was doing?"

"He got tied up with Al and a coupla guys from Washington who are trying to hustle things. I managed to duck out of it."

"Oh, dear. That probably means he'll be in a bad mood again." She stepped back to survey her handiwork, then walked round into the kitchen to inspect the bubbling pan of beef stroganoff. "He seems to get awfully moody these days, Aub. Are things really getting so bad?"

Aub pivoted round on the stool to face her, his mouth jerking momentarily downward at the corners beneath his beard.

"Yeah, he gets pretty upset about it, I guess. He's into some theoretical thing with Zim's eggheads that he wants to spend all of his time on, especially now we've got the Mark II machine running. Trouble is, the brass is getting impatient for its ironmongery. They figure that since they paid the check for most of it, they oughta be getting a bigger slice of the action."

"And that doesn't bother you?"

"Me?" Aub shrugged. "I guess I can just ride along with it. If I have to come up with a few ideas here and there to keep things smooth, that's okay. I'll get in enough of my own thing too. Brad's problem is he's too much of a purist. He has to have it all his own way or nothing. Y'see, he's got these principles he feels strongly about . . . whether science dictates politics or the other way round. If it looks like things are going in what he figures is the wrong way, he won't have any part of it." Aub shrugged again and sighed. "He oughta remember the ice ball."

"You don't think he'll get restless again, do you?" Sarah asked apprehensively.

"Restless? You mean take another walk?"

"Yes."

Aub pursed his lips for a few seconds. "Well . . . to be honest about it, if things get much worse . . . maybe."

"That's my Brad " Sarah sounded resigned but with no hint of bitterness. "I'd just grown to like this house too. Oh, well, what does it say in the book of Ruth . . . *Whither thou goest I will go* . . ."

"Huh?"

"Doesn't matter. Here—I'll take that can."

"Thanks. You know something . . ."

The house shook and a noise like thunder echoed up the stairs as the front door slammed. Elephantine footsteps pounded in the entrance level below.

"Oh, jeez," murmured Aub.

"Is that you, sweetness?" Sarah called. No reply.

A minute later Clifford appeared in the door of the dining room, glowering. He mumbled perfunctory greetings, stamped across to the bar and began pouring himself a large measure of Scotch. Sarah emerged from the kitchen and walked over to stand just behind him. He turned, glass in hand, to find her confronting him with hands on hips and lips pouted expectantly. He scowled back at her for a few seconds, then emitted a sigh of exasperation, grinned, and kissed her lightly.

"Hi."

"Should think so too," she said, and marched back into the kitchen.

Aub smirked through the serving hatch. "Man . . . wait till I tell the guys about this."

"You shut up if you don't want to end up eating at McDonald's." Clifford inclined his head in the direction of the bar. "Want a drink?"

"Cheers. Rye and dry."

Clifford turned to the bar once more as plates began appearing. Aub ambled round into the dining room and transferred them from the counter to the table. A few seconds later Sarah followed.

"My acute perceptiveness tells me we have problems," Aub said as they sat down.

"They want the project run their way—formal schedule of timetabled objectives, regular progress reports, resident liaison man from Washington. The works. Just what I knew would happen."

"Well . . ." Aub tried to sound philosophical. "I guess they figure that they've made the down-payment and ought to be seeing some deliveries . . . delivery estimates anyway."

"I'll deliver everything I said I would, but I won't jump through hoops too. I can't work that way."

"You have to see it from their point of view, Brad," Sarah tried. "It's a lot of money to put down with no guarantees at all. Perhaps you're making it look a bit like they owe it to you to fund anything that interests you. Surely you can trade off somewhere with them."

Clifford grew irritable again.

"See it from their point of view . . . Why do I always to have to see it from their point of view? Why can't they try seeing it from mine? Their so-called management science is going to everybody's heads. When will they realize they can't manage human thinking like production lines for plastic ducks? I already said—I'll deliver. That should be enough."

Aub was beginning to lose his patience. "You know that, I know that, Al knows that, and Sarah knows that," he pointed out. "But maybe they don't know that, or at least, they don't believe it enough. Maybe we have to persuade them a bit harder, that's all. Like Zim always said—remember—it needs selling."

Clifford wasn't buying. "We've been through all that and look where it's led. Anyhow, I'm not a salesman and I'm not interested in becoming one. I'm a scientist. It's just another hoop to jump through. Why should we have to?"

After a short silence Aub asked: "So what happens if you end up telling them to get lost? After all, it's not really like last time. We're working for ISF now when all's said and done. There wouldn't be any question of the job going down the pan."

"True," Clifford answered. "But they could still pull the BIAC out . . . plus all the other stuff they've bought."

Aub stopped chewing and looked hard at Clifford with a stare of disbelief.

"You're joking, man. They'd do that?"

"They're already threatening to. That's what held me up. They've got Peter Hughes over a barrel—he plays ball or they pick up their marbles. They've been getting at Geneva too, so things won't look good for pal Peter if he decides he doesn't want to play. That puts Al on the spot. He's on our side, but his hands are tied now. He's just having to hand it down the line."

Aub thought the problem over.

"So we play ball," he offered at last. "That way we've still got a project. The other way we haven't got a project." He looked from one to the other. "End of problem. There's nothing to decide."

Sarah said nothing. She knew better how Clifford's mind worked.

"It's not the way," Clifford replied slowly, shaking his head. A strange light had crept into his eyes. "It'll always be the same for as long as we knuckle under. I don't mean just here—everywhere. The whole damn world's gone crazy. The very people who are capable of finding out the ways of solving the real problems are all being muscled into making the problems worse. And the people who are doing the muscling don't even understand what the problems are." He looked at Aub appealingly. "Did you ever see films of what went on in Nazi Germany in World War II? Some of the best scientific brains in Europe being herded around like slave labor by a bunch of thugs. Well, it hasn't gotten that bad yet, but that's the direction it's going. I won't do anything to help it along, and that's what you're asking me to do."

"So you walk out," Aub tossed back lightly. "What the hell? Who cares? The world goes on anyway. Nothing changes. Only you lose out."

"Something has to change." Clifford sounded far away. He looked straight through Aub as if he were not there. "Once and for all there has to be a stop to it . . . the whole lousy situation . . . permanently . . ."

"*You're* gonna change it?" Aub laughed. "What'll you do—run for President? I think you'd be disappointed even if you made it. He, too, seems a bit stuck for answers right now."

Aub stopped smiling when he saw that Clifford was

not reacting. Clifford's mind seemed to be a million miles away.

"I don't know . . ." he said after what seemed a long time. And that strange light was still burning in his eyes.

Late that evening when they were relaxing over coffee to the background of Beethoven's Fifth Piano Concerto, Clifford, who had hardly spoken a word since dinner, turned suddenly toward Aub. "Do you remember when we were talking to Al about a week ago . . . about the technique that's used in the GRASER to induce annihilations? You said that you thought it might be possible to use the same principle to control the coordinates in normal space of where the return energy is delivered."

"I remember. What about it?"

"In other words, you figure that you could focus the return energy at a point . . . instead of having it spread out all the way to infinity."

"Maybe. Why?" Aub put down the magazine he had been browsing through and looked puzzled. Clifford ignored the questions.

"What would be involved to do it?"

"How d'you mean—as a sorta lab test?"

"Yes."

Aub thought for a moment. "Well, I suppose all the hardware you'd really need is already there. . . . It would just have to function in a different way. I guess you'd need to reprogram the modulator-control computers and the supervisory processor . . . plus a few bits of rewiring in the front-end electrics. That should do it."

"How long do you reckon it'd take?"

Aub suddenly looked alarmed. "Hey—you're not thinking of trying it, are you? That could be dangerous; nobody knows what to expect. You might end up blowing a hole in the middle of Sudbury."

"Not if the beam was wound right down to minimum power. All I want to do is prove the point.

We should be able to get the annihilation rate down to a few kilowatts."

"Al would never okay it," Aub protested. "The theory's still got too many unknowns in it. Suppose there's some imbalance that you and Zim's guys haven't figured out yet, and the space integral isn't unity. You might find that a lot more comes out than you put in." Aub was looking worried. "Anyhow, where were you thinking of focusing the return energy?"

"Right there in the lab. I'm happy the integral is unity."

"In the lab! Christ! Al will never buy that in a million years. Peter'd have the mother and father of all heart attacks."

"So we don't tell them about it. We set it up nice and quiet and run it late one night like a routine piece of overtime. What's the matter—don't you trust me any more?" Clifford was grinning in a crooked kind of way. "I thought you were supposed to be the adventurous one. Have a ball."

Aub stared as if Clifford had taken leave of his senses. He looked imploringly at Sarah, who was following the conversation, and threw out his hands.

"It must be all these English females," he said. "He's finally flipped. Brad, get this straight. There is absolutely no way I'm gonna come into the lab with you, late one night like some kinda crook or something, and run that kind of experiment."

Four weeks later at about an hour before midnight, Clifford's car eased to a halt outside the GRASER building of the Sudbury Institute. Two figures got out, presented their credentials to the police guards at the main door, and disappeared inside. By three in the morning the huge generators that supplied the GRASER were humming and the banks of equipment racks stacked around the reactor sphere were alive with patterns of winking lights. An array of heat sensors, radiation detectors, ionization counters and photomultiplier tubes had been positioned around a ten-foot-diameter circle that had been cleared near one of the walls, about thirty feet away from the sphere. Clifford and Aub were sitting at a control panel, facing the circle from behind the battery of instruments.

Aub adjusted the parameters of the GRASER to produce just the faintest trickle of particles through the beam tube and into the reactor. Then he switched on the annihilation modulators. The readings on the display screens on either side of the panel confirmed that a microscopic reaction was taking place inside the sphere. The particles were disappearing out of space to be transformed into hi-waves that propagated instantly to every point in the universe, where they subsequently reappeared as energy through secondary reactions. So far, it was an everyday GRASER run.

Clifford nodded. Working together, they started up the sequence of specially written programs that they had loaded into the system earlier that day. One by one the additional modified modulators were switched in and brought up to operating power, compressing the return energy into an ever-decreasing radius centered on the middle of the empty circle. The energy that would normally have been distributed infinitesimally sparsely throughout the whole of space was now being focused within a volume no bigger than a beach ball.

The screens showed that the instruments were detecting radiation. Counters registered the ionization of molecules of air. The infrared scanners indicated a rise in temperature. As Aub increased the beam power a fraction, dust particles began scurrying across the floor of the lab toward the center of the circle, drawn inward by the convection of the rising, heated air. A cool breeze made itself felt on their skin.

At higher power an incandescent glow appeared, elongated upward into a shimmering column of fiery radiance by the rising currents. It burned dull red at the outside, changing through brighter shades of orange to a core of brilliant yellow. Clifford and Aub watched spellbound. They were witnessing something that no men in history had seen before; energy was materializing in space out of nothing, from a source that lay thirty feet away—and it was traversing the distance in between through a realm of existence that lay beyond the dimensions of space and time.

After a few minutes Clifford, having satisfied himself that the recording instruments had captured everything, nodded and raised a hand. "That'll do. Don't take it any higher."

"Okay to cut?"

"Yep. That just about does it."

Aub took the system through its shutdown sequence. The glow died from the center of the circle and silence gradually descended as one by one the huge machines became quiet and the last row of lights went out. Aub sat back and wiped the perspiration from his forehead.

"Phew," he said. "Okay, I'll buy it—the space integral is unity. And you tried to tell me you weren't a salesman. Jeez." He shook his head.

"C'mon, it wasn't that risky and you know it," Clifford taunted. "If it wasn't unity, the detectors would have spotted an excess long before we wound the power up. There was no hazard really."

"Okay, you've made your point. We've proved we can focus the return energy. Now what?"

At once Clifford's grin snapped off and his mood became serious. "Tomorrow we talk to Al and Peter and put them in the picture," he said. "It doesn't matter now if there's hell to pay because this is rapidly going to become a lot bigger than both of them. What Peter has to do is get in touch with Washington and fix us an appointment for as soon as he can with Foreshaw and his merry men." He leaned across and slapped Aub on the shoulder. "You keep telling me I have to be a salesman, my friend. Okay—I, or, rather, we, are going to make the most mind-blowing sale ever. No salesman ever walked into the Pentagon with anything like what we've got. They want bombs? We are going to give them a bigger damn bomb than they ever dreamed of!"

Chapter 19

Clifford stood at the head of the large oval conference table and gazed along the line of unsmiling attentive faces. The Defense Secretary was seated at the far end with the rest—service chiefs, technical advisers, presidential aides, and defense planners—seated around on either side. Aub was at the end near Clifford, flanked by Morelli and Peter Hughes.

"Long speeches are not my line," Clifford began. His manner was unusually blunt and forthright. "The reason I'm standing here today is essentially to protest —to protest at a society that perpetuates a system of values that are becoming insane. Throughout history man's greatest enemies—from which practically all our other problems follow—have been two: ignorance and superstition. The most powerful weapon that man has developed to combat these enemies is science— the acquisition and harnessing of knowledge. And yet with every day that goes by, we see more and more science being used not to solve the problems of mankind but to aggravate them. Science is being progressively subordinated to the service of our lowest instincts."

He paused and looked around the room, half-expecting to be interrupted. But although a few aghast stares were in evidence, everybody seemed too taken aback to voice any comment, so he continued. "I am a scientist. I live in a world that is being torn apart by hatred and mistrust that I've had no part in making, and the reasons for them don't interest me. The situation is the making of people I don't know but who claim to act in my name. Those same people now presume the right to expect me to give up my own life in order to meet obligations that they feel I owe them. Just to make my position clear, I've never acknowledged any such obligations."

At the table, in front of where Clifford was standing, Morelli was massaging palms that were becoming moist. Next to him, Peter Hughes flinched and swallowed hard. A few sharp intakes of breath from around the room greeted Clifford's opening remarks. The gathering was not accustomed to being formally addressed so bluntly, and yet there was something about Clifford's compelling calm and poise—an assuredness of purpose that stemmed from somewhere deep inside him—that made them bite their tongues and hear him out. They sensed that the buildup was leading to something big.

After a pause that had its desired effect, Clifford continued. "During the scientific Renaissance in Europe in the sixteenth and seventeenth centuries, men found out for the first time how to distinguish fact from fancy, truth from falsity, and reality from dreams. From genuine knowledge came inventiveness . . . industry . . . intellectual freedom . . . affluence. Europe was unique among civilizations. This country was founded on that same tradition and our society was to be based on those same principles." He paused again and made no attempt to hide the accusing light in his eyes as he took in the faces before him.

Morelli hissed out of the corner of his mouth at Aub. "What's he trying to do—get us all deported?"

"He knows what he's doing . . . I think," Aub muttered.

Clifford carried on, refusing to be distracted. "But the tradition has not been followed. The promise of the Renaissance has not been kept. The same ignorance and prejudices that were there before are still with us today, but disguised; they still have the same power to inspire fear and suspicion in men's minds. First it was religious terror; today it's political terror. Nothing's changed. The knowledge that was gained and which should have become the birthright of all men has been perverted to more sinister ends, and the rest of the world has not been permitted to follow the path that Europe laid."

Nobody spoke while Clifford paused to drink from the water glass on the table in front of him. Foreshaw was regarding him through narrowed eyes, but had apparently elected to defer any verdict until he knew what this extraordinary address was leading up to. Clifford set the glass down and faced them once more.

"The lesson of history is that what you don't give, somebody will sooner or later take. Never mind the morality of it—those are the facts. The lesson is about to be repeated. The world is again all set to match brute force with brute force in an attempt to solve a problem that can't be solved that way. Only wisdom and understanding can solve it.

"I appreciate that nobody in this room made things turn out that way; neither did the government you represent. You've inherited the results of centuries of mismanagement, and you can't go back in time and change what's been done. Now it's too late to worry about how it might have been different anyway. We're stuck with it.

"I am convinced that as things are, mankind has run itself into a blind alley. The world is paralyzed by a military-technological deadlock that has existed on and off for over a hundred years. History has shown the futility of hoping that this deadlock will ever be dissolved by rational and civilized means, but while it continues to exist, there can be no meaningful progress for the world."

Clifford began pacing himself, getting ready to make his final point. "In other words it's too late now to avoid the deadlock, because it's happened, and it's painfully obvious that it's not going to go away. Even World War III won't solve anything. All that'll happen is that each side will wear the other to a standstill just as in 1914–1918, and within fifty years the same situation will emerge all over again."

Clifford took a long pause to let his words sink in, and then drew a deep breath.

"The only alternative then is that this deadlock must be smashed—smashed totally, finally, irrevocably and for all time! That's what I am here to offer."

A murmur of surprise ran around the room. Puzzled but intrigued frowns spread across their faces.

"Up until now, the very fact that the deadlock has persisted has ruled out any such alternative. But today I can offer you a weapon more potent than anything previously dreamed possible—a weapon that will pale your missiles and your hydrogen bombs into insignificance and enable this deadlock to be ended once and for all."

He paused to allow his words time to take effect, and then resumed:

"Make no mistake, I am not doing this for any reasons of loyalty, duty, ideology, or creed, or for any other such delusions. I am doing it because it is the only way left to restore science to a position of freedom and dignity, and to allow the human race a chance to cast off finally the yoke that is driving it toward total spiritual destruction. It seems to me ironically fitting that the cure for mass insanity should be the ultimate insanity.

"Gentlemen, you have repeatedly reaffirmed your obligations to counter the threat to the Western world that is posed by the alliance of nations and races pledged to destroy it. By powers vested in you, you have sought to compel my involvement in this. Very well—so be it. I will place at your disposal the means of eliminating that threat permanently. This time we will finish it. If I am to be involved, it will be this or nothing." He looked around the audience and finally let his eyes come to rest on Foreshaw. "That is the deal. Do you want me to go on?"

Foreshaw returned the look and drummed his fingers on the table for a long time before replying.

"I think you have to, Dr. Clifford," he said quietly at last.

"This had better be good," breathed a glowering, ruddy-faced Air Force general seated three places farther along to his right.

Clifford stepped forward and drew from a folder, lying on the table, a set of glossy, color computer prints, each measuring about a foot square. He held the top one up so that everybody could see the pattern of dull orange, from which a series of fuzzy, irregularly sized rectangles protruded upward against a background of black.

"The New York City skyline," he informed them simply. He handed the plate to Aub and indicated that it was to be passed around the table. It was followed by a whole series of familiar landmarks, geographic features and other oddments whose names he announced one by one before passing them on. They included the Rock of Gibraltar, Table Mountain, a cross section of the Dardanelles Strait, city profiles of London, Paris, Peking, Bombay, and Sydney; a picture of the eighty-mile-thick slab of oceanic crust of Earth's Pacific Plate plunging at the rate of seven centimeters per year down into the mantle beneath the Mariana Islands; a large iceberg in the Antarctic Ocean and a blob that represented the Americano-Russian *Cosmos V* space station, two thousand miles up.

Excitement and awe began to mount.

"Every one of those images was obtained at Sudbury, using the new Mark II system," Clifford stated. "And we should be able to improve on these examples. Once the correct coordinates have been computed, they can be stored and recalled instantly at any time. So much for target identification and fire control. Now for the weapon itself."

Clifford scanned the faces assembled before him, then continued. "You may remember that the principles by which these pictures are formed involve a new kind of wave that is generated inside any piece of matter and which propagates instantly throughout ordinary space. In recent experiments, we have succeeded in transporting energy from one place to another, using those same principles . . . at least, you can think of it that way. And in the same way that we can select information from any point we choose to construct those images, so we can select precisely where in space that energy will be delivered.

"Think what that means. In a thermonuclear explosion, the amount of nuclear material actually converted into energy is tiny—in the order of a fraction of 1 percent—and yet the results are devastating. In the process I am talking about, the effective conversion efficiency approaches 100 percent. From one central reactor capable of producing the power required, destructive forces of unprecedented strength can be instantaneously directed and focused on to any part of Earth's surface or beyond."

The stares that fixed him had by now frozen into wide-eyed masks of stunned incredulity. The silence, when he paused, was absolute.

"Furthermore, the means by which the target was being assailed would be completely undetectable by any surveillance or defensive system that exists in the world today. There is no method by which the weapons system I am describing could be interfered with or countered. Interception is impossible. As weapons of attack, the ICBM and the orbiting bomb are as outmoded as the battering ram."

A chorus of murmurings erupted from all around. Foreshaw waved for silence. "You're saying that from one single center, you could bomb any point on Earth's surface . . . without the enemy even knowing how you were doing it . . . without any way of anybody being able to stop you . . . ?" His face registered incredulity. "A superbomb that just comes from nowhere . . . ?"

Hughes stared aghast at Morelli as the words came home to him. "What are we getting into?" he asked above the rising hubbub of excited voices. "Has Brad gone mad?"

"First I knew about this," Morelli said, shaking his head, bemused. "I knew those two had something big . . . but this . . ."

"That's exactly what I'm saying," Clifford thundered above the clamor. "It'll not simply 'bomb' any point on Earth out of nowhere. . . . It'll annihilate it! And above Earth, too . . . It'll wipe out anything that comes inside a thousand miles of this country . . . and the other side will have no way of even knowing how we're doing it, let alone of stopping it. All their weapons and their numbers count for nothing now. That's how you can smash this deadlock. That's how you can smash it once and for all!"

When a semblance of order had returned to the room, Foreshaw had a question. "Dr. Clifford, what you've just told us sounds incredible. You are certain that a device of this nature could become a reality?"

"Quite certain."

"You can see no fundamental reason why it couldn't be built?"

"None." Clifford stood with his arms folded, composed and confident.

"What do you envisage it would take to do it?" Foreshaw asked.

"It would require a large power source to provide focusing energy—ideally a fusion reactor. There would be a matter-beam generating system feeding a black hole sustained in a more powerful and modified version of the Sudbury GRASER. For specific target location and fire control we'd need a detector arrangement bigger and better than the Mark II. I envisage that the Mark III detector system would require three BIACs running in parallel for adequate data processing and control."

"How long?" Foreshaw inquired.

Clifford had evidently come prepared. Without any hesitation, he replied, "If nothing was spared in making the requisite resources available, I estimate that the system could be operational in one year."

The four scientists from Sudbury stayed overnight in Washington and went back to the Pentagon next morning to answer further questions. Then they returned to Massachusetts while an advisory committee, specially convened by the President, examined the proposal and studied the report that Clifford had prepared. Ten days later they were summoned back to Washington to face the committee, restate the case, and answer more questions. In the afternoon they met the President.

Alexander George Sherman, President of the United States, rose from his chair at the table in the White House Cabinet Room and walked across to stand by the window. He stayed there for a long time, contemplating the scene outside, while he recapitulated again in his mind the things he had learned during the previous ten days. Behind him, still seated around the table, the four visitors from Sudbury, Vice President Donald Reyes, Defense Secretary William Foreshaw, and Secretary of State Melvin Chambers remained silent. At last the President pivoted on his heel and spoke to the room from where he was standing, addressing his words primarily to the four from ISF.

"Our latest intelligence reports and strategic forecasts do not paint a cheerful picture. The initiative is slowly but surely passing to the East, and once a critical point is reached, a major outbreak of hostilities will be inevitable. The only thing that would avert a full global war would be the granting of a long list of diplomatic, territorial, and political concessions by the West."

"That would be just the beginning," Chambers remarked. "Once you set any precedents like that, you simply get squeezed harder. The West would either be slowly reduced to complete impotence, or forced to fight it out later anyway, but on less favorable terms."

"Hardly a long-term answer, then," Peter Hughes commented.

"Precisely," Chambers nodded. "Appeasement is out."

"I must make a decision now," Sherman said to them. "I have three choices open to me. First—strike now, strike first, and strike hard while the balance is more or less even. The consequences of that would be catastrophic for the world whatever the final outcome, and I'm sure I don't have to spell them out. Second—I can do nothing. I can allow things to continue on their present course, in which case the end of free democracy as we understand it will be almost certain." He moved a pace back toward the table. "The third thing I can do is stake everything on this new weapon that will require a year to become a reality. But the world will not stop turning for our convenience. If I stake my bet that way, I naturally wouldn't want to run any risk of anything getting out of control during that year, before it was time to collect the winnings. In other words I'd be obliged to make whatever concessions the other side demanded. At the end of that year, if the bet didn't pay and the weapon turned out to be a dud, I'd have allowed the whole world situation to tip against us, irreversibly, and I'd have nothing to show for it. If that happened, things could only snowball for the worse after that." He walked back to his chair, sat down and regarded the others soberly.

"The third choice sounds like a big gamble," he said. "What evidence can you offer me to justify my taking it?"

Silence reigned for a while. The circle of faces stared grimly at the table. At last, Clifford quietly supplied the answer. "You have nothing whatsoever to lose by it."

"How so, Dr. Clifford?" Sherman asked.

"The weapon can either work or not work," Clifford replied. "If it works, it can either be used or not used. If it's used, it can either succeed or fail." He swept his eyes round the table. "The logical consequences of those statements are that there is nothing to lose. If it doesn't work or isn't used, the result is no different from that of choice two. If it's used but fails, the result is no worse than the worst-case of choice one. Either way, the West loses in the long term. . . . The only alternative to that is if the weapon is used and succeeds, and the only way of making that a possibility is to select choice three."

Clifford and his colleagues stayed that night in Washington while the President and his staff conferred. The next day they returned to the White House to meet Sherman, Reyes, Foreshaw, and Chambers in the Cabinet Room again.

"The decision is *Go*," Sherman informed them. "You have first priority for whatever equipment, materials, personnel, funds, or other resources you need. Code name for the project is *Jericho*. It will commence at once. As I mentioned yesterday, we may be forced to make unpalatable decisions in the course of the next year or so; therefore our Western allies will have to be informed of the reasons."

Even before the ISF scientists had left the White House, some of the presidential advisers had already dubbed the new weapon the *J-bomb*.

On the plane back to Boston that night, Clifford's mood was one of grim satisfaction. Aub, for once, seemed subdued and withdrawn.

"What's the matter?" Clifford asked him. "It's what you've always said you wanted, isn't it—unlimited government funds and resources. Why doesn't it taste so good now?"

Chapter 20

Once it had received official approval and been accorded highest priority, Jericho swung into motion with frightening speed. Home of the project was to be a place called Brunnermont, a complex of concrete and steel levels that went down for over a mile into solid rock beneath the Appalachians and which had originally been designed and built as a self-sufficient, bombproof survival center for VIPs and as a communications and command headquarters.

Here the thermonuclear power plant that had been designed to keep Brunnermont functioning for decades if need be was modified and pressed into service to feed the fearsome beam of concentrated matter into the new reactor. A level above the generators and the reactor, in a specially redesigned and sealed off top-security zone, the Mark III fire-control and direction system slowly began to take shape. Above that was installed a full-scale strategic command nerve center linked into the network of global surveillance, defense, strike and counterstrike systems, integrated command centers and war rooms of all the Western allied nations.

During the early months, Taiwan was invaded and occupied without opposition from the West, apart from routine protests and denunciations. After a series of large-scale battles on the borders of India, appeals for Western support and intervention failed to produce any decisive response. Encouraged by this demonstration of apathy or indifference, political subversion and agitation in that country rose to new heights of activity and found many receptive ears among a people who saw only impotence and betrayal beneath the ideology preached by their own government and its friends. Six months after the commencement of Jericho, the whole of India was engulfed in a bitter and savage civil war. Hard-pressed at the front and harassed from the rear, the border armies fell back to the Indus Basin in the west and to Calcutta in the east. Predictably the war had now become a "struggle for the liberation of the oppressed peoples of India," as the slogans of 1992 were once again shouted around the world. Air attacks on Indian cities became everyday news items; Calcutta burned under encircling laser siege-artillery; Bombay, Madras, and a score of other ports were blockaded by mine and submarine; famine and disease claimed hundreds of thousands. The West did nothing.

The time came for those scientists from the Institute who had volunteered for and been accepted to work on Jericho to bid farewell to Sudbury. With their families they were moved into the residential sector of the Brunnermont complex, where schooling, hospital care, recreation, entertainment, and all the other requisites of the modern style of living were provided. They came to accept as normal ingredients in their lives the discipline, the tight security measures and the isolation from society that Brunnermont demanded. They became a self-contained society-in-miniature of their own, charged with the custody of the greatest secret of all time, and sealed off from the world of prying eyes and ears by the electronically guarded three-mile-deep perimeter zone, the Marine Corps and Ranger squads that flitted like phantoms among the greenery of the surrounding hills, the gun pits that covered the approach roads and the silent, probing radar fingers that searched the skies above.

The roles of Clifford and Aub somehow became interchanged. Aub, once the epitome of enthusiasm and energy, had grown reserved and apprehensive, fearful of this thing that had intruded upon and was now taking over their lives. Clifford became the tireless driving force, dominating the project and sparing nothing and nobody in his relentless determination to meet ever more demanding schedules. Everything he had ever been and everything he had once stood for seemed to have been sacrificed to the voracious and insatiable new god that was taking possession of his being.

Like an immense iceberg, the larger part of the Brunnermont complex lay submerged deep in the Precambrian heart of the Appalachian mountains with just its tip breaking the surface. From the air this tip had much of the appearance of a scenically sculptured ultramodern village, with knife-edge-styled houses, chalets, and communal buildings clustered but secluded amid a carefully balanced setting of trees, shrubs, pathways, and lawns, broken by the occasional ornamental pool or flower bed. All this was intended more to relieve the harshness of the reality that lay below ground for the colony of inhabitants and to make some concession to their need for psychological relaxation than to conceal the nature of the establishment. Even the most amateur photographic interpreters would soon have noticed the impenetrable perimeter defenses, the ramps down which the access roads descended to subterranean destinations protected by steel doors and the disproportionately high volume of aerial and road traffic that constantly arrived and departed—though these things would reveal nothing of the installation's true purpose.

One evening, some months after their arrival at Brunnermont, Aub and Sarah were strolling among the trees in a shady corner of the so-called village, enjoying the scents and the freshness carried down from the hills on the first cool breezes of autumn. Had it been another time, another place, it would have been a dreamland. As things were, their mood was heavy and strained.

"Why did it all have to turn out this way, Aub?" Sarah asked, after several minutes of silence.

"Mmm. What?"

"You, me, Brad . . . us. This thing that's happened. I mean . . . I know what's happened . . . but I still don't really understand why."

"Yeah . . . I know what you mean." The ebullient Aub of earlier days was gone.

"I was thinking about it all earlier today," she said, kicking a stone absently. "How different it all used to be. Do you remember when you first came marching into our house, the one we had in New Mexico . . . the day that Brad quit that job at ACRE? We never laugh now the way we used to laugh then. . . . You and Brad used to get drunk every night . . . we all went out together. Remember?"

"I remember."

"What happened to those three people?"

Aub stared at the ground in front of his slowly pacing feet as he sought a reply that would neither hurt nor deceive.

"I guess . . . they had to grow up sometime."

"But it's not a question of growing up, is it? We were always grown-up enough; that wasn't so very long ago. It's more of a change. Brad has changed. He isn't the Brad we used to know any more. And his changing is making us change. I thought I knew him, Aub, but I don't. I don't know what made him change so suddenly."

They stopped and stared out across the pool to which the path had led them On the porch of a chalet on the opposite side somebody was bobbing gently back and forth in a rocking chair. The strains of pop music came floating across the water.

"He's doing the only thing he can to preserve the way of life he believes in, I suppose," Aub said. "At least, that's how he sees it."

"But it's not what he believes in. He's never wanted any part of all this before. He'd have died first. He always said that one human life was too much to

pay for all the causes in the world put together. That
was the Brad I knew. And now . . ." she cast an arm
about her to take in their whole surroundings, "this.
Everything you can see is part of one huge, horrible
machine that's being built for the sole purpose of
slaughtering people by the millions. And Brad has done
it all." She raised a hand to her lips and bit her
knuckle.

"Yeah, I know," Aub said quietly. "C'mon, let's
move on. It's getting chilly."

They walked on, taking a fork in the path that led
toward the warm, homely glow among the shrubbery
that marked the position of the bar and social club.

"What about you?" she asked. "You don't seem
happy about the whole thing either, and yet you still
play a big part in it. Why, Aub? Why do you choose
to stay mixed up in it?"

"Why don't I just quit?"

"If you like."

He scratched his head for a moment and pulled a
face.

"Well . . . I suppose I don't really have much of a
choice any more. When I signed the papers to join
Jericho, they said it was for the duration. Even if I
decided I didn't want to work on the project any
longer, I can't see my being let out to walk the streets,
not knowing what I know now. So . . ." he shrugged,
"might as well press on. At least I'm busy. Guess I'd
go nuts otherwise."

They stopped again outside the clubhouse. Dance
music from Brunnermont's own Marine combo was
coming through the open window.

"Is that really the only reason?" she asked. Aub
reflected for a while.

"Not really," he admitted. "There is something
else . . . kinda difficult to put into words, you know.
It's just that I still feel the old Brad down there under-
neath somewhere. I just can't see him letting Jericho
be used for real. Somehow there has to be a big bluff
behind all his bravado . . . something he's figured out

that he hasn't told even me about. All the time I was feeding him the dope on what was happening at Berkeley, he never once let me get implicated . . . and we didn't really know each other then. But he came across right from the start as the kinda guy you can trust—know what I mean? I felt I could trust him then, and I was right. It may sound crazy, but I still feel I can now."

"If you knew how much I needed to hear you say that." A shadow of her old smile brightened her face a fraction. "Come on—let's go inside. I'll allow you to buy me a drink and, if you're very good, to have the honor of a dance."

Chapter 21

One year and one month had gone by since Jericho was conceived. Deep in its rocky womb the fetus was now fully formed, its nuclear heart beating strongly. A miniature flying armada from Washington converged on Brunnermont, bringing the fathers to witness the birth.

In fact, a number of test firings of the J-bomb had already been successfully made; this was to be the first to be at all public.

As a prelude, Morelli conducted the deputation of Pentagon officials and Army, Navy, and Air Force senior officers on a guided tour of the restricted, lowermost levels of the complex. He showed them the duplicated system of fusion reactors and generating equipment, capable of sustaining all the machines in Brunnermont independently of outside sources of power for years, although under normal circumstances demands could be met from the national distribution grid. He explained that the amount of matter that was actually fed via the beam into the annihilation chamber of the J-reactor was really quite small; it was the technique employed for modulating, controlling, and focusing the delivery of the return energy through hispace—in order to achieve adequate accuracy of aiming the weapon—that required such enormous amounts of power.

The visitors inspected the battery of accelerators and massive electromagnets inside which the beam originated and followed the transmission tube, wreathed in its elaborate sheath of coils and coolant pipes, that conveyed it into the sphere of the J-reactor itself—there to be somehow squeezed by forces they were unable to comprehend out of the very universe. The party's mood grew somber. Hardened as these men were by daily exposure to the harsh realities of systematically engineered methods of mass destruction, they found themselves daunted and apprehensive as the full meaning of the things they saw on every side percolated through to their understanding.

Finally they saw the "brain" by which the entire operation of this awesome ensemble was coordinated and directed—the computer room where the three mighty BIACs (mighty in performance, that is; each machine occupied just two six-foot-high cabinets) presided over several hundred assorted slave processors and cubicle after cubicle of attendant electronics.

The operation of every component and subsystem that went to make up this aggregate was controlled ultimately from a single nerve center designated simply CONTROL ROOM. Here where all the data and control channels from every part of the vast machine were finally brought together in tiers of instrument panels and monitor screens, and where the command interface with the BIACs was situated. From here, every facet of system operation—control of the reactors and generator banks, beam modulation, target identification and location, direction of the fire-control computers—was orchestrated by just two human operators. The Control Room could, in an emergency, be sealed off from the inside, and with it the critical sections of the weapons system. Thus, regardless of what went on in other parts of the Brunnermont complex, unimpaired operation of Jericho could be guaranteed at any time.

The raised gallery that gave access to the Control Room looked down over the panorama of the Operational Command Floor—the new war room of the Western Democratic Alliance. In this brightly illuminated setting ' of communications consoles and thickly carpeted surgical cleanliness, enormous mural displays presented the global picture that was revealed from the combined inputs of a network of orbital and ground-based surveillance systems, the interconnected radar and early-warning chains of a score of nations, high-flying robot drones above the Siberian tundra and the Gobi Desert, and ships dotted all the way from Spitsbergen to the Ross Sea. From these surroundings of superficial calm and tranquillity, the integrated war machine of the Western powers could be unleashed in minutes. This was where the men from Washington and the observers sent by the governments of Europe, Russia, Australia, and Japan eventually assembled to see the end-product of Jericho in action.

Clifford and Aub had taken up their positions inside the Control Room, leaving Morelli to attend to the guests. While Morelli was describing the various facilities that were available on the Operational Command Floor, they put the system through a routine checkout drill. Everything was working fine.

The first item on the agenda was a demonstration of the resolving power of the Mark III detector to show how it was used for target registration; also it would give the spectators an insight to the meaning of dynamic real-time control via BIAC interaction between the operator and the machine.

"Just to recap for a moment on some of the things I said earlier, every piece of matter in the universe gives rise to hi-radiation that appears instantly at every point in space." Morelli spoke in a loud voice to make sure that his words carried to the back of the crowd of attentive faces arrayed before him. "Right at this moment, hi-radiation is pervading this room—radiation that is being generated in the mass of Earth, on the Sun, in Jupiter, in every star in our galaxy and every galaxy in the universe." He turned slowly to take in the fascinated expressions all around.

"This hi-radiation that originates from objects large and small, near and far, can be made to produce a measurable response by means of the instrument that you have just seen. The intensity of this radiation falls off rapidly with distance from its source, in spite of its traveling instantly between points in ordinary space, but it does carry information from which certain characteristics of the source object can be reconstructed. The amount of information that comes from each source also becomes less the farther away the source is.

"This means that although the detector in theory receives hi-wave information from every object in the universe at the same time, in practice the amount that is contributed from beyond comparatively small distances . . . at our present state of the art, a couple of hundred thousand miles or so . . . is so small that you can neglect it. There are exceptions to that—for instance the Sun and some other bodies appear abnormally 'bright' for their distance—but by and large what I've said is true. Any questions so far?"

"Just one." The speaker was a tall, swarthy man wearing the uniform of a Vice Marshal of the United States of Europe Air Force. "If I remember correctly, you said earlier that this hi-radiation that exists everywhere gives rise to conventional background energy by a process which, I believe, you called 'secondary interactions.' This background is immeasurably small even on Earth, because by astronomical standards Earth is really very tiny."

"Yes. That's correct."

"Fine. Does this mean then that near other, much more massive astronomical bodies, you would see greater amounts of background radiation . . . ones that were readily measurable?"

"Precisely so, and it does happen," Morelli responded. "In fact, the black holes in space have very intense radiation halos. This could never be explained by classical physics, and was one of the things that led to k-theory being recognized in the first place."

"I see. Thank you."

There were no further questions, so Morelli resumed his lecture. "The detector, then, responds to hi-waves that originate, to all intents and purposes exclusively, from objects situated in the nearby regions of space. Now, by using very sophisticated computer-processing techniques, we are able to extract from the information they carry, sufficient data to single out one portion of the composite hi-wave signal . . . we can zoom in, if you will, on any region that we care to select out of the whole volume in space that the total signal is coming from. Within limits, that region can be as large or as small as we like. Moreover, from the information that we have extracted, we can derive spacelike solutions to the equations involved, which enable internal and external visual representations of the selected object to be constructed."

"Another question, Professor Morelli," a voice called from the back.

"Yes?"

"What are the limits that you mentioned? What range of sizes of object can you resolve?"

"At the small end it gets worse the farther away the object is . . . also, don't forget, what we're really seeing is a measure of the difference in mass-density between the object and its surroundings. We're not looking at any kind of optically generated image, so you won't see normal visual contrasts and details. What you will see are contrasts in density.

"But to answer your question—if you swallowed a .22 caliber lead bullet, we could pick it up if you were standing a mile away. For an object sitting on the other side of the world—somewhere in the southern Indian Ocean, say—if it were solid steel standing up in air, we could go down to a size of, aw, twenty, twenty-five feet. So, you see, we could identify a tank.

"At the big end, well, we're only limited by the effective range of the detector itself . . . in other words, its sensitivity, since the signals from places that are farther away get smaller. But as I said earlier, there are some quite strong radiators a long way away. Up until about a year ago we did start to make pictures of things such as the Sun—nothing detailed, all you saw were smudges—but that was with an earlier model of the detector. The one we've got here would do a lot better, but I guess we've been too tied up with other things to bother much about taking it further."

A muttering of interest arose as some of the listeners realized for the first time the full potency of the system, if only as a means of surveillance, never mind as a weapon.

"Let's now have a look at some of the things I've been talking about," Morelli said. He gestured upward toward one of the huge screens above the floor. "This screen is coupled to slave off of the main BIAC monitor display in the Control Room. On it you will see an enlarged copy of what the BIAC operator can project on to his own console. Ready, Brad?" He addressed his last words to Clifford, who, he knew, was following events on one of the monitor screens in the Control Room.

"Ready." Clifford's voice came over the loudspeaker system above the Command Floor. An auxiliary screen, set below and to one side of the main display, showed the two operators in the room above.

"I'll hand the demonstration over to Bradley Clifford at this point, then," Morelli informed the group. "Brad, over to you. I'll leave you to do your own commentating. Okay?"

"Okay." Almost at once the main display came to life to show the hazy but unmistakable outline of a ship. It was positioned roughly halfway up the screen and was shown broadside; its bulk could be seen clearly floating in the ghostly haze produced by the water. "I've been tracking this ship for the past few minutes now, while Al was talking," Clifford's voice announced. "It's in the eastern part of the North Atlantic, between the Azores and the Bay of Biscay. If you want the exact position it is fifteen degrees thirty-six minutes west, forty-two degrees ten minutes north, course two hundred sixty-one degrees, speed thirty-five knots. From the general outline it's obviously a fairly large carrier, almost certainly one that's involved in the exercises being held in that area this week. If you watch closely, you will see a small dot rise from the left-hand end from time to time. These are aircraft being launched at this instant . . . there goes one now."

The audience had been well prepared with what to expect, but even so, gasps of astonishment and surprise rose around the floor.

"If I close in a little . . ." the shape rapidly enlarged, "you should just be able to make out details of the internal structure. In particular, note the brighter parts midships and toward the stern. These are the densest parts of the structure—the engines and propulsion machinery. You may be able to see also just the faintest hairlines of brightness inside the midships engine room. I'm pretty sure that the vessel is nuclear-powered and that those are fuel rods in its reactor. Note also the pinpoints in several compartments farther forward—probably fissile material contained in nuclear warheads that are parts of weapons included in the ship's armory."

The effect upon the watchers of actually being able to gaze inside a ship sailing on the high seas three thousand miles away was overwhelming. To a man they just stood and stared as coherent speech refused to come to their lips. Clifford's lazy, matter-of-fact drawl seemed only to add somehow to the effect.

"Another aircraft is just taking off. This time we'll follow it." A finger of pale orange, larger than the dots seen previously because of the enlarged view, detached itself from the bow of the carrier. The view closed in on the aircraft and the ship slid rapidly off the bottom edge of the screen. It seemed to gyrate around in space as the viewpoint altered to project it from all angles, finally zooming in to reveal the finely tapered nose and triangular wings.

"Again, the engines show up more distinctively than the rest of the structure," Clifford commented. "Also, it doesn't show up on the screen but I can see through the BIAC a slightly darker cone extending back from the tail. That is the result of the lower density of the exhaust gases. From the data contained in that pattern, we could compute the running temperature of the engines and make a fair guess as to what kind they are." He allowed them a few more seconds to watch the still-climbing aircraft before speaking again.

"You will have noticed that we are managing to track steadily a target that is now moving quite fast. What may not be apparent is that this is all being done completely automatically, without requiring any kind of continuous participation by either of us in here. When I made the decision to follow this target aircraft, I issued a command to the BIAC to lock on and track, using procedural routines that it has already learned. At this moment neither I nor my colleague here, Aubrey Philipsz, is interacting or communicating with the system in any way whatsoever. But as you can see, the target is being tracked and displayed faithfully."

Clifford began warming to his subject, and his voice took on a measure of excitement. "In fact, the system is capable of automatically following thousands of discrete, independent objects simultaneously, objects distributed anywhere within its range of operation. Moreover, I could instruct the machine to inform me when any of those objects reaches some predetermined point in its course—for example, the aircraft that you see is flying eastward now, toward the French coast; I could deposit an instruction to be informed if and when it gets inside one hundred miles of the shore; until that happens, the machine will do all the necessary work and I can forget about it. Similarly, I could command a general surveillance routine, whereby I would be informed of any aircraft or object entering French airspace . . . not just specific targets that I have previously identified, such as the one on the screen. In both those examples, I could, instead of being simply informed, program for the targets to be destroyed automatically. So too for all the other targets that the system is capable of tracking and detecting.

"You will appreciate therefore, gentlemen, that the surveillance and weapons-guidance capabilities of this machine are in no way limited to the number of events that one human brain can keep track of at any one time. The machine can make most of its decisions for itself, using generalized criteria that I give it. If you like, its functions include the duties of a whole regiment of staff officers."

Clifford then proceeded to conjure up a series of images of places and events taking place all over Earth, which included several examples of the automated facilities he had described. He finished the session by capturing the image of two U.S. spacecraft carrying out a prearranged docking maneuver while in orbit. While this was being shown on the main display, an adjacent screen provided a conventional view of the same sequence, which was picked up by a TV camera aboard one of the craft and transmitted down through the normal channels. The difference was that the conventional picture required a camera to be up there, on the scene of the event; the J-scope didn't.

Then it was Morelli's turn to speak again.

"So much for how we can guide the weapon. Now let us see exactly what the weapon itself can do.

"Hi-radiation gives rise to a secondary effect—conventional radiant energy that exists as a halo around every object you can name. For most objects this secondary radiation is so tiny that it exists more as a mathematical abstraction than anything you could hope to measure . . . but it's there." The faces were by now tense and expectant as the moment of seeing in action the weapon they had heard about for so long drew nearer.

Morelli continued. "In the J-reactor, we in effect amplify enormously what takes place in ordinary matter. The process causes secondary energy to materialize as a halo, which is most intense in the immediate vicinity of the reactor but extends outward . . . getting thinner all the time . . . throughout all of space. Now, the important thing to bear in mind is this. . . ." He paused for a moment to add emphasis. "Although the secondary energy is denser around the reactor, the *amount* of it is only a small fraction of the total—"

"I'm not quite with you there, Professor," one of the listeners came in. "Could you clarify that please?"

"Think of it as heat," Morelli suggested. "A red-hot needle is at a high temperature, but doesn't hold much heat. The water in the boilers of a power station is not as hot, but it contains a far larger *amount* of heat. Using that analogy, the energy in the vicinity of the reactor is more intense . . . 'hotter,' but when you add up all the 'colder' energy that's distributed all through billions of cubic light-years of space, you find that the *amount* is greater. In other words, forget the 'temperature'; most of the energy—most by far—that the reactor produces is spread out thinly across space . . . when you add it all up. Is that clearer?"

"Thank you, yes." .

"Fine." Morelli took a long breath. "The situation I've just described applies when the reactor is running with the focusing system switched off. By bringing the focusing system in, we can force all of that energy to materialize not all through space, but concentrated inside one tiny volume. One way of visualizing it is to imagine the mass consumed in the reactor as being converted into its energy equivalent and instantly appearing elsewhere. The effect is the same as that of a hydrogen bomb that suddenly appears out of nowhere. A big difference is that the mass conversion can be a lot higher than in an H-bomb, so we can produce effects far more devastating . . . not that there'd be a lot of point in that."

Morelli turned and gazed expectantly up at the main display. Scores of pairs of eyes followed his, tense . . . waiting.

This time the screen showed a normal TV transmission. It was a view from the air, looking down from high altitude on a desolate Arctic waste of snow, bleak rocky shorelines, inlets of sea and ice floes, with a range of broken, jagged mountains visible in the middle distance. An unfamiliar voice came over the loudspeaker.

"This is Foxtrot Five to Bluebird Control. Altitude fifty thousand feet, on course, target range two-two miles, bearing one-six-zero degrees. All systems checking positive."

Another voice replied:

"Bluebird Control. Dead on time Foxtrot Five. Maintain course and follow Plan Baker Two. Repeat —Baker Two. Redsox reports you're on the air now. Reception good. Countdown on schedule. Acknowledge."

"Foxtrot Five acknowledging. Wilco—Baker Two."

"You are looking at an area reserved as a military testing ground on Somerset Island, in the far north of Canada," Clifford's voice informed them. "The view is being sent back from an Air Force RB6 flying clear of the target area. The target is the high peak located near the center of the group now in the center of the picture. You might just be able to see a small patch of red against the background just above and slightly to the right of the target peak. That's a large marker balloon for visual identification.

"Back here, we have been starting up the reactor's beam energizers. I am about to switch on the beam into the J-reactor. . . ." A pause of a few seconds followed. "Not far below where you are standing, the beam is now on—pouring energy out across the universe. I have already preset the space coordinates of the target into the programs that are running in the fire-control computers. All I have to do now is activate the focusing modulators to direct the return energy on to some specific point. As soon as I do that, the fire-control programs will take over, and direct the concentrated energy to the coordinates supplied."

He waited for a moment, allowing time for the suspense to build up. "I am priming the focusing system to self-activate automatically and slave to the fire control programs ten seconds from . . . now." A numerical display, superimposed upon the target picture, appeared and began reeling off the seconds.

Nine . . . Eight . . . seven . . .

"Note that from now on I play no further part. All operations are automatic."

Three . . . two . . . one . . .

The whole room gasped in unison. The entire central portion of the mountain range instantly vanished in a brilliant blaze of pure whiteness. The familiar, sinister shape of a slowly swelling and rising fireball rose up out of the maelstrom that erupted where the whiteness had been. A writhing, swirling column of fire and vapors climbed up through the clouds and began spreading outward to form a boiling canopy that blotted out the surrounding landscape.

"Holy Moses, what was that?" yelled the voice of Foxtrot Five.

"Search me," came another voice on the circuit. "Musta been a ground burst. There was nothing coming in on radar."

"Cut the cackle, Foxtrot Five. You're still alive."

"Wilco."

In the next half-hour, Clifford repeated the performance on a series of other preprepared targets, including the burned-out shell of a shuttle booster that had been orbiting high above Earth for over ten years. In each case the results were as spectacular as the first. The shuttle booster demonstration showed that Jericho could be controlled right down to destructive levels that were far lower than the minimum unleashed by a thermonuclear explosion; it was vaporized in the equivalent of less than one hundred tons of TNT.

For his finale, Clifford brought up views of five different targets on separate screens, the locations being scattered across hundreds of miles of Arctic wilderness. Then he announced that, as already prearranged, ten dummy warheads would be launched toward various parts of the North American continent from orbiting space vehicles simulating ORBS satellites. As the mock attack was set in motion, the trajectories of the warheads were reported on an additional screen hooked into the regular tracking network.

"The fire-control computers have been fed the co-ordinates of the ground targets," he announced. "They are also being updated continually with the instant-to-instant positions of the incoming missiles, which are now being tracked automatically by the surveillance system. What I am about to do is activate the focusing system and set the fire-control routine to direct the weapon on to each of the targets in turn. It will fire on each target for exactly one millionth of a second. Focus will activate ten seconds from . . . now."

The countdown ticked by in a way that was by now familiar.

As *zero* flashed up, all five targets exploded together; at the same instant all traces of the attacking missile salvo were lost. The action had been effortless.

A stunned silence had taken over the room. Ashen faces registered the dawning of the first full realizations of what all this meant. The five menacing mushrooms were still spreading across the screens when Clifford's voice sounded again, still cool and dispassionate.

"Allow me to put what you have just seen into perspective. In the last demonstration, the J-reactor was operating at low power only, and the exposure time per target was one microsecond. With moderate power and a longer exposure, it would be perfectly feasible to wipe out a large city. Simple calculations show that, without taxing the system, one hundred selected enemy cities could, once the relevant coordinates had been fed into the fire-control programs, be totally destroyed in just over one hundredth of a second."

Hardly a word was spoken as one by one the screens went blank and the machines were shut down. Clifford emerged from the Control Room and looked down from the raised gallery over the silent upturned faces. His cheeks were hollow from the strain of more than a year of unbroken work, his eyes dark-rimmed from lack of sleep.

"You demanded my knowledge and my skills to be harnessed for the ends of war," he said. "You have them."

He said no more. There was nothing more to say.

Chapter 22

After testing the intentions of the West with nearly twelve months of escalating provocation, the Eastern Alliance nations had satisfied themselves that no serious attempts would be forthcoming to frustrate their designs in India. The Afrab and Chinese forces fighting on the frontiers, committed originally to defend the so-called People's Uprising, gradually assumed the role of regular armies of invasion. The internecine squabbles within the Indian nation were forgotten as rival civil factions united and turned to face the common threat, but by that time the country's cohesive power was draining fast.

Afrab armies took over all of the northwest plains and advanced southward to occupy the Kathiawar Peninsula, little more than two hundred miles from Bombay. In the east, the Chinese reached the delta of the Mahanadi River, and pushed along the basin of the Ganges to take Lucknow and Kanpur. Delhi was thus left precariously between the closing jaws of the pincer with both of its main arteries of communication severed, all the time becoming more isolated as the potential source of relief was compressed into the southern half of the subcontinent.

By then every armed satellite deployed by the West was being marked by at least two hostile shadowers. The strategic calculations of the Eastern bloc showed a tip in the balance that would preclude the West from so much as contemplating an all-out conflict, and developments in India seemed to confirm it.

The Vladivostok government declared its commitment to a crusade for the reunification of Siberia and Russia, denouncing the Moscow regime as unrepresentative. A mood of defeatism swept across Europe as Euro-Russian and Siberian armies clashed with renewed ferocity west of the Urals. The Afrabs struck northward from Iraq into the Caucasus; Americans and Europeans counterattacked from eastern Turkey.

The world braced itself.

Alexander George Sherman, President of the United States and cosignatory to the Alliance of Western Democracies, sipped approvingly at his whiskey and allowed his head to sink back into the luxurious leather padding of one of the armchairs facing the fireplace in the sitting room that adjoined the presidential study. The eyes that looked over the rim of his glass at the guest sitting opposite bore the marks of the burden of Atlas. And yet the expression in those eyes was calm and composed, mellowed by the compassion that comes with maturity and the wisdom of a thousand years.

"The provocations to which we are being subjected might seem to constitute a clear-cut justification for using the J-bomb without restriction," he said. "I am satisfied that were I to give the word, our enemies would be completely and utterly crushed within an hour. However, I must consider not only the heat of the moment today, but also the cool that will come when the world looks back from tomorrow."

Bradley Clifford tasted his own drink and looked back without speaking.

"The emotions that tempt us toward acting impulsively, however real they might be now, will soon be forgotten," Sherman continued. "History would never condone the indiscriminate use of a weapon of this kind, whatever the circumstances. If the West is to survive as the defender of all the things it has always claimed to stand for, it must uphold its principles even in war. It cannot and must not permit itself to precipitate the wholesale slaughter of civilians by this means, or to embark on an orgy of mass destruction by methods against which there can be no defense."

"But the deadlock has to be broken," Clifford replied at last. "Without an imbalance, it must remain a deadlock permanently."

"Yes, I agree with you. Clearly it would be absurd for us to concede any form of parity with the East now; your weapon should enable us to dictate any terms we choose. What I'm really saying is that the message is so obvious that there should be no need for us to let loose a worldwide holocaust to spell it out. I have conferred with our allies on this, and they agree. Europe, Australia, and Japan feel the same way; the Russians are all for going straight in with the bomb, but they're outvoted."

"I understand, of course," Clifford said. "But what did you have in mind as an alternative—some kind of token demonstration?"

Sherman shook his head slowly, apparently having been expecting the suggestion. "Mmm . . . no. We did discuss such a possibility, but we came to the conclusion that even that would be too risky. You see, Dr. Clifford, the kind of people we are up against are, shall we say, unpredictable. Much of the Eastern world has plunged straight from the Stone Age into the twenty-first century, without having any of the time to adjust in the same way the Western nations did— but even in the case of the West, the transition was far from easy. Many of their leaders still think and react in the manner of tribesmen rather than statesmen; that was why the UN collapsed and why any form of rational negotiation has been impossible for the last twenty years or more.

"But these people now possess enormous arsenals of the most sophisticated weapons systems known—apart from this latest, of course. It took our own experts a long time to realize the full implications of the bomb.

The problem with a demonstration is that our adversaries might react first and think afterward; they might see it as a bluff and try to call it. If they did, we could end up taking a lot of casualties on our own side before we convinced them, and that's the one thing I'm here to prevent if I can. I know that it looks as if the J-bomb would neutralize anything they tried to do, but we haven't actually proved that yet. Until we're more sure of that, I think we have to keep the element of surprise as an added insurance. That's one advantage that it would be foolish to sacrifice prematurely."

Clifford sipped his drink again and nodded slowly. None of this came very much as a surprise. He thought he knew what would follow next, but chose not to interrupt.

The President leaned forward and rested an elbow on the arm of his chair. "What I wanted to ask you about was the feasibility of using the J-bomb for a no-holds-barred surprise strike, but selectively. We want to be able to knock out the offensive capability of the other side in a single, lightning blow, especially the means of delivering any form of retaliation against our own territories. If we could first of all, without warning, eliminate their ORBS system, ICBM sites, and missile subs before they even knew what was happening, then it wouldn't really matter how irrationally they react, since they would no longer be in a position to do anything drastic.

"After that, if they saw sense, the whole thing would be over and only purely military targets would have been attacked. If they still refused to buy it, we'd just keep hammering at their ground forces wherever they're engaged in offensive actions against us until they did. Once again, the targets would be military; there'd be no mass killings of civilians, and we could take all the time in the world since there would be no threat to our own population or to our cities." He sat back and waited for a reply.

"That would be no problem," was all Clifford had

to say. He made the destruction of the military might of half the world sound like a simple matter of pest control.

"Easy, huh?" Sherman could not contain a thin smile as he gazed with a strange mixture of fascination and admiration at the young man, barely half his own age, who was casually accepting the challenge to take on virtually single-handed a thousand million fanatics equipped with every device of devilment that the armorers of modern warfare could provide.

"I wasn't meaning to be flippant," Clifford answered with sincerity. "I know what the machine is capable of, and what you ask is well within its limits. Have I ever failed to deliver anything once I've promised it?"

"No, you never have, and I don't think you ever would. You're not the kind of person who would promise something he didn't mean to deliver in the first place. So—I can carry on from here on the assumption that it's feasible?"

"You can."

Sherman caught the curious inflexion of the scientist's voice.

"You agree to being instrumental in the execution of a strategic plan along the lines I've just indicated," he stated, just to be sure.

"I didn't say that," Clifford replied quietly. "I said you could carry on and assume it's feasible."

Sherman looked at him with a suddenly puzzled frown as, for a few seconds, he backtracked mentally over the most recent part of the conversation. He was suddenly a trifle suspicious.

"Let's make certain we understand one another, Dr. Clifford. Exactly what is it that you are promising to deliver?"

"What I've always promised—an end to the power deadlock that is destroying this world."

"And exactly how do you see that being achieved?"

A long time seemed to pass while Clifford returned an unblinking stare. "I can't be any more frank than

I am being right now," he said, in barely more than a whisper that seemed to add to its firmness.

The eyes of the two men met and in a brief moment an indefinable understanding flowed between them that could not have been expressed in a thousand words. Sherman gazed into the unwavering stare of absolute composure, instinctively seeking to divine the purpose that the extraordinary mind behind was unable to disclose. He became acutely conscious that only a quirk of fate gave him the right to question and command a brain that could comprehend and harness the workings of mysterious realms of time and space that no man before had even suspected to exist. Could he presume to be the infallible arbiter of its deepest workings? For a long time his instincts grappled with the objectiveness and caution demanded by his office.

"I could rule that we don't use it at all," he said eventually.

"Then you would have won your gamble of a year ago, without collecting any winnings."

Another long silence ensued. The sound of the clock on the mantle above the fireplace and the subdued hum of the air conditioner became noticeable for the first time. The noise of a low-flying vehicle came from the darkness outside the window.

"Let me ask you a hypothetical question," the President said. "If you had a free hand to use the J-bomb in any way that you pleased and you set out to achieve the objective that you have specified by whatever means you consider it requires, would the situation that you visualize involve any unnecessary loss of life to any citizen of this country or of its allies, or the acceptance of any casualties that could be avoided by other means?"

"No."

"Would it entail any form of indiscriminate use against the civilian populations of hostile belligerents?"

"No."

Sherman took a deep breath and set his glass down on a small side table.

"If the people who elected me could hear what I'm going to say next, they'd probably kick me out of office without a second thought," he said. "I am not going to demand an explanation of what has been implied. I'm going to forget that we even said it."

Clifford remained expressionless and said nothing. The President thought to himself for a while before resuming.

"Earlier this evening it was reported that the Chinese and Afrab forces in northern India have begun using nuclear weapons on a limited scale in certain key areas. The Indians are retaliating in kind. Undoubtedly this will spread and escalate if things are left to run their course.

"It was agreed between myself and the heads of allied governments less than three hours ago that we would issue a joint ultimatum calling upon the invading forces to cease hostilities in all theaters and to withdraw immediately to the recognized international frontiers. This ultimatum will almost certainly be rejected, at which point it was our intention to proceed immediately with the first phase of our selective strategy I described—an instant J-bomb strike at their means of nuclear retaliation.

"Now, going back to our hypothetical situation, if you were free to use the weapon in the way that you visualize, would there be any reason for me to change my mind? Would there be any reason for me not to convey to the allied governments confirmation of my intent to endorse the ultimatum as planned?"

"No reason at all," Clifford replied. "In fact, if that were the position, it would be important that you did."

Chapter 23

TO
THE REPRESENTATIVES OF
THE GRAND ALLIANCE OF
PROGRESSIVE PEOPLES REPUBLICS

IN A SERIES OF ACTS OF INTERNAL SUBVERSION AND OVERT AGGRESSION THAT HAS BEEN PERPETRATED OVER MANY YEARS, THE CONSORTIUM OF POWERS TO WHOM THIS MESSAGE IS ADDRESSED HAVE REPEATEDLY AND BLATANTLY INTERFERED IN THE AFFAIRS OF NATION-STATES THAT HAVE EXPRESSED NEITHER THE WISH TO AFFILIATE THEMSELVES IN ANY WAY, POLITICALLY, MILITARILY, OR ECONOMICALLY, WITH THE OBJECTIVES OF THAT CONSORTIUM, NOR TO ACCEPT THE IDEOLOGI-CAL CREEDS TO WHICH IT SUBSCRIBES. THESE ACTS HAVE BEEN COMMITTED IN PURSUIT OF THE CONSORTIUM'S DECLARED GOAL OF SECURING FOR ITSELF THE STATUS OF DOMINATION OVER ALL OF THE WORLD'S PEOPLES, RACES, AND NATIONS, WITHOUT REGARD EITHER FOR THEIR WISHES OR FOR THE POLICIES OF THEIR FREELY ELECTED REPRESENTATIVES AND GOVERNMENTS.

REPEATED ATTEMPTS BY THE GOVERNMENTS OF THE FREE WORLD TO ESTABLISH A RATIONAL DIALOGUE WITH THE CONSORTIUM NATIONS AND TO ACHIEVE THE PEACEFUL COEXISTENCE OF ALL NATIONS HAVE BEEN MET ONLY WITH HOSTILITY AND PROGRESSIVELY HIGHER LEVELS OF PROVOCATION. THE CONTINUING INVASION BY FORCE OF THE TERRITORIES OF INDIA AND RUSSIA MARKS THE ESCALATION OF THAT PROVOCATION TO A

257

LEVEL THAT THE FREE WORLD FINDS ITSELF UNABLE TO TOLERATE.

ACCORDINGLY, WE, THE APPOINTED REPRESENTATIVES OF THE GOVERNMENTS OF THE NATIONS THAT ARE SIGNATORY TO THE FORMAL ALLIANCE OF WESTERN DEMOCRATIC STATES, GIVE NOTICE OF OUR DEMANDS AS FOLLOWS:

1. THAT THE MILITARY FORCES OF ALL NATIONS THAT ARE INCLUDED IN THE ALLIANCE TO WHOM THIS MESSAGE IS ADDRESSED CEASE FORTHWITH THEIR OPERATIONS IN ALL THEATERS OF COMBAT.

2. THAT THE FORCES REFERRED TO IN (1) ABOVE WITHDRAW COMPLETELY ALL PERSONNEL, ARMAMENTS, MUNITIONS, AND MATERIEL TO THE APPROPRIATE INTERNATIONALLY RECOGNIZED FRONTIERS.

3. THAT THE ILLEGALLY IMPOSED REGIMES IN HONG KONG, TAIWAN, AND SOUTH KOREA BE DISSOLVED AND THAT NEW GOVERNMENTS BE ESTABLISHED BY PROCESSES OF FREELY CONDUCTED AND INTERNATIONALLY SUPERVISED ELECTIONS.

4. THAT AN INTERNATIONAL BODY BE CONVENED, COMPOSED OF REPRESENTATIVES OF BOTH THE EASTERN AND WESTERN ALLIANCES OF NATIONS, TO EXPLORE WAYS OF LIMITING AND ULTIMATELY OF TERMINATING TOTALLY THE DEVELOPMENT AND DEPLOYMENT OF STRATEGIC WEAPONS SYSTEMS OF ALL TYPES.

WE HEREBY GIVE NOTICE ALSO THAT IF FORMAL ACCESSION TO THESE DEMANDS HAS NOT BEEN RECEIVED BY 12:00 NOON, LOCAL TIME IN WASHINGTON, D.C., ON THE 27TH DAY OF NOVEMBER 2007, A STATE OF WAR WILL BE DEEMED TO EXIST BETWEEN ALL NATIONS INCLUDED IN THE GRAND ALLIANCE OF PROGRESSIVE PEOPLES REPUBLICS, AND THE NATIONS THAT ARE SIGNATORY TO THE TREATY OF THE ALLIANCE OF WESTERN DEMOCRATIC STATES.

ALEXANDER GEORGE SHERMAN,
PRESIDENT OF THE UNITED STATES OF AMERICA
WOLFGANG KLESSENHAUER,
PRESIDENT OF THE UNITED STATES OF EUROPE
MAXWELL JAMES DOMINIC,
PRESIDENT OF THE REPUBLIC OF CANADA
YURI JOSEF SASHKAVOV,
PRESIDENT OF THE REPUBLIC OF EURO-RUSSIA
MARTIN CRAIG-WILSON,
PRIME MINISTER OF THE FEDERATION OF
AUSTRALIA AND NEW ZEALAND
SIMIL KUNG YO SAN,
PRESIDENT OF THE MALAYSIAN AND INDONESIAN
FEDERATION
YASHIRO MITSOBAKU,
PRESIDENT OF JAPAN

ISSUED FROM WASHINGTON, D.C.
12:00 NOON, 25 NOVEMBER 2007.

Aub stared once more at the copy of the ultimatum
that lay on top of the console beside him. His eyes
still registered a stunned disbelief, even after two days,
and kept straying back to the document as if hoping
that some mystical agency might miraculously have
changed the grim message carried in its words. All
hopes were gone now, drowned in the dull sickness
that lay in the pit of his stomach. So now, after everything, it had finally come to this. The nightmare that
he had staunchly and trustingly refused to believe for
all that time was really happening. He felt bitter,
betrayed, and confused.

A few feet away from him, seated in the second
operator's position in the Control Room, Clifford was
engrossed with updating the fire-control programs via
the BIACs. Deep below them in the lower recesses of
Brunnermont, the dreadful machine that Aub had
grown to hate was primed and ready, generators humming and beam on and up to power, waiting to unleash
its holocaust. There were only minutes left to run before the ultimatum expired. For the past forty-eight

hours, Aub and Clifford had been taking shifts to maintain a constant readiness against the possibility of a surprise attack during the ultimatum period. But there had been no change in the pattern of activity across the global scene; there had been no acknowledgment of the ultimatum at all. Reports from the fronts were that the fighting was continuing unabated.

Aub attracted Clifford's attention and indicated his desire for Clifford to keep his eye on things alone for a moment while he took a final breath of air outside the Control Room before the action commenced. Clifford nodded his assent, whereupon Aub removed his BIAC skull-harness, stretched his cramped limbs gratefully, rose from the console, and walked out to the access gallery where he stopped to lean on the balustrade and stare out over the Operational Command Floor.

The scene that confronted him, with its air of calm, well-regulated efficiency and smooth organization, could have been the inside of the control center for a space mission . . . were it not for the preponderance of military uniforms. All the communications posts were manned; the display screens were alive; the duty operators were all at their assigned positions and attending to their well-rehearsed tasks, while groups of senior officers surveyed the proceedings from various parts of the room. To one side President Sherman, Vice President Donald Reyes, and Defense Secretary Foreshaw were standing at the center of a semicircle of aides in front of a permanently open communications console, ready for any last-minute response to the ultimatum. This all reminded Aub grimly of a prison warden in an earlier age standing by for an eleventh-hour reprieve before executing sentence on a condemned criminal. He doubted if there would be any reprieve of the death sentence that had been passed on mankind.

He asked himself again why he had failed to declare his dissociation from the business long before this. Why had he not walked out? Had it been simply because he had continued deep down to believe in the man he had once called a friend until it was too late? Or was it now just a case of animal survival? Was he, like the priests performing their rituals at the sacrificial altars below, just reacting to the subconscious knowledge that only the power of the new god they served could preserve them through the wrath that was ordained to come? But whatever things were written on the pages that Destiny had not yet disclosed, there could be no going back now; to quit at this stage would be merely to guarantee the greater disaster.

He gazed at the clock set high on the far wall of the Command Floor, its window at the extreme right showing the relentless flow of seconds. Uncontrollable fingers of ice caressed his spine, and nausea rose to his throat. Less than three minutes. Time to get tuned back in. He turned and re-entered the Control Room.

Clifford was looking toward the door as he came in, as if waiting for Aub to enter. Aub sat down dully and began positioning the BIAC harness.

"Aub." Clifford's voice was barely more than a hiss, yet it carried a strange note of urgency. Aub looked up and noticed the expression of earnestness. Clifford was leaning toward him, while at the same time holding his arm outstretched to keep a key on his panel depressed, thus temporarily cutting off audio and visual contact between the Control Room and the Command Floor below.

"Aub, it's not the way you think," Clifford said, whispering hurriedly. "There isn't time to explain now. But it was important that your reactions and Sarah's be absolutely genuine all the way through. Everybody has been under observation here, all the time. I couldn't risk anyone not acting out his part faithfully." Aub started to shake his head in bewilderment, but just then Clifford glanced at the clock and hushed him with a gesture of his hand.

"When the action starts, I want you to do everything I say without any questions. I know how you've been feeling. But it's gonna be okay. Trust me."

As if in a trance, Aub nodded mutely, his eyes wide and dazed, his jaw hanging limp. Before he could form any coherent reply, the auxiliary screen came to life above Clifford's head.

"Hello, Control Room. We've lost you on the primary channel. Switch to standby while we check for faults." The face of one of the operators below spoke out of the display. Clifford released the key he had been holding.

"Sorry, my fault," he advised. "Must have knocked the switch. How's that?"

The face of the operator glanced off screen for a second.

"That's fine. Clearing down standby." One of the two faces now showing disappeared; the other continued to stare at them for a moment and then, evidently satisfied, turned to attend to other chores.

Aub began to frame some kind of a question when a new voice came through the speaker above the Control Room doorway. "H-hour minus thirty seconds. Still no response to ultimatum."

After that there was no time to think of questions.

"Report status of weapon delivery system," ordered the voice of the operations coordinator from the supervisory platform below.

"Fire-control sequence primed and ready for Phase One Strike," Clifford replied. "Awaiting orders."

"Acknowledged. Stand by."

"Standing by."

General Carlohm, Supreme Commander of the Allied Integrated Command, approached the President, still standing by the open-channel console.

"Request confirmation of present standing orders," he said. Sherman nodded.

"No change."

Carlohm turned to his deputy, who was standing behind him.

"Confirm orders to all military forces. All units to

maintain a condition of armed alert. Defend as necessary if attacked, but otherwise do not engage in offensive hostilities." The deputy acknowledged, then walked over to a console operator to relay the message out to the global command chain of the Western armed forces.

Ten seconds.

The eyes in the group of tense, grim faces clustered around the communications unit were all fixed on the President. His gaze was riveted on the screen visible above the operator's head, his tongue running unconsciously back and forth across his dry lips. Nothing.

Zero. Still nothing.

"The ultimatum has expired," Carlohm reported formally. "I request confirmation of your approval to authorize Phase One." Sherman took a long, deep breath and turned at last away from the empty screen. Absolute silence had descended on all sides.

"Proceed, General," he instructed.

Carlohm passed the order to the deputy who conveyed it to the operational coordinator. The coordinator activated the channel that connected him to the Control Room.

"Authorization to proceed confirmed. Execute Phase One Strike."

"Proceeding," Clifford returned. "Executing Phase One Strike now."

What followed was practically an anticlimax. A second or two later, Clifford's voice calmly informed them:

"Phase One completed."

There was nothing more to it than that. The information coming in from a thousand tracking points all around and over the world told the story on the displays surrounding them: between the last two times that Clifford had spoken, every ORBS satellite and orbiting antisatellite laser deployed by hostile powers had ceased to exist. The immediate threat of any direct attack on the Western nations had been totally removed. That still left, however, the less immediate but nevertheless formidable threat of submarine, surface- and air-launched missiles. These had to be dealt with next.

The tension began to ease somewhat. The worst was over. The victory was in the bag. In one or two places, amused grins appeared at the thought of the confusion and consternation that would at that moment be breaking out in similar places on the other side of the world.

"Permission to authorize Phase Two?" Carlohm asked the President. "Missile subs and launch silos."

"Proceed," Sherman responded. The order reached the operations coordinator, who turned towards his panel. Suddenly his face knotted into a puzzled frown. He began jabbing repeatedly at the buttons in front of him. An assistant sitting slightly forward of him was turning and muttering, making helpless gestures toward his own console.

"What's happening?" came the voice of Vice President Reyes, sharply.

"I'm not sure." The coordinator looked perplexed. "We've lost contact with the Control Room. Primary channel's dead; standby's dead; backup systems aren't responding." He spoke into a microphone grille on the panel. "Control Room, Control Room. We've lost you completely. Do you hear? Come in please." He toggled more switches furiously and tried again. No response.

"You've got a fault," somebody said.

"Impossible. Triple redundancy circuits. Something funny's going on."

A low hum followed by the dull thud of a heavy object striking solid resistance came from above their heads. Every face turned upward. The massive steel door had closed in the far wall of the gallery, sealing off the Control Room. Indignant voices rose up on all sides.

"What in hell's going on?"

"Somebody's flipped."

"Christ! It's all gonna screw up."

Then one of the operators at a monitoring station a few feet away from the coordinator became excited. "Access doors to generator floors, accelerators, J-reactor, modulator levels, and computer floor have all closed. The entire system is sealed off and all local controls have been deactivated by Control Room override."

"What's he talking about?" Reyes demanded. The coordinator slumped back in his seat and showed his upturned palms.

"The whole system is being controlled by those two guys up there." He pointed up toward the gallery. "We can't get in, and they're not talking to us. We can't get at any part of the machine either."

"Well ... damn it ... what can you do?"

"Nix."

"Can't you pull the plug on the damn thing—or something?"

"Wouldn't do any good. It's got its own generating station below that can run for years. There's no way we can get in at that either."

Reyes spun round to confront the group of agitated Presidential aides. Sherman himself seemed to be taking the situation more calmly than anybody . . . unnaturally so. His reaction, or apparent lack of one, served only to confuse the Vice President more.

"I don't understand it," Reyes said. "Alex. What are you going to do?"

"You've just heard," Sherman told him. "It doesn't look as if there's anything we can do. So I guess we just have to do what the old lady said—if it's gonna happen anyway, lie back and enjoy it."

Carlohm, who had been conferring with his staff officers and studying the details of the reports coming in on the displays, interrupted. "Excuse me. Can I update you on our evaluation of the situation. Not all enemy satellites have been destroyed. Their strategic bombardment system and orbital lasers have been eliminated, but their capability for intercepting our own satellites with space-launched missiles is still intact. Since it looks as if we might not be able to rely on further J-strikes, I suggest we alert our conventional defenses to prepare for independent action."

"Very well," Sherman agreed. "From now on we treat this as a conventional operation. You now have sole command of all forces. Act as you see fit."

Carlohm issued a brief list of instructions to his staff, who dispersed to translate them into orders for the commanders of the Western defenses. Within minutes, salvos of missiles were discharged by the surviving enemy satellites; ground launchings were detected from Siberia to South Africa, which proved to be not ICBMs but interceptor missiles streaking upward to join in the assault on the unscathed Western satellite array. As the attacking waves closed in upon their targets, orbiting lasers and defensive missiles were brought into action to counter them.

During the next fifteen minutes the pattern of attrition unfolded: The enemy missiles were not getting through. All the calculations and simulations had shown that even with all the most favorable assumptions, the Western defensive system could never achieve the kill-rate that was being indicated on the screens. Something else was at work. That something could only be the J-weapon, which made it all the more strange for the two scientists to seal themselves in.

Then a new and inexplicable trend became apparent in the reports: a terrible toll was being taken of the friendly ORBS and laser satellites. The enemy missiles were not getting through to their targets, and yet the targets were being destroyed. Suddenly Carlohm realized what was happening.

"It's those two crazy bastards up there!" he yelled, turning purple. "They're wiping out *our own* satellites!"

At the end of an hour the situation was clear. Neither side was left with the means of delivering a strategic attack from orbit, both having lost their ORBS systems entirely. However, since the East had suffered the loss of its system in the first swift blow, it had been obliged to attempt to redress the balance by sending its anti-satellite missiles against the ORBS system of the West, which at that time had been still intact. This had forced the West to respond by firing off much of its stock of antimissile missiles.

The result was that the East was left with ample stocks of antimissile missiles, having had no attacking waves to contend with, while the West was not . . . at least, until the West had had time to redeploy its defenses. The implications of the situation slowly dawned on the military staffs present. A worried Carlohm explained to Sherman:

"Until we've had time to reorganize our defenses, we're wide open. Our antimissile systems have been depleted, and for the time being we've got nothing that would effectively stop a classical attack from subs and ICBMs. The problem is that the other side hasn't had any reason to fire off their antimissile systems, so the chances of success for a counterstrike by us wouldn't be too good. Those guys over there aren't stupid; the message must be obvious to them, too. If I were in their position, I'd hit now and hit hard."

His concern was soon proved to be well-founded. Reports began pouring in all over the Command Floor:

"Salvo of sixteen missiles launched from underwater, three hundred miles south of Nova Scotia. Climbing and turning due west."

"Launchings reported from four positions in the eastern Pacific. First course indications point to western U.S.A."

"Mass launch profiles in northern Siberia, heading north over the Pole. Launches in central Siberia directed west toward Europe."

"Missiles climbing over inshore regions of Algeria and Tunisia, heading north toward Mediterranean."

A peppering of red traces started to appear across the enormous map of the world that was framed by the largest of the mural displays. The apprehension of the watchers rose to a point bordering on panic. The calm and composure that Sherman had exhibited throughout at last broke down. He stared aghast at the thin red lines that were beginning to elongate on the map, his mind refusing to accept what was demanded of him now. The lines began consolidating into irregular arcs that covered the North American continent from three sides, Europe from the south and east, and Australia from the north. The arcs were converging, agonizingly slowly, but relentlessly.

"Initial computations of trajectories put first missile on target in four-point-five minutes," a voice announced. "Origin, west Atlantic. Impact point, New York area. Impacts in Spain predicted at four-point-nine minutes, Italy, five minutes, British Isles, five-point-three minutes. Further data coming in now."

Carlohm and Foreshaw faced the President expectantly, but Sherman just stood immobilized, his eyes glazed and his head shaking weakly from side to side.

"It's an all-out attack," Carlohm said after a few seconds. "You have to order full retaliation . . . now." Sherman slowly sank into a chair. The color had drained from his face; perspiration glistened on his brow.

"What will that achieve now?" he whispered in a strangled voice. "It can change nothing. Sheer, futile savagery . . . for no purpose . . ."

"You have to," Foreshaw said grimly. "It's the price."

Sherman brought his hands up to cover his face. He shook his head mutely and became paralyzed. Suddenly Reyes stepped forward and proclaimed in a firm and decisive voice:

"I declare the President temporarily incapacitated and unable to carry out his duties. I therefore assume Presidential authority and accept full responsibility for my decisions. General Carlohm, order a full retaliatory offensive to be launched immediately."

Carlohm hesitated for a second, then nodded to his staff officers. Within thirty seconds the whole strategic missile arsenal of the Western world was thundering skyward. On the map above them, chains of dots of bright green was added to the story that was already there. Both sides had now hurled in everything they had; the difference was that the longer traces in red, now closing in on the frontiers of their target countries, would be almost unopposed.

"First computed impact now confirmed as New York. Time to impact, thirty-two seconds. Further confirmed targets are Washington, D.C., Baltimore, Boston, Philadelphia, Montreal, and Ottawa. Los Angeles and San Francisco confirmed on the West Coast. Trajectories of following missiles being computed. We expect they will fractionate into independent warheads."

"What's the defensive situation?" Reyes asked Carlohm.

"They're firing what they can. Most emplacements aren't programmed for local interceptions, since that was supposed to be taken care of by the orbital defensive system."

"Report status now," Reyes called out.

"Object previously reported homing on New York was a decoy. Full salvo of interceptors expended. Missile following has now altered course toward same target. Area Defense Commander reports insufficient reserves to intercept. Revised time to impact, forty-three seconds."

"Jesus . . . !" Somebody breathed.

"Impact will coincide with arrival time of first expected on targets in southern Europe," the report continued. "More decoys causing uncertainties in previous predictions."

"Never mind them now," Reyes snapped. "Read me that one that's zeroing on New York."

"Due on target in twenty-two seconds . . . twenty . . . fifteen . . . CONTACT LOST!"

"What the . . . ? You mean we got it?" Reyes was nonplused.

"Negative, sir. There were no defensive missiles

near. It just seems to have . . . vanished." The voice came again, now sounding utterly at a loss. "Predicted impacts in southern Europe deleted from latest computations. Traces of incoming missiles have been lost . . . Disregard confirmations for Washington, D.C., Baltimore, Philadelphia . . ." The voice grew totally bewildered. "Disregard confirmations previously given for West Coast . . ."

All over the map the leading lines in red were stopping as soon as they got anywhere near their targets, as if an invisible eraser were working along the coastlines of North America. The same pattern developed along the approaches to Europe, Australia, and Japan. The attacking waves were being wiped out by the score.

"Your defenses aren't doing that?" Reyes asked, incredulous.

"They've fired everything they had left," Carlohm answered, equally bemused. "I doubt if there's more than a handful of serviceable missiles left in the whole of the West."

"They're being J-bombed!" Foreshaw exclaimed abruptly. "Can't you see what those guys are doing? They've lured the whole damn Commie missile force up into the sky at once; now they're J-bombing it out of existence."

"Not their whole missile force," Carlohm reminded him. "Only their attack force. Don't forget they still haven't used their antimissile missiles."

Soon the whole of the network of red lines had frozen into immobility, marking the limit of penetration that had been reached before the last warhead was vaporized. Not one had made it past the frontier of any territory of a Western Alliance nation. Only the green traces were left in motion now, crawling inexorably onward toward their own destinations. By now the leading ones, fired from patrolling allied and U.S. submarines, were getting close.

Sherman had by this time recovered from his despair and had gotten involved in the proceedings again.

"Nothing will threaten our security for a long time to come now." He turned toward Carlohm. "That attack that's going on there no longer has any purpose. It must be stopped. Order immediate remote disarming of all warheads."

Carlohm looked amazed for a second, then started to protest.

"But there's nothing to lose now. There'll never be another chance like . . ."

"Those weapons were conceived and built only as a deterrent. Now there's nothing left to deter anybody from using. Do it."

Carlohm gave the order. From a score of command centers around the world, the transmissions were broadcast to transform the most sophisticated instrument of total destruction that the world had ever seen into just so many free-falling chunks of harmless metal.

The green tentacles continued stretching their way forward to condense into a thorny girdle around the Eastern world. It was the picture of a little while earlier all over again, but in reverse. A speckled haze of red pinpoints began to appear, adorning the enemy coastlines and borders.

"Antimissile interceptors coming up," Carlohm observed, now just a relaxed and passive spectator, as were the rest of them. "They've got no way of knowing that those warheads have been deactivated."

The display produced by the defensive-missile screen put up by the other side was truly spectacular. The amused observers at Brunnermont lounged back in their seats and pictured the alarm that must have been rife on the other side of the world. The whole of the Eastern bloc was becoming outlined by vivid streaks of blood red as thousands of individual tracks merged together; everything that could move was, it seemed, being fired into the sky.

And then the J-bomb went into action again.

The swarms of interceptors were methodically cut to shreds and then obliterated. The attacking salvos from the West were allowed to penetrate just far enough—far enough to act as bait to draw up the last of the defending missiles; then they too were destroyed. The destruction of the West's own attack force did not produce any reactions of surprise or anger now; the watchers around the Operational Command Floor had already resigned themselves to being merely puppets in the design that Clifford and Aub were revealing. They had all played out their assigned roles on cue as unerringly and as surely as if they had been manipulated on physical strings.

Carlohm watched as the last scattered defenders were mopped up and the green attack pattern ground to a final halt.

"I wonder what they'll make of that," he commented. "They'll know that none of their interceptors were getting through. It sure as hell wasn't them that stopped it."

Then it was all over. The entire war machine, which had required forty years and the lion's share of the world's finance, industry, and talents to conceive and put together, had been wiped from the face of Earth in less than an hour. Not a single manned target on either side had been attacked successfully and, as far as anybody could tell, there had not been a single casualty.

Sherman stood for a long time gazing up at the now inanimate display, faithfully preserving its record of the things that had happened through every agonizing second of that hour. There was an expression of wonder on his face, a mixture of awe and almost reverence, as if he alone could divine a deeper meaning to it all. The rest of the room remained silent, still savoring the relief and the sweet taste of the reprieve that none had dreamed possible.

Suddenly the operator at the communications console sat forward as words began appearing on the screen before him. He read for a moment, then looked towards Carlohm.

"It's a reply to the ultimatum," he announced.

Carlohm strode over and looked over his shoulder.

Then the general turned. "Peking has ordered immediate cease-fires in India and Russia," he informed the room. "Also, they agree unconditionally to all the demands that we have put to them." Forgetting his formal duties for a moment he added wryly: "Boy—we sure must have scared the shit outa those bastards!"

Chapter 24

The atmosphere at the meeting, called on the afternoon of the following day at the White House, was still one of dazed bewilderment. To make matters worse, a completely new and unexpected complication had been added to the already unprecedented situation that confronted the men sitting around the table in the President's private conference room.

Vice President Donald Reyes leaned forward in his chair and looked at William Foreshaw with a mixture of noncomprehension and plain disbelief.

"Sorry, Bill, I'm not quite with you," he said. "Just say that again, will you?"

"I said," the Defense Secretary replied, "that they haven't just taken out the whole of the world's capacity to wage global nuclear war; they have totally and completely paralyzed the possibility of *any* kind of strategic military operations for at least the next hundred years! They've demolished the whole structure of the East-West political balance of power."

"That's what I thought you said. Now could you explain it?"

Foreshaw passed his hand wearily across a brow that had been creased with concentration for most of the previous twenty-four hours.

"Aw, hell, this all gets a bit technical. Pat, go through it again, would you?"

Patrick Cleary, the principal Presidential adviser on

computing matters, nodded from the far end and cleared his throat.

"Before they came out of the Control Room at Brunnermont yesterday, the last thing they did was activate an extremely complicated system of interlocked programs in the supervisory BIAC . . . that's the main computer that controls all the rest. It appears that the only person who knew that these programs even existed in the system at all was Dr. Clifford; he'd begun developing them even before he and his team moved from Sudbury to Brunnermont."

"You mean they're still running there now . . . that thing is still live?"

"Absolutely. There's no way anyone can shut it down . . . but I'll come to that in a minute. Let's begin at the beginning."

Reyes sat back to listen as Cleary continued. "The first thing that they do is limit the operating range of the J-bomb. The bomb is still functional, but it will only accept target coordinates inside North America and allied Western nations, and up to fifty miles beyond their coastlines and frontiers." He noted one or two looks of bafflement and explained hurriedly. "This means that, in effect, it can only be used as a purely defensive weapon. Any form of attack from another part of the world—whether by land, sea, or air . . . using conventional weapons or nuclear ones —can be devastatingly crushed before it gets anywhere near us. But since the range can't be extended into the homelands of the other side, the weapon has no offensive value whatsoever. We couldn't attack with it."

"What about space weapons?" General Carlohm asked.

"The J-bomb will fire inside an umbrella that extends for up to one hundred miles above all friendly territory. So, if the East wants to put itself to all the effort and expense it can build itself up a whole new ORBS system if it wants to . . . but the moment they try to drop anything on us, we can blow it out of the sky. Somehow I don't think they'll bother."

President Sherman raised a hand to hold Cleary at that point.

"There's something I'm not clear about here," he said. "You're talking about our being able to fire the bomb in defense if we need to. Who exactly do you mean by 'us'? Clifford and Philipsz are the only two who seem to really understand how the system works, and I've got a feeling they won't be sticking around for much longer. Who else do you figure could operate it?"

"They've taken care of that," Cleary replied. "Now that the special programs have been integrated into the system, any experienced BIAC operator can be trained to use them. He only has to input data; he doesn't have to know how they are structured or inter-connected internally."

"In fact," Foreshaw supplied, "as I understand it, the two of them are offering to stay on at Brunnermont for a period of eight weeks, solely to train the first team of operators for us. After that, they blow."

"Where to?" Sherman enquired.

"They haven't said. Back to get on with whatever they want to do at ISF, I guess."

To the continuing surprise of most of those present, Sherman merely smiled as if he found the whole thing a huge joke. His evident inclination to treat the affair with something approaching cheerful nonchalance . . . almost amusement . . . had been a source of puzzlement ever since the session began.

"Okay," Reyes conceded. "It looks as if they've got the Brunnermont machine locked into a defense-only kind of role. But our security policy still requires an effective means of attack." He swept his eyes around the table to invite support. "My suggestion is this: Since Brunnermont is ruled out, we get together another scientific team, probably with the nucleus from ACRE, and figure out how to build another one. After all, the design data for Brunnermont itself is all available; it shouldn't be too difficult."

Cleary pursed his lips and shook his head.

"I'm afraid it wouldn't work, Don. You see, the essential part of any other machine that's built to work on the same principles would be the artificial black hole that sits inside the J-reactor. The hole constitutes an intense emission source of hi-radiation; it would stand out like a lighthouse in the local regions of space."

"So?"

"The Brunnermont surveillance mechanism would detect it straight away. The whole system has been programmed to function as a never-sleeping . . . watchdog, if you like . . . in hi-space. It will fire automatically on any phenomenon of that kind that it identifies. In other words, if we build another J-bomb, Brunnermont will blow it sky-high the first instant we switch it on."

Reyes looked at him aghast.

"You mean here . . . in our own country? If we built one here and turned it on, we'd get zapped off the planet?"

"That is exactly what I mean."

Reyes thought for a moment; his face slowly formed into a frown. He looked up again.

"But that's crazy. It leaves us wide open. What happens if the other side hits on the same technology? Their system wouldn't have any of these lunatic programs. They'd be able to blow us all to hell over here, and we wouldn't be in a position to even turn on anything to hit back with."

Cleary was shaking his head again before Reyes had finished.

"Not so. Brunnermont would fire on any black hole that they tried to turn on as well. If they did make one, they'd never be able to use it."

"But . . ." Reyes was getting confused again. "But I thought you said Brunnermont wouldn't fire outside the West. You don't expect that Peking would set up their J-bomb in the Nevada desert or somewhere, do you . . . just to make it easy for us to wipe it out?"

"They've been rather cunning," Cleary replied. "Or rather, Clifford has. You see, the limitations on the range of the target coordinates that the system will accept only apply to fire commands issued through the operator interface programs; they don't apply to fire commands issued by the watchdog programs. So if the operator tries to hit a target, say, in Mongolia, the system simply won't work. But if somebody puts a J-bomb in Mongolia and switches it on, it'll get blasted automatically. It's neat. We can't build another one and they can't build another one."

"In fact, when you think about it, the whole thing is very subtle," Foreshaw came in. "There can be no question now of keeping a security blanket over our k-technology. If anyone anywhere in the world— maybe in some research lab somewhere or in a university in the middle of a city—quite innocently stumbles on the same thing and makes himself a piece of equipment similar to the GRASER that they built at Sudbury, Brunnermont will fire on it. We have to publish full details of all the facts—and fast."

"We're already working on a preliminary statement for communication through diplomatic channels and for all the news media," the Secretary of State informed them from his seat next to Sherman. "It should be going out any time now."

Reyes sighed with exasperation as he turned it all over again in his mind. The West had the world's one and only J-bomb, it was true, but it had no value as a tool for exerting international leverage or for extracting concessions, for it would only respond to deliberate commands if the West were physically attacked . . . or at least inside prescribed geographic limits, which amounted to the same thing. As long as Brunnermont remained functioning, there was no way out of it.

"Tell me again why we don't just turn it off," he said at last.

"Because we can't," Cleary told him simply.

"But, hell—it can't stay sealed off all the time. Every machine ever built has to be maintained. Somebody has to be able to get in sooner or later, if only to do routine maintenance on . . ." He caught the look on Cleary's face. "No . . . ? Why? Don't tell me it'll never need it."

"Oh, you're right enough about that. It's just that it isn't sealed off . . . for that very reason. You could walk right into any part of it now if you wanted to."

"Really?"

"Really."

"So why couldn't I just do that and pull out all the right wires while I'm in there?"

"Because . . ." Cleary's voice became very sober, "if you did that, you would completely eliminate the United States from the world scene as a viable military power."

"I . . . don't understand. What d'you mean?"

Cleary took a deep breath and placed his hands firmly palms-down on the table in front of him.

"All the critical components of the system have power regulators that will keep the voltages on the power lines high enough for the circuits to carry on functioning for a couple of seconds after the power supplies are cut. They are also equipped with sensor circuits that will detect the falling supply-line voltages and automatically transfer control of the computers to a power-down routine. The first function that that routine will perform will be to activate a special fire-control sequence for the J-bomb; its effect would be to blow up the White House, the Pentagon, and just about every major military base and installation in the country. In short, you don't tamper with it."

Reyes stared at him, openly appalled.

"That's insane."

"Those are the facts."

Reyes turned toward Sherman as if pleading for a note of reason to be reinjected into the conversation.

"Alex, you can't let them get away with that. They're both mad."

Sherman shrugged.

"What do you want me to do?"

"Well, damn it, you're the President. Use your Presidential authority. Order them to disarm it."

"There'd be no point, Don. I wouldn't expose the Presidential image to the public indignity of being told to go to hell. They wouldn't do it."

"Then you could shoot the bastards."

"They'd let me, too. I'm telling you—they just wouldn't do it and nobody else knows how to. Forget it."

Reyes looked wildly from one end of the table to the other.

"How the hell am I supposed to forget it?" he shouted. "If anything goes wrong with that psycho machine we could all be zapped right here in this room any moment. I could forget it like I could forget a cobra in my bed . . . ." He looked back at Cleary. "What's to stop its power-supply system from going faulty? How's it supposed to be able to tell the difference between a line just failing and somebody pulling it out?"

"Actually the risk of anything like that is so near zero that you *can* forget it," Cleary said in a voice that was calm and unperturbed. "Everything in Brunnermont was designed and constructed to the strictest military standards. The technology throughout features the most advanced concepts of reliability engineering, triple redundancy, and self-checking known. Every subsystem works on triple voting and has at least one backup that switches on automatically if a fault is detected. Even if outside power is cut off for any reason, its own generating complex will keep it running for years if need be. Any combination of component failures, right up to impossibly unlikely levels, can be tolerated for way beyond the worst-case repair times." He paused for everyone to digest these remarks, then went on.

"What it does mean is that if and when faults do develop, and common sense dictates that we have to assume they will, those faults will have to be fixed and fixed good . . . without any messing around."

"That's one of the other things we've also begun working on already," Foreshaw told them. "We're talking to the manufacturers and outside contractors that were involved in all aspects of the system so that we can get together a permanent team of highly trained maintenance engineers to be permanently resident on the Brunnermont site. A first-aid team has already been put in to cover in the meantime."

"To summarize, the system is as near fail-proof as makes no difference, and it's tamper-proof," Cleary rounded off.

General Carlohm spoke next. "So we still haven't solved the problem of our attack arm. But why are we assuming all the time that it has to be based on the J-bomb at all? After all, we got along okay before we had it. There's nothing to stop us building up our conventional ORBS and missile deterrents again. It'll cost us an arm and a leg, but . . . if that's what we have to do, it's what we have to do."

"I'm afraid there is something to stop you." Cleary was beginning to sound apologetic. "You see, the Brunnermont surveillance programs are very sophisticated. They can identify the characteristics and trajectories of an attack profile and distinguish an offensive missile from, say, a regular suborbital aircraft, space shot, or satellite orbit. You could set up another deterrent system, sure, just as the other side can, but the moment either of you tried to use it, you'd trigger off the watchdog. You saw what happened yesterday; nothing would get through if either side launched any kind of offensive missile strike against the other."

"It's back to the last century again then," Carlohm growled. "We'll have to start building B-52s again."

"Now, you know that would be crazy," Foreshaw responded. "For one thing, today's forms of conventional defense would leave any kind of classical attack like that with no chance; it would be like attacking machine guns with cavalry. And for another, the sheer numerical superiority of the East means we could never think of taking them on in any kind of unlimited war along the lines of 1939–45. Doing so would be suicide."

"Cruise missiles then?" Carlohm suggested. Foreshaw looked at Cleary. Cleary shook his head.

"Not when you think about it," Cleary said. "Cruise missiles were low-cost, mass-produced weapons designed to be used in large numbers to saturate the defenses. A saturation-attack profile would be easy to identify and the J-bomb would break it up in minutes. If you tried to conceal the pattern by sending them over piecemeal, conventional defenses would be able to pick them off easily. Not feasible."

"Biological weapons then?" Carlohm tried. "Gas . . . bugs . . . viruses . . . anything . . . ?"

"Too uncontrollable; too unpredictable," Foreshaw pronounced "We abandoned that line years ago and so has the other side. There's nothing to be gained for either of us by wiping out the whole planet. I can't see that being resurrected—not in a million years."

As Sherman listened to the exchange going on around him the horizons of his understanding slowly broadened to encompass the full meaning of the thing that Clifford had done. For the first time since he had last seen Clifford earlier that morning, he comprehended the reason for the light of triumph that had burned behind the scientist's tired eyes. At that time, Sherman had come away still somewhat shaken by the tide of recent events, but at a deeper level excited and exultant, eager to commence at once with the rebuilding of a new and sane world upon the foundations of salvation and opportunity that had been offered. No possibility could have been more remote than that all men could be anything but similarly inspired and exalted.

He saw now that, in spite of his worldliness and his

years, he had been naive; only the scientist, as befitted his calling, had seen and understood the true reality. He heard the words that men had uttered for a thousand years and he listened to minds that wallowed in the clay of a lifetime's conditioning and stereotyping. It was a microcosm of a world that would never learn.

And as he listened and his eyes opened, he marveled at the perfection of the web that the scientist had spun. Every question that was being asked had been anticipated; every twist and turn that the human mind could devise to escape from the maze was blocked; every objection had been forestalled. It was beautiful in its completeness.

Donald Reyes slumped back in his chair and slammed his hand down on the table in a gesture that finally signaled defeat.

Foreshaw then summed up the situation. "The East cannot hope to succeed in any form of offensive action against the West, nuclear or otherwise, because the J-bomb will stop them. We can't attack them with the J-bomb at all, and we can't attack them with any kind of missile strike because if we do the bomb will stop that. We can attack with outdated weapons if we like, but we won't because we'd be sure to come off worst.

"The East can't break the deadlock in any way at all. We can break the deadlock, but only by trying to switch off the machine; however, we won't do that either because we'd wipe out practically all of our armed forces if we did—and be left with nothing to attack with anyway. And as long as it stays switched on, nobody can build another J-bomb."

"And it will stay like that until it self-deactivates . . . one hundred and eleven years from now," Cleary completed.

A solemn silence descended upon the room.

"It's just sitting there under those mountains," Reyes fumed after a while. "It won't switch off and we can't switch it off. It's . . ." he sought for the words, "it's like one of those movie things . . . a Doomsday

Machine . . . only this is the granddaddy of all of them."

"Hardly, Don," Sherman remarked affably. "Doomsday Machines are supposed to guarantee the end of the world. I'd say that this does exactly the opposite."

"Well, I guess the opposite of the end of the world is the beginning of the world," Foreshaw mused. "What's it called . . . ? Genesis . . ."

"Then that's what it is," Sherman declared. "A Genesis Machine." He looked slowly around the circle of faces. "Don't you think you're all missing the point? There's one obvious alternative strategy that nobody's asked about yet. After what nearly happened yesterday, it's the only thing that we ought to be talking about."

Perplexed looks greeted his imploring gaze.

"You've all been living under the threat for so long that you can't wake up to the fact that it isn't there any more," he said. "You've been hooked on missiles and bombs for as long as you can remember, and the idea of getting along without them just doesn't get through. It's over. Can't you get that into your heads? We don't need it any more—any of it. Everything that the West has publicly claimed to want for the last fifty years has happened. Doesn't it occur to you that we might be able to do something constructive with all those armaments budgets now?"

He stood up and made it plain that his part in the meeting was finished. Before turning toward the door, he concluded: "I am going out to take a long, quiet walk. You are going to stay here and start talking about how the people in this world are going to find ways of getting along with one another. It might be new to you, but you're just gonna damn well have to figure out how it's done. You haven't been left with any choice now."

Chapter 25

As with a man who awakens from the terrors of a bad dream to find only the serenity of sunrise and the joys of birdsong, so the realization slowly dawned on the world that the nightmare was over. And from a world that could now breathe free emerged a new understanding.

Delegations of politicians, generals, and scientists from Peking, Vladivostok, Beirut, Cairo, and Cape Town came to Brunnermont to gaze in wonder at the embodiment of the final triumph of reason. U.S. Army BIAC operators demonstrated for them the truth of the prophesies that had been pronounced. Unerringly they could direct cataclysmic bolts of destruction upon any point they chose in the domain of the West or to guard its approaches; they proved it with a selection of prepared targets in the northern wastes of Arctic Canada, the deserts of Australia, and the offshore waters of Europe and the U.S.A. But when they attempted to extend the range of the weapon to reach certain locations in the Sahara, the Gobi, and the far north of Siberia that the East had agreed could be used for the tests, the computers refused to obey. That was as much proof as anybody was prepared to ask for; neither side seemed immediately disposed to embark on the billions of dollar expenditure that testing out the rest of the system would require. Some of the predictions, without any shadow of a doubt, would never be risked anyway. And besides that, as time went by, the need to find out if the system could be outwitted somehow subsided. It didn't seem really important any more as the world began finding more pressing problems to turn its attention to.

Full details of the new physics that had made Brunnermont possible had, of course, been published throughout the world, and Clifford spent a busy period delivering a series of lectures on the subject to gatherings of scientists from all nations. In these he revealed a final piece of information about the Brunnermont watchdog, something he had neglected to mention previously.

The automatic surveillance system, programmed to fire immediately upon any strong source of hi-radiation that it detected in the nearby regions of space, would function only against targets located inside a distance of two hundred thousand miles. Beyond that radius k-technology could be developed and used safely.

He explained that it would not be feasible for a would-be aggressor to mount a J-bomb in a spacecraft with the intention of firing on or threatening terrestrial targets from outside Brunnermont's effective range. The target-location system aboard such a craft would be capable of "seeing" clearly from that distance only sources of intense hi-radiation, which in practice meant the solitary "beacon" of Brunnermont itself since no other source would be permitted to survive. But this beacon would be detected merely as a mathematical figment in the complexity of k-space, without yielding of itself the solutions of the equations that would be needed to mark its associated target coordinates in ordinary three-dimensional space. In other words, Brunnermont would not be vulnerable to destruction by these means. Before a J-bomb fire-control system could be accurately registered on selected targets in normal space, it was necessary to calibrate it with a reference framework of known locations derived from previously resolved sets of space-like images. But these images depended on the system being able to distinguish ordinary objects by virtue of the low level of radiation that was generated by the spontaneous particle annihilations taking place inside them; this was not practicable from distances outside two hundred thousand miles, and it followed that a hypothetical space-borne J-bomb would not constitute a workable threat to either Brunnermont or any other potential target anywhere else on the surface of Earth.

Clifford was of the opinion that technology would one day progress to a point where these restrictions could be overcome, but by that time the reasons for their having been imposed in the first place would long have gone away. In the meantime, scientists would be able to continue their researches into the new physics in laboratories on the Moon, anywhere else in the Solar System, and perhaps, one day, beyond. For the next one hundred and eleven years, however, as far as this kind of activity went Earth itself was quarantined. That was regrettable, but it seemed a small price to pay.

Chapter 26

The squat-nosed, ungainly surface-transport ship from Tycho Base slowed to a halt and hung amid the star-strewn black velvet of the sky over the observatory complex at Joliot-Curie, on Lunar Farside. In among the huddle of domes and receiver dishes that stood in the middle of the arid wilderness below, the massive steel shutters over the underground landing bay had already been rolled aside to uncover a splash of warm, yellow light and relieve the harsh monotony of the ash-gray dust. Its flight-control processors concluded their dialogue with the ground computers and the ship sank gently out of sight of the surface.

Inside the landing bay, after the shutters had closed and the bay had filled with air, an access ramp telescoped out to mate with the ship's entry lock as the last moans of its engines died away in the new world of sound that had come into being. The lock slid open and the small procession of new arrivals made its way down the ramp to the reception antechamber.

Professor Heinrich Zimmermann, his face wreathed in a smile of delight, stepped forward to greet the three young people as they approached him.

"How was your journey?" he asked as he shook each one warmly by the hand. "No unpleasant complications, I trust?"

"Very relaxing," Clifford told him. His face had filled out again and regained its fresh and healthy color. His eyes were shining brightly, just like old times.

"Starting to feel at home on this ol' dust ball already," Aub said.

"And what about you, my dear?" Zimmermann asked, turning toward Sarah. "Do you think you will enjoy living here on the Moon?"

"Who cares?" she smiled, snuggling nearer to Clifford. "I'm still getting used to the idea of having my husband back again."

Zimmermann smiled and turned to usher them in the direction of the far door of the antechamber. "First I must show you where the bar is and join you in a welcoming drink . . . just to keep our priorities correct. Don't worry about your baggage and so on; that will be taken care of. After that, we will show you to the living quarters so that you can clean up, settle in, and rest if you wish. I would like to suggest that we dine together later, in the main dining room at 2300 hours . . . in case you haven't got used to the local time yet, that's just over three hours from now. After that, I would be pleased to take you on a tour of the base and observatories. I warn you, it's a bit of a rabbit-warren underground, and newcomers here tend to be confused at first, but I've no doubt that you will get used to it."

He stopped and looked down at the sign that had been positioned across the doorway to which their torturous route had by that time brought them.

"Oh, dear—it appears that we cannot get through this way. The tunnel is temporarily out of use for maintenance." He sighed. "We will have to go back a little way, up and across into the next dome through the interconnecting tube on the surface. I am sorry about this. . . . This way . . ."

As they emerged from the access lock of the tube and entered the dome, Zimmermann called them over to a viewing port in the outside wall. From it they were able to see the limit to which the surface constructions extended on one side of the base. The professor pointed to the bare tract of dust and boulders that lay beyond.

"That is where you will be working," he said. "The area has been surveyed and we have completed preliminary designs for three additional domes to house the new laboratories. Initially they will all extend five levels down below the surface and be connected into the main complex, of course. The new GRASER will be built below the largest of them . . . roughly halfway between that prominent crater and that group of boulders . . . and the BIACs and associated equipment will be next door, about fifty yards to the left. The third is really for storage space at this stage; it will be useful should you require room to expand later."

"It sounds just great," Clifford said admiringly. "I think we're going to enjoy being part of your team here."

"I am sure that I am going to enjoy having you on the team," Zimmermann replied. "You will also be pleased to learn that headquarters has now signed firm contracts, and the initial shipments of materials to begin construction should arrive within two months."

Five minutes later, below ground level again, they settled themselves down around a table in the corner of the room that doubled as bar and informal social center for the base. It had a warm, friendly atmosphere enhanced by the background of piped music and the murmur of conversation from the dozen or so other persons already there. Zimmermann cast an eye around him as he sat down with a small tray of drinks and passed them around.

"I won't bother you with any introductions for now," he said. "There will be plenty of time for that later." He sat back and raised his glass. "And now, my friends, to what shall we drink? A successful partnership, I suppose . . ."

They responded.

"One word of advice," he said as they drank. "Take it easy with alcohol until you've had time to become acclimated. The gravity here can do strange things . . .

I suppose it's a case of being light-headed before you start . . . literally."

Clifford started to laugh. "Hey—I nearly forgot—Al and Nancy asked me to give you their regards. Al says he's sorry that they left things too late for them to make the same launch that we did, but they're all set for next month's."

"Yes, I know about that," Zimmermann nodded with a smile. "I understand that he found Nancy difficult to persuade."

"Aw, she'll be okay," Aub tossed in. "Especially with Sarah around; they get along fine. She just likes living next to that lake too much. That's all."

"Al's going off into the realms of science fiction," Clifford said. Zimmermann raised his eyes toward the ceiling.

"Is he really . . . ? What is it this time?"

"He's gotten all hooked up on the idea of beaming energy through hi-space. He figures that one day it'll be the way that energy will be piped to wherever it's needed, all over the Solar System . . . anywhere. He's got this picture of some enormous distribution network being fed from great big artificial black holes millions of miles out in space."

"Good lord . . ."

"He says it'll be the only way to power spaceships one day, too," Aub added. "Why should they bother carting their own energy around with them when they can have as much as they like beamed right at them wherever they want to go?"

"Well, I must say it will be entertaining to have Al with us," Zimmermann grinned. "I only hope that he doesn't start redesigning everything in sight the minute he arrives. What about you, Brad? What plans do you have until the new labs begin to take shape? It's going to be some time, you know."

"Oh, I'll be busy enough all right. I've got a year's lost time to make up, don't forget . . . on account of . . ." his face twisted into a crooked smile, "a certain minor matter that needed attending to. The main thing I want to do is pick up where I left things with you and your astronomers here. They're pretty keen to get to grips with that Wave Model that we started to talk about once. They've been carrying out a lot of observations over the last year, as you know, and one thing I have to do is get involved again and updated." He stopped and thought for a second. "In fact, I've been thinking ever since you mentioned that third dome you're planning . . . we're gonna need to build a specialized long-range detector system for studying cosmological k-data—a k-telescope, if you like. If you're not planning on using that dome for anything in particular for now, it sure would be a good place to consider putting it."

Zimmermann scratched his nose and grinned mischievously.

"As a matter of fact, strictly between ourselves, that was exactly what I had in mind. It's just that I haven't . . . ah, shall we say . . . quite gotten round to telling Geneva about it yet." He added hastily: "But I'm sure they will agree it's an excellent idea. I just think it would be better if the dome were actually there before I raise the matter. It keeps things simple, you understand. . . ."

"I understand too well," Sarah said. "If I ever saw three conspirators in league together . . . I'm beginning to wonder what I've let myself in for."

Aub had been staring far into space for the last minute or so. He returned suddenly and regarded them with a curious look, his head cocked to one side.

"You know, I've been thinking about something on and off for the last coupla months, too. It's to do with the way the GRASER modulators initiate the particle annihilations."

The others looked at him, waiting expectantly. "Well, the method that Al uses concentrates everything at one point in space," he continued. "That's what produces the intense spacetime distortion and gives you a simulated gravity effect . . . which, taken to the limit, gives you a black hole. It makes sense he should do it that way, since that's the kind of thing he was investigating in the first place. Sudbury is a gravitational-physics Institute."

"Great," Clifford conceded. "Al's methods make sense. Nice to hear it. What's new?"

"Al's way is fine for what he set out to do, sure, but I figure there's another way you could do it. I figure it would be possible to set up a distributed modulation and annihilation pattern that would take in a defined volume of space . . . and you wouldn't be talking about gravity intensities anywhere near like what you get around black holes, anywhere inside it. In other words, you'd be able to initiate the annihilation of a piece of matter . . . an object . . . not just of a focused particle beam."

"Why should you want to do that?" Clifford asked him, looking nonplused.

"Oh, all sorts of reasons . . . like, it would be a quick and easy way to excavate the holes under those new domes you were talking about, for instance. You just blow away all the rock you don't need into hi-space. But that really wasn't the point. The thing I had in mind was something more."

"Like what?"

Aub's expression took on a shade of earnestness.

"Well, this might sound way-out, but I can't see why it couldn't work. You know how the J-bomb director modulators focus all the hi-radiation on one selected target point. Well, I reckon that they could define a distributed pattern in space too, instead of just one point . . . in the same way that the annihilator modulators could."

Clifford screwed up his face and glanced at Zimmermann, then back at Aub.

"Still don't get what you're driving at."

"You could synchronize them both together!" Aub exclaimed, gesticulating excitedly. "It would enable you to project a piece of structured matter instead of simply a focused charge of energy. You'd be able to annihilate an object at one place in space and instantly reconstitute it, intact, somewhere else! That's what I'm driving at."

"You're crazy," Clifford told him. "I thought Al's science fiction was bad enough. This is science fairyland."

"I just can't see any reason why it couldn't work," Aub insisted. He looked appealingly at Sarah. She shrugged and pulled a face.

"Don't ask me. Sounds crazy."

"It's not crazy," Aub declared emphatically. "I tell you, it'd work."

"I hate to say it," Zimmermann joined in, "but while I have seen some examples of your unusual inventive abilities in the past, I do feel that what you are saying now is somewhat far-fetched. I am afraid that, were you approaching me as a potential investor, I would not for one moment consider putting any of my money into it."

"It's the drink," Clifford decided. "The gravity's getting to you already."

"Never you mind them, Aub," Sarah said soothingly. "I've changed my mind. If those two are ganging up on you, I'll come over to your side. I believe it will work."

"There you are," Aub retorted. He thrust out his bearded chin in an attitude of proud defiance. "I've got one convert already. I'm telling you—it'll work."

"Very well," Zimmermann raised a hand to quell the issue, "I have no wish for us to fall out so soon. We shall no doubt find out in good time." His eyes were nevertheless still twinkling with amused disbelief. "In the meantime, however, I insist upon getting you all another drink."

Epilogue

Bornos Karenski settled back into the enveloping luxury of his seat and closed his eyes while he pictured the life awaiting him and his family in what was to become their new home. There was so much land there and so few inhabitants that they grew and ate fresh food—grown in the soil itself. And they reared stocks of animals that they allowed to roam free . . . all over the sun-drenched meadows of open hills that tumbled down under their necklaces of silver streams all the way from the mountains. And what mountains! And the sizes of the trees in those forests!

He'd seen it all in the holomoviegrams that the immigration agency had shown them. And so keen was the government there to attract new immigrants that they had not only paid half the fare for the whole family, they had subsidized his purchase of the land to the tune of 70 percent and granted him a twenty-year, interest-free loan to cover the building of his new home and the provision of machinery and other equipment. His savings had bought him over two thousand acres with plenty set aside for contingencies. There would be no more claustrophobia in computerized, plasticized, conglomerized antiseptic cities now . . . no more rounds of garish parties designed as the last vain attempt to relieve the boredom of garish people . . . no more of the mass hysteria of screaming people packed in by the thousands into sports stadiums . . . no more drug-assisted going to sleep, drug-assisted waking up again, and drug-assisted everything else that went on in between.

Bornos Karenski was going to go back to living the life of health, honest hard work, and contentment that had once been the right of every man to follow if he so chose—the life that he had always dreamed of.

A sudden voice filled the huge volume of passenger cabin 3 on C deck and brought him out of his reverie.

"Hello, ladies and gentlemen. This is your captain speaking again.

"Well, while you were having your lunch we've been gaining speed and covering quite a lot of distance. We're well over a million miles from Earth now and have been under normal gravitic-drive acceleration all the time, which is why you will have been unaware of any sensation of movement.

"The power beam from Jupiter has been following us all the way and charging up our on-board boosters, and we're now into a region of sufficiently low gravity gradient to switch over to Philipsz Drive. Transfer into the system of Sirius will only take a second, but the process can induce a mild feeling of giddiness and we strongly recommend passengers to take their seats. Would all cabin staff now remain seated at their stations, too, please.

"When we exit from Philipsz Drive, passengers will be able to see Sirius A on the forward viewscreens in all cabins. Its companion star, Sirius B, will be partially eclipsed from our point of re-entry into normal space, but will be visible above and slightly to the right of the primary when we darken down the screens a little.

"Well, we're going to be pretty busy for a while now here in the control center, so I'm going to have to cut out. I hope you all have a pleasant trip. When I next speak to you, we will be eight-point-seven light-years from where we are now. Latest indications are that we should arrive at the planet Miranda on schedule, eight hours after re-entry.

"That's all. Thank you."

Signs illuminated in various parts of the cabin to announce:

TRANSFER TO PHILIPSZ DRIVE IMMINENT—
PLEASE BE SEATED

"Why do they call it such a funny name?" ten-year-old Tina Karenski asked from the seat next to him.

"Oh, well now," he replied, turning to look down at her. "That was the name of a very famous scientist who died a long time ago—long before you were born."

"Why do they give it his name? Did he invent it?"

"Not exactly, but he was the first man to discover how to make it work. He proved by what are called experiments that it was possible."

"How dumb can you get?" her twelve-year-old brother asked scornfully from the next seat. "Everybody's heard of Aubrey Philipsz. He was the friend of Bradley Clifford—the most famous scientist ever."

"Of course I've heard of Clifford," Tina retorted pertly. "He was the man who stopped everybody in the world from going crazy once. That's right, isn't it, Mommy?" She directed the last question at Maria Karenski, who was sitting on the far side of her brother.

"Yes, that's right, dear. That's enough questions for now. Look at your Sun on the screen there. You may not see it again for a long time."

Tina considered the suggestion.

"Won't there be any sun in Miranda then?" she asked as the awful implication dawned on her.

"Yes, of course there will, but it will be a different one."

"She's just dumb."

"Don't say things like that."

Suddenly the view on the screen seemed to flicker, and then it had changed. The sun that dominated the scene had moved to one side; it was larger and more brilliant than the one that had been there an instant before. And the background of stars had altered subtly. A chorus of *oohs* and *ahs* came from all parts of the cabin of the mile-long ship.

"My head feels funny," Tina said. "What happened?"

"It's nothing to worry about, dear," her mother replied. "Look there; that's your new sun."

Tina gazed for a while at the new image on the screen, eventually arriving, by the irrefutable logic of her years, at the undeniable conclusion that a sun was a sun was a sun. . . . Her mind turned to other things and she looked back again at her father.

"How did Bradley Clifford stop everybody from going crazy?" she asked.

Bornos sighed, smiled, and rubbed his brow.

"Oh, now, that's a little difficult to explain. He set up what was probably the biggest hoax ever in history."

"What's a hoax?"

"You'll learn all about it at your new school," her mother interrupted. "I think your daddy would like a rest now. Look—the signs have gone out. They'll be putting on more movies downstairs in a minute. How would you like to go and watch them?"

The two children squeezed out between the seats and disappeared along the aisle. Bornos was just settling back to resume his daydreams when his wife asked: "Was it all a hoax, I wonder?"

"Not all of it," he told her. "The J-bomb was supposed to be able to fire only at places inside the territories of the Western allies of the time . . . to make it purely defensive. That was certainly true; they tried to fire it at tests targets in Siberia and places like that, but it wouldn't work."

"And the rest of it?"

"Well," he said, rubbing his chin. "That's the mystery. Everybody believed for over a century that if they allowed the machine to lose power it would destroy places in America, and if anybody else on Earth built a similar machine, then it would be destroyed too. But lots of people say that this was just bluff to stop the world from rearming. If it was, it certainly worked. . . ."

She thought to herself for a while. "I must say, it

doesn't really sound like the kind of person you imagine Clifford as being . . . I mean . . . setting up a gigantic booby trap that could have killed lots of people . . . innocent people probably. It just doesn't sound like him at all."

"That's exactly why lots of people believe that part of it was a hoax," Bornos answered. "There was something funny about the whole thing anyway. The people who were actually there at Brunnermont on the day that the machine deactivated would never talk about what they learned. I'm pretty sure, though, that they'd have known. I'm sure it would have printed out something just before it switched itself off after all those years. . . ."

"Anyway, it doesn't really matter now," his wife declared. "The main thing is that neither the East nor the West were prepared to go to all the trouble and expense of testing it. *They* believed everything they were supposed to and they did everything they were supposed to. *That's* what matters."

"Absolutely right," he agreed readily. "It makes no difference now. How much of it was true and how much of it wasn't is something that I don't suppose anyone will ever know for sure now."

About the Author

JAMES HOGAN was born in London in 1941 and educated at the Cardinal Vaughan Grammar School, Kensington. He studied general engineering at the Royal Aircraft Establishment, Farnborough, subsequently specializing in electronics and digital systems.

After spending a few years as a systems design engineer, he transferred into selling and later joined the computer industry as a salesman, working with ITT, Honeywell, and Digital Equipment Corporation. He also worked as a Life Insurance salesman for two years ". . . to have a 'break' from the world of machines and to learn something more about people."

Currently he is employed by DEC as a Senior Sales Training Consultant, concentrating on the applications of minicomputers in science and research. In mid-1977 he moved from England to the United States and now lives in Massachusetts.